UNARCANA STARS

BOOK SIX

OF THE STARSHIP'S MAGE SERIES

This edition published in 2018 by:
Faolan's Pen Publishing Inc.
22 King St. S, Suite 300
Waterloo, Ontario
N2J 1N8 Canada

ISBN-13: 978-1-988035-40-6 (print)
A record of this book is available from Library and Archives Canada.
Printed in the United States of America
1 2 3 4 5 6 7 8 9 10

First edition
First printing: December 2018

Read more books from Glynn Stewart at faolanspen.com

STARSHIP'S
MAGE

UNARCANA STARS

BOOK SIX
OF THE STARSHIP'S MAGE SERIES

GLYNN STEWART

FAOLAN'S PEN
PUBLISHING
faolanspen.com

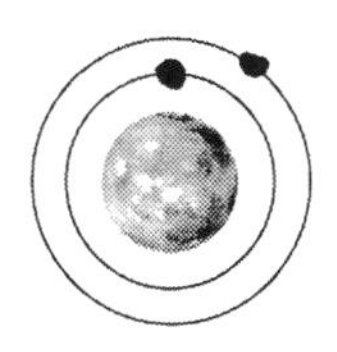

CHAPTER ONE

THERE WAS a recurring debate among constitutional scholars as to where the First Hand of the Mage-King of Mars fell among the five most powerful individuals in the Protectorate of said Mage-King. The bearer of that title, after all, wielded the full power and support of the Mage-King everywhere outside the Sol System, and the current bearer had been declared above even the Council of the Protectorate.

On the other hand, Damien Montgomery realized, constitutional scholars and kittens didn't speak to each other much.

"No, Persephone, you are not allowed on the desk," he told the ten-month-old black kitten measuring the jump. "We've had this conversation."

Persephone listened as well as she ever did. She landed on the touch-screen covering the desk, scattering the overlarge icons across the screen. Several flickered up onto the "glass" screen of the external window of the observation deck Damien had claimed as his office.

The First Hand of the Mage-King was a small man, barely a hundred and fifty centimeters tall and slight with it. The cat purring on his desk matched the color of both his hair and the suit blazer he wore.

He eyed Persephone for several seconds then reached out a hand. The black leather gloves he wore didn't conceal the unmoving state of his fingers. The gap between the gloves and his shirt showed the truth as well, the strange ridges of burn scars once again holding the shirt sleeve up.

Damien twitched his hand and conjured power. One moment, the kitten was purring at him from his desk. The next, there was a slight *pop* of air and she was on the floor.

Still purring.

He sighed and reached down to scratch her head. It was a careful, somewhat painful process, but it was why he even had Persephone. Petting an animal was good therapy for his burnt hands and fingers, so Kiera Alexander, the sixteen-year-old Princess of Mars, had found him a kitten.

"System, reset screens to forty-five seconds ago," he ordered aloud. The computer wasn't smart enough to recognize feline intervention, but it would follow orders.

Unlike the kitten.

From his observation-deck office aboard the Royal Martian Navy battlecruiser *Duke of Magnificence,* Damien could see the ships scattered through the void outside. His convoy was resting in deep space, waiting for the Mages aboard the various vessels to be ready to jump.

A second cruiser, *Glory in Honest Purpose,* was far enough away to be little more than a star. The computer screens in the observation window, however, happily added a subtle iconography to help Damien track his ships.

Between *Duke of Magnificence* and *Glory in Honest Purpose* hung fourteen freighters, a hastily gathered convoy carrying over a hundred and fifty million tons of grain, rice and other non-perishable food supplies.

The relief convoy was one jump outside of the Korma System, but Damien had ordered that they wait until they had *two* Mages ready to jump. He didn't want to bring the convoy into the Korma System until he was certain he could bring the convoy *out.*

Korma was one of the UnArcana World systems that had seceded from the Protectorate eighteen months before. Technically, Damien was violating the borders of the newly-founded Republic of Faith and Reason.

The colony on Kormar, however, had made the rather common decision to concentrate the majority of the planet's food production into the regions most accommodating to Earth-standard crops. A newly mutated bacteria had decided said crops were an amazing delicacy and, from the reports the Protectorate had received, *eaten* basically the entire food crop.

Famine wasn't normally a problem in the twenty-fifth century, but few Mages would jump a ship into a Republic where they were automatic second-class citizens at best. No one had ever found a way to travel between the stars that didn't require a Mage to teleport a starship, which meant the Republic was highly reliant on the few Mages who would take their money.

That wasn't enough ships to feed a world. One of those ships' captains, however, had reported what he'd learned about Kormar to the Protectorate...and now Damien was here.

He studied the readouts on his ships and teleported Persephone back to the floor in mid-jump, before she could mess with his icons. The kitten landed on the ground with a thump and a confused *mewp*.

He was bringing enough food to feed Kormar's populace for most of a year, more than enough time to get their crops back in order. His only real concern was how the Republic world would react to the help being offered by the Protectorate.

As far as Desmond Michael Alexander the Third, the Mage-King of Mars, was concerned, his protectorate was all humanity. The *nation* of the Protectorate might have shrunk when the Republic seceded, but the Mage-King's responsibility to guard humanity hadn't.

A grumpy meow distracted Damien from his thoughts, and he glanced aside to watch Persephone jump onto his desk from a completely different angle, where he didn't see her until she landed on the smooth surface. She skidded to a halt and met his gaze with sparkling blue eyes.

He sighed and raised one of his broken hands. There was a *pop* of displaced air, and Persephone dropped onto his lap. He carefully lowered a hand to scratch her ears, and she leaned into him with a purr.

"Don't worry, Persephone," he told her softly. "This is a relief mission. Even the Republic isn't going to cause too much trouble when we're here to feed a planet."

If only he truly believed that.

"Lord Montgomery."

Mage-Captain Kole Jakab was a tall man with the pale skin of a lifelong spacer. Contrary to his appearance, Damien knew Jakab had been born in London, on Earth. He also knew Jakab rarely traveled to Earth and *never* to England.

"Mage-Captain. Are we ready?" Damien asked.

"All of the convoy ships report ready to jump," the Mage-Captain replied. "*Glory* and *Duke* are at battle stations; all hands are prepared for the worst."

"I hope it doesn't come to that," the Hand murmured.

"So do we all, my lord," Jakab agreed. "But this is also the first time RMN ships have entered a Republic system since the Secession. This has every chance of turning into a diplomatic nightmare."

"And *that*, Mage-Captain, is why I'm here," Damien reminded him.

Before Jakab could reply, their conversation was interrupted by the arrival of Persephone on Damien's desk again. His controls were set to be used without having mobile fingers, so the cat was *far* too able to mess with his settings.

Fortunately, Damien managed to catch her before she managed to turn off the call. He winced as her purring weight settled onto his hand, and carefully brought his second hand to bear to carry the cat to his lap.

"How's the cat therapy going?" his Captain asked, manfully restraining his laughter.

"If nothing else, she's good for keeping my ego in check," Damien said. "It's nice to have one person around who doesn't follow my orders. No matter how much I beg."

"And your hands, my lord?" Jakab said, his voice suddenly gentler. "Are you...are you up for this, Lord Montgomery?"

Damien snorted.

"It's a little late to raise that concern, isn't it, Captain?" he replied. "I'm in better shape than I've been in for eighteen months."

Jakab arched an eyebrow at him.

"And how long before you're expected to have full function again, Damien?"

"At least another eighteen months," Damien admitted. "I cannot sit idly by and do *nothing*, Captain. I will not. Injured or not, I remain the First Hand of the Mage-King. I will do my job."

"If *I'd* lost the use of my hands, I don't think my doctors would have let me go back to work yet," his subordinate pointed out.

"Yes, but, well...I *am* the First Hand," Damien said with a chuckle. "Rank has its privileges, I suppose, and today those privileges include helping to save a world from famine. Shall we get this show on the road?"

"'Helping,' the man who organized the whole thing says," Jakab replied dryly. "We await only your order, Lord Montgomery."

"Then you have it," Damien said firmly. "Let's go save a planet, Captain. I'll be on the flag deck in five minutes."

The convoy Damien had put together would normally have had a flag officer attached to it. While he'd basically grabbed every ship to hand, including his normal ride in *Duke of Magnificence*, he'd missed acquiring a flag officer.

That put him in command himself. In theory, at least. Most of Damien's space battle experience consisted of sitting on his hands while Kole Jakab carried the day. The Mage-Captain was just about due to get kicked to flag rank himself, which was all but guaranteed by the glowing recommendation of the First Hand.

But *Duke* was Kole Jakab's ship, which meant the Mage-Captain was on the bridge. At the center of the warship, the bridge also acted as the simulacrum chamber, the nerve center of the magic that propelled the vessel between the stars.

Jakab's location meant the battlecruiser's flag deck went unused, so Damien had taken it over long before. The Hand had lived aboard the cruiser, off and on, for several years now. Jakab was used to having a Hand in his back pocket, and Damien was used to having a ship and crew he could rely on utterly.

"All right, Captain," Damien said as he slid into the Admiral's seat on the flag deck. The chamber around the big hologram was sparsely occupied. Damien didn't use a full flag officer's staff, and most of the Navy staff officers he *did* have knew perfectly well that he expected them to support Jakab, not him.

"What have we got?"

The Korma System rotated in his hologram, icons marking twelve worlds. Damien categorized them almost absently: four gas giants, eight rocks, no significant asteroid belt. One habitable and inhabited planet, Kormar.

"About what we were expecting," Jakab told him. "We had to jump in at the freighters' safe distance, so we're a good day from orbit of Kormar. About a two-minute round trip for coms whenever you want to say hello."

"Warships?" Damien asked.

"Twelve Legatan-built *Crucifix*-class gunships," his captain replied instantly. "*Duke* or *Glory* could take them out in a single salvo if they decide to be troublesome."

"If that's needed, things have gone very wrong," Damien told him. "You are authorized to take whatever actions you see necessary to defend the freighters, though. Am I clear?"

From the way Jakab swallowed, he recognized that Damien had just handed him a blank check to start a war. Of course, Damien wouldn't have *given* him that authorization if he didn't trust the man.

"Yes, my lord."

"So, a dozen gunships, no fortifications?" Damien asked.

"Kormar didn't have anything significant before the Secession, and it doesn't look like they've upgraded. If there's anything here we weren't expecting, it's at Baghdad with the cloudscoop."

The closest gas giant to Kormar flashed on the hologram on the flag deck. There wasn't a lot of industry there, but with the UnArcana Worlds' refusal to use magic, a cloudscoop was a necessity. If you didn't have Mages producing antimatter, then you needed hydrogen and helium for fusion generators.

And if you were running a fleet, you'd need the same to keep your ships fueled. If there was a Republic force in the system, it would be at Baghdad.

Damien's intelligence suggested that the Republic had *maybe* sixty Mages who'd been tempted into working for them by vast piles of cash. Any Republic force would inevitably be small in numbers—though he suspected the Republic had surprises for them.

The core of the Republic was Legatus, after all, and Legatus was the single most industrialized Core World, second only to Sol itself in human space. They might only have sixty Mages, but if they put each of them on something equivalent to the RMN's battleships, well...

"Keep an eye on Baghdad, then," Damien ordered. "For now, though, I need to make a call. We need to let the locals know their groceries are here."

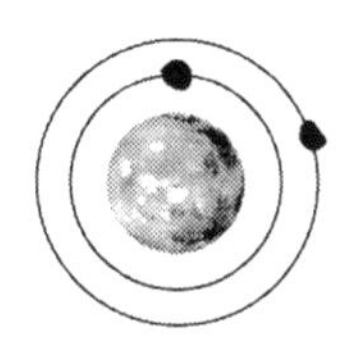

CHAPTER TWO

"THIS MESSAGE is for the government of Kormar," Damien told the camera. With over a light-minute between his convoy and the planet, there was no point in attempting to have a live conversation.

"I am Damien Montgomery, First Hand of the Mage-King of Mars. News of the damage to your agricultural zones has reached us via one of the ships that visited earlier this month. We organized this convoy as quickly as we could.

"I am attaching a manifest of our cargo, but to summarize: we are carrying just over one hundred and fifty million tons of non-perishable food supplies. I also have a specialist team of microbiologists who have volunteered to help finish getting the bacterial problem under control."

In all likelihood, Damien knew, the problem was already under control. The resources of even a single world were immense, after all. They just couldn't conjure food out of thin air.

"My convoy consists of fourteen freighters of various sizes and two Royal Martian Navy cruisers under my direct authority," he continued. "You have my word that we are not here to harm anyone, but I cannot justify allowing the convoy into Republic space without an escort."

He smiled sadly. That wasn't something he'd even thought of on his own. He'd originally only intended to bring *Duke*, but Jakab had pointed out that the Republic was hardly friendly space these days.

"I make our ETA into Kormar orbit approximately twenty-five hours," he told them. "We have sufficient shuttle capacity to deliver the cargo to distribution centers identified by you in roughly ten days. We do not know how the situation has progressed, so any information update you can provide us will allow us to help you more effectively.

"If we need to complete the delivery more rapidly, we will need assistance from local transport.

"I await your response."

He cut the recording and hit Transmit, leaning back in his seat to study the hologram as he waited.

"Do you think there'll be trouble?"

Damien looked over at the head of his bodyguards, Special Agent Mage-Captain Denis Romanov of both the Protectorate Secret Service and the Royal Martian Marine Corps. Romanov had a similar slim and dark-haired build to Damien himself but was over forty centimeters taller than his boss.

"I *want* to say that this is a humanitarian mission," Damien replied. "I want to believe that the Governor and his people will be reasonable and accept our help in the spirit it's offered in."

"So do I," Romanov agreed. "But?"

"I'm expecting trouble," the Hand confirmed. "I'm hoping for just some bureaucratic pushback and chest-thumping bullshit. Maybe some 'spontaneous' demonstrations when the shuttles touch down—and potentially some legit food riots when we're making deliveries."

"We have Marines assigned to every drop," his bodyguard pointed out. "Assault shuttles flying cover, with Nix-Seven supplies and SmartDarts. We can neutralize any riots without casualties."

"With minimal casualties," Damien corrected. Both Nix-Seven—Neutralization Solution Seven—and the auto-calibrating taser SmartDarts were almost guaranteed not to actually kill anyone. It still wasn't reasonable to knock large swathes of people unconscious without expecting *some* injuries and deaths.

"In all honesty, I'm worried about the Republic," he continued. "We have a surprisingly complete lack of intelligence on the classes or numbers of the new Republic Interstellar Navy. Without knowing what our potential opponent has in terms of capabilities, I can't predict how they're going to jump."

"So we watch and wait," Romanov replied.

"Exactly." Damien shook his head. "Hell, Denis, I don't even know who the Governor of Kormar *is* right now." He gestured to the camera with a half-frozen hand. "All I can do is wait for them to get back to me and hope they decide to be cooperative."

"There's what, eighty million people on Kormar?" his bodyguard asked. "That's a *lot* of reasons to be cooperative. I don't care how big of an asshole the Governor is—they can't get reelected if their constituents are *dead*."

The minimum round-trip time for a communication had already passed by the time Romanov had reached his conclusion, but Damien hadn't expected an immediate response. It would be over a day before they reached the orbit of Kormar, so the locals had time.

Time to go over his message and scans of his convoy with a fine-toothed comb. Time to panic, to argue and to decide what they were going to do.

In the end, it took them over an hour to respond to his message. Their response was tightbeamed directly to *Duke of Magnificence*, where Jakab's crew relayed it to the flag deck.

"System, play the recording," Damien ordered after it arrived. The repeater screens on the admiral's seat simply didn't have enough space for the expanded icons and control schemes he currently needed. The voice commands weren't perfect, but they were enough.

The image that appeared in the main holotank was of a petitely attractive blonde woman flanked on both sides by grim-looking men and women around a dark red conference table. The hologram picked up the interface touch screens and tablets scattered across the table, though an automatic filter on the transmitting end blocked their screens.

"Hand Montgomery, I am Governor Rozalia Motta. I am the elected leader of the planet of Kormar under the authority of the Republic of Faith and Reason."

Motta let her words hang for several seconds before she gestured at the men and women with her.

"These are my Cabinet, the men and women I rely on to help govern Kormar. Our greatest task in recent months has been to deal with the growing crisis overtaking our world."

She grimaced.

"You offer hope, Hand Montgomery, but I know who you are. The First Hand does not lightly cross between stars, and I can not blindly accept whatever price you demand for this aid. My duty is to my people first.

"So, tell me, Montgomery, what does the Mage-King demand for his help today?"

The recording froze and Damien nodded.

"System, record for transmission."

He focused his gaze on the camera and smiled sadly.

"Governor Motta, the Republic may have left the Protectorate, but realize that I am not your enemy," he said gently. "If you know who I am, you know my word is good. I know you have no reason to trust me today, but there is no price for this help. This is a purely humanitarian effort. We may have drawn a border between us, but we all remain human.

"It would neither serve our purposes nor fulfill our ethical burden to allow your people to starve. We offer aid the only way my King or I see as right: as neighbors, with open hands.

"I will not leave innocents to suffer while it is within my power to help."

Damien shook his head.

"You do not *need* to trust me, Governor Motta. I must simply ask you: what kind of monster would dangle hope in front of your people and hold it hostage? And do you truly believe me to be that kind of monster?"

He tapped the one command he *could* easily control, to end the recording, then sent it on. It would still be most of a day before they made it orbit. He had time to convince Motta to trust him.

And, like he said, he didn't need her to trust him. He just needed her to let him feed her people.

The next message—just over an hour later—that Damien received was a recording from the same elegantly-decorated conference room. Unlike before, however, this time the Governor sat alone.

Of course, it was entirely possible her Cabinet was just out of sight of the camera, and it was almost certain there were still bodyguards in the room, but the effort was being made to suggest she was speaking to him in confidence.

Damien didn't believe it for a second, but she was at least *trying*.

"Hand Montgomery," Motta greeted him. "Understand, first of all, that I do not—that I *can*not—acknowledge your authority. Even to the extent of granting you the honorifics you would be given in the Protectorate. I am bound, as I'm sure you realize, by the policies and dictates of the Republic and the Lord Protector."

George Solace had handily transitioned his role as President of Legatus into Lord Protector of the newborn Republic. Damien wasn't entirely certain just how much, say, *voting* had been involved in that transition.

He was becoming a cynic at the grand old age of thirty-odd.

"Regardless of my opinions of the Protectorate, however, well...I ordered planetwide rationing fifteen days ago. Even with the controls and restrictions, it is likely we will see serious shortfalls inside the next month. We are...at least six months from any kind of homegrown crop relief. And *that*, Hand Montgomery, is dependent on either a breakthrough in dealing with this bacterial infestation or pure luck in the success of quarantining the new fields we're breaking now."

Damien winced. They were worse off than he'd thought. Even as he'd made sure to *have* a team of microbiologists and their equipment so that he could help deal with the bacteria, he'd still assumed that Kormar had solved the problem themselves.

"We need the food your convoy is carrying. We need your help. But I *cannot* sacrifice the choices my people made in willingly joining the Republic. If you are truly here as neighbors, then you are welcome and I am grateful for your help.

"But realize that I have no choice but to watch your every move with the greatest of caution. I *will* defend my people."

Governor Motta laid her hands on the table and faced the camera head on.

"Until you give me reason to disbelieve your assurances, however, you and your convoy are cleared to enter Kormar orbit. We will have distribution center locations for you to begin delivery to by the time you're here, and I will make certain we have a detailed breakdown of our available shuttlecraft as well.

"Thank you."

The recording ended and Damien breathed a sigh of relief.

"Make sure that's passed on to Mage-Captain Jakab and the rest of the convoy," he ordered. "Let's get this done, people."

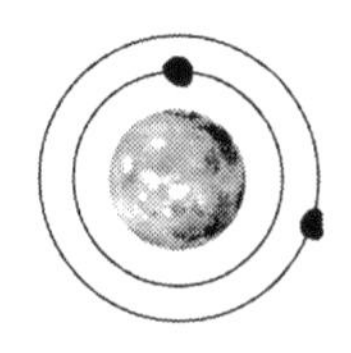

CHAPTER THREE

GLORY IN HONEST PURPOSE led the way into Kormar orbit, the silver spike of the Martian cruiser glowing bright white in the exhaust plume of the engines around her. Freighters followed her, establishing a neat globe formation as *Duke of Magnificence* took up the rear.

The cruisers on either side of the freighter formation were probably where the gaze of every military professional in the system was focused. Damien's focus, however, was on the shuttlecraft the freighters were already deploying.

One hundred and fifty million tons of cargo meant fifteen thousand standard ten-thousand-ton cargo containers. Even the most capable heavy-lift shuttle couldn't deliver more than four of those to the surface in a single pass.

Across Damien's entire convoy, he had roughly two hundred and fifty shuttles with a total capacity of five hundred containers. Each flight would take eight hours, which meant off-loading his convoy would take over a week.

There was a cargo station in Kormar orbit, but even if Damien was prepared to attach any of his ships to the local space station, it wouldn't get anything down to the surface any faster.

"Any word from the locals on shuttles?" he asked Jakab as he joined the Mage-Captain on the bridge. With the ship securing from maneuvers, he didn't need to worry as much about jostling the older man's elbow.

"Vague promises and unclear timelines," his subordinate replied. "You wouldn't think they were going to starve if we didn't deliver this food."

"That's strange," Damien murmured. "We were promised assistance. They can run the numbers on how long it will take to offload the cargo just as well as we can. What about the gunships?"

"They pulled them all back to their refueling station. That sits at a Lagrange point with the moon, L3-equivalent. Not out of range, but they've locked the ships down."

"We didn't even ask for that," Damien said. That was more of a gesture of *surrender* than of cooperation.

"I suspect the Governor doesn't trust her Republic-funded defenders not to do something stupid," Jakab replied. "I've passed the order that no Mages go down to the surface, sir. We're here to help, not cause trouble."

The UnArcana Worlds had uniformly banned the practice of magic on their planets, a reaction to the Compact that gave Mages special rights on the worlds of the Protectorate. Damien wasn't sure what the *Republic*'s rules on Mages were, but he doubted they were any gentler.

There was no reason to court trouble.

"Good call, Captain," he confirmed. "Anything looking suspicious in the rest of the system?"

"Not yet," Jakab said. "We're keeping our sensors online, though, and doing occasional active sweeps." He shook his head. "I'm finding myself wishing we'd picked up a couple of destroyers on the way. More eyes would help with this itch down my spine."

"You too, huh?" Damien studied the screens that covered every surface in the simulacrum chamber bridge. "My read on Motta is that she's on the level. She wants to help her people, and she's willing to let us help her."

He was silent for several seconds, looking at the planet below them.

"I'm hearing a *but* there, my lord," Jakab concluded.

"Yes. Motta was the Governor before the Secession. She isn't due to stand for reelection for another year—and she predates the Republic. Before the Secession, I'd say the final decision was hers. Now...I have to wonder what *Republican* authority is in this system."

Damien shook his head.

"In their place, I'd at least have someone keeping an eye on her—hells, on all of the Governors, but especially on anyone who hadn't been vetted by a Republic-supervised election. I wouldn't put it past the 'Lord Protector' to have someone in Korma who can override the local Governor."

"A Hand-equivalent?" Jakab said with a chuckle.

"Yeah. Except His Majesty would be *pissed* if I interfered in a humanitarian mission like this...and I'm not so confident in the opinions of Lord Protector Solace."

The shuttles were underway within the hour, five million tons of food heading towards sixty-two distribution centers scattered across the two inhabited continents.

Even from orbit, Damien could see the damage done by the new bacterial problem. Most of the images he had on file of Kormar had a glowing golden heart just north of the capital city. That heart was a massive prairie that supported enough food for a world of eighty million souls, along with a readily exportable surplus.

The massive collection of farms had been visible from orbit. They still were, he supposed, though it was a sick blue-black color now, not golden. It was almost grotesque, and he was sure the bacteria were spreading into the cities, too. The destruction of trees and gardens wasn't a crisis like the loss of thousands of square kilometers of farmland, but it would have its own impact.

"We'll want to coordinate getting Dr. Aputsiaq's team down to the surface as soon as possible," he told Jakab. Dr. Itzel Aputsiaq was the Earth-native microbiologist leading the team he'd "borrowed" from Tau Ceti's main university.

"Already working on it," the Captain replied. "The locals are making me nervous, my lord. Until about an hour before we hit orbit, everything was going smoothly and everyone was being perfectly helpful and cooperative.

"Then, suddenly, we couldn't get a straight answer out of anyone about anything except the DCs."

Damien nodded slowly.

"Keep it quiet," he told Jakab, "but bring both warships to status two. I don't think we'll see an attack from the planet, but *something* wicked this way comes."

"Yes, my lord."

"Lord Montgomery, you need to see this," a young dark-haired Lieutenant suddenly reported. Damien took a moment to process where she was and attach a name and role to the face: Lieutenant Sarah Wayan, a Tau Ceti native—and *Duke of Magnificence*'s junior communications officer.

"What is it, Lieutenant Wayan?" he asked as he crossed to the woman's station. She seemed almost taken aback that he knew her name, and he managed not to visibly shake his head.

The Lieutenant was one of the few officers on the bridge actually younger than he was, but he'd also made a point of at least knowing the main officers in each of *Duke*'s departments.

It made his job easier.

"We're receiving a request for an encrypted and scrambled tightbeam channel," Wayan told him after a moment. "It's coming from a satellite we hadn't picked out as unusual from the regular orbitals, and the codes are...odd."

"Odd how?"

"They flagged as expired, so I double-checked what they were," she admitted. "They're the *Protectorate* gubernatorial codes for Korma. All of those were deactivated in our system, but I still have them and can activate the protocols."

"Protocols the Republic would only have access to if Governor Motta had given it to them," Damien murmured.

"Exactly, sir. I might be able to trace the relay back to the original source, but it may take some time..."

"Do it," he ordered. "Since I suspect I can guess the origin, however, connect Governor Motta to my office while you're doing that. Full encryption, full scramble, maximum tightbeam. I don't want anyone in this star system to know we're in communication."

He looked over at Mage-Captain Jakab.

"Governor Motta is going quite a bit out of her way to speak to me in confidence," he noted. "The least I can do is return the favor."

Damien was completely unsurprised to find Persephone asleep on his desk when he returned to his office. There was a small cat door in the wall between the observation deck and his quarters, and the kitten could get between Damien's two main spaces with ease.

"Okay, cat," he addressed her. She rose and stretched, blinking slowly at him as she started purring. "Work time. Get down."

He was about to teleport her to the floor when, to his surprise, she calmly leapt down onto the chair and then the floor. Shaking his head, he settled into his seat—and Persephone promptly curled up on his feet.

He activated the channel that Wayan had sent up, and smiled slightly as his guess was confirmed. Governor Rozalia Motta looked out of the screen, sitting in a small office with the blinds drawn behind her.

"You know, we did deactivate those codes, Governor," he noted conversationally.

"I assumed you had," she agreed. "I also assumed you had them on file just in case. It was a gamble, Hand Montgomery, but it seems to have paid off. No one on my side knows I'm speaking to you."

"That's a gamble all on its own, isn't it, Governor?" he asked. "Some might say that's treason."

"They'd probably be right, but sometimes, the people I'm supposed to work *with* decide to be bloody morons," she snapped. "I've been ordered—*ordered,* Hand Montgomery—to hold all of my shuttles on the surface. The ground teams at the distribution centers have instructions to delay your shuttles on the ground as well."

"That seems...less than efficient at getting your people taken care of," Damien said slowly.

"That's because that isn't the point. There's a gunship carrier at the cloudscoop, Hand Montgomery," Motta told him flatly. "They can't get my people food, but they can sure turn up warships to cause trouble when someone else does."

Damien wasn't even entirely certain what a "gunship carrier" *was*, but he suspected they were about to find out in far greater detail than he could ever hope.

"They're going to attack."

"Technically, your warships' presence here is an act of war," she reminded him. "So, the esteemed Admiral Emerson Wang has decided to destroy your cruisers and seize the freighters. He thinks he can take your two ships without much difficulty, especially with the advantage of surprise."

"An advantage you are taking away," Damien noted. "I suspect, Governor, that that *is* treason. Why are you helping us?"

"Because you're helping me," Motta told him. "Given the choice between the arrogant bastard who's giving *me*, the elected Governor of this damn star system, orders, and the people who showed up in my people's hour of need with a hundred million tons of food..."

She sighed.

"I swore an oath, Damien Montgomery, and it didn't say a single damn thing about Republic *or* Protectorate. It said a lot about defending and serving the people of the Korma System. Admiral Wang is not under my orders; his chain of command goes straight to Legatus. I can't do more than warn you, but...I can't *not* do that, either."

"I understand. Thank you, Governor Motta," he told her. "I wish it hadn't come to this."

"So do I." She shook her head. "Do what you must, Hand Montgomery. But if you possibly can...don't let my people suffer for this."

"If I possibly can, at all, Governor, I won't."

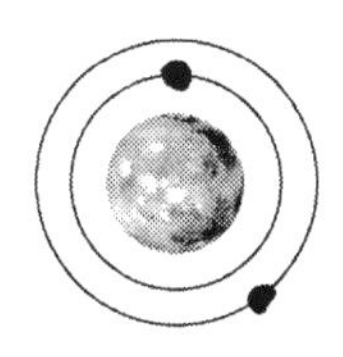

CHAPTER FOUR

"A GUNSHIP CARRIER?" Jakab asked Damien after he was filled in. "What the *hell* is that?"

"I'm going to guess a jump-ship that carries gunships," Damien replied with a forced chuckle. He stepped back into the flag deck as they were speaking, moving into the flag officer's seat and checking over the hologram.

"I know we've seen ships used to carry gunships before," he continued. "The whole mess at Antonius—and some of the crap I got involved in before I was a Hand. It's a logical step forward, given their limitation on Mages. They've got a small number of big ships, but to make up the difference in hulls and flexibility, they give them a few squadrons of, say, *Crucifix*-type gunships."

"Speaking of which, the orbital patrol is staying right where they are," Jakab pointed out. "Whatever's coming down the pipeline, they're not getting involved."

"Thank God for small mercies," Damien said. "Bring *Glory* out to join *Duke* in formation. They're not going to try to hit the freighters, but we don't want to risk even one misguided missile going that way."

"How do you want to play this, my lord?"

"This is their star system, Mage-Captain. *Find* them, hail them...but they have to fire first. You are authorized to do whatever is necessary to defend your ships and the convoy, but we cannot initiate the engagement."

"That could end very, *very* badly, my lord," Jakab said.

"I know," Damien admitted grimly. "But our presence here *is* a provocation, so we will minimize that as best as we can. We'll play with kid gloves—but not enough to risk our ships; am I clear?"

"Yes, my lord."

"Kole?"

"Yes, my lord?" Jakab asked carefully. Damien rarely used his first name, but it was a useful tool for making the officer stop and take careful stock of what the Hand was saying.

"Am I wrong?" Damien asked. "I'm looking at the political situation here, but you're the military officer. Is this the wrong call?"

The Mage-Captain sighed.

"No, Damien, you're right," he conceded. "It just...goes against the grain to know I have to let them get the first swing in."

"Find them, Mage-Captain. The better we know the threat, the better we can adjust to it. Plus, just knowing we're watching might be enough to make everyone stop and think."

"You know that's unlikely, right?"

Damien grimaced.

"Yes, Mage-Captain, I know. We do what we must."

"I don't have any unusual heat signatures," *Duke*'s tactical officer, Commander Kristopher Cisternino, reported. "There's nothing out there running engines of any kind except the usual collection of in-system clippers."

Damien was looking those over as the tactical officer spoke. Korma was classed as a MidWorld, which meant they had quite a bit of in-system traffic. A dozen ships of similar size to the freighters in the convoy but lacking jump matrices were the crown jewels, each hauling four or five million tons of cargo between various platforms and outposts. Another hundred or so smaller ships were scattered around, personal yachts and small transports and suchlike.

None of those civilian ships were heading toward Kormar. What traffic was moving around the system was, rather intelligently, avoiding the warships. They might have done the same even before the Protectorate ships had counted as vessels of a foreign power.

Now, well...Damien had seen enough of the news and fearmongering being distributed in the Republic. Even knowing the Protectorate had no intention of invading the Republic, he'd still have given the cruisers a wide berth in the locals' place.

"I doubt the Governor went to that much effort to warn us for nothing," he murmured. "So, what are we missing?"

"Not much," Jakab replied. "They've turned their engines off, and while we *can* pick up a ship by its operating heat signature, we need to be much closer. They're trying to be sneaky."

"I figured that much out." Damien studied the hologram. "But they're almost certainly coming from Baghdad, correct?"

"Agreed," the Captain said. "Depending on how far out they are, we might be able to identify them with a focused sensor pulse. There's no way we can do that without them knowing what we're doing, though. They'd know they were detected—and they'd know we had a reason to be looking for them."

"We don't have a choice." Damien shook his head. "The cloudscoop and the naval position there are the most likely source of an enemy force, regardless. They might be suspicious, but it's not an unreasonable course of action.

"Pulse them, Mage-Captain. Stand by to bring both ships to battle stations."

"Understood."

The sensor scan was shown on Damien's hologram as a white bubble, arcing out in the direction of the gas giant Baghdad. Every second it traveled was two seconds before he'd see any response, but after the first twenty seconds, they at least knew they weren't in laser range of the Republic force.

"Got them!" Cisternino snapped, then swallowed audibly. "I make it twenty light-seconds, one hundred individual contacts...make that one-fifty."

"Damn," Damien murmured. "Do we have any details?"

"Negative, all I can tell you is that they're out there and they're not very big," the tactical officer admitted. "Maybe twenty meters across, thirty to fifty meters long. None of the rotational pods of a *Crucifix*."

"Specifically designed for this," Jakab concluded. "How long have they been planning this?"

"At least since the Antonius Incident," Damien pointed out. "Record for transmission."

He faced the camera and smiled grimly.

"Republic gunships, this is Hand Damien Montgomery aboard the Protectorate battlecruiser *Duke of Magnificence*. We are on a humanitarian mission to deliver food and technical assistance to Kormar. We are *not*, I repeat, *not* on a hostile mission and mean no harm to anyone.

"I have authorized these ships to defend themselves, but there's no need to start a fight here today," Damien said softly. "We're here to help Kormar. You're here to protect Kormar. Those don't contradict each other.

"Please. Let me help these people. Then we'll leave. That's all I ask."

The message left and he shook his head.

"Think it will help?" Jakab asked.

"Maybe. Legatus had a number of intelligent, reasonable officers and crews," Damien reminded himself. "I can only hope that the Republic had similar recruiting standards."

"Well, that's an answer, I suppose."

The gunships had flipped in space, launching missiles and accelerating away from the Martian cruisers.

"No communications, I presume?" Damien continued, trying and failing to get a feel for the numbers showing on his hologram. "Someone want to fill the glorified civilian in?"

"No coms," Jakab confirmed. "One hundred and fifty gunships, six launchers apiece. Nine hundred missiles, accelerating at ten thousand gravities. That's an upgrade on the last numbers we had for Legatan antimatter birds, but I can't even guess their flight time."

"Enough to reach us seems reasonable." Damien was running numbers on the part of the scenario he did fully understand. "Their new course is going to keep them outside of our laser and amplifier range. They're playing it cautious."

"Agreed," Jakab replied. "Your orders, my lord?"

It was arguable whether the Republic had just declared war on the Protectorate—Damien's convoy was in their space, after all—but they had declared war on this flotilla.

"I already gave them," Damien said quietly. "Defend the convoy, Mage-Captain Jakab. This part is your job."

There were three Runes carved into Damien's skin that made him a far more powerful Mage than Jakab, but the simulacrum chamber that co-existed with *Duke*'s bridge was linked to an even more powerful version of his Runes of Power.

From the simulacrum chamber, Damien had once worked magic few other Mages could—but even Jakab could use the amplifier to terrifyingly and incredible effect. And Jakab was more experienced at using a warship amplifier than Damien was.

So, Damien would leave the fighting to the professionals. Even as his burned hands twinged in pain at the memories of the times he *hadn't*.

He had, after all, had *five* Runes of Power at one point.

CHAPTER FIVE

THE TWO CRUISERS had already positioned themselves between the incoming Republic vessels and the convoy. Now they accelerated outward, toward the missiles.

The runes providing the Protectorate ships with gravity also worked to counteract acceleration, up to about ten to fifteen gravities.

Those ten gravities were a tiny thing against the ten *thousand* gravities the incoming missiles were pulling, but it bought them more space and time to protect the freighters.

Damien watched in silence as his ships launched. Both of his ships were *Honorific*-class battlecruisers: big, tough ships, among the most modern the Royal Martian Navy possessed. They overwhelmingly outmassed the gunship flotilla thrown at them, but most of their advantages would be seen in the exact type of drawn-out engagement the gunships were avoiding.

Four salvos blasted into space in just over a minute, and then the warships' launchers were silent. Even with each battlecruiser carrying eighty missile launchers, that probably wasn't enough to take out the retreating gunships...but Damien suspected that wasn't Jakab's plan.

The missiles' vectors quickly proved him right. They weren't charging after the gunships—Jakab was clearly assessing their risk as lower than their already-launched missiles. Damien wasn't sure he agreed with that, but it was the Mage-Captain's decision to make.

The earlier Legatan gunships he had data on had carried multiple missiles for each launcher, capable of at least some sustained engagement, and Damien didn't think these new ships were *that* much smaller.

They were, however, falling back away from the convoy.

"First missile intercept in ninety seconds," one of the handful of techs on the flag deck announced. "Last in one hundred forty seconds. RFLAM range in one hundred fifty seconds."

Damien nodded his understanding.

Rapid-Fire Laser Anti-Missile turrets were the key component to his ships' defenses. Each of his cruisers mounted a hundred of them. All of the freighters in the convoy had at least two or three, though hopefully, the Republican ships weren't targeting the convoy.

"Still no communication from the Republic ships?" he asked.

"Nothing. Just missiles."

The Hand shook his head. He hadn't expected to avoid a fight, not once the Republic force had sent gunships out at him, but he had expected them to at least talk to him.

The tactical affair of dealing with the incoming fire was Jakab's job. The Mage-Captain was focusing his attention on defending his ships. Damien could order an attack on the fleeing gunships and Jakab would obey, but that...was contrary to his actual objectives there.

Which, of course, was why Jakab *wasn't* firing on the gunships. It was a rather large gesture of goodwill, and one that could easily cost the RMN force badly.

Damien hoped the bastards saw it that way.

"First missile intercept. Seventy-two percent success rate," the tech reported. Damien took a moment to study the man, a dark-skinned Chief Petty Officer with McQueen, Akash embroidered on his uniform.

"Thank you, Chief McQueen," he murmured.

"Second intercept...less effective," McQueen continued.

"That's normal, right?" Damien asked. He'd been in more than a few space battles by now, but usually, he'd been sitting on Jakab's bridge. This was the first time he'd been completely separated on the flag deck, and he was realizing he didn't like it.

It was a lot harder to judge how the battle was going by the Captain's demeanor when you couldn't see the Captain, after all.

"Yeah, we've got an ugly radiation hash out there from the antimatter warheads," McQueen confirmed. "The Republic birds are big, ugly weapons, too. Two-gigaton warheads to our one."

The third intercept was slightly more effective than the second, Damien thought, but it was hard to tell. Like McQueen had pointed out, the antimatter warheads were making a mess of the space in front of the Martian flotilla. Each weapon that detonated made it harder to track the rest.

There were still *far* too many missiles out there for Damien's peace of mind. Apparently, the cruiser Captains agreed, as both ships began spewing missiles again. They were using multi-million-dollar weapons systems as glorified flak, detonating the warheads in the middle of the incoming salvo even as the RFLAM turrets came to life behind them.

Then the missiles reached the distance at which the amplifiers allowed the Mage-Captains to unleash their own power. Arcing "lightning" flickered across the incoming fire, detonating dozens of missiles at once.

And still they kept coming. The sheer range of space-to-space weapons meant that Damien and his people watched the missiles come in for almost ten minutes, and while everything they threw at the incoming fire worked, there were just too many missiles.

Two missiles exploded around *Duke of Magnificence*, barely avoiding direct hits but still sending shockwaves and radiation pulses hammering into the big cruiser's armor. A few icons on Damien's screens flashed yellow, but *Duke* continued unharmed.

Glory in Honest Purpose wasn't so lucky. At least three missiles scored direct hits, multi-gigaton explosions going off in contact with her hull. The battlecruiser lurched in space, spewing atmosphere and vaporized metal—but she was still there.

This was the *exact* threat her armor had been designed for, after all.

"*Glory* reports heavy damage," Jakab told Damien a few seconds later. "Most of their missiles and defense turrets are offline. Engines are still mostly functional and they still have the amplifier." The Mage-Captain grimaced.

"She can run, my lord, but she can't fight."

Damien waited roughly five minutes to be sure he had all of the information on the status of his ships. None of it was good. *Duke* was combat-capable. *Glory* wasn't. The only good news was that less than a dozen missiles had missed the cruisers and gone for the freighters. None had come close enough to be a threat before they were destroyed.

"What's the status of our shuttles?" he asked Romanov.

The Special Agent wasn't in charge of the Marines aboard the convoy, but Damien would freely admit he used the man as an interface with Colonel Petrik Dean Popov. Popov was a solid, reliable soldier, but he and Romanov spoke what felt like a completely different language to Damien.

"The locals are causing trouble, as the Governor warned us," his bodyguard said. "The off-loading seems to be progressing on schedule, but the shuttles that have completed off-loading are being held up."

"Wonderful." Damien unconsciously tried to open a channel to Jakab from the repeater screens on the arms of his seat. For half a second, his fingers let him—then the scar tissue locked up and cramps tore through the muscles.

The Hand swallowed an undignified curse as he remembered himself.

"System, open a link with Mage-Captain Jakab and Colonel Popov," he ordered the computer aloud as he gently shook his aching hand. The screens lit up with the two officers' images before Romanov could inquire about Damien's health, which was a benefit.

"My lord," Jakab greeted him. Popov gave him a wordless half-salute.

"Jakab, what's the status of the gunships?" Damien asked.

"Outside our weapons range now, falling back towards the cloud-scoop. I'm guessing there's somebody else out there," the Captain warned.

"So am I," Damien agreed. "Colonel Popov, how much trouble are the locals giving us?"

"So far, they're keeping it to claiming they can't sort out flight clearances due to other traffic," the Marine replied. "Of course, unless said traffic is *invisible...*"

"That's what I figured. I want every shuttle headed back for orbit in fifteen minutes," Damien ordered. "If they can possibly dump their cargo and leave sorting it out to the locals, they're to do that. I want to get as much of this damn food on the surface as possible.

"Assuming they can make the fifteen minutes, how long until the entire shuttle fleet is back aboard their transports?"

"Three hours, give or take about twenty minutes," Popov answered instantly. "It would take about half an hour for them to refuel and pick up cargo—"

"They're not picking up cargo," Damien told them. "We're recalling everybody, right now. Colonel..."

The Hand shook his head and grimaced. Only part of it was from pain.

"Your Marines are to do whatever is necessary to get those shuttles back to their transports," he ordered. "I am specifically including firing on local aircraft and ground troops; am I clear?"

Popov nodded grimly.

"Yes, sir." He paused. "I hope it won't come to that, but...thank you, sir."

"I won't lose anyone else if I can avoid it," Damien told the two officers. "Jakab, I want eyes on those gunships from now until Judgment Day. There's a mothership out there and I don't want to play. Find her."

"Yes, sir." The Mage-Captain hesitated. "What do we do when we find her?"

"Unless we can negotiate some kind of ceasefire, we are leaving this system as soon as the shuttles are aboard," Damien said flatly. "The food we already delivered will buy them another month, with careful rationing.

"If the Republic won't let us deliver food, then the Republic will have to save its own people."

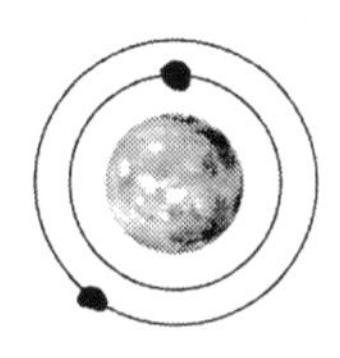

CHAPTER SIX

TO DAMIEN'S RELIEF, the shuttles managed to get clear without bloodshed. They even managed to get all of their cargo landed safely for the locals.

Five million tons of food wasn't much when weighed against eighty million appetites, but it would buy the people of Kormar time. Time to solve their bacteria problem and grow new crops. Time to get help from the Republic that seemed so damned determined to make sure that no one *else* helped.

"Threat alert!" McQueen reported sharply.

Damien found himself looking at the wrong part of the displays. His focus was on the planet, and he was half-expecting to see that the Republic military had launched aircraft or something to take down his retreating shuttles.

"Leaving Baghdad, my lord," the tech told him after a moment. "We have multiple major energy signatures heading out to rendezvous with the gunships."

Damien adjusted the main display, zooming in on Baghdad and the orbital platforms there. Five massive energy signatures were now plainly visible across the entire star system, immense plumes of fusion energy from ships that were far larger than he'd been expecting.

"How much detail do we have?" he asked, sounding far calmer than he felt.

"CIC is working on it, but it's definitely five capital ships using fusion engines. One's somewhat bigger than the others, but we're still isolating energy and acceleration to identify mass."

Damien nodded and looked at what data he had. Fusion drives were normally a civilian system. Both the gunships and the missiles the Republic had thrown at him had been using antimatter drives.

On the other hand, antimatter in the Protectorate was the product of Transmuter Mages. Converting matter into antimatter was a straightforward, if draining and dangerous, process for Mages in general. Damien himself was known to use it as a weapon, though that was a trick that required at least one Rune of Power to pull off.

The Republic's sole source of antimatter was a massive particle-accelerator ring wrapped around Legatus's largest gas giant. They obviously had decided to prioritize where they were committing it.

"I think we can assume that their missiles are also antimatter-fueled, don't you?" Damien murmured. A verbal command linked him to Jakab. "What do you make of it, Captain?"

"Carrier group," the Mage-Captain replied instantly. "Old wet-navy doctrine. They're using the gunships as a force and hull multiplier, but they've got escorts to protect the carrier herself. We'd need additional data on them, my lord, to say more."

"There's only one way to get that data, Mage-Captain," Damien pointed out. "My reading says we're still breaking down the energy signatures, but we're definitely outmassed and outnumbered. Which means almost certainly outgunned."

He shook his head.

"I won't sacrifice your ships or this convoy for tactical data we have no way of getting home," he continued.

The only form of faster-than-light communication available to the Protectorate was the Runic Transceiver Arrays, massive constructs of magic and runes that took years to build and could project a speaking Mage's voice to another RTA. They were too delicate and too large to be attached to ships or fleets, which meant that Damien could only send messages home aboard a ship.

"How long until the shuttles are aboard?" Damien asked.

"Seventy minutes," Jakab reported. "We've got time, my lord. Scans show them accelerating at roughly four gravities."

"They don't have magical gravity, so that makes sense. I can't imagine they use their Mages for much other than jumping the ships."

"Where did they even get the Mages for this?" his Captain asked.

"Some people will do anything for money," Damien pointed out. "It's not like our crime syndicates have ever had a notable shortage of Jump Mages, after all. I'll admit, though, I was expecting one big ship. Not five smaller ones."

The sudden sick expression on Jakab's face warned him before the Mage-Captain spoke.

"How about five big ones?" he asked. "CIC makes the carrier forty million tons. Escorts are thirty apiece. Any one of those ships could probably take both *Duke* and *Glory*."

"Get the convoy ready to move, Mage-Captain," Damien ordered. "We were here to help people, not fight a war—even if we *could* fight these people, I don't want to!"

The carrier group continued to accelerate toward Damien's convoy. Their acceleration might have been slow compared to what his cruisers could manage, but it was better than most of his freighters could pull off.

On the other hand, they'd started a *long* way away. If they accelerated the whole way and cut across his course at just the right angle, they could at least force a missile engagement as the Martian forces withdrew.

That wouldn't get them the freighters, however, and Damien was certain that the Republic had every intention of trying to seize his fleet.

"Do you think they're really willing to doom Kormar for this grandstanding?" he asked Romanov.

"I'm not sure, my lord," his bodyguard admitted. "I wouldn't. There's nothing in our files on this Admiral Emerson Wang, though."

"I know. I looked," Damien agreed. "He's enough of a hard case to try and blow us to hell and capture the convoy with his gunships, but so far, all it has cost him is a diplomatic incident we're both probably willing to smooth over."

It would be a disservice to his dead, but Damien would do it anyway. The Royal Martian Navy had never been intended as a true warfighting force. They only had three types of warships, and there were less than twenty battleships in commission. A war would fall almost entirely on the cruisers and destroyers, and the entire RMN had a strength of under three hundred ships.

The carrier group on their screens would slice through any cruiser squadron in the Protectorate, and there were *very* few formations or fleet bases with more than a cruiser squadron in place. If the Republic had a carrier group there in the Korma System, then Damien had to conclude they had at least three such groups. Almost certainly more.

Which made the armament programs taking place in the Sol and Tau Ceti Systems utterly critical—and it would still be a year before any of the new cruisers were commissioned, let alone the battleships or truly new warships.

Destroyers were starting to come out of the yards in small but increasing numbers, but Damien was now grimly aware of how short those million-ton warships might come up against their potential new enemy.

Both Damien and his King were more prepared to see the Republic go its own way than they were to fight a war—but if they had to fight a war, the Protectorate needed to complete their construction program.

"What happens if he pushes it?" Romanov asked.

"Most likely?" Damien shook his head. "We die. *Duke of Magnificence* and *Glory in Honest Purpose* can't stop those ships, so if they force a missile engagement, they'll take us down. They won't be able to stop the convoy escaping, though. If they really want an atrocity to kick everything off, they might be able to destroy half or more of the freighters, but not all of them."

"Someone would get home," the Marine concluded.

"Exactly. And there'd be a war...and Kormar wouldn't get the food they need, either."

Damien looked at the hologram and the five ships hurtling toward him.

"Admiral Wang has to know that," he admitted. "At least part of him is playing chicken, because I don't care how much of a hardcase he is. He almost certainly isn't going to let eighty million of his own people starve."

"So, what do we do?" Romanov asked.

Damien looked down at the controls on his seat and sighed.

"We get someone to set up a com channel for me so I don't hurt myself," he replied. "And then we'll see if I can talk some sense into the good Admiral."

The coms officer, Gwen Rustici, flashed Damien a thumbs-up as the recorder started.

"Admiral Emerson Wang of the Republic Interstellar Navy," Damien greeted the Republican officer. "I am Damien Montgomery, First Hand of the Mage-King of Mars."

He forced a smirk.

"Of course, we both know who the other is, but the niceties are required, aren't they? Just like I have to *ask* why your battle group is headed towards my convoy. I'm sure there is a long list of justifications you've written up for the press and your superiors, but we both know the truth.

"You are heading toward my convoy to steal what was meant to be freely given, to destroy the ships I brought to protect that cargo, and likely to force the Mages and crews of the ships in my convoy into the service of the Republic.

"This. Will. Not. Happen."

Damien bit off each word, then forced a smile.

"We have made one delivery to the surface, approximately five million tons of food. Give or take, six weeks of food for the population of Kormar. The local scientists have not developed a countermeasure to the bacteria that ate their crops. Their best plan is to plant crops somewhere else and *hope* that there is no contamination.

"I have a team that could help them. I have enough food to carry Kormar through an entire growing season. I came here to do those things, but I will not—I *cannot* do them under threat.

"Unless we come to some agreement or you pull your ships back to your docks at Baghdad, I have no choice but to evacuate this system. I'm not going to pretend I can fight your battle group with two cruisers. I will simply withdraw, and between you and me, we will have damned the people of Kormar."

Damien let that hang as he gave the camera his most level look.

"I would rather that you and I come to an agreement, save a world and eighty million people, and show both our nations that we *can* work together. But so long as your fleet is advancing, I have no choice but to withdraw.

"The next step is yours, Admiral Wang. I am prepared to negotiate. Are you?"

He waved his hand and Rustici cut off the recording.

"Do you want to review it, my lord?" she asked.

"No. Just send it," he ordered.

She nodded and set to work, and Damien leaned back in his seat. He wanted to massage his temples, but he couldn't do that. He wanted to massage his hands, but he couldn't do that, either.

Eighteen months wasn't long enough to get used to barely having any use of his hands.

"What happens if he isn't prepared to talk?" Romanov asked quietly.

"Then we leave," Damien replied, his voice equally soft. "I'll hate myself for it; don't get me wrong. But I won't sacrifice the lives of our people for nothing."

"If it feeds a world, is it nothing?" the Marine said.

"No," Damien admitted. "It isn't...but my first duty is to the people I brought out here." He shook his head.

"PO Rustici, how long until we hear back?"

"He's six light-minutes away and closing," she reported. "Minimum twelve minutes."

"More likely twenty or thirty," Damien said. "He's going to play for time, try to see if he can lure me into a trap."

"Why are you so sure of that?" Romanov asked.

"Because if I was stuck with his horrific set of objectives, that's what *I'd* do."

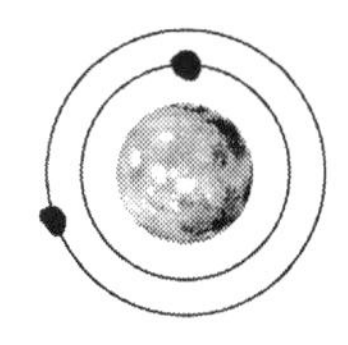

CHAPTER SEVEN

HALF OF THE TIME left before the shuttles made it aboard had passed before Damien finally heard back from the Republic officer.

"Incoming transmission. It's a pulsed recording," Rustici reported.

"Play it," Damien ordered. "Loop in Jakab and Popov. Let's keep everyone informed."

"What about Mage-Captain Flipsen?" Rustici asked and the Hand paused.

He shook his head at his own forgetfulness. Nuria Flipsen was the commanding officer of *Glory in Honest Purpose*. Jakab was the senior officer and the designated commander of the convoy, but Damien should have been including Flipsen already.

"Include her," he agreed. "And...send her my apologies. I'm out of practice, it seems."

The Petty Officer didn't quite chuckle at the Hand's error, but she did smile as she set to work.

A few seconds later, the holographic tank in the middle of the room dissolved into the image of a heavyset man barely taller than Damien. Emerson Wang seemed nearly as broad as he was tall, with a thick epicanthic fold and heavy jowls as he glared down at his audience.

Given Wang's height, Damien knew that was only possible by careful positioning of the recorders. He had to arrange things so he wasn't looking *up* at everyone. He'd never have set it up so he was looking down, however, and he felt a chill running down his spine.

"I know who you are, Damien Montgomery," the Admiral said calmly. "Your reputation for deception and trickery has made it to the Republic. We remember the man whose lies shattered the unity of the human race."

"Lies, facts, it's all the same, isn't it?" Romanov murmured in Damien's ear.

Damien had been the one to find and present the evidence connecting Legatus and the UnArcana Worlds to the covert war they'd waged against the Protectorate for over half a decade. He'd laid those crimes at the feet of the Legatan Councilor in a session of the Council of the Protectorate—and the response had been the Secession.

No one had blamed him for the Secession to his face yet, but he wasn't particularly surprised by the Admiral's tack.

"Your presence and the presence of your warships in this system are an act of war against the Republic of Faith and Reason. If your mission was as humanitarian as you say, you hardly needed warships to see the cargo delivered.

"Your own presence represents a provocation the Republic cannot ignore. You will either surrender yourself, your ships, and your convoy to internment, or I will be forced to engage and destroy your ships."

The recording ended.

"Well, that's wonderfully helpful, isn't it?" Damien said aloud. "Nice to know that I'm apparently the Republic's public enemy number one."

He couldn't help but feel a twinge of guilt, though. If he'd sent someone else to deliver the cargo, perhaps they would have managed it without all of this trouble. Only his desire to see the task done—and, he supposed, to take credit for it—had needed him to be there.

"How long until the shuttles are back aboard?"

"Thirty minutes," Jakab replied instantly. All three of Damien's senior military officers were on the channel, and his hologram split into three screens showing their faces. All of them looked as grim as Damien felt.

"My CIC says there's no course where we can prevent him ranging on us unless his missiles are much shorter-ranged than we expect," Flipsen noted.

"They know the capacity of our Phoenix VIII," Damien said. "There's no way their new main-line missile doesn't at least match its delta-*v* and powered range, if not necessarily its acceleration. All we can do is assume their weapon is comparable."

"So, what do we do, my lord?" Jakab asked.

"We proceed as per the last plan," Damien ordered. "Get the shuttles aboard and run for space clear enough to jump. We use the cruisers to cover the freighters against long-range missile fire, and we use our own weapons entirely for defense."

"And the Republic?" Flipsen said.

"We're not here to start a war," he replied. "If I thought we could engage them without risking our charges, I'd order it at this point. But we're going to need every missile we've got to cover our own asses. Our priority is getting the convoy out."

"What about Kormar?" Popov said grimly.

"There's nothing we can do," the Hand told them. "Not unless Wang decides to back off and let us unload. I'll make one more attempt to convince him to stand down, but...I don't have much hope."

"My lord, may I borrow a moment of your time?" Flipsen's request was soft-spoken, almost hesitant. Even in the hologram, the Mage-Captain's skin seemed to blend in with her black-and-gold uniform, but her gaze was level as she met Damien's eyes.

"Of course, Mage-Captain," Damien replied. He needed time to marshal his thoughts for the message he was about to send. Any distraction would be worthwhile.

"My lord...no Captain likes to admit this, but *Glory* is not combat-capable," she stated flatly. "I'm not certain that we would even be capable of assisting in the missile defense of the convoy, other than by providing an additional target.

"If that is your order, we will do so, but..."

"But your responsibility is to your ship and crew," Damien agreed. He paused thoughtfully. "Is your amplifier matrix intact?"

"I have Mages reviewing the damaged sections of the ship right now, but I believe so," Flipsen confirmed. "I can use the amplifier to great effect if given the opportunity, my lord, though I worry that—"

"They won't get close enough, Mage-Captain," Damien cut her off. "I had something very different in mind. An amplifier, Captain Flipsen, can jump from a significantly stronger gravity field than a regular jump matrix."

And if he sent one of his ships away now, it would help make his point to Admiral Wang very, *very* clearly.

"I want *Glory* to start moving immediately," he ordered. "As soon as you've confirmed your amplifier is safe to use, you are to jump to the rendezvous point and wait for us there."

Flipsen winced.

"I..." She hesitated.

"You do not want to appear a coward and you don't want to be useless," Damien said gently. "But you are correct. I will not commit a ship into action that is not capable of defending herself, let alone others. Plus, Mage-Captain, I have a use for the demonstration I'm asking you to undertake."

He smiled.

"How much are you willing to bet, Mage-Captain, that our good Admiral Wang isn't nearly as comfortable with his knowledge of the limitations of a jump matrix as you and I are?"

It took Flipsen a moment to add up the pieces he'd given her, but her answering smile was cold.

"And you intend to educate him?" she asked, then nodded. "*Glory in Honest Purpose* will be underway in the next few minutes, Lord Montgomery. We'll give you your demonstration."

Glory in Honest Purpose vanished four minutes later, a *pop* of magic teleporting the starship a full light-year away.

Damien regarded the icon of the jump flare on his holographic map for several moments.

"So, Mage-Captain Jakab," he said slowly. "What's the key to the Navy jumping out closer than the merchant ships?"

"My lord?" his subordinate said carefully.

"I've jumped a freighter with an amplifier from planetary orbit. Never tried it with a civilian jump matrix, but I wonder...like I said, what's the difference?"

"It's the amplifier, isn't it?" Jakab asked.

"No." Damien was one of the few people who could be absolutely certain of that. He was a Rune Wright, one of the incredibly tiny number of Mages who could read the power flow in a set of runes at a glance. That freighter he'd jumped had had an amplifier because he'd realized that the jump matrix and a full amplifier matrix were functionally *identical*, except that the jump matrix had additional runes to restrict it into only amplifying the teleport spell.

Converting a matrix to an amplifier wasn't easy, even knowing that. Damien wouldn't trust anyone who wasn't a Rune Wright to make the conversion, even if he gave them full diagrams.

But the *jump* function of the two sets of runes was identical.

"If it isn't the amplifier, then what?" Jakab said after a few seconds of silence.

"The amplifier is part of it. There's an additional spell we can use to absorb some of the turbulence, and the amplifier will handle that," Damien admitted. "A lot of it is power. The Navy, in general, recruits more powerful Mages than are generally found aboard merchant ships."

He smiled as his thoughts ran to their conclusion.

"The biggest piece, however, is training," he told Jakab. "We teach civilian Jump Mages that they have to jump that far out. It's safer, yes, but not required."

He heard the Mage-Captain swallow.

"Are we going to try and jump the convoy from orbit?" Jakab asked.

"No. But we *will* jump the convoy before we are actually in danger from Wang's missiles," Damien replied. "That gives us time to play with. The risk of an unstable jump is less than the risk of a few hundred antimatter warheads. Don't you agree, Captain?"

"Having never made that type of jump with a civilian matrix, I can't be certain," *Duke of Magnificence*'s Captain said levelly. "But I trust your judgment on these matters, my lord."

"We'll be underway as soon as the last shuttle is aboard, Kole," Damien ordered. "We've now demonstrated that Wang can't stop us leaving. Let's see if I can convince him to see reason.

"If we can't...well, my first responsibility is to the citizens and spacers of the Protectorate."

Jakab was silent for several seconds.

"I don't like it," he admitted. "Coming all this way just to leave with the food these people need?"

"I hate it, Captain. But I can't let Admiral Wang commandeer our ships and forcibly enslave our Mages. So, we leave."

"Yes, my lord."

The Republic battle group was still hours away from being able to fire on Damien's ships. They hadn't even crossed a full light-minute of the six separating them yet. They'd have seen *Glory* leave and Damien hoped Admiral Wang understood the message that sent.

"Admiral, I have received your message," he told the Republic officer. "I have no intention of surrendering my ships, my cargos, or myself to the Republic. If you are determined to *continue* your unprovoked attack on a humanitarian mission, then I have no choice.

"Since it appears I cannot trust you to honor a ceasefire, I will be evacuating this system in the next thirty minutes. As demonstrated by the departure of my damaged warship, you can't stop me. All you can achieve today, Admiral Emerson Wang, is to aggravate the crisis growing on the planet beneath me."

Damien paused, considering his next words carefully.

"What is more important to you? The point of pride and doctrine you're attempting to enforce or the eighty million people on Kormar?"

"Withdraw your ships to Baghdad, Admiral, and I will continue the delivery of our cargo. Once that is done, my ships and I will leave. There is no need for this to become worse than it already has.

"The choice is yours. I don't want to abandon Kormar's people, but at best, I could leave another million tons of food floating in orbit while I retreat. If we are to save these people, I need you to let me."

He stopped, then gestured to Rustici to send it.

"There's nothing more I can say," he admitted. "Either he lets us deliver our cargo or he doesn't."

"If we leave, will we come back?" the communications Petty Officer asked quietly.

"I can't see any reason they'd withdraw Wang's fleet." Damien shook his head. "I can't justify committing an *actual* act of war just to deliver food, Petty Officer."

He'd need at least two cruiser squadrons, and preferably a battleship or three, to tangle with the battle group under Admiral Wang's command. It was possible that with enough force, he could convince the man to stand off, but most likely, he'd have to engage and destroy the Republic force.

There were probably at least fifty thousand people on those ships. If the only way to save the eighty million on Kormar was to kill them all, he might have to do it. But he wasn't even sure he could pull together that much firepower before it was too late.

"Last shuttles beginning their approaches, my lord," McQueen reported. "Five minutes."

"Ten before we'll hear back from the Admiral, at least," Rustici told him.

"We're underway as soon as the shuttles are aboard," Damien ordered. "Everything after that is up to our Republican friend."

Engines flared across the convoy, fifteen massive ships bringing their drives online and accelerating out of Kormar orbit. Damien watched it all in silence, his hands resting uselessly on his lap as he struggled with the feeling of failure.

He hadn't heard anything more from Governor Motta. He hadn't even officially advised the planetary government of what was going on. If Wang wanted to cause this disaster, he could damn well bear that burden.

"All ships are online, matching acceleration of two gravities," McQueen reported. "All vectors online; we are on course."

Damien nodded. Somehow, he felt this moment deserved his attention and his silence. He was about to abandon eighty million people to an uncertain fate and he wished he could see another option.

"Vector change!" McQueen suddenly shouted. "Vector change on the Republican battle group; all ships are reversing course."

"Show me," Damien ordered, rising carefully from his seat and walking to the hologram.

The three-dimensional image flickered, zooming in on the five big Republic warships. All of them had flipped in space, massive fusion engines now blazing at the same force as before to reduce their velocity toward Kormar.

"We wait," he ordered. "Continue on course until we hear from Admiral Wang."

"Passing that to Captain Jakab," Rustici confirmed, her voice quiet.

It took only a few seconds for an image of the Mage-Captain to appear at Damien's elbow.

"Are you sure?" he asked.

"It *looks* like Wang is conceding, but I want to hear him say it," Damien told his subordinate. "A few minutes now won't make any difference to whether or not we can feed Kormar—but it could make all of the difference when it comes to getting our people out safely."

Jakab nodded grimly.

"Standing by for further orders, then."

Damien waited. Seconds ticked by as the Republican ships continued to accelerate away from him, but he needed to be sure.

"Incoming message."

"Play it," he ordered.

Admiral Emerson Wang appeared in the holotank again, superimposed over his retreating ships. There was something...odd to his expression. He wasn't smiling, his face seemed as grim as it had before, but there was a spark to his eyes that hadn't been there before.

"Hand Montgomery, you must understand that my orders are to intern your ships and you specifically," he said, his voice almost conversational. "You are high on the list of people the Republic wants to have a very long discussion with."

Wang paused thoughtfully as Damien considered his words.

Had Wang received orders since Damien had arrived? If so, *how*? For that matter, how had the Republic known he was coming? Something wasn't right there, but it wasn't today's problem. Today, Damien needed Wang to stand down.

"However, I remain a flag officer of the Republic Interstellar Navy. I understand my duty as well as my orders, and my carrier group is stationed here to *protect* Kormar. That is my duty and my priority.

"Since it is impossible for me to achieve my orders in the face of your movements and you appear to be holding eighty million citizens of the Republic somewhat hostage, I see no choice. My fleet will return to our anchorage.

"As a compromise, may I request that I be permitted to reinforce the gunships stationed in Kormar orbit? That way, I can ascertain the security of the planet I am duty-bound to protect."

Wang shook his head and Damien was *very* sure now. The smile might not have reached the Admiral's mouth, but his eyes were dancing.

"That would also allow me to use the gunships as fuel tankers to deliver my fleet's shuttles to Kormar, where they can assist you in off-loading the cargo.

"I think that the sooner we get those containers on the ground, the sooner you can leave and the happier *everyone* will be."

He paused, then bowed his head slightly.

"Well played, my lord Hand. Well played, indeed."

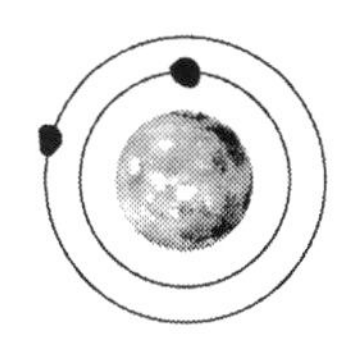

CHAPTER EIGHT

MAGE-ENSIGN ROSLYN CHAMBERS was tired. That had been a rather default part of the athletic redhead's life since reporting to the Royal Martian Naval Academy in Tau Ceti two years earlier. Somehow, showing up with a personal recommendation letter from a Hand of the Mage-King of Mars hadn't smoothed her way.

Quite the opposite. Her instructors seemed to have taken Damien Montgomery's assessment that she'd be an amazing officer as a challenge to make her the best she could be. That process had involved a *lot* of coursework, formal and informal testing, coaching and work.

To her surprise, however, she'd met every challenge they'd thrown at her and earned the grades necessary for her current posting. Every cadet had an Ensign cruise, a six-month tour of duty aboard an RMN warship to see if they were cut out for the shipboard life—it came after the first two years of their training and before the last eighteen months.

Most of those cruises, however, were aboard ships kept in the security fleets at Tau Ceti or Sol. Only the best students were actually assigned to ships the RMN expected to do serious work—and the destroyer *Stand in Righteousness* was on anti-piracy patrol.

"Ensign Chambers, are we keeping you up?" Commander Onyeka Katz asked brightly. The destroyer's tactical officer wasn't a Mage, which meant the black woman would likely never command a starship. She was pointed in her critique, often brusque in her manner, and crisp in her dress and deportment.

Roslyn had also watched her manage the destroyer's weapons through a short and ugly encounter with a pirate ship a week before and had basically decided she wanted to *be* Commander Katz when she grew up.

"No, ma'am," she replied crisply. "Scanners are clear; there's no one out here."

The likelihood that any pirates were waiting for prey one jump along the normal travel routes from the Nia Kriti Fleet Base was low, in Roslyn's opinion. Nonetheless, right now, one Mage-Ensign Roslyn Chambers was crewing *Stand in Righteousness*'s main sensor console.

She realized that the Commander had crossed from the Captain's seat beneath the semi-liquid simulacrum of the destroyer to stand behind her shoulder.

"Shipboard life takes some getting used to," Katz murmured. "Time will help with most of that fatigue, Ensign, though I'll note that actually getting *sleep* in your bunk is also known to help."

Roslyn flushed bright red and looked up at the Commander. Katz winked at her, then calmly returned to the command seat. Ensign Michael Kor was on an engineering track and serving in a completely different section of the ship. They weren't violating any regulations—she'd *checked.*

Her one turn in a juvenile prison had managed not to wreck her life, mostly thanks to Hand Montgomery. She damn well wasn't throwing away her chance in the Navy.

Her and Kor's shifts didn't align perfectly, however, and the Commander was quite right. They had lined up the previous night, and she hadn't got much in terms of actual sleep.

And instead of making trouble about it, Commander Katz had *teased* her. While still making her point.

Roslyn had seen the woman in battle and in team-supervisor mode, and now she was seeing her in counselor mode. She shook her head with a smile.

She *definitely* wanted to be Commander Katz when she grew up.

An hour later, Mage-Captain Salut Martell entered the bridge. The tall brunette strode across the runed floor with a confidence that Roslyn could only wish she shared, and settled into the command seat under the simulacrum.

"Status report, Commander Katz?" Martell asked.

"One freighter jumped in about thirty minutes ago," the tactical officer reported. "She's one of ours: on the list of ships contracted to supply the Fleet Base. ID checks out, so I let her be. She's about thirty light-seconds out, in any case."

"Nice, quiet jump point. That's how I like them," Martell agreed. "No sign of the regular patrol?"

"We haven't been here long enough," Katz replied. "If we stuck around another half-day or so..."

Nia Kriti was a key component of the Royal Martian Navy's deployment near the Fringe Worlds. The cruiser squadron and attached destroyers there were the backup to a dozen star systems, and Nia Kriti's Runic Transceiver Array was where any emergency message would be delivered.

Any star system nearby that had trouble would send a ship here, and it would be reported back to Mars and the rest of the Protectorate. Since the Navy had over twenty ships here, it would be a rare problem the Nia Kriti base couldn't deal with themselves, too.

Part of that task was sending ships out on long-distance anti-piracy patrols, like *Stand in Righteousness*'s current mission. Another was sending ships out to sweep the closest usual jump points along most routes to the system.

Pirates learned not to show up in spots like this.

Roslyn was keeping her attention on the jump freighter half a light-minute away. There wasn't much *else* out there for her to bother with, and carefully tracking the ship with her passive scanners was good practice.

"Mage-Ensign," Martell said calmly. "Come here, please."

"Yes, sir." There wasn't much else a not-quite-larval officer could say in response to the Captain. Approaching the Captain's seat, Roslyn realized that Martell had set it in jump position, lifted up next to the liquid silver simulacrum that controlled the ship's amplifier.

She also wasn't sitting in her chair, standing next to it with an almost impish grin on her face as she gestured Roslyn to the seat.

"Take the con, Mage-Ensign Chambers. The jump is yours."

Roslyn almost froze. She was trained to jump a starship, but she'd only jumped warships in carefully-controlled circumstances around Tau Ceti. According to what she'd read, *nobody* let an Ensign jump a warship of the Royal Martian Navy.

On the other hand, no one argued with a starship's Mage-Captain, either.

"Are you sure, sir?" she asked, very carefully.

"Sooner or later, Ensign Chambers, you are going to jump one of His Majesty's starships," Martell told her. "At some point, you may even be required to do so under fire—or even *into* fire. Today will be neither of those things. Nia Kriti is a safe haven, with an entire fleet on hand if something goes wrong."

She smiled.

"There is no better time to start getting experience in the real thing, Mage-Ensign. The ship is yours."

Roslyn swallowed hard and nodded. She stepped past the Captain and lowered herself into the seat. The chair adjusted to her instantly, invisible scanners adapting the cushions, arms and height of the seat into perfect positions for her.

The simulacrum now hung directly in front of her, a fifty-centimeter-high silver pyramid that exactly duplicated *Stand in Righteousness*, right down to the barely-visible-at-this-scale scar where a meteorite had stripped off a line of armor two weeks before. As turrets and sensors moved in automatic patterns on the outside of the ship, the semiliquid silver of the model flowed to mirror the movements of the real ship.

In a very real sense, the silver pyramid in front of Roslyn *was Stand in Righteousness*. Runes formed and disappeared across the surface, but she could easily see the spots on the model where the matching runes inlaid into her palms would go.

"Calculations are on the screen to your right," Martell told her. "Standard one-light-year jump. No complications, nothing strange."

Roslyn nodded again and glanced away from the simulacrum to her hands. Silver glittered in her palms and she clenched her fists reflexively at the memory of the ache when she'd woken up after getting the runes inlaid.

They weren't a tattoo. The runes were a two-millimeter-thick polymerized silver inlay, carved into her skin with a knife while she was under anesthetic. Waking up afterward had *hurt*.

That was a year before, but the memory stuck with her.

Taking a deep breath and unclenching her fists, she read over the calculations on the screen. It was as straightforward as the Captain said, but no Jump Mage was going to jump without being one hundred percent certain of what they were doing.

Certain she'd locked the numbers in her memory, she laid her palms on the simulacrum and inhaled sharply as the magic flowed into her.

Linked into the simulacrum and, through it, to the amplifier matrix woven through the ship, it was almost like Roslyn Chambers *became* the million-ton white starship. She could see with *Stand*'s sensors, feel the RFLAM turrets gently rotating in their standard patterns.

Holding the calculations in her head, she summoned her power and fed it into the simulacrum, feeling the runes absorb her power and double it. Triple it. The energy she commanded expanded a thousandfold, and she exhaled a long sigh as the power flowed through her.

Then she *stepped* and *Stand in Righteousness* jumped. The empty void around them and the freighter drifting half a light-minute away vanished in a flash of blue light, and when the light faded, they were...somewhere else.

A wave of exhaustion swept over Roslyn and she released the simulacrum. Amplifier or not, the jump spell was one of the most demanding tasks a Mage could take on.

"Navigation?" Captain Martell asked. She offered Roslyn a hand, helping the young Mage out of the command seat.

"We are bang on target," another officer reported. "We are in the Nia Kriti System, exactly nine million kilometers from the Fleet Base in orbit of Samos."

"Good." Martell took her seat back and smiled at Roslyn. "Lieutenant Sanders, send our bona fides into the base and request a docking port. We'll need to refuel and restock, and the crew needs some time off. Lieutenant Diamond, get me a zero-zero course to the station."

The officers got to work and Martell held her gaze on Roslyn.

"Well done, Mage-Ensign Chambers. Now go rest. I'm not going to make you stay on duty after jumping!"

With a tired salute and a glow of accomplishment, Roslyn obeyed.

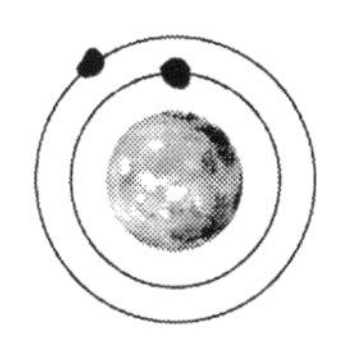

CHAPTER NINE

BY THE TIME Roslyn woke up from six hours of sleep, feeling mostly recharged, *Stand in Righteousness* was slowing down into orbit of Samos. The Nia Kriti Fleet Base itself hung in geostationary orbit above Samos's equatorial capital city. The core of the Fleet base was a massive space station assembled from prefabricated components, a set of gantries, tubes and rotating rings roughly five kilometers long.

Six cruisers were nestled into the docking cradles at the top of that station, but there was easily space for twice that many more. Gantries sprawled out from the base, each with the umbilicals and fueling systems for half a dozen destroyers.

The Nia Kriti Fleet Base was home to six cruisers and fifteen destroyers, three and a half squadrons of the Royal Martian Navy. It had been provided with the infrastructure, however, to fuel and maintain over three times that many.

Roslyn looked over the data feeding to the ship's scanners from the comfort of her quarters. Kor was still on duty, and she wasn't scheduled to go back on duty for another four hours, which left her with some studying to do...and a junior tactical officer's access to the sensor feeds.

She'd thought there'd been a lot of work going on at the Fleet Base when they came through last time, and it had only increased since then. Many of the extra docking cradles and refueling gantries had been functionally in mothballs when *Stand* had first arrived, but there had seemed to be work in progress.

Now it was obvious. Docking ports that probably hadn't even been inspected in ten years were swarming with workers, and new prefabricated station components were hanging in orbit nearby.

The Fleet Base was expanding, and rapidly. Someone was expecting to need to reinforce the Fringe, and soon.

Roslyn wasn't a full-fledged officer yet. She'd still ended up helping the Hand Damien Montgomery via a few juvenile delinquent–esque tactics before she'd ever joined the Navy. She kept up with the news, and it wasn't like the Secession had been easily missed.

There was only one possible enemy the Protectorate could be preparing for war against, but her own sparse but continuing correspondence with the First Hand told her the Protectorate's leaders didn't *want* a war. They weren't planning on starting one.

Which meant that if the Royal Martian Navy was preparing for war, either someone in the Navy was going against the intent of the Mage-King—or those same leaders were expecting the Republic to start one.

Roslyn's next shift saw her under Commander Katz's command again, part of a skeleton crew as most of the ship's crew were sent off on shore leave. From her brief conversation with Kor before reporting for duty, the other Ensign was remaining aboard as well.

Rank had its privileges, and if said rank was that you were still in training, those privileges included continuing your training.

Having full access to the scanners only confirmed what she'd seen from her quarters: Nia Kriti was in full refurbish-and-expand mode. There were no more warships on the radar than there had been the last time they'd been there, though. Just an expansion of the logistics base.

"Sir," she said carefully as Katz approached her console—the Commander made a habit of walking around the bridge at least once an hour. "Does it seem odd to you that we're expanding Nia Kriti this much? I don't see any other ships or, well, wars on the horizon."

Katz chuckled, but there was a sad tone to it.

"Really, Mage-Ensign?" she asked. "You see *no* wars on the horizon? Peace forever, huh?"

Roslyn flushed.

"I know *we* don't want a war with the Republic," she said. "I know they may be less peaceful-minded, but still...this seems like a lot of work."

"It is," Katz confirmed. "I don't know where the decision came from, Ensign, and that would be way over your head even if I did. But you're right. We don't want a war. That said, the presence of the Republic increases our threat levels out here on the Fringe, so the call was made to increase our force levels."

"I guess that makes sense," Roslyn said, looking back at her scanners. "Where are those ships, then?"

From the Commander's repeated chuckle, she wondered if she was asking more than she should be.

"From the updates we got when we arrived, Mage-Admiral Palmeiro will be arriving in the next few days. He'll take over from Mage-Admiral Castello as the commander of the Fleet Base, and he's bringing another squadron apiece of cruisers and destroyers."

Katz shook her head.

"I'm glad I don't have to be on the wall when Palmeiro takes command, though," she admitted quietly. "Castello is *senior* to him, but she's been stuck in Nia Kriti for a decade and he's been explicitly placed in command above her."

That sounded like a level of politics above Roslyn's pay grade, but... like everything else, politics were something an Ensign had to learn.

"May I ask why, sir?" she asked.

"She pissed off a Hand," Katz said bluntly. "Our Mage-Admirals are among the most powerful people in the Protectorate. Castello isn't the first Admiral to forget who she answers to. She won't be the last, either."

Roslyn shivered.

"I can't imagine arguing with a Hand," she admitted. "Have you *met* one?"

"No," Katz replied. "You have, right? You got into the Academy on a letter of recommendation from one, didn't you?"

"I got dragged into some kind of op that Hand Montgomery was running on Tau Ceti," Roslyn confirmed. "Went downhill pretty badly at the time but managed to get me into the Academy despite a stint in juvenile detention for being an idiot."

Helping Montgomery had got her gassed and briefly kidnapped. Worth it in the end...but she could not *imagine* getting on the wrong side of that terrifyingly-intense man.

"Huh." Katz regarded her levelly, then smiled. "For your reference, Ensign, that you were *ever* in juvie isn't in your Navy file. I suggest not mentioning that to your superiors in the future."

"Yes, sir. Of course, sir." Roslyn was surprised. She'd assumed that *had* been in her file.

"The Navy thinks you have great potential, Ensign Chambers. Hand Montgomery's recommendation may have caused people to look at you more closely, but you've shown that potential yourself."

Katz shook her head.

"But for today, you shouldn't need to worry too much. We'll stick around Nia Kriti until the Mage-Admiral arrives, then we'll head out on another patrol. Keep your eyes open, Ensign. We've got work to do."

Roslyn was back on duty the next day when the reinforcements arrived. Her screens flashed with warning icons as jump flares lit up the space nearby.

"Jump flares," she reported briskly to Commander Katz, exactly per the book. "Sensors are resolving twelve individual icons." She paused, studying her screens.

"Sir, I have some odd backscatter. Can you take a look?"

They were expecting twelve ships, six cruisers and six destroyers. There was an odd flare behind them, though, like there was more Cherenkov radiation than there should be.

"Do we have IDs on our jumpers yet?" Katz asked as she mirrored Roslyn's screen.

"IFFs are resolving out of the jump-flare static right now," the Ensign responded. "Running them against the warbook as the system cleans them up."

There were no real surprises in the IFF codes for the twelve ships.

"IDs confirmed: Ninth Cruiser Squadron and Eleventh Destroyer Squadron. Flagship is *Honor of Liberty*, beacons confirm Mage-Admiral Palmeiro in command." She looked up at Katz. "There's also a message sent to the main fleet base. We got the fringes of it, but I can probably decipher it."

"Leave it be, Ensign," Katz ordered. "It's almost certainly just a hello, but one doesn't eavesdrop on Admirals' coms." She chuckled. "Not without suspecting something more serious is going on, anyway."

The Commander was silent for several more seconds.

"You're right, Ensign. That backscatter is odd, but I'm not seeing a source for it. Looks like background radiation, really."

Which was a polite way of saying *it's a sensor ghost*. The downside of running systems as sensitive as those aboard a modern Martian destroyer was that they saw a lot of things that weren't relevant.

Background Cherenkov radiation was odd, but...not unheard of. Katz would know better than Roslyn, in any case.

"Yes, sir. Thanks for taking a look."

"When your junior sees something they don't understand, your job is to double-check it," the tactical officer told her. "For two reasons: one, it's my job to educate you and it'll be your job to educate your juniors in future; and two, sometimes your junior sees something of concern you might just dismiss."

"Yes, sir."

"By which I mean, keep an eye on that, Ensign Chambers," Katz ordered. "I would have dismissed it if you hadn't flagged it, but it's strange enough to deserve more attention."

Admiral Palmeiro's fleet was clearly in no hurry to make Samos orbit. Five gravities of acceleration was beyond even the emergency standard for most civilian ships, but every Royal Martian Navy ship had enough Mages aboard to keep the gravity runes refreshed.

Without those runes, they had no gravity and nothing to counteract acceleration. With those runes, RMN ships could push ten gravities easily. Fifteen in emergencies.

Five gravities saved fuel, however, and if Admiral Palmeiro wasn't expecting to need to be anywhere soon, well, it made sense.

Roslyn had to wonder, though, if his upcoming meeting with a senior officer he'd been placed in command of had anything to do with the slow pace.

That was going to be an awkward introduction, from what Commander Katz had said.

The background radiation from the jump seemed to have finally dispersed as well. Her focus was remaining on the ship's sensors, however. It was as good an excuse as any to dig into the systems and learn as much as she could about them.

Stand in Righteousness had some esoteric toys buried in her systems. Her primary long-range sensor systems were infrared-based, scanning for heat sources across empty space. She also had extraordinarily sensitive radiation receivers, capable of picking up Cherenkov radiation from a jump flare at a light day or more.

For that matter, she could pick up the miniscule radiation leakage from the two fusion plants in the mountain above New Athens, the Samosian capital. Given how carefully shielded and directed a fusion plant was, that was impressive.

Of course, on double-checking, she realized that one of the fusion plants was leaking above the regulated maximum. It was adding the equivalent of an extra couple dozen bananas a year or so to the rad dosage in the city, but there were radiation rules for a reason.

Roslyn flagged it for Katz to consider—it was hardly important enough for even the Ensign to be spending time on. The report would bounce its way through an automated notification system down to the plant, where a tech would probably go tighten three valves and fix the problem.

She was about to move on to the next system when something else flashed on the radiation scanner in the mountains. It was a tiny pulse of rads, too intense to be natural but too small to be anything else.

It had to be a ghost. The scan data made no sense—and then a *second* strange pulse occurred, several kilometers away from the first. It was like there was a more intensive source that was being muffled, which made no sense.

A third pulse triggered and Roslyn stared at her three datapoints, wondering what she was missing.

Then a *new* alert wiped the strange data from her mind.

"The seismic stations in New Athens are going nuts," Katz snapped. "Where the hell did that come from?"

Roslyn was about to mention the strange rad sources, but then she looked at the feed coming in from New Athens and lost everything she was thinking of.

They were receiving visual data from a number of sources, with a computer algorithm identifying the most important image to focus on on a moment-to-moment basis.

At that moment, it was focusing on the downtown core of New Athens, a collection of skyscrapers over thirty stories high that held the key government and corporate offices for a world of two hundred million souls.

Roslyn was only vaguely aware of the building codes involved in building hundred-plus-meter towers, but she was pretty sure they weren't supposed to be swaying like trees in a stiff wind.

Stand's bridge was silent, every member of the skeleton crew's gaze riveted on the screen as the inevitable happened. The Spire, New Athens' tallest and most prestigious building...broke. The bottom hundred meters of the tower continued to sway as the top two hundred meters *sheared* off and fell.

Other towers were already falling, and the debris from the Spire hammered into its neighbors.

"My god," Katz murmured. "It's midday there. Those buildings are..."

Packed. Full. There were a hundred words Roslyn could have finished her superior's comment with, but they all meant the same thing. The horror they were watching wasn't just the loss of buildings but the deaths of *thousands.*

"Sir! The RTA!"

It was the petty officer running the communications console who'd seen it first, but the computer algorithm picked it up as well. The feeds from the surface refocused, bringing an image of Samos's Runic Transceiver Array to the front.

From above, the RTA was a large black stone dome. The satellite feeding them the image didn't have enough resolution to show the runes visible from the outside, and most of the runes were inside the obsidian hemisphere, in any case.

It took a few seconds for Roslyn to see what the NCO and the computer had picked up, but at the point that the dome split in two, no one could miss it. A fault line had apparently run directly underneath the RTA but been quiet enough that no one had even considered it.

The RTA was built into a plateau just west of the city of New Athens, and as Roslyn watched in horror, half of the plateau *slipped,* falling away from the other half and taking a third of the construct that gave Nia Kriti interstellar communications with it—as it fell on New Athens's suburbs.

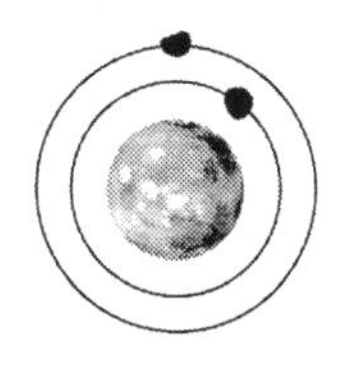

CHAPTER TEN

"ALL SHIPS in orbit will deploy their shuttles to assist in the rescue efforts immediately," Admiral Palmeiro said grimly on the hologram. The same message playing on *Stand in Righteousness*'s bridge hologram tank was playing on every screen and receiver in the fleet.

"The Ninth and Eleventh will deploy their small craft as soon as we arrive."

The screens on Roslyn's console told her that the incoming ships were no longer lazily traveling in-system at five gravities. Every ship in Palmeiro's force was now accelerating at fifteen gravities, an emergency maximum rarely deployed outside of battles.

Or, Roslyn supposed, massive crises.

"All leaves and furloughs are canceled," Palmeiro continued. "Personnel who are not currently aboard their ships are to report to the nearest police station to coordinate with local search and rescue. We will be collating lists of missing Navy personnel as rapidly as possible.

"I have already informed the government of Samos that the Navy stands by to assist in any way possible. We will shortly be asking for volunteers from all ships to assist in rescue efforts on the ground, but we'll start with the people already down there."

The graying Admiral shook his head.

"New Athens's situation is dire. We will do everything in our power to prevent it getting worse. The Navy protects, people."

The recording ended and Roslyn shivered.

No one was sure how bad it was yet. Half of the downtown core was in ruins, and the falling plateau with its interstellar transmitter had covered thousands of homes in debris.

They knew it was bad, but from what Roslyn was hearing from the surface, the locals were expecting to discover that it was much, *much* worse.

"Sir, permission to volunteer for the surface parties," Roslyn said to Katz. "A Mage can be of major..."

The tactical officer was already shaking her head sadly.

"Ensign, there are only two Mages aboard *Stand in Righteousness* right now," she pointed out gently. "Mage-Captain Martell is on the surface...hell, she was in downtown New Athens, so we don't even know if she's still alive.

"Mage-Commander Herbert sent the rest of the Jump Mages on shore leave, which means that you and the XO are the only Mages aboard this destroyer, and regs forbid us to have less than two Mages aboard."

"Which means you and I are stuck, Ensign," a familiarly accented voice said calmly.

Roslyn turned to see Mage-Commander Philip Herbert enter the bridge. *Stand in Righteousness*'s executive officer was an Earth native with an English accent recognizable even to someone who'd never visited the homeworld. He was portly and balding, with a fringe of shockingly white hair around his head.

If the Ensign saw tears in the XO's eyes, she'd never admit it to anyone.

"Unfortunately, Commander Katz, the same goes for you," he continued. "You and I are the only senior officers left aboard. Both Mage-Captain Martell and Commander Farrier are on the surface, and I can't help but feel our chief engineer, especially, is going to find her hands very full."

He smiled sadly.

"So, we'll keep the lights on up here and make sure that if there's anything we can do, it is done. But none of the three of us get to go down there and help with our own hands."

Returning to her quarters at the end of her shift, Roslyn found her fellow Ensign, roommate and lover packing. Kor was tossing uniforms into a duffle as quickly as he could, though he stopped when she came in to give her a tight embrace.

"You're going down to New Athens," she said. It wasn't really a question. *She* would be going down to New Athens if she could.

"Not exactly," he admitted, not letting her go. "*Dance of Honorable Battle* is dropping into a low orbit and being used as a shuttle tender. They want everyone who knows which way a shuttle engine is supposed to point aboard her to help turn the birds around as fast as we can."

Dance of Honorable Battle was probably the oldest warship in the system, but she was still a cruiser. Kor would be safer there than in the disaster zone that had been a city.

"They won't let me go anywhere," she told her lover. "*Stand* needs two Mages aboard, even if we don't have enough crew to fight her."

"Regs are regs for a reason, usually," he replied. "I *can* go, so..."

"So you have to," Roslyn agreed. She wasn't sure when she'd picked that up. It was something the Academy tried to hammer into their students—but she was inclined to blame Montgomery for her own sense of duty.

"Yeah. You get it, right?"

She kissed him.

"I get it. Need help packing?"

"I'm out of time," he admitted, glancing at his wrist-comp. "This will have to do."

"I didn't mean to interrupt!"

Kor laughed and kissed her back fiercely. When they came up for air, he zipped up his duffle and winked at her.

"*Totally* worth it!"

By the time Roslyn was back on duty, barely eight hours later, the role of the crews remaining aboard the ships was clear. Roslyn manned the sensor station, providing air traffic control for a specific volume of the space above New Athens.

Between civilians, police, rescue services and the Navy, there were over two thousand spacecraft and aircraft swarming the air above the city. Hospitals in New Athens couldn't handle the need, so many of those craft were transporting the injured who could be moved to other cities or into orbit.

Dance of Honorable Battle was serving as a shuttle tender, but she was hardly the only warship turning out her decks for a purpose other than her designed combat role. Two more of Admiral Castello's cruisers hung in geostationary orbit above *Dance*, with most of the squadron's medical personnel aboard as they acted as impromptu hospital ships.

New Athens was a city of four million people. Most of them were alive and uninjured, but the injured were enough to require every scrap of help they could get.

Marines and Navy MPs were on the ground in their thousands, helping the police evacuate the damaged sections and helping get food and medical supplies where they were needed.

It was something entirely outside of Roslyn's experience, and she was frankly stunned at the speed with which the whole reaction had come together. Her classes had spoken again and again about the need for contingency planning and that the Navy needed to be ready for any scenario. It seemed Mage-Admiral Castello had taken that message to heart.

They might not have planned for *this* crisis, but there'd been a plan in place to provide major humanitarian assistance to the surface.

"Damn."

The curse word was mild enough, and Commander Herbert's soft English accent somehow softened it more. There shouldn't have been *any* swearing on the bridge of a Martian destroyer, however, and Roslyn turned to look at the XO.

"The Captain didn't make it," Herbert announced very steadily. "They just confirmed the identity of the body—she'd been staying downtown but was visiting somewhere in the outer suburbs. They only just got to sweeping that area for survivors."

Stand in Righteousness's bridge was very quiet in response. Even Roslyn was in shock. She'd known Mage-Captain Martell had been on the surface, but she hadn't truly expected to learn that the older woman had died.

It brought the loss and devastation on the surface home with painful certainty. The current best guess was that over forty thousand people had died in the earthquake. New Athens had technically been on a fault, but none of the studies had suggested a quake of this magnitude was remotely likely.

"Still, people, Salut would have been rather frustrated at us if we sat around and wept for her," Commander Herbert said after several seconds of silence. "Let's keep on our toes. We're the eyes in the sky for thousands of pilots trying to rescue people. We can't let them down."

Six hours of air traffic control was enough to fry anyone's brain. With over half of *Stand in Righteousness*'s crew elsewhere, there was no one to take over from Roslyn.

So, she kept going. The only real sound on the bridge was people talking into headsets, guiding the tiny percentage of the shuttlecraft currently having computer troubles. Her zone was currently clear and she took a moment to lean back in her seat and rub her eyes.

She was feeding sensor data to most of the other consoles on the bridge, allowing the destroyer to act as an ATC for about a hundred small craft. The rest of the ships were doing the same, and their attention was definitely focused on the planet below.

Mage-Admiral Palmeiro's ships would be in orbit in under an hour, doubling the number of military spacecraft and ships available. That would hopefully spread the workload out a bit further.

Roslyn checked over her long-range scanners to double-check the incoming ships' locations. "Best practices" said that she should be checking them anyway, and she wanted to make sure she built good habits.

She was very aware just how larval her current stage of officerhood was, and she was determined to be a *good* officer by building good habits.

Running the scanners left her scratching her head. Something wasn't right. She could see Mage-Admiral Palmeiro's squadrons exactly where they were supposed to be, but there was another group of icons beyond them.

She queried the squadron tactical network, to see if anyone else had noticed them.

The result gave Roslyn a minor flush of embarrassment. They'd been flagged over an hour earlier by the sensor crew aboard Mage-Admiral Castello's flagship, *Thunderous Roar of Justice*. Flagged, IDed and tagged as helpful.

Habit opened the full file, however, and a strange chill ran down her spine.

Thunderous Roar's sensor crew had picked up the contacts, yes. They'd done enough analysis to confirm they were too small and too numerous to be jump-ships...and that was it. The contacts had then been flagged as friendlies.

Roslyn could see the logic. They had to be sublight ships; they were running fusion drives, so they were almost certainly civilian...but she came back to the whole "best practices." Doctrine and regs said that a contact shouldn't be flagged as friendly without a solid ID.

As Kor had said when she'd complained about being stuck aboard *Stand*, regs were regs for a reason.

Stand in Righteousness could spare a radar emitter for a few minutes to salve her itchy nerves, she judged. With one eye still on her ATC duties, she retasked one of the emitters on the opposite side of the ship from the planet and targeted it at the incoming contacts.

They were still a good distance out, and it took most of a minute for the data to come back. She'd used a relatively weak pulse, but it was enough to get her some data from all of the ships.

They were identical. All of them. That didn't make any sense, not for civilians. If the cluster was civilian ships coming in to lend a hand—entirely likely and clearly what *Thunderous Roar*'s crew had assumed—there'd be almost as many different designs as there were ships.

Not hundreds of identical ships. Even as she was staring at that, however, she realized that she had managed to build some of the habits she was working—she'd automatically fed the data into the warbook and it happily popped back a response.

One that made no sense.

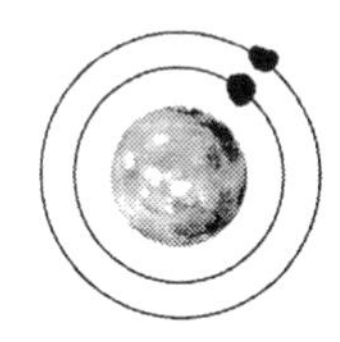

CHAPTER ELEVEN

"SIR, I THINK I need you to take a look at this," Roslyn said loudly as she stared at the impossible data. "The warbook is giving me a seventy percent probability that I'm looking at a flight group of Legatan gunships."

Herbert nearly teleported to her station.

"That's impossible," he noted slowly. "Show me."

She gestured to the screen and he looked it over. His florid face paled as he did.

"Two hundred and fifty identical ships," he whispered. "Dear gods, where did they *come* from?"

"I have to be misreading something," Roslyn told him. "I've fed something—"

"No, Ensign. You are reading it entirely correctly," he stated flatly. "Stay here."

She stared after Mage-Commander Philip Herbert as he calmly and steadily walked over to the Captain's seat and flipped up a covering panel to hit a button.

A flashing alert blared up and a recorded voice started speaking over the PA system.

"Battle stations. Battle stations. All hands to battle stations."

Herbert calmly took his seat and tapped a command.

"All ships, all ships. Bandits inbound, I repeat, Bandits inbound. Republic warships are in-system and making an assault approach on Mage-Admiral Palmeiro's fleet.

"I repeat, Bandits inbound. Republic warships are in-system and making an assault approach on Mage-Admiral Palmeiro's fleet."

Stand in Righteousness's acting captain rotated his chair, studying his skeleton bridge crew.

"Get us underway," he ordered. "Commander Katz will be on the bridge in a few minutes. Ensign Chambers, you're on tactical until she gets here. Lieutenant Pepper, vector us away from the gunships."

Confusion was reigning across the system, and Roslyn felt panic try to seize her throat. There were three squadrons of warships in orbit, and none of them were prepared for battle. All of them were under-crewed, their small craft and much of their staff helping in the disaster relief.

"Commander Herbert, what the hell is going on?"

Roslyn recognized Mage-Admiral Palmeiro's voice from the all-ships broadcast.

"What kind of joke is this?" the Mage-Admiral continued. "There's no Republic ships in this system. The only craft on our radar are local sublight ships!"

"They're not local, sir. They're gunships," Herbert said flatly. "I don't know how, I don't know why. But check your scans, sir. *Look* at the damn data before—"

"Missile launch," Roslyn cut him off, her report half-instinctual as her screen lit up with threat icons. "We can't resolve individual targets at this range." She swallowed. "Estimate forty seconds to impact."

She could barely make out the gunships now behind a swarm of at least a thousand missiles. Forty seconds wasn't enough time to maneuver, to bring ships to readiness. All that Admiral Palmeiro's people had to protect them was the automated defense sequence on the RFLAMs.

"I see," Palmeiro said quietly. He was clearly looking at much the same data as Roslyn and Herbert, and he faced the camera levelly. "By the time this message arrives, I will be dead.

"You will take your ship and whatever Mages you have aboard and you will leave the Nia Kriti System immediately. You will proceed to the Hoisin System and inform the rest of the Navy of events here."

And it finally sank in for Roslyn. The RTA had been destroyed in the earthquake. There was no way for anyone to tell the Protectorate what was happening there. An entire Protectorate fleet was about to be obliterated and the Mage-King wouldn't even know.

Unless they ran.

"These orders are non-discretionary, Mage-Commander. You will get underway immediately. Godspeed and good lu—"

Roslyn didn't even need to check her screens to know why the message had cut off. Mage-Admiral Palmeiro had run out of time.

The gunships were impossible. They were sublight ships, and even if the Republic had managed to refit them with jump matrices, where had they found *two hundred and fifty* Mages to jump them?

Even as she was questioning that the answer appeared as five massive ships lit off fusion engines in the outer system.

"Carriers," she half-whispered. "They've built themselves a fleet of carriers."

Stand in Righteousness was the only ship already at battle stations, and Roslyn was grimly aware of how understrength they were. Panic coiled through her and it took every scrap of self-control she'd learned in jail and the Academy alike to keep her breathing under control.

"Commander Katz has gone to the secondary bridge," Herbert told her. "She's taking up the XO's seat. You're acting tactical officer, Ensign. What have you got for me?"

Roslyn swallowed hard. She wasn't ready for this...but she was the one on the spot.

"Mage-Admiral Palmeiro's force is gone," she told him, her voice only breaking a little. "The gunship swarm is still heading our way and continuing to accelerate. They'll pass Samos traveling just over one percent of lightspeed. Presumably, they still have missiles and most of our ships won't be mobile yet."

"And they're undermanned and unready," her new Captain said quietly. As he spoke, the destroyer's engines *finally* flared to life beneath them. "Our orders are non-discretionary, people, and Palmeiro had the authority to issue them.

"We run."

Only silence answered him. Even Roslyn couldn't muster up anything to say. It was wrong. It *had* to be the wrong call...but the incoming gunships were only ten minutes at most from missile range, and the fleet wasn't going to be ready.

"Chambers, make certain you have operational RFLAM turrets and missile launchers," Herbert ordered. "If you need people to man the mounts, let me know ASAP. The only thing with higher priority than our missile defenses is our engines. If we don't make it out of here, no one is going to know what happened until it's too late."

"It's war," Roslyn breathed. "They've declared war."

"They've started one, that's for sure," the Mage-Commander agreed. "Somehow, I doubt they've been so polite as to *tell* anyone." He shook his head. "Once we have guns, focus on the sensors. Get me everything you can on those gunships and the warships, Ensign. Every scrap of data we have will be worth this ship's weight in gold."

Roslyn nodded and got to work. Her list of tasks was short, but none of it was simple. None of her weapon mounts or turrets had their full crews, but even *she* knew the full crews weren't actually necessary.

How many people her guns actually needed, though... There was an easy way to answer that question. She'd only physically met Chief Petty Officer Chenda Chey, the senior noncom for *Stand in Righteousness*'s tactical team, once, but she knew the woman's duty station was Missile One.

"Chief Chey, are you there?" she asked, pulling on a headset and opening a channel to the weapon mount.

"I'm here. You're left in charge, Ensign?" Chey asked bluntly.

"Herbert's in command and Katz is running secondary control," Roslyn reeled off. "Chief, we're undermanned and our missile defenses are the most important thing we need running. What's the *minimum* we can run the RFLAMs and launchers with?"

"Strip the battle lasers and we've got sixty-one of our people aboard," Chey told her. "We need at least three people per missile launcher and one per RFLAM."

Twenty-four missile launchers and thirty-six RFLAM turrets. A hundred and eight people—and they had sixty trained weapons crew.

"Can you sort out who we've got and get them in motion?" Roslyn asked.

The Chief chuckled.

"That's supposed to be an *order*, sir," she pointed out. "I'll make it happen. If you can get me another forty-odd hands, though..."

"I'll talk to the Commander," the Ensign promised, flushing at the Chief's correction. "Everyone we get, I'll send to you."

"I'll get them where they need to go, Ensign. See you on the other side."

Roslyn cut the channel, swallowed down the acid taste of fear in her mouth again, and turned to talk to Mage-Commander Herbert.

At full crew, *Stand in Righteousness* had just under six hundred spacers and Marines. As she fled Samos orbit, she had just over two hundred souls aboard.

By the time they had minimum crew everywhere they needed it, there were only three people left on the bridge itself. One Chief was flying the ship, Mage-Commander Herbert was trying to coordinate everything, and one underqualified Ensign was running the tactical console.

Kor was aboard *Dance of Honorable Battle*, and the swarm of engineers aboard the old cruiser had made her the first ship actively online. Her orbit was so low, however, that it would take her the entire time before the gunships reached the planet just to safely get out of the planet's gravity well.

The system might be about to fall to the Republic, but that still wasn't enough to justify firing a cruiser's antimatter engines that close to an inhabited planet.

Roslyn was probably one of the few people in the star system with the time and sensors to know what was going on. She had a timer running on one side of her screen, showing the countdown to the estimated range of the missiles carried by the Republic gunships.

Her current focus was on the Republic warships, hitting them with every active sensor the destroyer commanded. There was no subtlety to what she was doing, but there wasn't much to be subtle about.

Stand was running. Their job was to warn the Protectorate about what had happened, and she was going to learn as much about their new enemy as she could.

"They must have come in on a direct line behind Admiral Palmeiro's fleet," Katz said over the link from secondary control. "That way, we thought their jump flare was backscatter to Palmeiro's." The XO shook her head on the screen.

There was only one other person in secondary control with her. *Stand*'s bridge was her simulacrum chamber. If something happened to that room, the destroyer wasn't leaving. All Katz would be able to do at that point is fight—and probably surrender.

"That's impossible," Herbert replied. "They'd have needed live data on Palmeiro's fleet and a complete itinerary. That would need them to have...I don't know, someone aboard his ships who could tell them in real time what he was doing."

Which was impossible. And yet...

"And yet they did it," Roslyn whispered and a sudden horrifying thought hit her. "Sirs...could they have triggered the fault? With...say, nuclear bombs?"

"It's theoretically possible," Katz said after several seconds of silence. "Why?"

"I'd forgot, with everything that happened, but I picked up some odd rad pulses just before the quake."

"Sweet God," Herbert said in shock. "All of this was planned. They wrecked a city to take out the RTA and weaken the fleet."

"I'm not even sure weakening the fleet was required," Roslyn admitted. "I'm forwarding you both everything I have on their task group."

She tapped a command, looking over the data herself.

"The central ship is the size of our battleships," she told them. "At least fifty million tons, possibly sixty. She's got two main hulls on either side of what I'm guessing is her recovery-and-launch deck, and they're big enough that's she's probably got rotational gravity decks *inside* her armor."

Roslyn shook her head.

"She's almost certainly primarily a carrier, but I wouldn't want to tangle with her with less than a battleship of our own. Her escorts are almost as bad. Two are half again the size of our cruisers, fifteen million tons."

"Big enough for internal centrifuge decks, like the carrier," Katz noted. "The other two don't look smaller."

"No. Forty million tons apiece, maybe bigger again," Roslyn told them. "Like the smaller ships, I'd say they're direct combatants. Battleships."

Assuming the ships were a ton-for-ton match for the Martian Navy, at least outside of amplifier range, Admiral Castello's fleet was outmassed and outgunned—and undermanned and outmaneuvered.

Roslyn was grimly certain she was going to have to watch her boyfriend die.

Only half of the destroyers had their engines online by the time the gunships opened fire. Only two of the cruisers had managed it, and *Dance of Honorable Battle* was still struggling up from low orbit.

"Ten thousand gravities," Herbert noted. "Didn't notice that before; that's quite the upgrade. Last data we have on their Excalibur missiles was eighty-five hundred, but they'd pushed the flight time out to match our Phoenix VIII in range."

"Assuming this is their max range, they'd have a range of about eight million from rest," Roslyn replied. "I doubt that assumption is valid."

"No." Herbert shook his head. "How many are targeted on us?"

"None," Roslyn admitted. "It looks like they're sending everything at the cruisers."

Silence filled *Stand*'s bridge.

"Any chance they'll survive?" the Mage-Commander asked.

"I have no idea, sir," Roslyn said. "That's two hundred and fifty missiles per cruiser. They could handle that in three or four salvos, but just one..."

A second salvo blasted clear of the gunships as she spoke. How many missiles did those little ships carry? They were only about fifty thousand tons apiece, smaller than any Legatan gunships they had in the warbook.

The computer was assessing them as basically the core hull of a *Crucifix*-class gunship without the living pods. Their crews almost certainly lived aboard the carrier instead of their gunships, and they probably had less fuel aboard, too.

"And the battleships and cruisers are coming in fast," Herbert concluded. "Watch for any missiles coming our way."

"Yes, sir." Roslyn paused. She felt very young and very small right now. "Couldn't we...jump away now?"

Their presence wouldn't change what was about to happen. She hated herself for it, but she didn't want to watch it.

"We could," the Mage-Commander said, very gently. "And I understand why you want to, Ensign. We just don't have a choice. Someone needs to see what happens. We need to know how this ends."

Roslyn nodded and turned back to her console. She understood. She didn't *want* to understand, but she did.

The first salvo fell on the fleet like the hammer of an enraged god. The cruisers might not have had engines yet, but they'd brought most of their defenses online and the destroyers were trying to cover them.

The inability of most of the cruisers to dodge was their doom. Even wrecked missiles left trails of vapor and half-annihilated antimatter, and even as the defenders shattered the vast majority of the incoming fire, that debris collided with its targets at over fifteen percent of the speed of light.

Mage-Admiral Castello presumably died with her flagship. *Dance of Honorable Battle* survived, the oldest of the squadron's cruisers shielded from the worst of the debris by the atmosphere. The cruiser *Rise of Dancing Manticores* took a beating but continued to maneuver.

"*Rise of Dancing Manticores* has taken over the tactical network," Roslyn reported, then swallowed. "They're sending us a full feed."

Manticores' Captain clearly understood what *Stand in Righteousness* was doing. She was sending them every piece of data she could.

It wasn't for very long. The second salvo crashed home on a mere two cruisers, and it didn't matter that most of the destroyers were maneuvering now.

Roslyn closed her eyes as the download from *Rise of Dancing Manticores* cut off—and both cruisers vanished from her screens.

The gunships didn't seem to have any more missiles now, but the speed at which they were closing with the remaining destroyers suggested they still had weapons to play with. This time, however, the Martian ships actually had a chance to engage.

Missiles flashed out from the eight surviving destroyers and the battered remnants of two squadrons formed up to try and push through the gunships to make space flat enough to jump from.

Eight destroyers, unfortunately, didn't fire enough missiles to get through even half-effective defenses on two hundred and fifty platforms, and the gunships swept into battle-laser range.

The destroyers carried over a hundred and sixty lasers and filled deep space with coherent light. The gunships carried over *seven* hundred individually weaker weapons.

It was over as soon as light could travel between the two fleets. For the first time since they'd arrived, the Republic paid for their victory, but the destroyers had focused their fire to guarantee kills. Two dozen gunships disappeared, but the remnants of the defenders of the Nia Kriti Fleet Base went with them.

"I'm..." Roslyn paused, swallowing down a sick taste in her mouth as she looked helplessly over at Mage-Commander Herbert. "I'm picking up what the warbook is calling Legatus Self-Defense Force Space Assault transports, battalion-sized."

"Why would the Republic build something new when the LSDF had a tried-and-tested design?" Herbert asked rhetorically. "The base will surrender. That's policy. The Protectorate doesn't want a scorched-earth war, so we won't blow a space station with fifteen thousand people aboard."

Roslyn winced at the thought. It hadn't even occurred to her—even if she had just watched over forty thousand men and women wearing the same uniform she did die.

"We're done here, Ensign," the Mage-Commander continued. "I'm guessing the Republic is starting to pay attention to us now?"

"One of the cruisers is changing their vector," she confirmed. "They won't get to us anytime soon, but if we don't jump, they'll cut us off eventually."

Herbert nodded and laid his hands on the simulacrum.

"Let's get out of here."

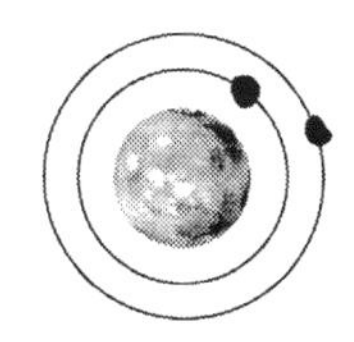

CHAPTER TWELVE

"THAT'S IT, my lord," Romanov reported. "The last shuttles have off-loaded their cargo and are heading back to the convoy."

Damien nodded silently, his hands resting on his lap as he studied the image displayed on his office's immense window. Persephone head-butted his leg for attention and he sighed, then reached down to pat the cat's head.

"As soon as the shuttles are aboard, we are getting out of here," he said quietly. "Make sure Mage-Captain Jakab and the freighter captains are advised."

"That's been the plan for two days, my lord," his bodyguard pointed out. "Everyone knows."

Damien chuckled bitterly, looking at the icons of fifty Republican gunships orbiting on the opposite side of the planet from his fleet.

"Has Wang moved at all?" he asked.

"Not from what anyone is telling me. His ships are still sitting at Baghdad. He'll get the update that we're nearly done soon enough."

"And I'm sure we'll hear from him then," Damien agreed. Persephone shoved her head more firmly into his hand, which unfortunately did not work with his injury. Pain went spiking all up his arm and shoulder, and he pulled himself back up to sitting with a hiss.

"My lord?"

"Just...my hands." The kitten mewed pitifully and butted his leg in what he thought *might* have been an apology. Damien sighed and gestured gently with the hand that wasn't currently hurting. Magic flared through him and the kitten was on his lap.

She looked surprised for a moment, then curled up and started purring.

"Mage-Captain Jakab doesn't need me to remind him of the plan, you're right," Damien conceded. "I want to know the instant any of the Republican ships so much as twitch."

Romanov didn't even get a chance to respond before a chime announced an incoming message from the bridge. Damien gestured his bodyguard to a seat and tried to tap the Accept command.

Even with his system adapted for his current needs, though, he didn't manage it without overstretching his scarred forearms. His whimper of pain was met with soft paws poking at his arm and a purring head shoved gently into his stomach.

"Persephone says, 'Use the voice command,' my lord," his bodyguard said in a perfectly professional tone.

Damien chuckled and shook his head at both his subordinate and his cat.

"System, accept incoming call," he ordered aloud.

Mage-Captain Jakab appeared in front of him, the video feed appearing next to the tactical plot on the screens laid onto the observation deck window.

"My lord, we have an incoming transmission from Admiral Wang," he reported. "I'd guess that his people advised him we were nearly done."

"Of course they did," Damien acknowledged. "Send it to my screen, Mage-Captain. Make sure you're in the loop. No point in my summarizing his posturing for you, after all."

His window dissolved into the image of the heavyset Republican Admiral. Wang was glaring at the camera and there was a new, determined set to his jaw.

"My people inform me that by the time you receive this message, you will have completed your off-loading. Your only excuse for being in this system is done, Montgomery. If you have not left the system by midnight tonight, Olympus Mons Time, I will engage and destroy your ship.

"This is no longer discretionary. You will leave or you will be destroyed."

He shook his head.

"There is nothing more to say, Montgomery."

The message cut and Jakab's image reappeared.

"That was...brusque," the Mage-Captain noted.

"That was what I was expecting," Damien replied. "Though that was shorter than I was expecting." He shook his head lightly, studying the screen showing him the positions of the ships in the system.

"What I find fascinating, though, was his descriptor of his plan," the Hand continued. "'This is no longer discretionary.' Which sounds, to me, like it's no longer at *his* discretion."

"Even the Governor said she can't override him," Romanov said. "So, who in this system is giving him orders?"

"No one," Damien agreed. "And that's the interesting part, isn't it? We've had evidence before that Legatus has some kind of interstellar communications. Our friend Wang should have been more careful with his words.

"For now, however, that's merely a curiosity. What is truly *concerning* is the overall hostility of Admiral Wang's force, not to mention its firepower. We'll head to rendezvous with *Glory in Honest Purpose*, but from there, we'll leave the convoy with *Glory* and make our own way."

"Where to, my lord?" Jakab asked.

"The convoy is supposed to return to Tau Ceti," Damien replied. "There's an RTA there and I could report it, but only at the cost of several days' travel time. We spent enough time here. What's the closest array?"

"Ardennes," Jakab replied. "I'm sure we'll be welcome there. Governor Riordan and Minister Amiri will be pleased to see you."

Damien chuckled. Julia had been his bodyguard before Romanov, but her whirlwind romance with the now-Governor of Ardennes had eventually taken her to different duties. She was her husband's Minister of Defense, responsible for rebuilding the Ardennes System Defense Force.

Of course, the reason the ASDF had needed rebuilding was that an RMN force operating under Damien Montgomery's orders had blown the entire fleet to pieces while removing the previous Governor.

There'd been reasons—good ones; the Protectorate couldn't stand by and allow massacres by governments, after all—but it was an open question how welcome Damien would actually be in Ardennes.

"And others won't be," he concluded. "Nonetheless, it's the closest RTA. We can be there in two days. Tau Ceti is six."

"We'll get you there, my lord," Jakab promised. "This whole situation makes my skin crawl."

"You too, huh?" Damien murmured. "Yeah. Something doesn't sit right. There's no way Wang would have been this aggressive without backing from the Lord Protector."

"That could mean war," his ship's Captain noted.

"We've been expecting it since they responded to our charges of treason with secession," the Hand said. "More time would be better, but this has been coming since the beginning.

"The Lord Protector needs *something* to justify the existence of his Republic. Fighting the Protectorate is the only idea on the field that I'm aware of."

The last of the shuttles was tucking themselves into their motherships' docking bays when a new communication request came in on the encrypted com channel the Governor had used before. This time, Damien's people connected Governor Motta to him instantly.

Once again, she was in the quiet office that was probably her working space. Motta looked tired, leaning on her desk with both hands as she gazed levelly at the camera.

"Lord Montgomery," she greeted him. "On your way, I presume?"

"Within the next ten minutes or so," he confirmed. "Admiral Wang has made it clear that our limited welcome has expired."

"Admiral Wang is under very different pressures than I am," she said. "We ran the numbers, Montgomery. Almost two tons of food per person per standard year. You've bought us over a year of breathing room... I... There are no words, Lord Montgomery. Your scientists didn't manage to do much, but they gave us some key places to start—and you made sure my people will survive until we can get it fixed."

"I intended to do more, but I can't leave Dr. Aputsiaq's team behind in what is potentially hostile territory," Damien admitted.

"It's not potential," she said quietly. "I shouldn't tell you this, but I can't imagine it's a surprise: the Republic Assembly has given the Lord Protector the authority to go to war against the Protectorate. I don't know when he'll pull the trigger, but...it's coming."

"We could hope," he replied, his tone equally soft. "We don't want a war with the Republic."

"I figured that when you showed up with enough food to save my planet from famine." She shook her head. "I have no authority to oppose the Republic, Lord Montgomery. Opinion polls show a sixty percent majority of my people are pleased to be part of it, though it's a much smaller component that's really happy about secession."

"It's done, anyway," Damien said. "We have to live with it. I don't want a war, Governor, but don't make the mistake of thinking that means the Protectorate won't fight one."

"I know. I'm going to keep my eyes and ears open," Motta told him. "I know which side I'm on, regardless of what I may think of some of the Republic's plans, but you've handed us a miracle. If I can convince some folks to consider peace who might not have otherwise, well, I'll talk their damn ears off."

"I appreciate it," he replied. "You have a job to do, Governor Motta: take care of your people. That's what they elected you for, and that's all I need you to do, too."

"Maybe. But I owe you, Damien Montgomery," she said. "My entire damn planet owes you, and things may be tense right now, but we will remember what you did for us.

"God speed you, Hand Montgomery. We may never meet again, but know that we will remember you."

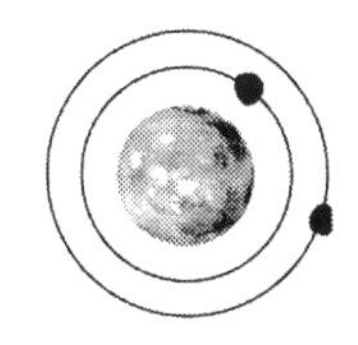

CHAPTER THIRTEEN

THE TRIP to Ardennes was as fast as humanly possible. The Mages aboard *Duke of Magnificence*, from Mage-Captain Jakab on down, were clearly feeling the same pressure and worries as the Hand giving the orders.

They crossed the thirty light-years from the rendezvous point to Ardennes in a day. That was...too fast, Damien knew. Even Navy Mages weren't supposed to jump more than every six hours. To travel thirty light-years in one day, the six Mages aboard *Duke* had jumped every four and a half.

He hadn't given any orders to push that hard, but he couldn't argue with the need. In other times, he'd have achieved the same goal by stepping into the jump rotation himself, but the jump runes on his palms had melted along with the Runes of Power on his forearms.

"Mage-Captain Jakab," he said calmly as he opened a link to his bridge. "I see we are already in Ardennes. That seems...fast."

"They volunteered, my lord," Jakab admitted. "And once my juniors had pushed themselves that hard, what was I to do but push myself harder?"

Damien shook his head.

"If I see or hear of you—or any of your jump Mages—on duty in the next twenty-four hours, I will be *most* upset," he said quietly. "I've walked too close to the line of fatal burnout myself to blithely allow my subordinates to risk it. I trust you and your Mages to have been careful—but you *will* rest now.

"Am I clear?"

"Yes, my lord." Jakab inclined his head. "I wouldn't have let them do this if we were going further. We need at least that level of rest."

"Yes. You do," Damien agreed. "Now go sleep, Mage-Captain. And thank you."

He dropped the channel and looked at the map. They'd arrived quite close to the planet, less than four hours' flight at the standard acceleration of the battlecruiser. Not quite close enough for a live conversation, but it wouldn't be too bad.

"System, get me the Coms Section," he ordered. The image of a young man in a Lieutenant's uniform promptly greeted him, the officer saluting crisply as he recognized who was calling.

"How may we assist, Lord Montgomery?"

"Lieutenant Parker, I need a link to Governor Riordan as quickly as possible. Can you get that for me?"

"Yes, sir!" Parker agreed instantly. "I'll get in touch with his people and let you know as soon as I have him on the line."

"Damien Montgomery, it's good to see you," Mikael Riordan greeted him a few minutes later. The former rebel rabble-rouser turned politician was an almost spectacularly unremarkable man. He could blend into any crowd.

Until, in Damien's experience at least, he opened his mouth. He'd been a recruiter for the Ardennes Freedom Wing during their revolt, and he'd talked his way into a position with the new, Mars-appointed Governor after Damien had used that revolt to overthrow the corrupt previous government.

"You may not be as pleased to see me by the time you're done getting the news," Damien responded. "We were attacked by Republic forces while carrying out a humanitarian mission in the Korma System. We eventually managed to get a rough truce allowing us to complete our mission, but..."

"Damn. You need the RTA," Riordan said after a few seconds of light-speed delay. "At least this time, we don't have to arrange a distraction, huh?"

During the rebellion, Damien had helped the Freedom Wing to break into a high-security prison holding a number of their people, as a distraction to get him access to the RTA.

"Not unless you've got something going on I don't know about," Damien agreed. "We'll be in orbit in a few hours and I'll be dropping immediately. Can you make certain the RTA is available for my use?"

"Of course. Any assistance that Ardennes can provide is yours, Lord Montgomery. We have not forgotten your service."

"I may take you up on that," the Hand replied as he glanced over the scan data showing him the ships of the Ardennes System Defense Force. "I see Julia has been busy."

There was a major Navy refueling station in the outer system there. It had once been host to an entire squadron of Martian cruisers, but the Navy was starting to feel the pinch of the various losses inflicted by Legatus's shadow war.

They'd only *had* fifteen squadrons of cruisers—ninety ships—to begin with. Now, until the new construction came online, they were down to eleven squadrons and a handful of extras like *Duke of Magnificence*. Seventy ships. Ardennes's Martian defenders now consisted of two squadrons of destroyers.

The ASDF, however, had two destroyer squadrons of their own *and* three cruisers. All Tau Cetan–built, if Damien recognized the designs.

Tau Ceti shipyards built many of the Royal Martian Navy's ships. They also built "export" versions of similar hulls with only jump matrices for the many system militias in the Protectorate.

"I gave her a budget," Riordan agreed. "I'm not entirely sure how she got fifteen warships for that budget, but I know when not to ask questions of my wife!"

"I'll want to sit down with both of you once I've spoken to His Majesty," Damien told the Governor. "Unless Julia has changed dramatically in the last two years, she almost certainly is better up to date than

I am. I've been out of the loop for two weeks, and I'm worried the galaxy may have changed behind my back."

"If it has, Julia will know," Riordan agreed. "I'll get our intel people talking to the Navy squadrons, see if we can pull together a briefing for you. I think you're bearing the biggest news, my lord, but we'll see what we scrape up when we poke at the barrel."

A robed Transceiver Mage ushered Damien into the central nexus of the Runic Transceiver Array. She'd already given the spiel about shutting down the rest of the space, and he gently waved her away as she paused hesitantly.

"Thank you, Mage O'Malley. I know how this works," he told her.

She glanced at his hands.

"Will you be all right, my lord?" she asked.

"I don't need interface runes for this, Mage," Damien reminded her. "I know my limits; don't worry. Now, if you don't mind..."

She bowed her way out and he shook his head with a smile. It seemed like most of the people around him were more concerned about his injuries than he was. Despite how they wanted to treat him, he was most definitely *not* a cripple.

He just had crippled hands. He was sure there was an important difference in there somewhere—one the fact that he remained the third most powerful Mage alive made very relevant.

Resting his hands gently against his sides, he reached out for the construct surrounding him with his power, linking energy into the layers upon layers of runes that made up the RTA. Silver inlays in the obsidian around him flared to life in his sight, his Rune Wright gifts allowing him to trace the flow of power.

Long practice allowed him to shape the energy, directing it toward the Sol System. Only one RTA could be built in a star system, because the catchment area for the transmission was actually somewhat larger than most systems.

The one in Sol was on Mars, on the slopes of Olympus Mons, where the Mage-King could rapidly reach it.

"Solar RTA, this is First Hand Damien Montgomery," he said aloud. The magic picked up his voice and flung it across the stars in the blink of an eye. "I need to speak with His Majesty if he's available. I am at the Ardennes RTA and will remain here until I hear from him."

"Hand Montgomery, this is Transceiver Mage Rodriguez," another voice answered him. "We will make the connection with His Majesty and begin securing the Solar RTA. We will advise as soon as we have a timeline on His Majesty's arrival; please hold on."

With the arrays secured on both ends, both Ardennes and Sol were now removed from the Protectorate communication network. Incoming coms outside of the secured line would be magically routed to a side chamber where they would be recorded for review once the lockdown lifted.

The Protectorate had learned a long time before that the only thing that would be transmitted was a Mage's voice. It didn't even seem to be their speech so much as their *intention* to speak. No data transmission, no video communications. Just the voice of one Mage on each end.

"His Majesty will be here in roughly five minutes, my lord," Mage Rodriguez informed him. "Please hold on."

"Of course."

Damien wasn't watching the time closely, but he suspected it was less than five minutes before the familiar voice of Desmond Michael Alexander the Third, the Mage-King of Mars and Protector of Humanity, sounded in his ears.

"Damien. It's good to hear from you. How did the Korma mission go?"

"Strangely and dangerously," Damien replied. "First and foremost: we came under attack by Republic forces. They appear to have perfected the gunship carrier concept that their agents were working with during the Antonius Incident, and are deploying carrier groups reinforced with heavy warships somewhere between our cruisers and battleships in weight.

"I don't know where they're getting the Mages for them, but it makes some sense. A five-ship group can run with five or ten Mages, and if that group outguns any of our individual formations..."

"We could be in trouble," Alexander agreed. "And Kormar?"

"We managed to negotiate a truce long enough to deliver the food, but *I* am apparently specifically persona non grata in the Republic of Faith and Reason."

"That's not really a surprise," the King pointed out. "You pissed them off pretty badly."

"I'm checking intelligence reports after this, but their aggression in Korma worries me," Damien said. "I can't see their local commander being that aggressive unless they were already moving towards war. The Governor of Korma warned me that their Assembly has already voted to give Solace the authority to wage war on us."

"Damn. Our intelligence networks in the Republic are a disaster right now, Damien," Alexander told him. "We didn't know that."

"Their local commander also seemed to be receiving orders directly from Legatus in something approximating real time," Damien added. "I think we need to double down on the assumption that they have some form of technological FTL communicator."

"Capturing one of those is going to be a high priority once this war starts."

"I think the war may have already started, my liege," Damien said grimly. "We haven't heard anything yet?"

"Nothing," Alexander confirmed. "I'll double-check reports on my side as well, but I think we'll want to investigate our systems along the border without RTAs. I'll see the orders passed to the Navy."

"I'm going to check in with the border RTAs myself," the Hand promised. "Potentially via taking *Duke* out to investigate. This whole situation is making the back of my neck itch."

"Mine hasn't *stopped* since the Secession," the Mage-King said. "We're months away from new ships. A year from the dreadnoughts. It's on you for the moment, Damien. Ardennes and the other fleet bases along the border are essential.

"You have my authority to do whatever is necessary to hold."

"I always do," Damien said quietly. "I'll protect our people, my liege."

"That is what I pay you for," Alexander said with a chuckle. "Good luck, my Hand."

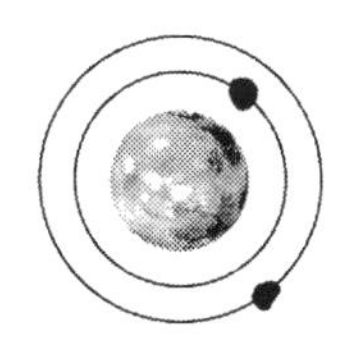

CHAPTER FOURTEEN

ROSLYN LIFTED the personal locker onto the second bed in her room and punched in the override code the XO—now Acting Captain—had given her. She tried not to look at Michael Kor's possessions too closely as she carefully and gently packed away the scattered personal items that always made their way out into one's room.

Their relationship had been as much one of opportunity as anything else. They'd met in the Academy and she'd thought he was cute, but her focus there had been on proving herself worthy to belong in the Navy.

With just the two of them sharing a room on the destroyer, however, there'd been an opportunity to act on that impulse without it getting in the way of her career. Neither of them had had any illusions it would last beyond the end of their tour of duty together—*maybe* through to the end of their time at the Academy.

But he'd been gentle and caring and funny. And now he was dead. She'd watched *Dance of Honorable Battle* come apart in Samos's upper atmosphere. There hadn't been any escape pods, and there was only a tiny chance anyone could have survived the debris falling to the surface.

As she finished packing his possessions away, there was a sharp rap on the door.

"Come in," she replied, then scrambled fully to her feet as Mage-Commander Herbert stepped into the room.

"Are you finished with his things?" he asked gently.

"Yes, sir," she replied crisply.

"Good. We'll put them in storage for his family. We'll move you, as well," he told her. "Even if you hadn't been lovers, asking you to stay in this room would be cruel. Besides, there *are* specific quarters for the tactical officer."

"The...what, sir?" Roslyn asked, confused.

He held out a black velvet jewelry box.

"Commander Katz is now acting as my XO. Every other officer in the tactical department was elsewhere when the penny dropped. They're MIA at best, presumed KIA."

She took the box in shaking hands, opening it to reveal the silver bars of a Royal Martian Navy Mage-Lieutenant.

"I'd say congratulations, but this kind of battlefield promotion sucks for everyone," Herbert said frankly. "You're going to have to take on responsibilities and duties you wouldn't be expected to take on for years yet. Thankfully, you have Chief Chey, but neither Katz nor I will be able to provide you the support you'll need.

"You'd preferably spend at least a year as the junior ATO on a bigger ship before you became assistant tactical officer on a destroyer, let alone the tactical officer...but we don't have time. I need someone in secondary control and I need someone on tactical."

Roslyn was frozen, staring at the insignia. Taking the insignia would skip the entire last year of her Academy training. She'd be a fully-commissioned officer in the Royal Martian Navy—and that acceleration would probably haunt her career for the rest of her life.

"You can turn it down," he reminded her.

"You need me," Roslyn finally said. "Someone's got to do the job. I won't let down my shipmates or the Protectorate, sir." She swallowed hard and took the box. "I'll do my best."

"Having seen your best, Lieutenant Chambers, I think we'll be fine," Herbert told her. With the box open, he took the silver bars out and gestured her closer to him.

"Allow me."

He carefully removed the ensign's pips on her collar and pinned the new bars home, flanking the golden medallion that declared her as a

Mage of the Guilds of the Protectorate. She swallowed hard, then stepped back and saluted crisply.

"I won't let *you* down, sir," she told him.

"I don't expect you to," he replied. "But we're all running short and hard right now. We're still two days from Hoisin, and I need you to make half the jumps.

"Are you up for it, Mage-Lieutenant Chambers?"

"Without question, sir," she said firmly.

Chief Petty Officer Chanda Chey was significantly taller than Roslyn, a dark-skinned athletic woman with short-cropped black hair and brilliant green eyes. She surveyed Commander Katz's old office with a calm gaze, clearly unsurprised to find Roslyn sitting behind the desk.

"Have a seat, Chief," Roslyn instructed. "I'd offer you coffee but, frankly, I don't even know where the coffee machine *is* in here. Commander Katz finished moving out about ten minutes ago."

Chey chuckled and pointed.

"That cupboard there. Shall I?" she offered.

"Sure."

The Chief popped the cupboard open to reveal a standard Navy coffee machine. A few moments later, it was happily burbling its way toward coffee for them both.

"Commander Herbert has promoted me to Lieutenant and made me acting tactical officer," Roslyn told the other woman after the coffee was going. "I had to actually look up if he could *do* that; it's sufficiently rare for us."

"So is war," Chey said bluntly. "The RMN has never fought one. Two centuries of police actions and anti-piracy. No wars."

"Exactly." Roslyn shivered. "I know enough about being an officer to know that I can't show hesitance or uncertainty in front of the crew, Chief, but if I can't be honest with you, we're all already doomed.

"I *think* I can do this, but I know how underqualified I am."

"Well, that's three right statements out of three, so you're not doing too badly," Chey said with another chuckle. She poured two cups of black coffee, then paused, studying the cabinet the coffeemaker was tucked away in.

A practiced slap opened a concealed compartment that Roslyn would never have guessed was there, and the Chief produced a mostly empty bottle of whisky.

"Thought so," she said with satisfaction. "Tradition says you leave the booze behind for the next officer." Without even asking, she poured the alcohol into both coffee cups and then put one in front of Roslyn.

"So, boss," Chey said calmly, "if you know how far out of your depth you are, you've got me in your office because you have a plan."

"I do," Roslyn confirmed. "First off, I want you to flag two Petty Officers that we're going to jump to second-class Chiefs and stick on the bridge. I can run defense, sensors, or missiles on my own. I can't run all three, and that's why we have a bridge crew."

"You don't want me on the bridge?" Chey asked carefully.

"Want? Sure. Need? No. I *need* you on Missile One, making sure the gunnery crews know everything is still running smoothly. I need you on a closed channel with me if you think I'm screwing up—but I also need you to follow orders and keep the department ticking until we get things back under control."

The Chief grinned.

"That, Mage-Lieutenant Chambers, is my *job description*," she pointed out. "We'll make this work, I think."

"We have to," Roslyn admitted. "If we don't make it to an RTA, Chief, the Protectorate may not know we're at war until it's far too late."

Chey's grin faded.

"Hoisin, then?"

"Exactly," Roslyn agreed. "We're the harbinger, Chief. But if we don't carry our message, the Protectorate might fall. And we both swore an oath about that, didn't we?"

CHAPTER FIFTEEN

STAND IN RIGHTEOUSNESS jumped into the Hoisin System and Mage-Commander Herbert sagged against the simulacrum. Roslyn watched in concern as he straightened and extracted a pair of small blue pills from a package and swallowed them.

"If we have to jump, it's on you," Herbert told Roslyn. "But these will let me stay awake." He shook his head. "After Nia Kriti, I think we're allowed some paranoia."

They'd waited long enough after the last jump to make sure that Roslyn was able to get them out. She wasn't sure that was a necessary step—Hoisin had both a Navy refueling base and an RTA. Without some kind of trick like they'd launched at Nia Kriti, it should be safe from the Republic.

"Transmitting IFF to local control and requesting orbit clearance," Lieutenant Armbruster reported. The broad-shouldered blond officer glanced back at Roslyn and Herbert. "I'm seeing proper protocols on the radio waves."

"Chambers?" Herbert asked.

"Usual traffic," she said as she went over the scanners. "I've got in-system clippers. The main orbital is running traffic control, as Lieutenant Armbruster says. No jump ships on the scanners."

Roslyn checked their position versus the orbits.

"The Navy refueling station is on the other side of the star," she continued. "We'll have to relay our report to them via the satellite network."

"The priority is getting to the RTA on New Bangkok," Herbert replied. "Armbruster, get our report onto the satellite network and make sure that the locals know we need RTA access immediately, emergency priority."

"Should we relay our report through the Transceiver Mages?" Armbruster asked.

Herbert hadn't quite mastered the impassive face a Captain needed. Roslyn recognized his moment of hesitation, possibly aggravated by the amphetamines keeping him awake, before he spoke.

"No," he finally ordered. "And encrypt the report sent into the satellite network under Orange Cream protocols."

"Yes, sir." Armbruster looked confused but he didn't argue.

"Orange Cream" was the highest level of encryption protocol *Stand*'s crew had access to. They didn't even carry the *decryption* protocols for it; those were only available to flag officers and base commanders.

The station commander there in Hoisin would be able to decrypt their report. Their subordinates, however, wouldn't be—and if, by some currently unknown disaster, the Republic now held the Hoisin Navy Station, they *definitely* wouldn't be able to.

Roslyn continued to go through her scan data. Something wasn't adding up.

"Commander," she said slowly. "Do you know how many ships were assigned here?"

The pills were not doing enough to keep Herbert fully functional. It took him at least ten seconds to even process her question.

"No," he admitted. "Should be in our records, though. Might be out of date, but we should keep the number constant."

Roslyn nodded, hiding her concern for the Acting Captain's health as she dug into the records. She wasn't as experienced with the broad Navy files as she probably should have been, but she managed to find the listing for the Hoisin Navy Station eventually.

Four destroyers. Not a world-shattering number by any stretch of the imagination, but enough hulls that there should have been a ship in orbit of New Bangkok.

Wait.

There was an addendum, a convenient link to the Navy's files on the Hoisin System Security Flotilla. She looked at that listing for thirty seconds, processing the details listed for the sixteen ships the Hoisin System had purchased to protect themselves.

"Sir," she said slowly. "There should be two destroyers and four non-jump-capable guardships in orbit of New Bangkok, even ignoring the Navy flotilla. I don't see them *or* the ten corvettes that should be backing them up."

The stats said the guardships were Legatan-built, four-megaton ships with rotating habitats hidden "under" their hulls. The destroyers were Tau Cetan–built, proper export ships with rune matrices for jumping and artificial gravity.

The system was missing *eighteen million tons* of capital ships.

Seconds ticked by as Roslyn waited for Herbert to respond. Too many seconds; she turned to look at the Acting Captain and realized he was frozen, staring blankly forward into space.

"Sir?" she snapped. "*Sir?*"

Armbruster caught the tone in her voice and all but ran to the command chair, feeling for a pulse at the Mage-Commander's neck and then swearing.

"Chambers, get a medic!" he barked. Feverishly, he began unstrapping the belts holding the Acting Captain into the chair and lowering him to the floor. While the coms officer began CPR, Roslyn hit the ship's intercom system.

"Medic to the bridge, medic to the bridge! We have an emergency!"

Herbert's face was turning gray, even as Armbruster hammered on his chest. Roslyn grabbed the automatic defibrillator the coms officer hadn't had time to pick up on his way to the Captain.

"Damn it, sir, *breathe.*" Armbruster nodded to her as she dropped the defibrillator next to him, but he was focusing on his CPR.

The clear tasks complete, Roslyn froze. Their Captain was dying, potentially dead—but the ship was in critical danger. She'd let *one* odd scan result slip her mind in a crisis, and thousands had died for her mistake.

It wasn't going to happen again.

A ragged breath escaped Herbert's chest, and Armbruster sighed in relief as he took the chance to grab the automated defibrillator and start slapping its patches on. He continued to administer care, compressing the officer's chest again as the Mage-Commander didn't *keep* breathing.

Roslyn swallowed and rose. The coms officer was doing everything that could be done for Mage-Commander Herbert. *She* needed to make sure the rest of the ship survived the trap they'd walked into.

Commander Katz would be asleep, the acting XO taking every scrap of rest she could get when she was off-duty. There was no time for that, and Roslyn started tapping commands on the Captain's repeater screens.

Herbert had been logged in with his codes, and the computer wasn't smart enough to realize the Acting Captain was on the floor, dying. Roslyn used his overrides to trigger an emergency alert in Commander Katz's quarters.

"Commander Katz to the bridge," she snapped into the microphone. "Mage-Commander Herbert is down, Commander Katz to the bridge."

Then she swallowed down her fear and stepped into the Captain's chair. Herbert had been running navigation himself, and she had control of the ship's engines. They were accelerating toward New Bangkok at fifteen gravities, a rush to get to the RTA.

An RTA she had to now assume was either destroyed or in enemy hands.

A medic rushed onto the bridge and started helping with the Mage-Commander as Roslyn set to work. She wasn't entirely familiar with the controls for flying a destroyer from a Captain's repeater screens, but she *was* qualified to fly one.

The Navy insisted that if the only officer left aboard a ship was a Jump Mage, that would be enough to get everyone else home. Jump Mages were trained to fly everything from shuttles to battleships.

Stand in Righteousness reacted to her commands with alacrity, the million-ton white pyramid flipping in space to accelerate toward the outer system.

Sensors told her the worst of it. She was well inside of the unsafe jump zone. Roslyn *could* jump the ship, but it was risky—mostly due to her inexperience.

They'd been accelerating in-system for over an hour. It would take them just as long to slow to zero relative to the planet, and they'd be within missile range of the planet orbitals once they had.

"Stay right there," Katz barked as she charged onto the bridge. "I assume command, but you're the Jump Mage, Chambers."

Roslyn swallowed. The bridge wasn't designed for that. The Navy assumed that the person in command was the Mage—but with Mage-Commander Herbert on the floor with a medic kneeling over him, the only available Mage was Roslyn Chambers.

And she was *definitely* not qualified to command a warship.

"He's gone," the medic reported grimly several minutes later.

"What was it?" Katz, now Acting Captain Roslyn supposed, demanded. "Allergic reaction? I thought those pills weren't supposed to *do* that."

"They don't," the medic said flatly. "Overdose. I'd say that was at least the fifth set of pills he'd taken in the last twenty-four hours. He shouldn't have been given that many, but..." The young woman shrugged. "He was the Captain."

"Damn."

Katz's tone was almost broken to Roslyn's ear, leaving the young officer wondering if there'd been more between the two Commanders than she'd known about—or if the new Acting Captain was staring down the barrel of her responsibilities.

"We need to get out of this system," Roslyn said firmly. "Your orders, Captain Katz?"

A long silence hung over the bridge.

"You seem to be doing just fine, Lieutenant," Katz finally replied. "What's our ETA to safe jump?"

"Four hours, roughly," Roslyn confirmed. "A full hour to decelerate to zero, then three to get back to where we started."

"Keep us on it," the new Captain ordered. "I'll manage tactical and keep an eye on...things."

"Sir?" Roslyn asked, then glanced at the repeater screens on her current seat. "Oh."

A squadron of ten gunships had lit up their engines in New Bangkok orbit, accelerating out toward *Stand in Righteousness.*

Lightspeed delays caught up a few moments later, showing them the *other* squadrons deployed around the system. Four squadrons, forty of the little ships in total, were now accelerating toward the Martian destroyer.

"Lieutenant?" Katz said calmly. "You have navigation. Can we get away from them all?"

Roslyn was already running vectors. It took her longer than a fully-trained navigator, but she could do it.

"Yes, sir," she reported. "Vector up seventy-five degrees to the ecliptic and stay at maximum acceleration. We have almost double their engine power. They can't catch us."

"Do it," Katz ordered. She looked back at Roslyn from the tactical station and shook her head though.

"My math says at least one of those groups could have caught us on our original course. What are they playing at?"

"A trap?" Roslyn suggested.

Katz grimaced.

"Almost certainly. Are you okay to jump us, Lieutenant?"

Roslyn hesitated.

"I *could,* sir, but it would be hard on me. It's not going to get easier for at least an hour, though. Your orders?"

"We have time," the Commander noted, but she was studying the distances. "I'm firing up an omnidirectional sensor sweep. Let's see what they think we haven't noticed."

Stand in Righteousness's radar emitters came to full power, pulsing coherent radiation across the star system. They could see the gunships' engines clearly on infrared, but a ship without engines was harder to pick up at a distance.

Radar wouldn't necessarily work *better*, but it gave them a bit more of an edge. It would create another signature, however faint, and *Stand*'s computers were smart. If the sensors had two signatures in the same place from different scans that weren't enough to flag the detection thresholds on their own, it would still flag the location.

"And...bingo," Katz said grimly. "New contact right where we need to fly to get clear of the gunships. Too far away and cold for a hard signature, but I'm guessing that's not a gunship."

"No, sir," Roslyn confirmed. "It appears the Hoisin System has fallen to the enemy."

Silence was the only answer to her words, but Katz nodded slowly.

"Our ships and the local System Militia both appear to have been destroyed. The RTA is lost...I can't tell if it's intact from here, so it's *possible* the Navy has been warned."

"They had a plan for Nia Kriti," Roslyn said. "I doubt they didn't have one for Hoisin, not if they were here at all."

"Agreed." Katz sighed. "We apparently don't have time, Lieutenant. Jump this ship—then we need to decide where the hell we're going next."

Roslyn took a deep breath and laid her hands on the simulacrum. This would take even more out of her than an ordinary jump, but...it was that or run into the teeth of a Republic warship that almost certainly outgunned them.

She jumped.

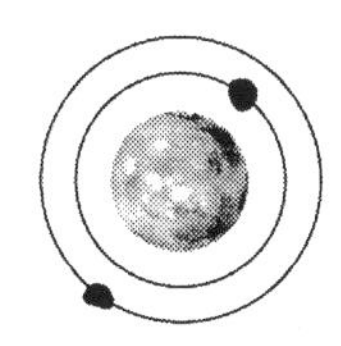

CHAPTER SIXTEEN

SIX HOURS LATER, an exhausted Roslyn joined the tiny handful of remaining officers aboard *Stand in Righteousness* in the conference room attached to the Captain's quarters, right next to the bridge.

There were only four of them left now. Commander Katz, once the tactical officer and now the Acting Captain. Armbruster, once the most junior officer of the communications department, barely senior to Roslyn, who hadn't even been commissioned yet then.

Lieutenant Scrivenor, on the other hand, was an older officer, a hard-edged woman promoted from the ranks. She'd been the second-in-command in Engineering and had been left behind when everyone else moved over to *Dance of Honorable Battle.*

And then there was Roslyn herself, the youngest person in the room and the only Mage. Her commission as a Lieutenant had been the emergency act of a now-dead man. Without her, the ship wasn't going anywhere—and she still didn't feel like she belonged in this meeting.

"Thanks to Lieutenant Chambers, we escaped the trap that was set for us at Hoisin without further losses," Katz concluded. "They knew we were coming and where we were coming from. There's no way that trap was set up that perfectly by accident."

"That's impossible," Armbruster replied. "Even if they had Mages willing to run the RTAs for them, which I guess they must, given they have jump ships, they wrecked the one in Nia Kriti."

"You're assuming they're working under the same rules we are," Scrivenor said in a hoarse half-cough. "Legatus has always put more research into what the rest of the Protectorate thought were dead-end lines of study. They've been searching for a technological answer to interstellar coms and travel for generations."

"And if they have it...then that would explain a lot," Katz said grimly. "If they don't need Mages, that would explain where their fleet came from—and if they have some other form of interstellar coms, then why would they care about wrecking RTAs? It'll hold us back even if we retake Nia Kriti, but it won't bother them at all."

"So they'd know where we were coming from and could even make a decent guess as to when," Roslyn whispered. "That means...we can't trust anywhere to have held. If they've launched a coordinated assault across the border..."

"Then we might have already lost this war," Armbruster said. "What do we do?"

Katz tapped a command, bringing up a map of the region.

"We have to try and report in. These two systems"—she gestured at a pair of stars marked with the icons of Navy refueling stations—"have neither RTAs nor sufficient defenses to have stood off major assaults. They don't have significant local militias, and neither was home to more than three of our destroyers.

"That leaves us Santiago or Ardennes," she stated, highlighting the two stars. "Ardennes is pretty far from the border, but..."

"Santiago may have an RTA but they don't have a Navy presence," Roslyn pointed out as she checked the files on her wrist-comp. "Local militia is understrength...a single Republic warship could have taken the system in an afternoon."

"And the Republican Navy seems to have agents on the ground to make sure no one calls for help," Armbruster noted. "Santiago doesn't look like a good option, Captain."

Katz visibly shivered at the title, studying the map.

"Eighteen light-years to Ardennes. Can you do it, Mage-Lieutenant?" she asked Roslyn.

"Stars," Roslyn breathed, looking at the course. "Five days. Maybe four and a half, but...it's just me."

"We know, Lieutenant," Katz told her. "It's more important that we get there than that we get there yesterday. I'm afraid the Republic has planned this for far too long, and so far..." She shook her head. "So far, I can't help but feel they pulled it off without a warning getting back to Mars."

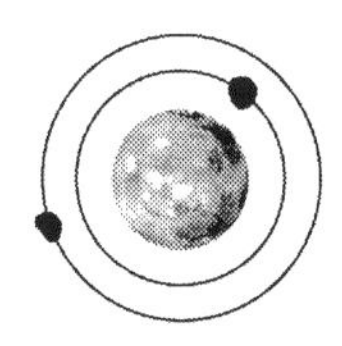

CHAPTER SEVENTEEN

"IT'S GOOD TO SEE YOU, DAMIEN," Julia Amiri told him. Ardennes's new First Lady and Minister for Defense was a tall woman with broad shoulders and short-cropped black hair. She'd also once been his bodyguard, serving as a member of the Protectorate Secret Service until Mikael Riordan had stolen her away.

"And you," he replied. "I see the political life suits you."

Amiri chuckled, gesturing him to a seat at the large stone table in the new Governor's House. The room and the table were designed for meetings of the Governor's cabinet or possibly grand affairs with major political figures or visitors from other worlds.

It *rattled* with just him, Amiri, her husband and Romanov.

His old bodyguard had filled in some of the gaunt hollowness and stress lines on her face. She didn't look relaxed per se but certainly the most content he'd ever seen her.

"More than I expected," she admitted. "Can't say I don't miss pulling your butt out of the fire on a weekly basis, though. It was never boring."

"Neither is running a planet, as Julia and I are discovering," Riordan added. He inclined his head to Denis Romanov. "Agent Romanov, I hear we have you to thank for the Hand still being with us. At least, oh, half a dozen times."

"That's the job," the Marine murmured. "Julia taught me well."

"Most of my staff is still in Tau Ceti or Sol," Damien told the two Ardennians. "Or scattered to the eight corners of the galaxy. I certainly didn't need a staff while in physical rehab, and my decision to get involved in the Korma mission was entirely out of the blue."

He shrugged.

"I was in Tau Ceti, and we learned they needed help. The bauble cut a lot of bullshit out of the way." He tapped the closed-fist symbol of his office, the only platinum Hand in the Protectorate right now.

Only three had ever been made, and the first two had been vaporized and buried with their holders, respectively.

Damien did not expect to die in bed. But then, it had been a *long* time since he'd expected that.

"The attack in Korma leaves me nervous," he continued. "I'm hoping you've found the time to go over the RTA logs?"

"I found the time to have people do it and brief me, at least," Amiri told him with a sigh. "There's no smoking guns, Damien, but not everyone talks to Ardennes. We're one MidWorld of twenty-plus, after all."

"And?" he asked. "I know that sigh, Julia."

Riordan chuckled. It wasn't an entirely humorous sound.

"We don't hear from everyone on a regular basis, so it didn't catch our notice until you asked us to look." He slid a hand across the marble tabletop, revealing part of the surface to actually be a screen mimicking the surface of the stone. A holographic image of the Protectorate and Republic appeared above the table.

"Only nine of the MidWorlds and three of the Fringe Worlds have RTAs," he reminded everyone. "At least, of the ones left after the Secession." Four stars flashed orange. "Closer to the border with the Republic than us, though scattered along the length of it, are Santiago, Hoisin, Nia Kriti and Tormanda.

"We also usually see a degree of shipping from these systems." Another five stars flashed pink.

"The shipping is the most definitive warning sign," Amiri said quietly. "We don't get a lot of ships from any one of those systems, but we haven't seen cargos from *any* of them in a week."

"And in the same time frame, we haven't seen any RTA transmissions from those four systems," Riordan concluded. "Any single piece of that isn't unusual, Lord Montgomery, but..."

"But if you add it all up with the attack at Korma, there's a pattern and I don't like it," Damien confirmed. He rested his hands on the table, careful to keep them motionless as he studied the map.

"I presume we've already made an attempt to make Transceiver contact with those systems?"

"It's being done as we speak," Amiri confirmed. "We'll have an update for you within an hour or so." She shook her head. "I wish we had better—or at least more useful—news."

"Unless you could tell me with certainty that I was wrong and just being paranoid about the Republic, you couldn't give me the news I want," Damien admitted. "Almost regardless of what we get from the check-in, I need to take *Duke* and investigate. I'll probably borrow escorts from the refueling station. We're not used to gunships in those kinds of numbers."

The married couple exchanged a glance, and Riordan made a "go ahead" gesture to his wife.

"We'll want to reinforce you from the ASDF," she told Damien. "We can spare a cruiser and a pair of destroyers. It's a good chunk of our forces, but...we *need* to know, Damien. If the Protectorate is in danger from the Republic, Ardennes is going to be on the front lines."

"I know," he replied. "And if it's bad as I'm starting to fear, I'll be right here with you."

"Lord Montgomery, this is Transceiver Mage Alanna O'Malley," the Mage from the RTA introduced herself again over the video call.

"I remember you, Mage O'Malley," Damien told her.

He was currently in the passenger compartment of a Royal Martian Marine Corps assault shuttle, about halfway out of Ardennes's atmosphere.

"I was tasked by Governor Riordan with making contact with the RTAs along the border with the Republic, my lord," she said. "He asked me to brief you on what I discovered."

"I appreciate both your work and you taking the time to brief me," Damien replied. "What did you discover?"

"Governor Riordan suggested that I try and 'keep things casual,'" O'Malley said. "He didn't want me to tip them off if something *was* wrong. It...wasn't really necessary."

"How so?" That didn't sound promising for this to have been unnecessary.

"Nia Kriti and Tormanda are offline," she said quietly. "It's not that no one is responding, my lord. The Transceiver Arrays themselves have been destroyed."

"Damn," Damien murmured. "How can you tell?"

"There are ways, Lord Montgomery. Few outside of full-time Transceiver Mages would have been trained in them, but we can tell the difference between a lack of response and not being received at all. Nia Kriti and Tormanda are completely off the air."

Runic Transceiver Arrays, gone. An RTA was a construction project to put orbital stations and interstellar battleships to shame, in complexity and difficulty if not size. The fastest construction of one on record was two and a half years, at Damien's homeworld of Sherwood.

"That's..." He stretched for any kind of description that could cover this news. "That's a disaster."

"That may be the *better* news, my lord," O'Malley admitted. "Hoisin is not responding. The RTA is intact, but there is no one there to send a response. We wouldn't let this happen if the Array was crewed, so I can't help but feel that something terrible has happened to my compatriots in the Hoisin System."

Damien nodded slowly, gesturing Romanov to him.

"Agent, can you bring up a map of the region?" he asked. The shuttle was *not* set up properly for his current needs. Fortunately, he had willing subordinates.

"What about Santiago?" he said to O'Malley.

"Santiago responded," she told him. "But it felt...wrong. All of the key phrases and everything were correct, but I *know* the Transceiver Mage who answered." She shook her head. "He was afraid, my lord. I think he was being watched and under threat if he betrayed any sign of trying to deceive his watchers.

"I fear for his safety and for the Santiago System...and the others. I don't know what's happened, Lord Montgomery."

"Neither do I, Mage O'Malley," he told her, looking over the map. As he'd thought, Santiago was the closest of the systems in question, twenty-six light-years away. Just over a day for a fully staffed Navy warship.

"What I can tell you, however, is that I'm going to find out," he promised her. "And if I can save the Mages at Santiago, I will."

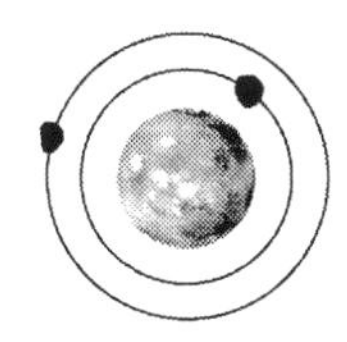

CHAPTER EIGHTEEN

MAGE-CAPTAIN JAKAB met Damien as he exited the shuttle onto *Duke of Magnificence. Duke* had been Damien's ship for a long time, and he and the Captain had long since come to an agreement on ceremony and such when the Hand boarded or left the cruiser.

The main point of the agreement was that there wasn't any such ceremony. Jakab had done an occasional end run around Damien on that point, but today wasn't one of them. The Mage-Captain was alone and fell into step beside him with a quiet nod as Damien headed into the ship.

"You got my message," Damien said. It wasn't really a question. If the messages from an RMMC assault shuttle to her mothership weren't getting through, then this whole game had gone even more to hell than he thought.

"I did. I spoke with Commodore Cruyssen as well." Jakab shrugged. "Well, traded messages anyway. He's a good three light-minutes away still.

"We'll have the destroyers *Bonnie Darling of Sherwood* and *Dance in Starlit Darkness* joining us for our trip. They can micro-jump to us or meet us at the one-light-year point. Your call."

"Have them micro-jump," Damien ordered. "We're also getting the cruiser *Andes* and two destroyers from the ASDF." He shrugged. "I don't know the destroyer names. We'll find out."

"I'll get my people on that," Jakab replied. "I'm guessing the locals are feeling twitchy, too?"

"I might be infectious," Damien said dryly. "Six ships to Santiago, just over three days there and back with most of a day to poke around."

"More than enough time to make sure the system is secure," his Captain agreed. "But what if it isn't?"

"If Santiago is in enemy hands, it's already done," Damien said. "The RTA appears to be under their control. The likelihood that the system is under siege or that we can even retake it is low. I hate to leave our people in the Republic's hands, but if Santiago is fallen, we won't be able to retake it with six ships."

Jakab grimaced.

"That...is your call, I suppose."

"It is," Damien agreed with a sigh. "Coordinate with the locals and with the destroyer Captains. I want every ship commander aboard *Duke of Magnificence* this evening for a working supper. You and I need to know who we're working with, and they need to know what I expect of them."

"I'll make it happen," Jakab promised.

"You're in command, obviously," Damien told him. "Should I be making you a Commodore or something?"

Jakab chuckled.

"Won't say I'd turn it *down*, but the Navy has always run on 'who the Admiral says is in command' rather than any real structure for task groups like this."

From what Damien understood, that was true all the way down. The Royal Martian Navy had a surprising paucity of ranks compared to most organizations like it in history.

"Well, in this case, what the Hand says goes," Damien said with a chuckle. "And the Hand thinks he's dragged you from one end of the galaxy to the other. Have someone make sure the appropriate paperwork makes it to my office in a way I can authorize without signing."

"My lord?"

"You're a Commodore now," Damien said with a vague gesture of his left hand. "Should have done that when I left you behind in Sol, but I half-expected the Navy to take care of it."

Jakab sighed audibly.

"I *was* joking, my lord."

"I know. But you've been my strong left arm for a while now, Kole, and if this mission to Santiago goes the way I'm afraid it's going to, I'm going to need you to command Navy ships for me again in the future—and I cannot afford there to be confusion over who is in command.

"It will be you. Mage-*Commodore* Jakab."

"Yes, my lord. Thank you, my lord."

"Persephone! You're not supposed to be in here!"

The scandalized tones of Damien's steward were, he supposed, the entirely correct background to a black kitten darting under the man's feet and *leaping* up onto the dining room table. The six officers had just sat down and had their drinks poured. Food hadn't even made it out yet—his steward was carrying a bread basket—and now there was a kitten sprawled indelicately in the middle of the table.

"I've got her, Jeff," Damien replied, starting to rise and reach for the cat. Unfortunately, his reach stretched his fingers just ever so slightly wrong, and he inhaled sharply as pain radiated down his hands.

Persephone was instantly up and next to him, gently nuzzling his hands as he tried not to audibly whimper.

"*I've* got her," Jakab said quietly, giving Persephone a scratch behind the ears as he picked her up. She headbutted Damien's shoulder as Jakab moved her, purring loudly as the Mage-Commodore took her out of the room and back to Damien's office.

"My apologies, Captains," Damien told the gathered strangers. Four women and a single man looked at him in confusion as Jakab closed the door and returned. "Persephone was a gift from Princess Kiera, strongly encouraged by my physical therapists."

He waved his crippled hands in mute explanation.

"She has exactly the personality you would expect an animal imprinting on me to have," he admitted with a chuckle. "Please, help yourselves. The main meal will be out shortly."

Damien waited until they were distracted, then floated his glass of water up to his mouth to take a delicate sip. His hands most definitely did *not* have the fine dexterity for glassware or cutlery at this point.

If any of his guests noted that his hands remained on the table as he drank, they were too polite to say anything.

The food arrived before further conversation was needed, thick slices of some pastry concoction filled with chicken and vegetables and spices. Damien's portion was precut, the explanation for anyone paying attention as to why the meal was in the style it was.

It was a lot easier for him to eat a meal contained in one dish than it was for him to use cutlery to eat multiple sides, for example.

Damien carefully levitated each piece of tart up so he could bite into them. Even after eating like this for a year and a half, he was still self-conscious about it. Nonetheless, his guests remained politely focused on their own meals until he finished eating.

Jeff Schenck, his steward, came through and filled wineglasses for everyone. Damien eyed his with a sigh, then reached out for it. He didn't actually pick up the glass with his hand, though. More magic lifted the glassware as he rose and offered a toast.

"Ladies and gentlemen, the Protectorate of the Mage-King of Mars."

"The Protectorate," they responded.

He looked around his companions. He knew Kole Jakab of old, and the newly-promoted Mage-Commodore was a brave, reliable man.

The two Royal Martian Navy Mage-Commanders were cut from similar cloth. To command destroyers at their current rank, both women had to be experienced, senior officers—and also skilled and trusted by their superiors.

Hanaa Boulos commanded *Dance in Starlit Darkness*. She wore a midnight-blue headscarf over pale blond hair that framed the usual faded parchment skin and mild epicanthic fold of the classic Martian mongrel. She was a descendant of the survivors of Project Olympus, Mars-born and raised among the traditions of an older culture.

Amelie Paternoster, the commander of *Bonnie Darling of Sherwood*, was actually a native of Ardennes. She was tall and slim with neatly braided waist-length blond hair. She was a Mage by Right to Boulos's Mage by Blood, identified by the Royal Testers who checked every child in the Protectorate for the Mage Gift.

The three Ardennes Self-Defense Force officers were clearly even less comfortable than the junior Martian officers. They wore dark green uniforms in contrast to the black and gold of the Martian uniform, and seemed quite unsure how to deal with their crippled host.

"Captain Brandt," Damien focused his gaze on the cruiser Captain, Liliana Brandt. "Do you and your fellow ASDF Captains have any questions before we get into more detailed planning?"

Everyone in the room was a Mage, but the three Militia officers had training closer to a traditional Jump Mage than the Navy officers' far wider—and more dangerous—skillset.

Brandt considered the question for a moment, seeming to roll it around in her head. She was a petite woman with a dyed-green stripe running across her black hair.

Her two subordinates, Under-Captains Wobbe Kaluza and Unai Groos both had similar stripes, in red and purple respectively. Given that all three had otherwise identical hairstyles, Damien suspected there was a dress code rule with regards to hair in the ASDF.

And since he suspected Julia Amiri regarded it with as much favor as her personnel did, that code was being stretched to the breaking point.

"We have not worked closely with the Navy before," Brandt finally said, her voice slow and steady. "There is still some bad feeling between the survivors of the battle and the Navy, regardless of how necessary what happened was."

"That's to be expected, Captain," Damien admitted. A lot of men and women wearing the uniform Brandt now wore had been killed by the Royal Martian Navy. They'd been ordered into battle by a commanding officer who'd committed crimes against humanity and, perhaps, should have refused those orders...but that didn't change what had happened.

"I have to admit, I am unsure of our mission," she continued after a few more moments of thought. "Santiago is a Protectorate System, and we are looking for Republic ships?"

"We have reason to believe the Republic may have attacked Santiago," Damien told her. "It's sufficiently fuzzy that I want to confirm it with direct observation before we take any drastic action."

"That would be an act of war!" Kaluza replied, her voice shocked.

"And that, Under-Captain Kaluza, would be what I mean by 'drastic action,'" Damien said dryly. "If Santiago has been attacked by the Republic, I have no choice but to assume that the other systems whose RTAs have gone silent have *also* been attacked.

"In which case, officers, we are already at war. We just haven't been told that yet."

Brandt swallowed.

"So, what do we do?"

"I believe you train with our tactics manual, correct?" Damien asked.

"We do," she confirmed. "About a quarter of our officer instruction is by personnel temporarily seconded from the RMN."

"All right. We're going to launch a standard recon sweep," he told them. "We go in at battle stations, with all hands on deck. I'd rather insult the locals and have to apologize than not be ready for a Republic counterstrike.

"If the Republic is present, we do everything within our power to ascertain their intentions and actions *without* engaging." He grimaced. "Based off the forces we encountered in the Korma System, our force is insufficient to challenge the Republic Interstellar Navy's new standard deployment group."

"If they've attacked a Protectorate System, we're just to walk away?" Paternoster demanded. "That goes against everything the Navy stands for!"

"Mage-Commander, the task group we encountered in Korma consisted of five ships with a total mass of over a hundred million tons," Damien said quietly. "We cannot risk assuming that the Republic has not built warships capable of matching ours on a ton-for-ton basis. I will not start a battle we cannot win.

"You are authorized to defend yourself, but outside of that, you will *not* open fire without my direct orders. Is that clear?"

Paternoster's interrupting might not have been planned, but it couldn't have worked better. Damien got to give the harsh orders he knew were needed *without* directing them at the militia officers he expected to have to handle with kid gloves.

"Now, are there any further questions with regards to our objectives?"

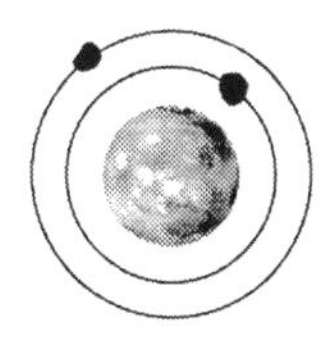

CHAPTER NINETEEN

DAMIEN HAD LOST TRACK of the star systems he'd visited at this point. It wasn't *that* many, he was sure. A dozen. Maybe twenty? He wasn't certain off the top of his head.

Even now, however, most of humanity never saw stars beyond the one they were born orbiting. Traveling between planets in that star system was more common, but it wasn't that unusual to have never left the surface of your homeworld.

Santiago was the latest in that long line, and he wished he could have visited under better circumstances. It was an unusually calm system, with asteroids and comets mostly limited to an outer belt beyond the system's giants. Three average gas giants in offset orbits shielded the inner system from debris, resulting in four unusually unmarred rocky worlds.

Only one of those planets was inside the liquid water zone, and Novo Lar was a tropical paradise across much of its surface, with archipelagos of gorgeous islands and beaches scattered across warm and calm seas.

The polar storm zones were less congenial, but it was those unending hurricanes that fed the currents that carried warmth and plankton across the world. Vast farms on the surface of Novo Lar's oceans raised plants and fish sourced from two dozen worlds for their taste or pharmaceutical properties.

One of the causes and consequences of that—Damien wasn't entirely sure which came first—was lax drug laws, even by the Protectorate's standards. Whatever high you were looking for, you could get it on

Novo Lar if you had the money—whether that high came from herbs, hyper-processed chemicals or simply sitting on a beach in unending sunshine.

Santiago's fourth planet was outside the liquid water zone, but its orbit was neatly synchronized with Novo Lars at exactly double the time. For most of the local year, transit between the two worlds was relatively straightforward, and Cova was rich in the minerals and ores that fuelled modern industry.

Cova's atmosphere might not be breathable, but that was often a benefit when industry moved in on a massive scale.

The combination of the two worlds allowed the system to grow rapidly. Santiago was one of the poorer MidWorlds—but it was also one of the youngest colonies to qualify for that status.

And the complete lack of shipping between Cova and Novo Lars suggested that growth was coming to a sharp and unpleasant end. That kind of interlaced symbiotic economy was never lacking in ships.

Today there were none, and Damien watched the plot of the system expand around his ships with grim certainty.

"We're not detecting any civilian shipping," Mage-Commodore Jakab reported. "We're closest to Cova, and we picked up a dozen gunships before they cut their emissions. A little late on their part, but it's not like they knew we were coming."

"Why not?" Damien asked. "They seem to have had warning of everything else we did."

He sighed.

"Unfortunately, the Santiago Star Guard *has* gunships," he pointed out. "Legatan-built ones, at that. They're mainly used as search-and-rescue ships, since the SSG always relied on Mars for their security."

Like they were supposed to. Officially, the Protectorate was opposed to the continuing proliferation of System Militias, but the Charter tied their hands.

Unofficially, the Mage-King had seen a counterbalance to Legatus in those Militias. *And* his hands were tied. No one wanted to be renegotiating the Charter at this point.

"Get coms with the refueling station," he ordered. "Then continue the recon sweep. If there's anything bigger than a gunship in this system, I want to know about it before they decide to get clever."

"Yes, my lord."

"Refueling station is gone."

That harsh report from Mage-Commander Boulos was probably all the evidence Damien needed. The data flowing in over the telemetry link was even more so.

Santiago's innermost gas giant had been host to a Transmutation facility, tasked with providing antimatter for both the star system's industries and the Navy refueling station. The refueling station had orbited the same gas giant for convenience, and two RMN destroyers had kept a careful eye on the station.

Both space stations were wrecks now. The refueling station was simply, as Boulos had said, gone. Thousands of tons of antimatter had gone up in what must have been a spectacular fireball—and probably an intentional one on the part of the station's crew.

The Republic was always going to have troubles sourcing antimatter. They'd almost certainly at least attempted to take the station intact.

The wreckage of the two destroyers was easier to pinpoint. The ships were armored against gigaton-range explosions, after all. There tended to be at least something left.

Radiation fields were still dispersing. That would let Damien's people date the battle, eventually.

"Took out the Transmuter station first, then swept around to hit the destroyers and try to capture the fuel tanks," Jakab concluded. "Probably figured that trying to capture a station full of Mages was asking for trouble, even if they are half convicts."

There were few enough Mages in the galaxy that the Protectorate couldn't lock even criminals away uselessly. Most Mage prison sentences were served on Transmuter stations, transforming matter to antimatter under strict supervision and isolation.

Convicted criminals or not, however, those Mages wouldn't have rolled over for the Republic.

"What are we seeing at Novo Lar and Cova?" Damien finally asked. "We'll want to set up for a fast pass between the two planets, see how much we can see."

"Yes, my lord," Jakab said calmly.

"Which you've already done and are humoring me, of course," the Hand replied, chuckling. "What's our estimated time?"

"We'll blast through them with about a light-minute to spare on either side in about an hour and ten minutes," the Mage-Commodore told him. "By then, we should really know everything that's going on in the system.

"We'll jump in just over three hours, heading back to Ardennes."

"We already know what we came to find out," Damien said with a sigh. "The Santiago System has been attacked and taken by the Republic. We're at war."

"Yes. The more we know, however..."

"The better off we are," Damien agreed. "Get me everything, Mage-Commodore. I want to know how bad it is."

Horrific was the correct answer.

"I make it the same style of carrier group as we ran into in Korma," Romanov said quietly. The Marine was acting as Damien's operations officer on the flag deck.

He supposed he was going to need to acquire a staff. Both his old-style one, for politics and covert ops, and a military one for the war it seemed he was going to have to fight.

"I've got what looks like a forty-million-ton ship and a twenty-million-ton ship in orbit of Cova," he continued. "Battleship and cruiser?"

"Probably," Damien agreed. They had more detailed data now than they'd had in Korma and he looked over the long-range visuals. "That's fascinating."

"My lord?"

"Look at them." The Hand gestured. The smaller ship was a long cylinder-like shape, presumably an outer armored shell around a rotating habitat. The larger ship, however, looked like *two* cylinders welded together.

"The big ship is basically two of the smaller ships connected," Damien noted. "They're building one, maybe two styles of hull. The cruiser is one of them, the battleship is two. The carrier is probably two of them with an extra connecting layer for the gunships.

"Efficient; about as close as you can come to mass-producing starships."

"Where are they getting the Mages?" Romanov asked.

"That's the question, isn't it?" the Hand murmured. "Or do they have a technological equivalent to the Mages? A jump drive of some kind?"

"That would explain their willingness to secede and go to war, I guess," his subordinate replied. "But we've been looking for that for centuries."

"We were looking for a technological FTL com for centuries, too," Damien pointed out. "We're almost a hundred percent certain they have that, so I don't want to rule out the possibility of a jump drive. It would explain a lot."

"The ships at Cova aren't maneuvering towards us," Jakab reported. "We can't say the same for the ones at Novo Lar, though. I make it a battleship and a cruiser guarding the carrier. The carrier is staying where she is, but the two escorts are coming our way with a hundred gunships or so."

"Wonderful."

Damien pulled up the visual on the carrier and nodded as it confirmed his thought. Two twenty-million-ton cylinders positioned about four hundred meters apart. The connecting section clearly served as a launch-and-retrieval deck for the gunships, with covered landing pads and refueling systems.

He realized that right now, however, those landing pads weren't deploying gunships. They were deploying assault transports, a new wave of ground troops heading to the surface.

"Have we made contact with the locals?" he asked.

"Limited," Jakab told him. "There is fighting continuing on the surface. So far, it sounds like the RIN is refraining from kinetic strikes outside *very* specific targets, but they've already landed twenty thousand troops."

"And if those transports map up to what I think, they've got another five thousand headed down." Damien shook his head. "Do you see any other transports, or are we just looking at the organic complement from the carrier?"

"I'm guessing the first twenty thousand were from another transport that left to pick up more troops," Jakab replied. "They can defeat organized resistance and take control of the government with twenty-five thousand soldiers, but they can't truly control the *planet* with that."

"Can those gunships and escorts intercept us?" Damien asked.

"No. They're just making sure we *do* leave, I think. Do you want to talk to them?"

Damien studied the ships heading his way. Five warships. The Republic had taken this system with five warships, and he didn't have the firepower to take it back from them. If he brought *everything* from Ardennes, including the ASDF...he'd still be outgunned.

The Republic hadn't declared war. They hadn't issued any ultimatums or demands. They'd just attacked, and Damien wasn't even sure how many systems had fallen.

"This is a date that will live in infamy," he quoted softly.

"My lord?"

"December seventh, nineteen forty-one," Damien replied. "The Japanese attacked the United States at Pearl Harbor, bringing the USA into the Second World War. There was no warning, no declaration of war.

"That date wasn't forgotten...and this one won't be either." He shook his head.

"No, Commodore, I have nothing to say to the Republic's Navy."

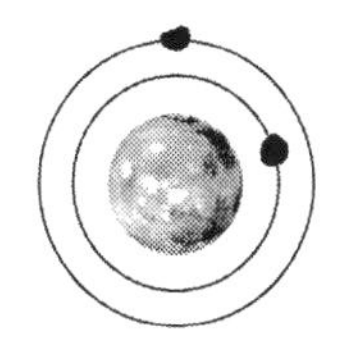

CHAPTER TWENTY

"JUMP COMPLETE," Roslyn reported, her words half-slurred in exhaustion. "Someone please tell me we're safe now."

Katz laid her hand gently on Roslyn's shoulder and squeezed.

"I think so," she said calmly. "Stick around a few minutes, Mage-Lieutenant. We'll know for sure."

Roslyn was in the seat attached to the simulacrum, usually the Captain's chair. With the odd setup for officers aboard *Stand in Righteousness* right now, it had been relegated to "the Jump Mage's" chair, with Katz commanding the ship from the tactical console.

The Commander's codes were apparently sufficient for her to remotely override the repeater screens around Roslyn's seat, updating them with the tactical plots of the star system as Roslyn looked with half-closed eyes.

She'd probably jumped as many times in the last few days as she had in her entire life before this, and she'd done so at shorter intervals than she ever had before. She was *awake*, yes, but she was riding the hard edge of nonfunctional.

And Mage-Commander Herbert's example meant that she wasn't going to take the uppers available to her—and she doubted that the overworked medic acting as ship's doctor would give them to her after the Commander's death, either.

Even through her exhausted state, however, she could make out the IFF codes being transmitted by the destroyers around the refueling station. Ardennes had a major Navy anchorage, barely a step short of a full fleet base, and ten destroyers were standing guard over it.

"The IFFs check out," Armbruster reported. "I make it the Sixteenth Destroyers and four ships of the Third Destroyers." He paused. "Confirming two cruisers and a slew of destroyers in orbit of Ardennes as well. Their IFFs read as Ardennes System Defense Force.

"Sir, the system appears to still be in our hands," he concluded.

"Good." Katz turned her gaze back to Roslyn. "Mage-Lieutenant Chambers?"

"Yes, sir?"

"Get your butt to a bunk and sleep. If you need help sleeping, talk to Sergeant Ryan. You're off duty for forty-eight hours, and I will by God *kill* anyone who tries to suggest differently. Am I clear, Mage-Lieutenant?"

"Yes, sir." Roslyn admitted. She half-stumbled out of her chair, but one of the POs Chey had put on the bridge with her caught her. "I'll be fine," she slurred.

"No, she won't," Commander Katz said firmly. "PO Karlson? Please see your boss to her quarters. Everybody on this ship owes her their lives. Let's make sure she gets the rest she needs."

When Roslyn woke up, her wrist-comp happily informed her that it had been just over thirteen hours since PO Karlson had bodily hefted her onto the bed in her new quarters and turned the lights off. She was still wearing the uniform she'd been wearing before she'd been sent off duty.

She had a short mental battle between *shower* and *catch up on what's going on*—but *shower* won pretty handily.

By the time she was cleaned up and dressed in a fresh uniform, she was feeling something close to human. She still had over a day off-duty according to Katz's orders, but she also needed to know what was going on—and the best place to find that out was the bridge.

To her surprise, however, *Stand in Righteousness*'s bridge was very quiet when she entered it. Commander Katz was holding down the command chair, but there was no one else in the room.

"Ah, Mage-Lieutenant," Katz greeted her. "If you so much as twitch toward a console, I'll have to find a Marine to escort you back to your quarters."

"That doesn't look like it would be easy, sir," Roslyn replied. "Where is everyone?"

"If they're following orders, asleep," the Commander told her. "I crashed after sending a report in to the Ardennes Station, leaving Armbruster in command until an hour ago. We're taking single-person watches until we make Ardennes."

"Is that safe?" the much-younger woman asked—and was surprised when Katz chuckled and gestured to the screens around them.

"Pretty safe, yes," Katz said. "Meet our new friends, Mage-Lieutenant: the ASDF cruisers *Appalachian* and *Himalaya*."

Roslyn blinked. She hadn't even checked the screens around them for other ships, but she saw them now. *Stand in Righteousness* was an even-sided pyramid, a hundred meters on a side. Her two escorts were *much* bigger.

"Export ships," Katz continued as Roslyn tried to scale the four-hundred-meter-long spikes in space against her own destroyer. "Tau Ceti–built, no amplifier, but missiles and battle lasers for days. I think we're safe, Mage-Lieutenant."

"I'd have to agree," Roslyn admitted with a chuckle of her own. "*Cruisers*, sir?"

"Our report is being relayed to Mars already," Katz told her. "RTA transmissions are already sent and a courier left the system with our entire sensor records two hours ago. I think the Navy is feeling twitchy about us, though, and asked the ASDF if they could borrow some *big* guard dogs."

Roslyn nodded.

"It's been a bad week," she said in a small voice.

"It'll get better," her boss promised. "It won't get more peaceful, though. Commodore Cruyssen has confirmed your commission. Last

I heard was that he was scrambling to put together a replacement crew for *Stand*, but I've been assured that you and I are remaining aboard."

Katz sighed.

"For my sins, I get the XO slot. From the sounds of what Cruyssen is saying in terms of his available hands, I think you're staying at Tactical, too."

"That's...a hell of a jump from 'I haven't graduated yet.'"

The Commander grimaced.

"Welcome to war, Lieutenant Chambers."

"It's certain, then?" Roslyn asked.

"The relayed message from Mars arrived just before you did. It's going out across the entire Protectorate—the Mage-King has drawn his sword, Lieutenant.

"The Republic doesn't know what they're walking into. The Protectorate has *never* gone to war."

"They were ours, once," Roslyn pointed out quietly. "Doesn't that mean they knew *exactly* what they were walking into?"

Roslyn joined Katz and the rest of *Stand in Righteousness*'s shattered officer corps in standing at attention as the shuttle came to a gentle halt. Cooling vents blasted air over the spacecraft, bringing the temperature down to where the safety barriers could retract and the boarding ramp extend.

There were, to Roslyn's understanding, about forty people on the shuttle. Only four stepped down immediately, all officers with the gold medallions of Mages. A Mage-Captain with skin almost as dark as her uniform led the way, and three Mage-Lieutenants followed her.

"Commander Katz," the leading woman greeted the acting captain. "I am Mage-Captain Indrajit Kulkarni. I have orders for you."

She passed a datapad over to Katz, who thumbed it and glanced down the screen.

"As expected, Mage-Captain," Katz said loudly. "I stand relieved."

"I relieve you, Acting Captain," Kulkarni told her. She stood at parade rest, surveying the handful of officers standing in front of her.

"All of you have been through hell," she said calmly. "We're reinforcing *Stand*'s crew, but we won't be back up to establishment." She gestured behind her. "These are all the Mages we're getting, people. Five Mages where we should have six. We're going to have less than two dozen officers where we should have thirty, barely three hundred crew where we should have six hundred.

"But you have given this ship a reputation to uphold. The Commodore is still reviewing the files and he's asked me to go over everything as well, but I guarantee you that there are going to be a stack of decorations coming down the pipeline. You have risen to the call of duty and gone far above and beyond anything we could ask of you."

She shook her head.

"In happier times, we'd be taking this ship back to Tau Ceti or Sol and sending you all on well-earned leaves. These aren't happier times. We're going to take *Stand in Righteousness* back into the line of duty almost immediately."

Roslyn shivered. She hadn't expected anything else, but it was still painful to hear.

"Before all that, however, there are two tasks that I have been charged with, very specifically, by the word of the Mage-King himself," Kulkarni stated calmly. "Mage-Ensign Roslyn Chambers. Commander Onyeka Katz. Step forward."

Roslyn swallowed hard and obeyed. Kulkarni was the first person to call her *Ensign* in a bit, which wasn't promising.

"Commander Katz. Rarely do we call upon non-Mages to command warships of His Majesty's Navy, but it seems that every time it is necessary, we are reminded that the lack of a medallion does not indicate a lack of talent or ability. I am tasked to present you with His Majesty's personal thanks for your service."

That was...a big deal. The Mage-King's thanks ranked above a good number of decorations for service and went on an officer's permanent record. That meant that Katz was almost certainly up for promotion to Captain as soon as they could spare her from running *Stand in Righteousness.*

"Your service was exemplary, above and beyond what we would ask, but it was still within the scope of your duties and actions," Kulkarni noted, exchanging a firm handshake with the other black woman.

"What is *not* within the scope of the expected duties and actions, however, is for an Ensign on a glorified internship to step up to the duties of an officer of His Majesty's Navy. We know perfectly well that the young officers-in-training we send out on Ensign cruises are not officers—they are students.

"We tailor our expectations to that. We do *not* expect them to step up as tactical officers or Jump Mages—let alone for them to single-handedly bring a Royal Martian Navy destroyer home after all of the ship's other Mages were lost."

The Mage-Captain had produced a large velvet box and Roslyn was lost. She was on the edge of panic and she wasn't sure what the *hell* was going on.

"Please kneel, Mage-Ensign," Kulkarni ordered.

Roslyn knelt, only to stare in shock as Kulkarni opened the box to reveal a deceptively simple medal.

A length of blue ribbon held a stylized rocket ship cast in gold. No gems or text or decoration. Just one simple symbol—that represented the Mage-King's Medal of Valor.

"Mage-Commander Herbert already saw to your promotion, so I don't have collar tabs to give you," the new Captain told her. "Your promotion has been confirmed, countersigned by Commodore Cruyssen and the Mage-King himself.

"I am also, under His Majesty's direct orders, tasked to hang this trinket around your neck, to remind *everyone* that we do *not* expect an Ensign to rise to the occasion as extraordinarily as you have—and that we recognize the value of one who does."

The medal felt surprisingly light around her neck.

“We expect great things from you, Mage-Lieutenant Chambers,” Kulkarni whispered. “But I also understand how unprepared you are. We’ll get through this the only way we can: as a team. As a crew.”

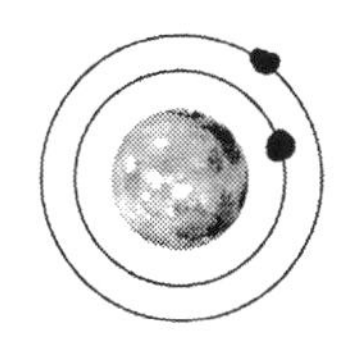

CHAPTER TWENTY-ONE

SIX RANDOM jumps away from the Santiago System, Damien's little fleet had to stop. With the full crew of Mages, they could jump six times in sequence. They just had to let all six Mages rest for a quarter of a day after that.

It made for a decent way of getting clear of the enemy. If they jumped along the normal route to Ardennes, they had a not-insignificant chance of being followed. Making six entirely random jumps meant that even if the Republic somehow had a technological equivalent to the rare human Trackers who could follow a jump, they wouldn't find the fleet before it moved on.

The downside was that they were less than two light-years from Santiago. That *shouldn't* have been a problem—even a single light-year was an almost incomprehensible distance for the human mind—but with everything going on, Damien wasn't taking that as a given.

"Commander Ferber," he said calmly into the video call. "What's *Duke*'s status?"

Commander Tamatha Ferber was a heavyset woman with a shaved scalp. She was also the operations officer aboard *Duke of Magnificence* and the most senior non-Mage aboard the ship. With the rapid-fire jumps, the Captain, the XO and the tactical officer were all asleep, recovering from the spells.

"We're running regular operations," Ferber told him. "Sensor sweeps are clear. Bravo shift is on duty." She shook her head. "Not much going on, my lord. We're out in the middle of nowhere, after all."

"We are," Damien agreed, looking at the chart on his flag deck hologram. "And yet the Republic keeps surprising us."

"My lord?"

He sighed.

"Take the task group to Alert Bravo," he ordered. "Man all weapons, load all launchers, pre-charge all capacitors."

"Sir...there's no way they can find us out here," Ferber protested. "All of the Mages in the task group are asleep and most of our crew have joined them. The trip through Santiago pushed us to our fullest."

"I know," Damien agreed. "And you're going to take the task group to Alert Bravo anyway. I would rather have our people tired and angry at me than vulnerable and dead. Am I clear, Commander?"

He didn't raise his voice. He knew perfectly well that he was a small man and raising his voice was hardly intimidating. For most people, though, he'd found that simply talking over them in calm, level tones was more than enough to achieve his purposes.

Ferber bowed her head.

"Yes, my lord. Of course, my lord."

"You don't need to agree with me, Commander, and I hope I'm being paranoid," Damien told her. "But let's humor my paranoia. We have to be prepared for anything."

"Yes, my lord."

The icons of the cruisers and destroyers on Damien's tactical plot slowly added amber carets to their green cores. The amber marked them as Alert Bravo, a couple of steps short of full battle stations. Two-thirds of the crew was awake and on-duty, with minimum crews on all of the weapon mounts.

The ASDF ships might not use the same terminology, but they had an equivalent status and knew the RMN term. It took longer to get all six ships up to ready than Damien would have preferred, but the empty darkness remained calm and silent.

For now.

"Are you going to sit on the flag deck and watch the scanners until we leave?" Romanov asked, the bodyguard leaning against an empty console.

"That's basically it, yes," Damien agreed. "I can't count on the Republic not having any more surprises for us. We didn't think they had jump ships, and we've been proven thoroughly wrong."

"I wish we knew more about those," his bodyguard admitted. "That's a wrinkle I don't think any of us were expecting."

"Right now, I'm honestly presuming they have a small number of Mages who were either kidnapped or like money more than ethics," Damien replied. "That's enough for them to support a relatively small number of the massive warships we're seeing."

The Marine stepped up beside him, tapping a command to bring up a map of the border area next to Damien's view of the space around them. The UnArcana Stars were marked in red now. The Santiago System had a red marker around it, declaring it as lost.

Other stars were marked with yellow, a line of systems from Nia Kriti down the border. Stars where either RTAs had gone silent or shipping had suddenly stopped.

"If they took all of these systems," Romanov said slowly. "That's not a few ships, my lord. Even assuming they're staging a small number of carrier groups through multiple systems, that's still multiple groups."

Damien sighed.

"And the carrier group at Santiago was still there, covering the landings," he concluded. "It's entirely possible each star system was hit by a separate group, which means we're looking at...eight to ten battle groups. Plus the one at Korma, and presumably at least one at Legatus, too."

Romanov was silent, the Marine staring at the map.

"So...sixty ships. Maybe more."

"At our best case, one Mage per ship," Damien concluded. "Strategically and tactically slow, but their command-and-control loop is tighter and more flexible than ours. We know *nothing* about this FTL com of theirs except that it exists, but I'm guessing a shipboard installation."

"And if they're using some kind of technological jump drive, we don't know what its rules and limitations are," Romanov said. "I'm starting to feel underequipped for my job, Damien. Keeping you alive is starting to look like it's going to require dragging you away from the front in chains."

Damien snorted.

"We both know that isn't happening," he replied. "You just need to watch my back. The Navy will keep whatever ship I'm on safe; we just need to be wary for assassins."

"You think we have traitors aboard?" Romanov asked.

The universe decided to answer the Marine's question for them. In the middle of the last word, three jump flares appeared on the screen, and Damien swallowed a curse.

"I'd say that yes, we do," he said grimly. "And that their FTL com can apparently be concealed on *our* ships.

"Commander Ferber—take the fleet to battle stations! We have incoming!"

Jakab struggled onto the bridge a couple of minutes later, the Mage-Commodore looking utterly drained.

"Report," he ordered. Even as he was giving orders to his bridge crew, he looked at the channel to Damien.

"As usual, paranoia turns out to be accurate," he said dryly. "What's your guess, my lord?"

"Spy with an FTL communicator, probably aboard *Duke* herself," Damien said grimly. "Because what we needed was a fucking *witch hunt*."

Jakab grunted and Commander Ferber reported.

"We've got three Republic warships at fifty light-seconds. They're accelerating our way at five gravities. No gunships on the screens, but it looks like a forty-megaton battleship and two cruisers, fifteen and twenty megatons apiece."

"I'd make jokes about the Lord Protector compensating for something, but I'm feeling rather notably outgunned," Jakab replied. "Do we know *anything* about these big bastards' armament?"

"No," Ferber told him. "I guess we get to find out."

"Lucky us," Damien murmured. "How long until they're in weapon range, Commander?"

"If we do nothing and they continue to accelerate: thirty-four minutes and some change for our Phoenix VIIIs," the Operations Officer replied. "We can't jump for at least four hours."

"You have ten gees on them," Damien pointed out. "We can avoid engagement, can't we?"

He wasn't sure that was the *right* plan, but he wanted all of the options.

"They jumped in with a thousand KPS of base velocity towards us," Jakab replied. "If we run, we buy about ten minutes—and we don't know what their range is."

Seventy-five million tons of Republic ships versus less than twenty-five million tons of Protectorate warships. Even Damien could do that math.

"Anyone feeling comfortable with the bet that our ships are three times as good as theirs?" Damien asked. Both the Mage-Commodore and the Operations Officer looked at him in horror.

"That's what I thought." Damien looked grimly down at his hands. Once, he could have teleported at least *Duke* away. Combining his Runes of Power with the amplifier, it wasn't even impossible that he could have moved the entire fleet.

It would have *hurt*, but he could have done it. Now, however, he couldn't even link with the amplifier to augment his range and power. He was the most powerful Mage in the fleet, but without the ability to link with the amplifier, Mage-Commodore Jakab could do more in the space battle.

"It would be over two hours to amplifier range, even if we go right for them at maximum power," Jakab murmured, as if he was following Damien's thoughts. "We'd wipe them out if we got any of the Navy ships to within reach of the amplifiers, but I don't know if we'd survive an hour of missiles to get there."

Damien sighed.

"I can help stop their missiles," he told the two Naval officers, "but without interface runes, that's all I can do. The command is yours, Mage-Commodore. If I come up with any clever ideas, I'll let you know, but right now I'm afraid the best thing I can do is get out of your way."

Jakab snorted.

"You'd be surprised, my lord," he admitted. "Keep your eyes and ears open."

The Commodore gestured Ferber back to her station.

"In the absence of brilliant ideas, however, let's start by keeping the range open. Get me a tactical network, Ferber. We have a battle to fight."

All six Protectorate ships flipped in space and brought their engines fully online.

As Damien watched, one of the key weaknesses of the Protectorate warships' design struck him. The Royal Martian Navy had never really expected to face an equivalent or superior enemy, and the Militias had copied the RMN's designs.

While the cruisers and destroyers had some of their RFLAM turrets around the base of the pyramid, able to fire forward or backwards, they carried no offensive weapons and few defensive weapons on the base of the pyramid. Missiles could handle the course change easily enough, but lasers fired in a direct line.

So long as they were running, they were limited even in their ability to protect themselves. Once the missiles started flying, they were going to have to turn—and at that point, they wouldn't be able to run anymore.

With the magical gravity runes throughout their ships, they were pushing fifteen gravities to the Republic ships' five. The Republic's starting velocity was more than enough to get them into missile range, though, and Damien found himself simply...waiting.

"They've got us pretty badly outgunned," Romanov murmured. "Not seeing any clever options, either."

"I have a couple," Damien admitted. "Entirely defensive, though."

Unless the incoming ships had a *lot* more missile launchers than he expected, he actually had a decent chance of making up the difference in their missile defense.

"I'm okay with living through this," his bodyguard replied.

"Me too."

The Hand looked over the holographic map of the system and was once again struck by the fact that he very much needed a staff if he was going to run a war from this ship—and unless he died today, he was going to be running a war from aboard *Duke of Magnificence.*

"I'll never get used to the waiting," he admitted. "Been a long damn time since the first time someone fired missiles at a ship I was aboard, but I still hate the wait."

"War is ninety-nine percent boredom, one percent absolute terror," Romanov told him. "That's what my first drill sergeant told us, back when even we larval officers and Mages were going through the same boot camp as everyone else.

"Working with you seems to up it to about ninety-seven / three, but the same rule applies."

Damien chuckled.

"I spent a year and a half in rehab. That can't have been *that* bad!"

"Nah, that was fine. The couple of months before that more than ma—"

"*Vampire!*" Commander Ferber's exclamation echoed across the link. "Range is thirteen point one million kilometers and the Republic has launched. Estimate four hundred and fifty, repeat, four five zero, missiles incoming."

The Operations Officer coughed.

"They're all targeting *Duke of Magnificence.*"

"Yeah," Damien said calmly. "We've got a mole on board. Mage-Commodore?"

"I can work with this. I can't work with being outside of my weapon range, my lord."

"If we can't outrun them, then let's take it to them," the Hand suggested.

"With your permission, my lord?" Jakab asked.

Damien laughed. "Shove your fleet down their throats, Mage-Commodore. The call is yours."

For the first time in its existence, the Royal Martian Navy faced an enemy with superior range. Not necessarily, Damien knew, superior *weapons.* Just longer-ranged ones.

They were assuming that the Republic weapons could reach them, of course. The missiles accelerated noticeably slower than the Protectorate's equivalent weapon, but everyone aboard *Duke* was assuming they had the extra sixty seconds of endurance that would make up the difference.

Once the Martian ships flipped, however, the math changed. Not so much for the missile flight time—the fifteen gravities the cruisers and destroyers could accelerate at was a pale shadow of the *ten thousand* gravities the missiles were pulling—but for when the RMN's missiles would be in range.

With the incoming missiles still ninety seconds out, Damien's force returned fire. The two hundred and thirty-six launchers on his fleet were badly outnumbered by the enemy's weapons, but they'd known that from the moment the enemy opened fire.

"They had three salvos in space before we returned fire," Jakab reported. "They have less confidence in their weapons than I would—against our force, that's easily a full salvo wasted."

"Well, I intend to prove their *lack* of confidence quite justified," Damien replied. "I'm linked in to your sensors and preparing my calculations. How do you want to play this, Commodore?"

The battlecruiser vibrated under their feet as a second salvo launched into space.

"Hard and fast. Hit them with everything we've got, lasers and Mages alike." The Commodore grimaced. "We have about fifty seconds to take them out and that window is opening...well, now."

The Mage at the amplifier stopped talking, Jakab locking his hands on to the simulacrum of his ship with a grim focus. Damien knew how worn-down the other Mage was from jumping less than two hours before.

This was *probably* safe. But only probably.

His own range without the amplifier was more limited, and he kept a careful eye on the scanners as the lasers opened fire as well.

Three fully-trained Navy Mages were unleashing the full power of their amplifiers, blasting missiles out of space by the dozen. Lasers flared as well, hundreds of beams calmly drawn onto Damien's holographic display as neat white lines.

The missiles continued to crash forward through the defenses, and the Hand took a deep breath. He closed his eyes and brought up his power.

Without an amplifier, few Mages could do more than take down a handful of missiles in their last second or so of flight...but Damien Montgomery was a Rune Wright, a Hand of the Mage-King of Mars with three Runes of Power despite everything that had gone wrong.

He was running off the ship's sensors with a series of screens which inevitably made him less accurate than the Mages using the amplifiers. Unlike them, however, he didn't *need* to be accurate.

Balls of electrically charged plasma materialized in deep space, each arcing off "lightning" toward the missiles nearby. He couldn't produce as many or as powerful of the ball-lightning strikes as he could normally, but he could still scatter them through the densest remaining parts of the salvo.

Explosions lit up space and the sensors dissolved into static as big, ugly antimatter warheads went off in their dozens—their hundreds.

"We're clear," Ferber reported. "None of them made it through."

"Are they continuing to target us exclusively?" Jakab asked.

"Yes, sir."

"Interesting," the Mage-Commodore murmured. "All right. Drop our acceleration for a half-second, pull us behind everyone else. If they want to ignore the rest of the task group, let's make them shoot *past* our friends to hit us."

"At least one more of their salvos is going to hit us before our fire hits them," Ferber said. "We're dropping behind the rest of the ships, but we're still going to take a lot of missiles."

"Buy us what time you can." Jakab met Damien's gaze. "Are you having the same suspicion I am, my lord?"

"If our mole is aboard *Duke of Magnificence*, they're trying to get *off* of her right now," Damien said. "Is that the one?"

"Yes, sir."

"Fight your ships, Commodore. I'll deal with our spy."

"Yes, my lord."

Damien kept most of his attention on the hologram, watching the next missile salvo plunge into the outer portion of Jakab's defenses.

"Romanov." He called the Marine over. "Keep this off the radio channels, but I want you to take a team of *our* Secret Service agents and lock down the escape pods. Pull in any Marines from *Duke* that you trust, but we're ninety percent sure we've got a mole onboard.

"They're using the mole's FTL transmitter as a targeting beacon. It isn't helping them much, yet, but we need to find the mole and we need to find the transmitter."

"My job is to protect you, my lord."

"And right now, you can protect me best by making sure we catch that spy," Damien ordered. "And that they haven't sabotaged *Duke of Magnificence*!"

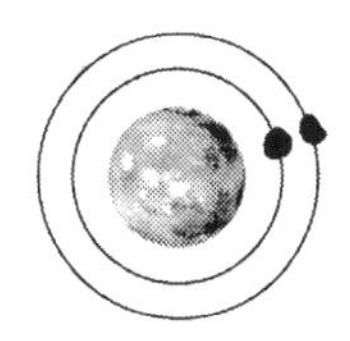

CHAPTER TWENTY-TWO

DAMIEN'S FOCUS was on the incoming missiles. He trusted Jakab and the other ship Captains to do their jobs and put their own missiles where they'd do the most good. He trusted Romanov and *Duke*'s Marines to handle any attempt by the spy to escape.

His own contribution was making sure they all survived. For the first time since he'd melted the runes in his hands, he felt *powerful* again. It was all too easy to compare his skills to the Mage-King's or even what he'd been two years ago.

Today, however, he unleashed the miracles of a Rune Wright trapped in a corner, and he knew that few others could match what he was doing. Ball lightning danced across the incoming fire like an angry will-o'-the-wisp, and he could *see* that his power was turning the tide.

Enough missiles were making it through the outer layers to the final terminal maneuvers where he could reach them to make his contribution necessary. His power spoke to the universe—and hundreds of missiles died.

He had enough attention to spare to watch the first of Jakab's salvos go in. The Republic hadn't skimped on defenses for their new ships either, but even from the number of launchers, it was clear the rotational gravity habitats inside their hulls cost them mass and volume alike.

On a ton-for-ton basis, even the Ardennes ships, Tau Ceti–built "export" ships, had more missile launchers and defensive lasers. The

Ardennian ships wouldn't normally carry the Phoenix VIIIs he'd ordered loaded aboard them before they moved out, but the Republican missiles were still longer-ranged.

Of course, the smallest Republic ship out there had three million tons of mass on *Duke of Magnificence* and over five million tons on *Andes.* The tonnage made up *plenty* of the difference.

But the Republican battle group didn't have Mages. Over a thousand missiles had reached the Royal Martian Navy force, and none had struck home. Less than two hundred and fifty missiles replied...but some of them made it through.

The battleship at the heart of the Republic formation lurched in space. Damien wasn't sure how many missiles had struck it—at least two, probably more—but there were a thousand tools in the arsenal of a twenty-fifth century-Navy to withstand an antimatter warhead.

She was hurt, but she was still in the fight. First blood, however, had gone to Damien's people. His confidence in their ability to at least survive this battle was rising.

Then he heard the distinct cracking noise of the penetrator carbines carried by his own Secret Service detail. The weapons were designed to punch through exosuit battle armor but still be human-portable. They were expensive, overpowered...and probably shouldn't have been fired aboard ship.

But both Damien and Romanov trusted their people's judgment enough that they'd left the team with the penetrator carbines—and *no one* else on the ship had the guns.

If a penetrator carbine was being fired, it was one of *Damien's* people shooting.

Damien had enough time to realize that with Romanov off hunting spies, he was alone on the flag deck. The Marine had clearly left at least one guard outside the room, but there was no one in there with him.

They hadn't considered the possibility that if there was a Republic agent aboard, well, the First Hand of the Mage-King was probably a fantastic opportunity target.

There was a security lockdown for the flag deck. Damien even knew where it was, but it was under a plastic shield to avoid accidental triggering. There was no way he could remove it with his half-frozen fingers.

He had to take a moment to recalibrate his power. There was a vast gap between the amount of energy needed to remove a plastic cover and the amount needed to generate balls of plasma seventy thousand kilometers away—and even Damien would be in trouble if he tried to use the latter inside the ship.

By the time he'd adjusted his mental throttle and torn off the cover on the button, it was too late. The much-flimsier normal doors were ripped apart and a vague figure dove into the room. Only the blur of motion allowed Damien to pick out the stealth-suited spy from the background—and they moved fast.

Too fast. Somehow, the Republic hadn't merely infiltrated a spy onto Damien's own ship. They'd infiltrated an Augment, a cybernetically-modified and heavily-trained Mage-killer.

Damien threw up a shield of solidified air in front of himself, barely in time to turn aside the first shots from the penetrator carbine the Augment carried. Recognizing the weapon sent a chill down his spine—it wasn't a Republic weapon and it wasn't integrated with the suit. The Augment had taken it from one of Damien's bodyguards.

The Augment kept moving. He knew that Damien needed to localize him to hit him with magic and that the shield couldn't be made spherical without cutting off Damien's air supply.

Damien threw lighting at the cyborg anyway, diving out of his own seat as the Augment managed to get around the initial shield.

A thought slammed the button for the security doors down and the doors crashed shut. Damien was now trapped in the room with his assassin.

This time, he "threw" the solidified layer of air that made up his shield. Barely visible walls slammed down around the Augment, sealing the cyborg inside exactly the kind of defense—and trap—that Damien had used to stop the tungsten penetrators a moment earlier.

The Augment bounced off the invisible wall, then fired into it experimentally. The stealth suit flickered as Damien rose to his feet, studying his enemy, and he clearly saw the cyborg give him a mocking salute.

Then *pain* wracked his body as the Augment slammed *something* into the bubble Damien had trapped him in. He'd never encountered anything like it—it was the opposite of one of the runic artifacts his gifts allowed him to build. It yanked energy out of the spell he was trying to maintain. He could keep the spell up, but only at the cost of agony.

The spell collapsed as Damien hit the floor panting in pain.

"Huh. That's even more effective against a Hand than a regular Mage," the cyborg said in an oddly-level, nearly-mechanical voice. None of the Augments he'd met before had spoken like that—and there was no way the cyborg had infiltrated his ship sounding like that.

No. The Augment was still expecting to get out of this alive. Damien was peripherally aware of the spy raising the penetrator carbine again...

Then, without Damien contributing to the defense of *Duke of Magnificence*, three missiles made it through her defenses. Hammerblows rocked the massive ship and the Augment stumbled.

A bullet whizzed past Damien's head, and he was still distracted by the aftermath of the pain. He couldn't attack or defend himself—but there was one spell he'd learned by heart over the years he'd been a Jump Mage.

He teleported, leaving the Augment trapped inside the heavy security doors of *Duke*'s flag deck.

Damien reappeared on the observation deck he used as an office, one of the few places on the ship he knew the location of relative to the flag deck. The pain from whatever the Augment had used to disrupt his spell was still running through his system, and he collapsed to his knees, vomiting across the floor.

"My lord!" Jeff Schenck exclaimed, the steward bustling into the room. "Are you okay? How did you get back here?"

"Battle still going on," Damien gasped out. "Get me a link." He coughed. "To the bridge."

Schenck might have been a steward and assigned to take care of the Hand, but he was also a Royal Martian Navy Petty Officer. Damien would have been shocked to learn that the man *didn't* have bodyguard training—and even more shocked if he wasn't able to bring up a communication channel.

"My lord, what is going on?" Jakab demanded. "We're taking hits, Damien. I need you."

"Commodore, lock down the flag deck with the maximum-security codes you have," Damien ordered. "Our spy killed one of my bodyguards and came after me. Augment, with some tricks I haven't seen before." He grimaced and forced his body to work well enough to open up the oversized icons on his personal console.

"I trapped him on the flag deck and teleported to my office. I'll have a feed set up so I can help defend the ship in a moment—but make *damn* sure that agent doesn't escape. I want to have a *long* conversation with him when this is over."

Jakab didn't even hesitate.

"Dropping secondary security seals. We didn't even have camera feeds in there, my lord. We didn't know what was going on at all. I'm instructing the ship to lower the oxygen content in the air," he told Damien. "We'll take him alive. Even Augments need to breathe."

"Eventually," the Hand replied, the sensor feed he needed unfolding on the screens in front of him. He grunted as he channeled power again, dropping ball lightning into the middle of a salvo that was already far too close.

It took him three tries to adjust for his new location within *Duke of Magnificence*, and a missile made it through while was doing so. The ship lurched again, but then Damien had the rhythm.

"He'll have an oxygen reservoir in his lungs," the Hand continued. "Not to mention resistance to stunguns and almost certainly a complete willingness to wreck the ship to escape."

"Marines are on their way. Combat Mages, too," Jakab replied. "Brief them on those 'tricks' you mentioned." Both men's focus turned to the incoming missiles for a few seconds.

"I don't know what these bastards are using for a jump drive, but I'm hoping they're able to run," the Commodore admitted. "With your help, we can stand off most of their missile fire, and we're landing hits, but...not enough. That battleship can keep taking missile hits all week, it seems. I *want* the man who designed her armor..."

"I'd rather not discover what they're mounting for lasers," Damien agreed. "What can we do?"

"I'm not sure I can even keep us out of range. We're still hours from *us* being able to jump, so...it's down to them. If they want to press this to the knife, we're gonna have a knife fight."

Damien grimaced, scattering more ball lightning across space as he did.

"I don't know if I can keep this up that long," he admitted. "I don't know what that Augment had, but he's left my magic more than a little fried."

"Fill in the Combat Mages," Jakab repeated. "This part of the battle is my job...and for all that I'd *rather* they ran, I'm willing to take that knife fight to see what happens.

"Brutal as it is, I'm quite sure that those three ships represent a *lot* more of the Republic Interstellar Navy than my three do of the RMN."

"We want him alive, Marines," Damien ordered grimly. "He probably won't cooperate, but the crew is running the oxygen content in the room down, and there's a setup for pumping in a knockout gas."

"Augments are usually protected against that," the Marine Mage-Lieutenant warned. "We'll do what we can, my lord."

"He has some kind of anti-magic weapon," the Hand continued. "It short-circuited my magic, threw my own power back against me. My guess is he can only use it on one Mage at a time and, well, if he's using it instead of a gun, your Marines have an advantage."

"That they do," the Marine confirmed. "We have this, my Lord Hand. If he can be taken alive, we will."

Damien nodded.

"Carry on, Lieutenant."

The Marine cut the channel and Damien turned his attention back to protecting his flagship. He could *feel* his energy reserves flagging, hammered surprisingly hard by whatever trick the Augment had pulled.

None of the ships in his little fleet were untouched now, but all six of them were still in the fight. The range was continuing to drop, and the Republic ships were starting to take long-range testing shots with their lasers.

Interestingly, all three ships were using the same class of laser. Both the Navy and ASDF destroyers were using a three-gigawatt battle laser, but the two cruisers used different levels of power.

The Republican ships were uniformly equipped with a twenty-gigawatt weapon, far more powerful than anything except what an RMN battleship carried.

"There's some interesting patterns to their design," he said to Jakab. "It's all standardized parts."

"I agree. Two hulls, larger ships built with multiple hulls connected together. One missile launcher, one battle laser, one defensive turret." The Mage-Commodore shook his head. "I have to wonder how long they've been mass-producing components, hoping they managed to pull off an FTL drive."

"And yet...they still can't have many of them," Damien pointed out. "Even Legatus only has so much industry and money. They can't throw away...There they go."

Jakab's guess that the enemy would act to preserve their ships in preference to a knife fight they *might* win was right. At six million kilometers, still well out of laser range, the Republic battle group disappeared.

"Jump flare," Mage-Commodore Jakab observed. "Like when they arrived. Identical to what I'd expect from a Mage-jumped ship." He shook his head. "Timing suggests that they have at least three Mages aboard each ship, though, and I'll be *damned* if I believe the Republic could find that many Mages willing to fight for them."

"It's possible," Damien said. "But unlikely, I agree. There's something else going on here, and frankly, they have duplicated other magical feats with technology in the past."

"Like what?" Jakab asked.

"Antimatter production, for one," the Hand reminded him. "They may have built a particle accelerator that wraps around an entire gas giant to do it, but Legatus was one of the largest antimatter producers in the Protectorate before the Secession.

"I believe they could find a technological solution." Damien shook his head. "I just don't see why they'd then go to war with us. We don't want to fight them."

"They're afraid," Jakab said quietly. "They think we'll want to reconquer them, to 'put the mundanes back in their place.'"

"I wish all I had to do was tell them we don't *want* them." Damien chuckled sadly. "But they won't believe me."

"No." The two men were silent for a moment, and then the Mage-Lieutenant from the flag deck came back onto the channel.

"Sirs? We got into the flag deck."

The Marine was in contact far too quickly. There was no way it had been that easy, and Damien sighed.

"He was already dead?" he asked.

"Yes, sir. Suicide charge built into the implants." The Marine coughed. "Hard to say, but it may have been remotely triggered."

"It might have been," Damien conceded. "But I wouldn't bet on it. Legatus has always had a supply of fanatics. I can't imagine they went away when they founded the Republic."

The feed from the bridge was quiet and Damien met Jakab's gaze.

"Have the body autopsied," he ordered. "And see if we can track down his FTL com. I'm guessing it was wired to the same signal that killed him, but the pieces will at least tell us how large the device is."

"And then, my lord?" Jakab asked.

"Then we get ourselves back to Ardennes," Damien replied. "If things are as bad as I fear, Ardennes just became the last possible launch pad for operations against Legatus."

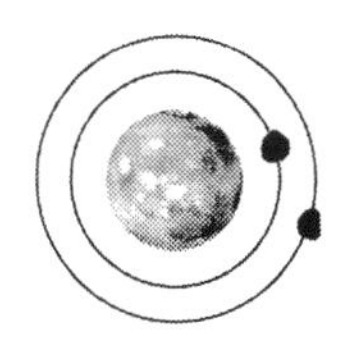

CHAPTER TWENTY-THREE

DAMIEN WAS reviewing the damage reports and casualty lists when they finally made it back to Ardennes. None of the ships he'd taken to Santiago with him were undamaged, but *Duke of Magnificence* had taken the worst of it.

A hundred and fifty-six people had died. All but ten of those had been aboard *Duke*, but for all that, the battlecruiser was still almost entirely combat-capable. She was missing a lot of armor and had large chunks of several decks open to vacuum, but all of the missile launchers save one were online, and her offensive and defensive lasers were intact.

The ASDF ships had damaged armor and that was it. Some wounded, but the remaining dead were aboard the Navy destroyers. The casualty list was far shorter than it could have been, but each entry was a new scar on Damien's soul.

A lot of men and women had died at his orders over the years, but it had been over a year since the last time he'd dealt with it. Some of the necessary calluses of his work had faded, and the new losses were a punch in the gut.

Still...he'd also forgotten just how unbelievably tough a Royal Martian Navy battlecruiser was. The report Jakab had sent him said the cruiser had taken seventeen hits while Damien had been fighting off his would-be assassin.

Seventeen two-gigaton warheads had detonated within a hundred meters of *Duke*'s armor. There were ablative-armor sections and energy-dispersal networks and electromagnetic fields designed to reduce that damage, but it was still a mind-boggling amount of energy that the ship had effectively shrugged off.

Of course, the Republic ships had taken just as much of a hammering, and Damien wasn't sure they'd been any more damaged by it.

"My lord." Romanov's voice pierced his thoughts.

Damien looked up and Persephone took advantage of his relaxed attention to leap onto his lap and demand pets. Chuckling, he looked over to his bodyguard.

Three Secret Service agents were *in* the room with him and Romanov now, the head of his detail clearly feeling grimly paranoid after the assassination attempt.

"Agent?" Damien asked, carefully petting Persephone's head.

"The system is on full alert. We've got an ASDF cruiser group headed our way, demanding IDs and IFFs."

"That's...good," Damien allowed, tapping a command with his non-cat-occupied hand. "That's a war footing," he realized aloud.

"Yes, my lord."

"We didn't tell them yet, so someone else made it here," Damien concluded. "That's good, I suppose."

The observation deck office was silent for a minute or so, both men watching the approaching cruiser group. The course and posture change from "intercept" to "escort in" was subtle, but it was one Damien knew enough to recognize.

"How bad is it, my lord?" Romanov finally asked.

Damien didn't answer him initially. He'd noticed a new IFF and was pulling it in.

"That's *Stand in Righteousness*," he told the Marine quietly. "The Commandant touched base with me when they sent Miss Chambers on her Ensign cruise—that's her ship."

"My lord?"

"*Stand* should have been doing anti-pirate patrols out of Nia Kriti," Damien told Romanov. "A system that should have two *squadrons* of cruisers. If a lone destroyer is here..."

He sighed.

"If *Stand in Righteousness* is here, alone, and Nia Kriti's RTA is offline, then I think the entire border is now in Republic hands."

"Nia Kriti is confirmed to have fallen to the enemy," Commodore Cruyssen said grimly over the multi-point link. "As has the Hoisin System. You've confirmed the Santiago System. This...this does not look good."

"I think we can assume that the Tormanda System and, sadly, everywhere else within about fifteen light-years of the Republic has also fallen," Damien told the rest of the call.

The two Navy Commodores looked tired. Probably for different reasons—Cruyssen wasn't a Mage, so he wouldn't have been jumping his ships around. On the other hand, he'd been the one staring down a potential invasion with only a dozen RMN destroyers and a System Militia.

"Those losses make Ardennes the closest remaining Protectorate system to key Republic positions, including Legatus," Damien continued. "This means that, even more so than our regular standard, Ardennes *must not fall.*"

Governor Riordan and Julia Amiri looked somewhat reassured by his statement. Julia, at least, should have known Damien well enough to realize there wasn't going to be much chance of that at all.

Admiral Forrest Vasilev, the commanding officer of the ASDF, looked less reassured. Unlike his political masters, Vasilev probably understood just what Damien was about to ask of him.

"I need to touch base with His Majesty and RMN High Command to see what resources we can deploy to reinforce this system," Damien told them. "We need to make certain that *Duke of Magnificence* and the other ships that went to Santiago are repaired as quickly as possible.

"We also need, much as I hate the potential consequences of this, to make sure there are no further saboteurs or FTL communicators aboard our starships." He shook his head. "It's going to be a witch hunt, people, but we had an Augment assassin with a direct link to the Republic Interstellar Navy aboard my flagship. We don't have a choice."

"That is going to be a pain in the ass," Cruyssen agreed. "We'll need to clear our MPs first, then have them carry out the investigation."

"We have a few teams of space-experienced personnel on Ardennes that I'd trust beyond reason," Riordan offered. "We can use them as a starting point to sweep the MPs aboard all of our ships."

"We have a few reliable teams ourselves," Damien said, "but the more people we start with, the better." He shook his head. "Admiral Vasilev, what does your munitions production look like?"

"We have the production lines to turn out roughly a hundred Phoenix VIIs a day," Vasilev replied. "It's not much versus the ammunition needs of our combined forces."

"No, and we'll need to retool it for Phoenix VIIIs," Damien confirmed. "Commodore Cruyssen, Mage-Commodore Jakab, I want you to get your staffs on pulling together every piece of logistics infrastructure we have.

"If we *can't* triple that production number in Phoenix VIIIs with a few days' work, I don't know Navy engineers as well as I think I do."

"We'll make it happen," Cruyssen promised. "We also do have a major stockpile of Phoenix VIIIs here still. Ardennes always was a logistics base, so we have those supplies on hand."

"We're going to need them," Damien said. "We're going to be moving a lot of ships into Ardennes, people. What we have can't hold against *one* of these damn carrier groups, and if I were the Republic, I'd be pulling multiple groups together as soon as I realized we knew they were coming."

"We'll do everything we can," Vasilev promised. "We don't have any ship construction facilities here, though. Just repairs."

"You can't build a fleet in a week, Admiral," Damien said quietly. "But I'm pretty sure I can find one in a week."

"What happens if they don't give us that much time?" Amiri asked, pointing out the hole in his plans, as always.

He shook his head at her.

"Then we do everything we can," he promised. "But...I can tell you that Ardennes must not fall. I can promise you that I will move the stars themselves to get reinforcements here in time...but if the RIN arrives with three carrier groups tomorrow, we can do nothing but surrender the system.

"If they give us time, we can assemble a defense to challenge them. If they have the ships to absorb the dozen systems they'd conquered and still throw multiple carrier groups at Ardennes?"

Damien shrugged.

"If they have that many of these new ships, people, we may have already lost the damn war."

The Ardennes RTA had apparently decided that Alanna O'Malley was going to be Damien's point of contact. At least, he doubted it was coincidence that it was the same Mage who met him when he landed at the massive black structure and left his assault shuttle.

She seemed a little taken aback by the Combat Mage and exosuited Marines who exited the shuttle after him, and he gave her a small sad smile.

"Someone tried to kill me aboard *Duke of Magnificence*," he told her. "My security is being paranoid. Shall we?"

Romanov and his heavily armored companions fell in around Damien and O'Malley as she led the way into the RTA.

"Usual security procedures are in place," she told him. "There are recorders running in the secondary receiving chambers, but otherwise, the Array has been evacuated. We'll review the recordings to make sure they're sanitized of your conversation."

"That's the standard, yes," Damien murmured. "Denis?"

The Secret Service Agent and Marine nodded.

"We'll be reviewing the recordings ourselves, Mage O'Malley," he told the younger woman. "We would prefer to trust your people, but we have evidence that the Republic has agents in places we thought were impossible."

O'Malley looked shocked, but she nodded.

"I understand, Agent Romanov. It's unusual, but the procedures exist for it. I can show you to the review office now or...?"

"After the Hand has made his call. We'll get it sorted."

"My liege."

"Damien. How bad was it?" Alexander asked bluntly.

"Bad. Santiago has fallen," Damien confirmed quietly. "Another five-ship carrier group, like we saw in Korma. Worse: they had an agent aboard *Duke of Magnificence* with an FTL com of some kind. We random-jumped to evade any possible pursuit, and then they just jumped to right where we were."

"What happened to the spy?"

"He was an Augment and tried to kill me. Suicided when we trapped him and blew up the communicator." Damien shook his head. "We *found* the communicator—or what was left of it, anyway. We're going to have some real nightmares over that, my liege."

"Smaller than we feared, I take it?" Alexander said quietly.

"Fits in a closet, basically." They'd pulled the shattered wreckage of the device, whatever it was, from a utility closet near the electronics shop where the spy had worked. "No special components that we could see, but it was also laced with about a dozen small explosive charges. No serious damage to *Duke*, but completely wrecked the com."

"So, any of our ships, any of our stations, could have an FTL communicator talking to the Republic at all times," the Mage-King concluded.

"Yes."

The stone chamber was silent.

"With Santiago confirmed taken by the Republic, Ardennes is now the flashpoint," Damien warned his King. "From here, we can strike at Legatus in forty-eight hours. Everywhere closer is now in the hands of the Republic.

"We have some time. They were still landing troops and fighting on Santiago; I can't imagine many of our systems rolled over instantly."

"I also would not expect our people to fight to the death," Alexander replied. "This isn't a war to the last man standing, Damien, and I refuse to let it become one if we can avoid it. You have a plan?"

"They're going to hit Ardennes with everything they've got. I say we let them. We can concentrate enough ships here to make this system a trap they won't escape."

"And they'll know what you've assembled and build a force to match it," the King pointed out. "We can no longer assume that the Republic isn't watching our every move. We cannot be weak anywhere, Damien."

"We cannot be strong everywhere," he countered. "They have to hit us here. The more force we concentrate at Ardennes, the better chance we have."

"That makes sense," Alexander admitted slowly. "But I'm not a military expert, Damien. Neither are you."

That...also made sense.

"And what are our military experts suggesting?" Damien asked.

"Reinforce all critical systems as heavily as possible," the King said. "We have no way to know whether or not they have any greater or lesser strategic flexibility than we do. We have to secure our production lines and shipyards against deep strikes...and the Navy simply isn't that big."

"And only Tau Ceti actually has a significant Militia of the Core Worlds," Damien concluded.

"Exactly. And the size of the enemy deployments is terrifying, too," Alexander admitted. "We're talking multiple battleships or cruiser squadrons to offset them, and..." The Mage-King sighed. "We only had fifteen cruiser squadrons to begin with, Damien. We didn't even replace the squadron we lost in Cor's mutiny in Ardennes.

"With damaged ships and lost ships and one crisis and another, we're down to only sixty cruisers. I'm not sure our destroyers are worth *anything* in this fight—and it would take fifteen of them to match the tonnage of the smallest ship the Republic seems to be deploying!"

Sixteen battleships. Sixty cruisers. Two-hundred-odd destroyers. Damien knew the numbers almost off the top of his head.

The carrier groups he'd tangled with had been a carrier, a battleship, and three cruisers. Over a hundred million tons of warships, equal to basically half the entire destroyer fleet of the Protectorate on their own.

If the Republic had even *ten* such groups, it was possible the Republic Interstellar Navy outmassed the entire Royal Martian Navy.

"What about the new construction?" Damien asked quietly.

"Months for the cruisers. A year for the dreadnoughts. More for the new battleships. We have destroyers rolling out of the yards already, but..."

He could feel his King's despair.

"I didn't truly expect them to start a war, Damien. We were willing to let them go. If they have a technological FTL drive, what do they even *want?*"

"I don't know," Damien said quietly. "All I know is that my oath to you says I fight. If you can send me a fleet, I'll hold. If you can't...I'll find one. Somehow. But I must fight."

"I'll make sure you get *something*. A couple of battleships at least." Desmond Alexander chuckled bitterly. "They may have their opinions and I trust their judgment, but my Admirals *do* follow my orders."

"I'll find something. Somehow," Damien promised. "I swear it."

"I know. You have my faith, Damien Montgomery, and you bear the platinum hand. You speak with my authority in all things, in all places. I have no intention of jogging my fleet command's collective elbow as they try and fight a war—or of letting you do so—but anything else..."

Damien snorted, counting on the magic to carry it to the other star system.

The only thing he needed was a fleet. If the Royal Martian Navy wasn't going to get him one, he had no idea what he was going to do.

"What purpose is our Protectorate if we do not protect people?" he asked his King.

"I don't know." Desmond Michael Alexander was silent for several long seconds. "I just don't know anymore."

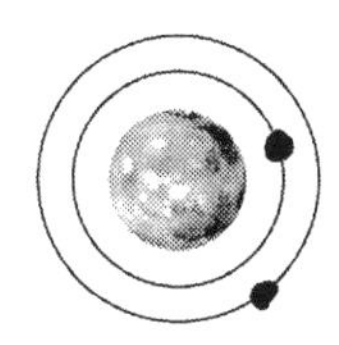

CHAPTER TWENTY-FOUR

THIS TIME, Damien had gathered his key players in person at the Ardennes Governor's House. It was a quiet meeting and he was relatively sure that Amiri was holding Riordan's hand under the table as a reassurance.

Two RMN Commodores, an ASDF Admiral, the First Hand of the Mage-King of Mars and two members of the planetary government surrounded the long table. A hologram hung above the table, gently rotating as it showed them the ship strength available to Ardennes defenders.

Thirteen destroyers and *Duke of Magnificence* from the Royal Martian Navy. Twelve *Lancer*-class destroyers and three *Phoenix*-class cruisers, all Tau Ceti–built, from the Ardennes System Defense Force.

"In all honesty, my lord, I can't help but wonder if we would be wiser to evacuate Ardennes," Admiral Vasilev said quietly. "Without reinforcements from the Protectorate, we cannot hold."

"His Majesty has promised reinforcements," Damien replied. "Not as grand or as overwhelming as we might hope, but even a single battleship has turned the tide of entire wars in the past."

The Royal Martian Navy had only *had* twelve battleships until very recently. Four had been commissioned since Damien had become a Hand less than three years before, the largest amount of new construction deployed in decades.

There were *another* twenty now under construction, but those wouldn't see commissioning for years. Even Project Mjolnir and its secret warships would commission first, and those were the ships Damien actually expected to turn the tide of this war.

Damien would back the RMN's battleships and their fifty million tons of armor and weapons against any individual ship he'd seen the Republic deploy. Until he had five of them at his back, however, he didn't know how the next battle would go.

"Thanks to Mage-Lieutenant Chambers and the rest of *Stand in Righteousness*'s crew," he continued, "we now know as much as we're likely to about the capabilities of our enemy. The Republic has better missiles, lasers, ships and gunships than we thought Legatus had.

"Much of that was likely built in Legatus, in the reservations they blocked from Mages." He shook his head. They should have found that more suspicious in hindsight, but even *knowing* that Legatus was waging a shadow war against the Protectorate hadn't caused them to think the UnArcana Stars were building a fleet.

"They're better than we thought they had," Cruyssen agreed. "But they're still not as good as ours, in a lot of ways. Most of those trace back to our having a more reliable and expandable supply of antimatter than they do. Our ships and missiles accelerate faster, are more maneuverable and have greater endurance. We have amplifiers and magical gravity. They don't."

"We're going over the data from both battles that we have sensor records on," Jakab said. "Their armor is better and their electronic warfare systems are better. Their lasers are the same as ours, but their targeting software is superior. They've made up a lot of the defensive shortfall they face from not having an amplifier.

"Ton for ton, they lose out because of using fusion engines and having to provide rotational pseudo-gravity," the Mage-Commodore concluded. "Otherwise, they're using superior software and systems to make up much of the difference."

"What about command-and-control loops for their missiles?" Vasilev asked. "What happens if they're including an FTL component?"

The room was very quiet. Even Damien could see the consequences of that.

"Their firing patterns don't suggest they are," Jakab replied. "I don't know what limits they have on production of their FTL coms. The fact that they had one aboard *Duke of Magnificence* suggests that they have enough to equip their spies with them."

"On the other hand, one com per planet would provide them a lot of information," Amiri pointed out. "And, well, bluntly, Mage-Commodore, everyone knows you command Damien's personal transport. If I was going to put an agent *anywhere*..."

"Agreed," Jakab admitted. "That's my hope, at least."

"The ASDF will do everything within our power to defend our system and support the Navy," Vasilev assured them. "Any data and technological assistance the RMN can provide us is, of course, more than welcome, but this is our star system. The Militias exists to defend our home ground."

"And we will defend Ardennes with you," Damien promised. "I will find a way to get more ships, people. The battleships I've been promised should suffice to stand off any rapid strike the Republic can mount, but... we'll need more for their real push."

The return to *Duke of Magnificence* was almost painful. They'd converged as much of the two fleets as they could above the planet, leaving only a trio of destroyers to guard the logistics base. The missile-production lines they'd jury-rigged together in orbit of the gas giant Lyons were critical...but they weren't essential.

It would hurt both the Protectorate and the defense of Ardennes if the logistics base and its production were lost, but they'd survive. They'd have to. Losing *Ardennes*, however, was unacceptable.

So, destroyers and cruisers hung above the planet and Damien's shuttle weaved through them. Ardennes did have repair slips for their ships, and *Duke of Magnificence* was currently occupying one of them. Drones and workers swarmed over the big ship, replacing armor plating and sealing breaches.

Twenty-nine ships against whatever the Republic could gather. Thirty-one if he got the "couple of battleships" the Mage-King had promised.

There was a key there, something niggling at the back of his mind that would change the equation. Part of him was certain he was staring directly at it, but it wasn't coming to him.

He was too tired, too stressed, to produce a miracle today.

He recognized *Stand in Righteousness* as his shuttle passed the destroyer, and smiled. *That*, at least, seemed to have been something he'd done right. He'd met with Roslyn Chambers at the request of her counselor, Kole Jakab's cousin.

She'd served him well on Tau Ceti, dealing with a conspiracy inside the Protectorate. His authority had then seen her ushered into the Academy *immediately*, bypassing exams and everything else to drop her into the class she would have been in if she hadn't failed the ethics part of the entrance exam.

And, well, been two weeks out of juvenile detention when she took the exam. That wouldn't have weighed against her *that* much, though someone without that background might have had a marginal fail on ethics bumped to a pass.

The reports he'd read on Nia Kriti suggested she was the only reason anyone had escaped—and she'd been the only Mage left aboard her ship when they'd arrived in Ardennes. Watching a mentor and superior officer overdose couldn't have been easy, either.

She'd well earned her battlefield commission.

Damien was more comfortable with her handling that role than he was with the fact that everyone expected *him* to save the day.

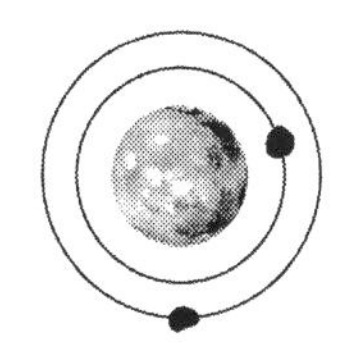

CHAPTER TWENTY-FIVE

ROSLYN SIGHED as she looked at the Petty Officer standing in front of her. PO Madelina Wendell had been transferred to *Stand in Righteousness* from another destroyer's tactical department, and Roslyn was now quite certain she understood why.

Wendell's record was clear: she was an *amazing* team lead, capable of garnering fervent loyalty from her crew and achieving noticeable increases in efficiency for the weapon mount she was in charge of.

What clearly hadn't made it into her record was that the tall woman with the short-cropped red hair had a massive attitude problem, which was hardly helped by being expected to report to an officer ten years her junior.

"Well?" Roslyn asked.

"*Well* what?" Wendell demanded.

"That would be 'well what, *sir*,' Petty Officer," Roslyn said calmly, carefully *not* glancing over at Chey next to her for support. This was her first in-department disciplinary hearing, and she knew damn well that leaning on the Chief too much would hurt her.

Even if she had no idea what to do with an exemplary NCO who'd pissed off three other Petty Officers and started a fight in the mess that had, thankfully, managed to avoid any serious injuries.

Wendell was silent.

"PO Wendell, the purpose of this hearing is to decide whether you face administrative punishment at this level or get bounced to the Captain for a full Mast," Roslyn said. "Explaining what you were thinking when you took a swing at PO Arbor is potentially your best bet of avoiding actual assault charges. So. What the *hell* were you thinking?"

This time, Roslyn let the silence stretch out.

"You really want to know?" Wendell finally demanded. Roslyn met her gaze for several seconds, then the PO grudgingly added, "Sir."

"My alternative is to bounce you to Mage-Captain Kulkarni for a full Mast, so, yes, PO, I really would like to know."

"They were a bunch of idiots who think you walk on clouds," the PO said bluntly. "Told them the truth, that no nineteen-year-old kid is worth even a butter bar. They told me I hadn't been with you in Hoisin and got personal. I took offense."

Roslyn had wondered if it was something like that when she'd seen that the three other POs had all been in her department when they'd escaped the Republic at Hoisin.

From Wendell's expression, she had been poking at the Petty Officers before the fight—and was poking Roslyn now.

The young Mage-Lieutenant grinned. What Wendell didn't realize was that Roslyn Chambers had spent time in street gangs *and* prison. She knew how to play *this* kind of dominance game.

"And you want to see how I react to the fact you got in a fight attacking my honor, is that it?" she asked sweetly. "I wanted to know why you got in a fight. Now I know. And it was, as I expected, a dumb reason."

Wendell looked more curious than intimidated now.

"But no one was hurt, so I see no reason to escalate this. You are restricted to quarters when off duty for three weeks and are fined ten days' pay."

Roslyn might have been phrasing it as mercy, but that was the maximum punishment she could levy in a departmental disciplinary hearing.

"If this occurs again, you *will* go before the Mast," she warned Wendell. "Keep doing your job as well as Mage-Commander Trill says you do, and I'll forget this after your restriction is up.

"Understood?"

Wendell cocked her head, looking curiously at the Mage-Lieutenant, then nodded.

"Understood. Sir."

There was less hesitation before the title this time, at least.

"Just what the hell am I supposed to do with someone like that?" Roslyn asked Chey bluntly when they were alone a few minutes later. "Is this *normal* for a PO?"

Chey laughed.

"It's normal for that type of PO, yeah," she confirmed. "The type that *should* be a Chief and *would* be a Chief if they didn't have a chip on their shoulder about something. Often about *not* being a Chief."

Roslyn sighed and shook her head.

"Wonderful."

"That said, I think you handled that well," the Chief continued. "I'd have hammered her and sent her on up to the Captain, kept our tier of administrative punishment for the people in the fight who got swung *at*."

"I watched the video, Chief," Roslyn pointed out. "There was plenty of swinging to go around. Now I know what the fight is about, the next few hearings will go faster."

Chey snorted.

"What, they get off easy for defending your honor?"

"No," Roslyn said flatly. She didn't even need the Chief to tell her that was a bad idea. "They didn't start the fight, but they definitely didn't try to deescalate, either. Don't care why. I will *not* have my Petty Officers brawling like dockyard drunks.

"They'll get less than Wendell did, but they're getting restrictions and fines, too. Should make my point, I think."

"That it should," the Chief agreed. "You might get through this okay, Lieutenant."

"People don't change," Roslyn observed. "Environment doesn't matter; they group, they clique and they cause trouble. Sometimes, you got to hit someone with a hammer."

"I'd have said it differently, but yeah." Chey shook her head. "Ready for the next one?"

No wasn't really an available answer, Roslyn reflected. This was part of the job.

"Yeah, let's get PO Virden in here and keep working our way down the list."

With the hearings done, Roslyn dismissed Chey and returned to her office to face the never-ending stack of paperwork that came with her new job. Normally, she'd be the *assistant* tactical officer and learn the paperwork while keeping her boss from being overwhelmed by it.

Without a senior *or* junior, she was struggling to make the distinction between paperwork she could delegate to an NCO like Chey and paperwork she needed to handle herself. She was pretty sure she was erring on the wrong side, and her sleep was suffering for it.

She had an hour before she had to be on the bridge for her watch, however, so she dove back into the current stack. This one was the transfer records for the personnel they'd brought over from the other destroyers. Her tactical teams were still understrength, but there were now two hundred men and women under her authority.

There was a reason the tactical officer was usually one of the three Commanders aboard a starship, along with the executive officer and the chief engineer. Right now, though, *Stand in Righteousness* had one nineteen-year-old Mage-Lieutenant.

One of the new messages in her queue was a short note from the First Hand, congratulating her on her promotion...and thanking her for what she'd managed to do.

Everyone seemed to think that she'd done something incredible. So far as Roslyn could tell, she'd *survived*. She'd always been reasonably good at that. Sometimes with a bit more acting out than even she would prefer in hindsight, but she'd always survived.

"Mage-Lieutenant, this is Chey," the Chief's voice interrupted her paperwork.

"Yes, Chief, what is it?" Roslyn asked.

"Need you in Cargo Four. We may have a problem."

When you are a brand-new Lieutenant and your senior Chief Petty Officer says they need you, you get there.

Cargo Four was mostly empty. A pair of standard ten-thousand-cubic-meter containers were currently docked with its airlocks, and Roslyn had to think about why Cargo Four was registering as "her problem."

Right. One container was general replenishables for the ship, but the other was missiles. A full reload for magazines that had been fired off before they'd returned to Ardennes.

Chief Petty Officer Chenda Chey stood by the door, with an addition to her uniform that Roslyn had never seen the Chief wear before: a standard Military Police shoulder holster with a stungun in it.

"Chief? What's going on?" Roslyn asked.

"We had a security breach on the missile container," Chey reported. "My readouts say nothing has been removed, but the cameras say nothing even came into Cargo Four around when the container's door alert went off."

"And we don't have any MPs," the Mage-Lieutenant said grimly. Which wasn't *entirely* true, but given there were only ten Military Police on the ship, it may as well have been.

"Backup would be great, and rumor says you Navy Mages are combat-trained," Chey told her.

Roslyn chuckled and touched the gold medallion at her throat. Like any Mage, hers was inscribed with symbols dictating her qualifications. Like any *Navy* Mage, however, all hers had were the three letters *RMN*. If she'd had a standard medallion, however, it would have included the Sword of a trained Enforcer Mage.

"Yes," she confirmed. "Shall we go take a look, Chief?"

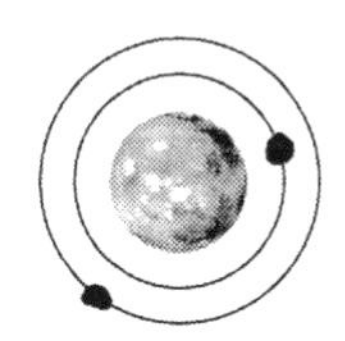

CHAPTER TWENTY-SIX

"I SEALED THE CARGO HOLD as soon as the alert went off on the container," Chey told Roslyn as they reached the small personnel access to Cargo Four. "Cameras weren't showing anything on the ship, but it's a straight mechanical connection on the container. Easy to short-circuit if you know it's there, but it's only standard on *missile* shipping containers."

"So, our ghost shut down every alert they knew about and botched the one that wouldn't be there on another container," Roslyn agreed. She conjured energy in front of them, a shimmering shield of solidified and heated air protecting them from incoming fire.

"Open it," she ordered.

Chey hit a command on her wrist-comp. The doors slid open into the dimly lit cargo hold.

There was no movement visible.

"Lights?" the Chief asked.

"Go on," Roslyn agreed, stepping into the hold. She could see the two cargo connector locks. Both were closed, but she didn't disbelieve Chey's discovery.

Light panels in the roof went from minimum lighting to full power, a stark white brightness that cut stark lines of shadow in the floor.

"If you're in here, you may as well surrender now," Roslyn said loudly. "We know you're here and the exits are secured."

As she spoke, the entrance they came through locked down behind them. No one was getting out of there until Chey decided they were.

A moment of chill paranoia ran down Roslyn's spine, but then the Chief was right beside her with the stungun drawn.

"I don't think anyone wants to be that cooperative," she said cheerfully. "What do you think, Lieutenant?"

Roslyn grimaced.

"This is so far outside my experience, I have no clue," she admitted. "Let's check the missile container. We have the exits locked down, so even if they're hiding in the other one, they can't go anywhere."

The cargo airlock connected to the missile container slid open easily, revealing the massive expanse of one of humanity's standard shipping containers. Ten meters wide, ten meters tall and a hundred meters long, the ten-thousand-cubic-meter containers were ubiquitous across both the Protectorate and the Republic.

Most of them weren't full of neatly stacked missiles, stacked two wide and five high on each side of a narrow-looking gap leading down the center of the container.

"No gravity in the container," Chey warned.

"I'll take care of it," Roslyn replied, conjuring more magic to hold their feet to the deck as they moved forward. Whispering nonsense words under her breath—a child's focusing trick but still a useful one—she conjured a ball of light and tossed it down the central path.

It drifted down the container, seemingly only a light...and then halfway down the hundred-meter-long void, it started to drift to the side. It moved faster and faster as it approached the heat source—almost certainly a human in there—until it stopped and hovered in place next to someone's hiding spot.

"We know where you are," Roslyn shouted down the container. "Surrender now and—"

Chey slammed into Roslyn bodily, detaching both of them from the deck as her spell collapsed. They both went flying as gunfire echoed toward them.

"Yeah, not happening," the Chief snarled. She turned in the air with the grace of an experienced spacer, opening fire with the stungun. The SmartDarts it was loaded with were supposed to calibrate their shock to avoid lethal overload of any human.

They still had to *hit*, however, and the expensive smart munitions smashed into the chassis of the missiles down the container.

Roslyn leapt forward herself. She didn't have the Chief's experience or grace...but she had magic.

A shield of solidified air led the way, sweeping bullets out of the air as their "ghost" fired down the hallway. Magic slammed her into the side of a missile as she reached her still-floating orb.

Their intruder was tucked into a neatly assembled cubby between the missiles. There were a hammock, a computer, a small locker of personal effects—and a disturbingly large machine gun now pointed directly at Roslyn Chambers.

She shattered the gun with a flash of power. The spy pulled *another* gun, a heavy pistol of some kind.

Roslyn didn't wait to find out what it was. Electricity arced down her hands and across the space between them, flinging the spy against a wall and leaving him convulsing.

She landed next to him and pinned his gun hand to the wall with her foot and magical gravity.

"This would have been so much easier of a conversation before you started shooting," she pointed out grimly, a bar of overstrength magical gravity pinning the man's other hand to the missile. "But I think this will still work."

Chief Chey brought herself to a halt next to the cubby, producing a pair of manacles from somewhere inside the many pockets of an RMN utility uniform.

"I'm sure the Hand is going to *love* having a chat with you," the Chief informed their prisoner...and then the man's entire body spasmed. His eyes disintegrated in explosions of blood, and Roslyn had a horrified moment to realize a series of tiny explosives throughout the man's body had just gone off.

"We need to get out of here!" she barked. She was already working magic, wrapping bands of force around them both and flinging them toward the entrance. "You have the codes, Chief. *Eject the container.*"

They hit the cargo hold fast, Roslyn barely having enough control to keep them from breaking bones. She left ejecting the container to Chey as she opened a channel to the bridge.

"Get us away from the container we're ejecting," she ordered, without even checking who she was speaking to. "There was a spy aboard and it may be rigged to blow!"

There wasn't much antimatter inside a missile in transit. Most of that would be loaded from the ship's own storage tanks while arming the weapon. There were, however, enough *other* explosives and volatiles in even an unarmed missile...

She hoped she'd been fast enough.

For just over a minute, nothing happened, and Roslyn began to think she might have just cut short her career by giving orders to the Captain.

At the same time, her wrist-comp showed her every ship in orbit accelerating away from the container as it drifted away from Ardennes. She might be wrong...but it didn't look like anyone else was going to take that chance.

Then something sparked. The container started to disintegrate and it looked, from Roslyn's low-resolution view, like several of the missiles were about to *activate*...

They didn't get a chance. As soon as the container started to disintegrate, four destroyers opened fire with every laser in their arsenal. Volatile or not, the contents of the container were *much* less dangerous reduced to vapor than being fired through rocket nozzles.

She still held her breath, waiting to see what happened next. The debris cloud "sparked" visibly in her holographic screen as antimatter reacted with the rest of the vapor, spreading the cloud wider. More laser beams cut through space as the Navy ships carefully contained the cloud to avoid further damage.

"Well, Mage-Lieutenant," Mage-Captain Kulkarni said calmly from the bridge, "it seems you have once again stumbled into the middle of it, haven't you? And saved the day, at that."

"No, sir," Roslyn said firmly, looking over at Chief Chey. "This was all Chief Petty Officer Chanda Chey, sir. She recognized the alert, locked down Cargo Four and called for my assistance."

"What are you *doing*?" her subordinate hissed.

"I am *not* carrying all of this, Chief," Roslyn said cheerfully. "If you want to be a hero, you get to bear that burden."

Chey sighed.

"Yes, sir."

"Well, get both of you up to the bridge," Kulkarni ordered. "For your sins, you get to talk to every MP in the fleet.

"You caught one of these buggers. We need to make sure we catch them *all*."

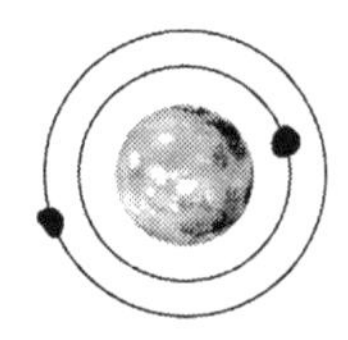

CHAPTER TWENTY-SEVEN

"I WISH we at least had some way to detect their communicators," Jakab complained. "We can't be sure that the agent who was trying to sneak aboard *Stand* had an FTL com or not."

"Have we traced how he made it aboard that cargo container?" Damien asked. He and Jakab were sitting at a small table in Damien's observation deck office. Commodore Cruyssen was present by hologram.

"I have military police tearing the logistics base apart," Cruyssen replied. "But..." He shrugged. "We've confirmed that container was sitting out there for a while. It was delivered in a resupply shipment from Tau Ceti over a year ago.

"We can be reasonably sure our spy wasn't living in that container for a year, so he was infiltrated recently. If he was targeting *Stand* specifically, he would have had to sneak aboard within the last twenty-four hours."

"But if he just wanted to make sure he was aboard *one* of our ships, he could have inserted himself into that container anytime in the last few weeks," Damien concluded grimly. "Can we check the rest of our logistics infrastructure for moles? At least in theory, there shouldn't be much in terms of heat signatures in our missile containers."

"We're sweeping as we speak," the Commodore in charge of the base confirmed. "This one is on me, my lord. Either my people missed him going aboard or some of them helped him get aboard."

"I don't care whose fault it is. I want to make sure it doesn't happen again. If someone intentionally caused this, *then* I care," Damien said dryly. "Otherwise, I have no intention of assigning blame for blame's sake; am I clear?"

"Yes, my lord."

"In better news, the Transceiver Mages have forwarded a message from Tau Ceti," Damien told the two Commodores. "An old friend is on his way: Mage-Admiral James Medici has taken command of Task Group *Peacemaker* and is headed here.

"At this point, we're all being insanely paranoid about what we're transmitting, even via the RTAs," he continued. "I'm not entirely sure what Medici is bringing with him—but *Peacemaker* is the RMN's newest battleship. If we're lucky, we're getting *Peacemaker* and *Pax Marcianus*."

Those were the two *Peace*-class battleships, laid down in orbit of Terra the day the body of Hand Alaura Stealey was brought back from Ardennes for burial. Until Project Mjolnir completed, they were the most powerful warships in existence.

"Even if we're not that lucky, *Peacemaker* herself will turn the balance of power here," he continued. "Their ETA is three days. Once Medici is here, he'll take command of the combined force, second in authority only to me."

"I only know Admiral Medici by reputation," Jakab admitted. "But his reputation is good."

"He saved my life once," Damien replied. "I can't say I know him well, but that's definitely a solid introduction to a man."

"So, if the Republic waits for three days, we win," Cruyssen suggested.

"Maybe," Damien allowed. "Three days and they can't take this system with one carrier group. In their place, I'm not sure I ever would have planned to. If they bring two and Medici has a pair of *Peace*-class ships? We can hold them.

"If they bring *three*?"

"We'll bloody well give them a fight they won't forget," Jakab promised. "But I won't pretend I'd turn down a miracle."

"So far, evidence suggests we should ask young Lieutenant Chambers about that," Cruyssen said. "Where did you find that young woman, Lord Montgomery?"

Damien chuckled.

"In a juvenile detention center, looking down the barrel of an absolutely ruined life," he told Cruyssen. Jakab already knew the story. "I accidentally dragged her into Protectorate politics and got her in trouble, so I exercised the privileges of my rank to give her a boost."

He shook his head.

"Given what she's pulled off lately, I think that might be one of the best calls I ever made."

Intelligence was continuing to trickle in. The limitation of the RTAs to basically voice communication meant mass information only traveled quickly when it could go by ship. Protectorate couriers were jumping around like madmen, updating every command on what information was flowing back.

None of it was good.

The timelines that Damien was looking at were fuzzy at best, but they suggested that while *he'd* been playing games with an RIN carrier group in Korma, other carrier groups had been hitting at least five systems.

Nia Kriti wasn't the only system where the RTA had been taken out by preemptive sabotage, either. Santiago was odd in that the RTA was intact. Damien wasn't sure how that had worked, but he doubted it had been overly pleasant for the Mages in the structure.

The Martian Interstellar Security Service was run off their feet, chasing spies and operatives. Some of the people MISS had flagged and arrested had been in place for decades. How could you secure your infrastructure against an enemy who'd been laying the groundwork for thirty years?

Damien could already see the chilling effect of those discoveries on communications. His last data package from Mars had been hand-delivered by a nervous-looking courier captain, a civilian Mage who probably didn't even *want* to know what he was delivering.

Less and less information was being transmitted or even sent by RTA. The Protectorate was not ready for war.

They'd thought they had been. They'd *expected* the Republic to move...but eighteen months of peace had lulled them into a false sense of security.

Persephone head-butted his leg, and he sighed and patted his lap.

"Come on up, kitten," he told her. He was honestly surprised by how well the cat could account for his limitations. He couldn't really pick her up, but she was perfectly capable of getting into his lap.

The report he had up on his screen told him that specialty MISS ships were being deployed into Republic space, trying to learn as much as possible about the enemy. He suspected at least some of those ships had already been there, but what they'd been able to learn had clearly been far too limited.

His *minimum* estimate was that the Republic had eight to ten carrier groups. He'd guess they were holding at least a third of their ships back to defend their territory, and attacking the Protectorate with at least five carriers and twenty cruisers and battleships.

It was possible, in his worst-case calculations, that their *offensive* force was ten carrier groups—one per system that had already fallen to the Republic. In that case, he'd expect that they had five more in defensive positions in key systems.

And if the Republic had fifteen carrier groups, the only option available to the Protectorate was a desperate holding action until Project Mjolnir finished.

"I need more data," he said aloud as he carefully scratched behind Persephone's ears. "I don't know enough about my enemies...or my own people."

He sighed. What was the Art of War quote? If you knew yourself and your enemy, you would win every battle, but if you didn't know either, you'd always lose? Something along those lines.

Two days. He needed the Republic to give him two more days.

He wasn't really expecting to get them.

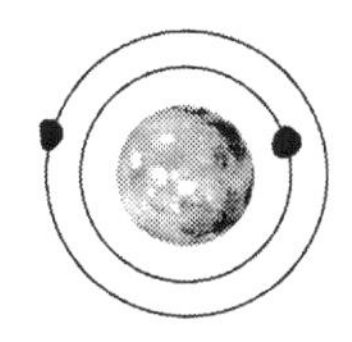

CHAPTER TWENTY-EIGHT

"SO, HOW MANY TIMES have we checked these calculations?" Kelly LaMonte, commanding officer of the Martian Interstellar Security Service's covert operations ship KEX-26, *Rhapsody in Purple,* asked her wife sweetly.

Right now, *Rhapsody* drifted in deep space one light-year from the Santiago System. They'd reached their home port in Tau Ceti after a long and incredibly boring sweep of the UnArcana MidWorlds, and been turned around *immediately.*

Normally, they got at least a few days, but Kelly had agreed with her superiors' urgency.

"I've checked them three times myself," Jump Mage Xi Wu, *Rhapsody*'s senior Ship's Mage and Kelly LaMonte's wife, replied. "And *then* I had Joe, Liara and Mel check them all as well. We're coming in on the other side of the gas giant. No one is going to see us."

There was a strong tone of "teach your grandmother to suck eggs" in Kelly's wife's words. *Rhapsody in Purple* was just over two years old and her crew had been together since the beginning. They'd made a *lot* of covert insertions over those years.

"This is the first time we've jumped into a war zone," Kelly pointed out gently. "Normally, the worst we're going to get is shouted at, unless someone works out that we're not what we appear. This time, the RIN *will* just start shooting."

Rhapsody looked like a standard Protectorate courier ship. On a command from her Captain, however, a number of panels that artificially augmented her radar signature back up to where it should be would fold away, leaving her with her base hull. A hull covered in radiation-drinking paint that any twenty-first-century aircraft designer would *kill* for.

She could also retract her heat radiators and store heat in several massive heat sinks buried underneath her antimatter power plant, where a normal courier would have put their fusion core and its fuel bunkers.

Rhapsody in Purple and her sisters were as invisible as technology could make them—and unlike their civilian cousins, the *Rhapsodies* had full, unrestricted amplifiers. The final piece of Kelly's cloak of invisibility was her wife's Gift.

"I know," Xi Wu confirmed. "And I am well aware, my love, that both my wife and our husband are aboard this ship. I don't plan on getting shot at today. Can't say the same for Mike."

Mike Kelzin was the senior of *Rhapsody*'s three shuttle pilots and the husband of both women. His job was to make sure the elite platoon of black ops cyborgs tucked away in the barracks aboard *Rhapsody* made it to their targets intact.

It had been a surprise to Kelly to discover that Legatus and the Republic didn't have a monopoly on badass fanatical cyborgs. The Protectorate's Special Operations Command fell under the authority of MISS, not any of the military branches, and the Bionic Combat Regiment was part of PSOC.

"Unless something goes *very* wrong, we won't be sending Mike in today," Kelly replied. "You're sure on these calcs?"

"Sure enough to take myself and my two most precious people in the galaxy into hostile territory with them," Xi Wu said with a chuckle. "I don't think I can be more certain—and worse-case scenario, Mel is making the jump with Liara and I standing by to jump us right back *out* if needed."

Kelly chuckled.

"All right. Inform Mage Melanie Droit that she may jump the ship at her discretion."

A moment later, reality *twitched*—and Kelly LaMonte's ship was in enemy-held territory.

The Santiago System had three gas giants, and *Rhapsody*'s crew had picked the farthest-out of them to emerge behind. None of the three had significant infrastructure, beyond the one facility the Navy had protected, but Columbo had nothing. There were no ships, no stations and—most importantly—no sensors out there.

"We're clear," Conrad Milhouse declared after reviewing the sensors for several minutes. The tactical officer was a chubby blond man—and one of the few people Kelly had ever met who could keep up with her in programming.

Which was good, given that *Rhapsody in Purple* had a grand total of two missile launchers and a laser. Her sensors and electronic-warfare emitters, however, could put battleships to shame. She'd been designed for a very specific purpose.

"All right," Kelly said brightly as she tugged gently on a long lock of currently neon-pink hair. "Can you give me a safe zone for accelerating?"

Milhouse nodded, a few gestures across his console dropping a green cone behind Columbo on the main display. A larger amber cone surrounded it.

"Green, I'm ninety-nine percent certain no one will be able to see us. Orange, we've got a good chance of going undetected if we keep our burn low." He shook his head. "Outside those zones, our odds get very messy, very fast. Assuming they have ships at the cloudscoop and in orbit around Novo Lar, these areas are *definite* no-gos without full stealth."

Large sections of the system shaded into red. "Of course, that assumes they're watching," he concluded.

"I don't plan on hanging the survival of a hundred and twenty-six people on our enemies being *completely* incompetent," Kelly said calmly. "Check in with Engineering; make sure we have everything set up for stealth at my command."

As Milhouse set to work, she programmed in a course and flipped it to her navigator's console.

"Hilton?" she asked. "Any issues with this?"

Jennifer Hilton was already reading through it.

"Nothing, boss. It won't be a fast trip, though," she warned. "Biggest concern will be running out of heat-sink capacity before we reach Leonardo."

Leonardo was the next gas giant in, currently roughly four light-minutes away. The course Kelly had plugged in would take them just over thirty-six hours to reach it.

"Worst-case scenario, we rely on the Mages' stealth spell for a bit while we vent heat," Kelly responded. "It's not perfect, but it will let us reset the heat sinks."

"And if we're spotted?" Milhouse asked.

"We jump," she said instantly. "No games here, people. Hand Montgomery's data says there's a carrier group in the system—we're *guessing* the ships that came after him were from here, but validating that is part of our job."

"And what happens if they ambush us?" her tactical officer said.

"Unless Xi Wu jumps us before they can fire, we die," Kelly admitted. "Their gunships aren't FTL-capable, which means anything ambushing us is a cruiser or bigger." She shook her head. "A cruiser outmasses us about a hundred to one. If the Republic catches us with a warship, we're dead.

"So, let's not let that happen, shall we, people? We're here to find out what the RIN is planning."

If she was lucky, it would be obvious. If she was good—and she *was*—she could probably extract a lot of their plans from their radio communications, even from this far away.

And if the Republic was far better at communications security than anyone else she'd ever encountered, there was always the option of ambushing a ship in the outer system and discovering how her commandos stacked up against Republic shipboard security.

The acceleration burn was hard on *Rhapsody*'s crew. It took a *lot* of power to actually inflict a force on the crew of a ship with magical gravity runes, but it was doable. At twenty-five gravities, the runes were doing their best, but they weren't designed for this.

Eight gravities made it through, slamming Kelly and her crew back into their seats for a full fifteen minutes. Once they entered Milhouse's orange zone, the pressure released as the acceleration cut back to a "mere" five gravities.

They continued to accelerate at that rate for another fifteen minutes, and then cut acceleration entirely.

"Well?" Kelly asked.

"We appear to have gone unnoticed," Milhouse said after several seconds. "I'm not picking up anyone accelerating hell-for-leather in our direction, anyway."

"That's good," she allowed. "What *are* we picking up?"

"Not much yet," he told her. "We have some of the most sensitive passive sensors in the galaxy. They were *not* calibrated for a twenty-five-gravity burn, so it'll take me some time to get them aligned again."

"Then get on that," Kelly ordered. "Xi?"

"Stealth spell is in place," her wife replied. "We are invisible, Captain."

"That's a good feeling," Kelly said. "Thank you. Stealth systems?"

"Fully online," Milhouse said in a distracted tone. "Heat sinks are melting at standard rates. Vong estimates twenty-two hours till we will need to vent."

Duong Vong was the chief engineer, a Navy officer who'd been involved in the development of the stealth systems aboard the *Rhapsodies*. MISS had happily poached him when the ships had been commissioned.

If he left Engineering while they were underway, Kelly LaMonte didn't know about it. Vong was...dedicated, to put it mildly.

"All right. We're the invisible eye in the sky, Officer Milhouse. How long until we aren't blind?"

"We're not blind," he objected. "We just need...some optical nerve surgery. Things are blurry." He gestured expansively at the main display. "I can tell you where all of the planets are!"

"I could tell you that with a window, Milhouse," she replied. "Anything more for me?"

"There's ships in orbit and there's ships at the cloudscoop around Roberta," he told her. "Give me ten minutes, and I'll tell you how many.

Give me an hour, and I'll tell you the maiden names of their commanders' mothers."

"I don't need to break into their bank accounts, Milhouse," Kelly pointed out. "I need to know what they're planning."

Milhouse had been many things in his life. Currently, he was technically a convicted felon putting in community service to commute his sentence. He'd been convicted of hacking into bank accounts and funneling money to his own projects.

Since he'd been *good* at it—and had been a Navy officer before he'd fallen into his white-collar criminal career—MISS has offered him an alternative to ten years in jail.

"Well, for that, you'll need to give me at least that hour," he said with a chuckle. "And hope that at least one of them used their mother's maiden name as an encryption key!"

"Well, that's about what we were expecting," Kelly concluded as they looked over the ships in orbit of Novo Lar.

"Yeah. One carrier, one battleship, three cruisers and a couple of transports built on the same hull as the cruisers," Milhouse counted up. "That battleship has had a rough month, too. Someone kicked them in the nuts a few times with antimatter boots."

Novo Lar's local space was swarming with gunships, too, but that was also expected. The electronic intelligence Kelly was looking over suggested that the Republic had just dropped two army corps' worth of regular troops.

Not Space Assault troopers. Not cyborgs. Just a hundred thousand regular soldiers with tanks and guns. A true army, designed to take and hold a planet in the face of heavy resistance.

The Protectorate didn't even *have* an equivalent force. Marines and PSOC combined barely totaled a hundred thousand troops. There were more uniformed Navy personnel than there were trained ground soldiers in the service of the Mage-King.

"What's funny is that Damien's report made it very clear that the Republic was keeping a close eye on the cloudscoop when they came through," Kelly murmured. "Do we have a clean scan of that area yet?"

Her tactical officer looked at her in near-confusion for several seconds, then sighed.

"You mean Montgomery," he clarified. "Damien Montgomery. The goddamn First Hand of the Mage-King of Mars. Could you *not* refer to him like an old high school friend? It makes my neck twitch."

"Would you rather I called him my ex?" Kelly said sweetly. "Answer the question, Milhouse."

"No, we've got nothing on the cloudscoop, and that's weird, too," Milhouse said with an exaggerated shiver at her description of the First Hand. "I should have a clean shot at it by now, but it isn't there."

"You think they blew it up?"

"No." He shook his head, all humor gone now as he focused on his screens. "I think they moved it. And I think they moved it to make *exactly* what we're doing harder."

"Which means they have something to hide." Kelly shook her head as well. "But if we can see every ship that we know is here, then what are they hiding?"

"More ships?"

She snorted.

"I can't think of anything else they would move a cloudscoop around to help protect," she confirmed. "And if there's more ships here, we need to know. Clever ideas, Officer Milhouse?"

"They expected something like the course we took," he pointed out. "They moved the cloudscoop to be invisible from the outer system. We're not going to see anything on this course."

Kelly didn't like where that was leading, but she could see his point.

"We need to go deeper," she concluded aloud.

"How are you feeling about playing matador, boss?" Milhouse asked. "Because the only way we're getting the answer to your questions is to dive right past a Republic battle group."

She curled a lock of pink hair around her finger and smiled coldly. "Then it's a good thing I have the best crew in the MISS, isn't it?"

Even magic could only do so much when Kelly pointed her ship directly at the enemy and brought the engines online at full power. Antimatter met matter and created pure-white flares of annihilation that flung the covert ops ship deeper into the star system.

Xi Wu maintained the stealth spell around the ship, channeling the heat from the engines away from the Republic ships. With the engines online, it could only do so much. That kind of concealment worked a lot better with other ships to hide against.

Kelly LaMonte had once seen Damien Montgomery conceal a freighter running at full power, but they'd been in the middle of a swarm of other ships fleeing an attack on the station they were leaving. Out here, with nothing behind them, all Xi Wu could buy them was time.

"And...there we go," Milhouse confirmed. "We can stop running the stealth spell now, Ship's Mage. They see us."

Kelly checked. Almost half an hour of full-power acceleration. That was more than she'd expected.

"Are you sure?" she asked.

"Well, twenty gunships just rotated in space to point right at us and brought their engines online," her tactical officer replied. "They're coming our way."

"I figured. Time until we can see past Roberta?"

"Forty-five minutes," Hilton reported. "Do we have a plan for what we do *after* that?"

"We locate the cloudscoop. Find whatever ships they're hiding. Jump the hell out."

"They'll know we were here," Milhouse pointed out. "They'll guess what we are, what we've done."

"Yep," Kelly agreed. "And that's the price we're going to have to pay to *know* what's going on."

"What if we're guessing wrong? We could blow our cover to find nothing."

"It's a little late for that," she pointed out. "It doesn't matter, anyway. We may *look* like a regular courier, but the Republic isn't going to care. If they find us swanning around their systems these days, they're just going to blow us to hell.

"So, blowing our cover is irrelevant. Finding out what they're planning is everything."

"And you're the skipper, skipper," Milhouse allowed. He checked his data. "Good news is that the gunships won't range on us *before* we can see the other side of Roberta."

"And how long afterwards?" Kelly asked.

"Oh, about a minute," he told her. "These new missiles of theirs are among the longest-ranged things in existence. They'll take eight minutes to reach us, but..."

"But once we pass Roberta's orbit, we have eight minutes to learn as much as we can," she concluded. "Then we need to get the hell out of this star system."

"Or be blown to a million pieces," Milhouse confirmed cheerfully. "Which seems like it would make delivering our intelligence somewhat difficult."

"Why are all my crew smartasses?" Kelly asked aloud.

"Sir...have you *met* the people you married?"

Kelly and her crew had just spent three weeks ghosting through the outer edge of various Republic star systems, scanning for new shipyards, logistics stations and warships. It was almost exhilarating to do something more blatant and active.

Of course, the exhilaration wore off around half an hour before anything actually *happened*. They were accelerating at fifteen gravities. The gunships, lacking in magical gravity but clearly well equipped with acceleration couches and suchlike, were accelerating at ten.

They'd started far enough apart that even those incredible accelerations weren't enough to bring them into missile range in a timely fashion. Even once they *were* in range of each other, it would be so only for missiles that traveled at a thousand times their acceleration for seven or eight minutes.

Space combat was weird. It also wasn't Kelly's job and she had no intention of actually fighting anyone today.

"We are crossing Roberta's orbital line now," Hilton reported.

"Still a couple of minutes until we get a clear view of the inner hemisphere," Milhouse reported. "I'd guess they're running enough engine power to stay on the inside of the planet, but that cloudscoop *can't* go fast enough to evade us. Not without tearing some fragile bits that would render it nonfunctional, anyway."

Seconds ticked away.

"And there we are," the tactical officer concluded. "I've got new resolution on my original signatures from Roberta orbit and it looks like I've localized the..."

"Milhouse?" Kelly demanded a few seconds later, pulling up the scans on her own screens.

"Jump flare," he told her quietly. "I have five jump flares just inside Leonardo's orbit. Best guess is we're looking at carrier group number two for the system."

"Which is a carrier group more than we've ever seen in any single..."

This time, it was Kelly who trailed off, her attention still focused on Roberta as the computers continued their calm, rational, unflappable analysis of the data. There were a *hundred* gunships flying close air support around the cloudscoop, and she could see the reason why as well.

A "portable" 'scoop had been brought in from out-system and set up. It wasn't a permanent structure and would only stand up to the pressures of its task for a few months. That was all it needed to do, however, and for those months, it more than doubled Santiago's capability to refuel the Republic's fleet.

Thirteen warships hung under the gunship screen. All of them were *huge*. Six were the size of RMN battleships, and the remaining seven were almost twice as big as any cruiser she'd ever seen.

She swallowed.

"Can you validate individual IDs, Officer Milhouse?" she asked, her voice coming out far calmer than she'd expected.

"On it." He paused. "Incoming fire, skipper. From both our friends who left Novo Lar and the gunships in Leonardo orbit. Flight time is shorter for the Leonardo missiles."

"How long?"

"Six minutes, some change."

"Xi, you heard that?" Kelly asked her wife.

"Yes."

"Get us out of here in five," she ordered. "We can post-process data later, so long as we're *alive*."

"Wilco."

More seconds ticked by as *Rhapsody in Purple*'s scanners drank in every piece of data. None of the big ships were maneuvering, but they had files on the Republic's warships now. Those files *sucked*, but they at least allowed Milhouse to break it down by type.

"Looks like two carrier groups with some reinforcements," he finally concluded. "Two carriers, big ones, four battleships, seven cruisers. All of them are as large as we've seen the type yet."

Seven twenty-million-ton cruisers. Four forty-million-ton battleships. Two fifty-million-ton carriers.

And that was ignoring the *other* two carrier groups in the system.

"Confirmed, our jump flares are *also* a carrier group," Milhouse told her. "Can't ID specific units, but the carrier is at least smaller than the pair at Leonardo." He coughed. "Those missiles are still closing. Three minutes out."

"Can we get more by hanging around?" Kelly asked.

"Not really. We have enough to chew on for days while we go home."

"Xi, get us out of here," she ordered.

As the strange sensation of the jump swept over her, she turned her gaze to Milhouse.

"Start chewing, Tactical," she told him. "We're not going home. We're going to Ardennes."

"Why Ardennes?" he asked

"Because Hand Montgomery is at Ardennes with a fleet—and Ardennes is the last logistics base remotely close to Legatus. The only reason they're gathering this large a force is to pin the First Hand against a world he is sworn to defend, and smash as large a portion of the remaining RMN as they can in a single battle."

Kelly LaMonte shivered.

She was going to have to convince Damien Montgomery to run.

Age might have mellowed her ex-boyfriend...but she doubted it had mellowed him *that* much.

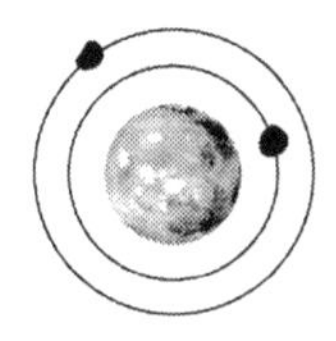

CHAPTER TWENTY-NINE

IT WAS CLEAR THAT, from Persephone's perspective, the immense magical might of a Rune Wright had one major benefit: her human could create a ball of light for her to chase around the office floor.

Damien had one eye on the data flowing across his screens and the view beyond them, but most of his attention was on the kitten. Medici was still at least eighteen hours out, but he trusted Jakab to run the fleet until the Mage-Admiral arrived.

Politics and symbolism required him to be there, but there was only so much for him to actually *do*. If the Republic came, he would challenge them and he would contribute to the battle, but until then...he found himself feeling rather useless.

Persephone had a very different opinion, at least, which helped. Watching her chase the ball around the floor, he slowly and carefully flexed his hands, running through the series of exercises he was supposed to do every time he remembered.

Between magic and voice recognition on his computers, he could do everything he needed to. But he still couldn't hold his own cup of coffee without using magic.

The black mug with *Duke of Magnificence*'s commissioning seal on his desk mocked him. He glared at it for several seconds before sighing and *willing* it over to him.

Drinking from the hovering cup, he reflected that there was at least one small positive: he'd finally mostly broken himself of the need to gesture to use his magic. That was *technically* only a habit, not a true requirement of magic use, but few Mages ever managed to break free of it.

A disgruntled meow from the floor informed him that he'd let the cat-toy spell lapse. Before he could resume it, however, several kilograms of large kitten landed in his lap. Persephone meowed at him again, head-butted his chest, and then wrapped herself around the hand he'd left resting on the chair arm and started aggressively grooming the glove.

While purring.

"And that, my furry little friend, is what *you* think of my moping," he said aloud with a chuckle. "And here I thought we adopted you as therapy for my *hands.*"

"My lord?"

Damien looked up as Denis Romanov entered the room.

"Agent?" The tone suggested a problem. On the other hand, there was *always* a problem.

"Local security forces just intercepted an attempt to bomb the Governor's Palace," his bodyguard told him. "The assassins' backup were Augments. Situation is under control, but over a dozen police were killed."

"Damn." Damien shook his head. That made sense, and yet... Even decapitating Riordan's government wouldn't impede the defense of the system, and the Republic seemed more direct in their covert operations than that.

"System: show me a map of Nouveaux Versailles. Mark the most recent Al-Assad class four or higher incidents."

A map of Ardennes's capital city flashed into existence on his window. Persephone stopped grooming his hand, the cat seeming to have an eerie sense of when to behave.

"That's the bomb attempt," Romanov said, tapping one of the red markers. "That's a class six incident by the Al-Assad standard. Why class four?"

Al-Assad was a standard created by an Arabic police reformer in the twenty-first century. Class six incidents were confirmed terrorist attacks. Class four was anything involving suspected terrorists or military-grade firearms or munitions.

"Distractions, Denis," Damien replied, studying the map. "They're concentrated around the Governor's House and the northwest quadrant. I'm guessing system and city police are moving to reinforce around the House?"

"I don't have that information, my lord, but almost certainly," Romanov told him. "I can find out."

"It's only a question of degree, not of what action they're taking," the Hand said grimly. "System, show me ASDF command stations in Nouveaux Versailles."

Three green icons appeared on the map. None of them, Damien noted, were the old Command Center that he'd wrecked during his first visit to the planet. One of them was in the far southeast corner, well separated from the Governor's House.

"System, identify the ASDF facility at grid 26-K," he ordered aloud.

"Ardennes System Defense Force Ground Command Alpha," the computer replied calmly. "Primary coordination center for orbital defense and search-and-rescue."

Damien studied the map for five more seconds. Then he was on his feet, magic gently carrying Persephone to the floor.

"My shuttle, Denis. Now."

"My lord?"

"They're going for the command center, and the fastest way we can get reinforcements there is to drop them from orbit."

There was some method to Damien's madness. His orders set Marines throughout the RMN detachment into motion, but while the warships were on alert and prepared to fight, that didn't include their assault shuttles.

They were on alert for a space battle, not a ground team feinting to draw the locals out of position for a decapitating strike on the local command facilities. There was one shuttle in the fleet, however, that was *always* kept fully fueled, with exosuit armor charged and on standby for a Marine detachment: Damien's.

Duke of Magnificence's crew had learned that having a Hand aboard meant that said Hand might need to go somewhere at the drop of a dime, and it was better to send him there in an armed spacecraft with heavily-equipped bodyguards.

Damien could no longer fly the shuttle himself, so he still needed to find a pilot when he left the ship. It was still faster to find a pilot than to fuel a shuttle capable of an orbit-to-surface-to-orbit flight and charge up a platoon's worth of exosuit combat armor.

Of course, there *were* other rapid-response forces, which meant that Damien's shuttle wasn't the only one dropping from space towards Nouveaux Versailles like a homesick meteor.

And that the commander of his bodyguard could still try and argue him out of this.

"There is an entire company of Marines dropping from orbit, my lord," Romanov pointed out calmly. "Multiple *battalions* locking and loading as we speak, ready to drop within ten minutes. Each of those companies has at least three Combat Mages."

"And which authority is cutting through air traffic control like a hot knife?" Damien asked brightly. He probably hadn't needed his First Hand status for that, not with a potential attack on the ASDF command in the air.

On the other hand, they had no proof of that attack yet. They were going on Damien's instinct and analysis.

If he was right, it was a good thing no one argued with a Hand. If he was wrong, well, it was good thing no one was really going to hold it against a Hand.

"Damien, it's Julia," his ex-bodyguard's voice sounded in his earpiece.

"Ground Command Alpha is supposed to be Top Secret. Most accesses are double-blind; people go in via underground tunnels from other locations."

He knew from experience she wasn't arguing with him about his analysis, so he waited to hear her point.

"That means the security posts are at those tunnels, not in the main facility," Amiri concluded flatly. "If they've located the site and are preparing to come in through the roof, we are in serious trouble."

"Rapid-response force is three minutes out," he replied. "I'm with them."

"Of course you are." He could *hear* her rolling her eyes. "I see the same pattern you do. I'm moving APA troops as we speak, but they're all outside the cities. "

Like any sensible military force, the Ardennes Planetary Army based itself well outside any urban area. It helped avoid a lot of potential problems—including, though no one talked about it much, collateral damage from kinetic strikes if someone attacked the planet.

It was a problem when you were suddenly expecting a serious threat in one of your cities, though.

"I don't care who they are," Damien told her. "They're about to learn what it means for a Hand to go to war."

The call was silent for a few seconds.

"Yeah, that's about what we need," she admitted. "Can I ask that you leave my command center intact when you're done, though?"

They were still over a minute out when the first explosion rocked the secondary commercial district that housed Ground Command Alpha. Evacuation orders had been issued, but there were no officers to enforce them.

Most people were smart enough to get the hell out when the police starting issuing even voluntary evacuation. The explosions weren't targeted at any of the civilian buildings, anyway.

They still blew out the bottom four floors of a bank office tower that Damien hoped had been fully evacuated. It took him less than two seconds to confirm that the explosion was directly above the command center.

"Get us on the ground," he ordered.

"Working on—"

"Threat detected. Threat detected." The mechanical voice of the shuttle's systems echoed through the cockpit, and Damien recognized the icons on the sensors before the pilot spoke again.

"SAMs incoming. Diving hard."

"No. Fly straight," the Hand ordered. "I'll put us down."

The pilot looked at him with fear and confusion in his eyes but obeyed. Even as the high-speed missiles blasted toward them, he stabilized the shuttle.

Damien closed his eyes—and then the shuttle was somewhere else. They were less than a meter above the ground now, blazing a trail directly toward the gap torn open in the tower.

The sensors flagged the man-portable surface-to-air-missile launchers firing at the incoming rapid-response force, and even as the pilot fired every forward thruster he had to slow their hurtling progress, he also tapped a series of commands with a half-free hand.

The assault shuttle had several different weapons systems available, but the pilot went for the simplest: twin thirty-millimeter railguns fired in atmosphere mode. The weapons were designed for deep space, but in atmosphere, they fired a fifty-gram aerodynamic "arrow" at five hundred kilometers per second.

Each round hit with the force of a hundred kilograms of modern explosives. The pilot walked a dozen shots across the already-wrecked lobby, and the threat icons from the man-portable SAMs disappeared.

Half a second later, the shuttle itself hammered into the ground with brutal force. Any of the saboteurs still up would have been burned to ashes by the flaming rockets.

"Go!" Damien ordered. "Sweep the site, secure the entrance. Legatus doesn't go for single-point-of-failure plans.

"There *will* be a second string to this mess."

There was still a first string, as it turned out. The Marines aboard Damien's shuttle were a platoon seconded to the Protectorate Secret Service as his bodyguards. While that meant they hadn't seen action in the last eighteen months, it *also* meant that they'd been training with the elite troops and Combat Mages who guarded the Mage-King of Mars.

They swarmed out of his shuttle expecting to be fired on, and the Republic ground team met that expectation. Most of the Republic troops were carrying regular small arms, however, and Damien's Marines were all in full exosuit armor.

Bullets ricocheted off the heavy body armor, and the two heavy penetrator rifles punched through. One of the Marines went down—and so did the two women with the anti-armor gear.

The Marines moved out with practiced efficiency, fire teams providing covering fire as other teams moved forward. The infiltrated attack squad were utterly outclassed—and the bodyguards had them outnumbered.

It was over in moments. Another Marine was wounded, but Damien's people now controlled the surface above Ground Command Alpha.

"Looks like at least a forward team has gone down," Romanov reported. "None of these people are Augments. I'd say local recruits."

"And the Augments are in the base," Damien agreed. "Send two squads down after them, hold the third up here. I don't think this is—"

It was funny. He'd seen, heard, or set off at least a dozen nuclear-equivalent explosions, but he'd never seen or heard an actual nuke before. Nonetheless, he knew instantly what had happened when the ground shook and a cloud of fire rose into the sky. The mushroom shape of the cloud was just confirmation.

"Julia!" he barked into his link with the Minister for Defense. "Where was it?"

"The RTA," she told him flatly. "I don't know enough to know if it's repairable; we may have intercepted it before they got it *into* the array..."

"In which case the shell should have protected it, but the array will still be temporarily offline," Damien told her. "My Marines are yours. Where do you need them?"

"I'm redirecting APA units towards the RTA but..." She choked off, then: "*Fuck.* Damien, the RTA is in a goddamn exurb of the city. I don't know how big the bomb was, but there are *half a million people* within twenty kilometers of that rock."

"We'll redirect all of the Marines in the air to search-and-rescue support," Damien told her. "We'll save them, Julia."

"We have to," she replied.

"My lord," Romanov interrupted. "I thought the Minister said the APA was outside of town."

"They are. Why?"

"Because our scanners are picking up exosuits. *Lots* of exosuits. They're coming our way."

And Damien had just ordered his reinforcements redirected.

"Damien?" Julia asked.

"That's my problem, Minister Amiri," he told her formally. "The Marines in the air are yours. Ground Command Alpha will be intact when this is over. You have my word."

"Thank you."

"I'll do my job, Julia. You do yours."

He cut the channel and turned back to the Marines with him.

"Agent Romanov, ladies, gentlemen," he said brightly. "Our reinforcements are going to go save people from that nuke, and it seems the Republic thinks that means we can be overrun.

"I don't think they know I'm here, and that's a mistake they're not going to survive making. Dig in and get ready. It seems like the war is coming to us."

The Marines saluted and got to work as Damien took a moment to assess the situation. He needed to *see* what he was affecting, which meant that he needed good sight lines.

"My lord, it's Commodore Jakab," another voice echoed in his headset, and Damien inhaled sharply as he realized there was only one reason Jakab would be contacting him right now.

"They're here, aren't they?" he asked.

"Full carrier group just jumped into the system," Jakab confirmed. "Your orders?"

"I'm down here. You're up there. Defend the planet, Mage-Commodore. I'll make sure they don't blow it up behind you."

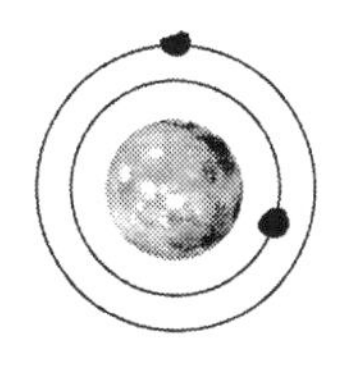

CHAPTER THIRTY

"BATTLE STATIONS! All hands to battle stations."

It took Roslyn a few seconds to separate the clarion call of *Stand*'s general quarters alarm in reality from the identical klaxon in her nightmare. She finally jerked awake, escaping one nightmare for another.

"Battle stations! All hands to battle stations," the automated voice screamed through the ship, and she rolled out of bed, the feel of the cold floor knocking the last of the sleep from her system.

A gesture and a wisp of power pulled her combat vac-suit from the closet and she pulled it on as quickly as she could.

The klaxon muted after the first minute, by which point she was already out of her quarters and heading for the bridge. The destroyer's corridors were controlled chaos, spacers heading for their stations at the carefully controlled run they trained for.

She wasn't even the last officer on the bridge, with a full minute left before the "acceptable" mark for a drill.

Except this was no drill. Five ugly red icons glittered on the display as she dropped into her seat and brought her systems online.

"What have we got, Tactical?" Kulkarni asked once she was up and running.

"We're in the fleet tactical network," she told the Captain. "We're making it a full heavy battle group, two twenty-megaton cruisers, two forty megaton-battleships and a fifty-megaton carrier." More icons speckled her display as she watched.

"Gunships launching. Computer makes it two hundred fifty, repeat, two-five-zero hostile gunships."

"Any orders from the flag?" Kulkarni asked Armbruster.

"Mage-Commodore Jakab is assuming full tactical command of the combined Navy and Militia fleet," the coms officer reported. "We are to move into formation Delta-Six along predesignated vector Oscar-Nine at fifty KPS, then hold velocity and vector for further orders."

"Helm? Make it happen."

"Yes, sir."

Their new helmsman was already on it.

"That puts us out in front, sir," he reported. "Are we sure we even know which end of the ship the missiles come out of?"

"I beg your pardon, Lieutenant?" Kulkarni asked.

The young man was one of the most recent acquisitions from one of the other destroyers. It took Roslyn a moment to even remember his *name*—Lieutenant Adrian Coleborn. Suddenly, she had a sinking suspicion as to why his old ship had been able to spare his services.

"This is a scratch crew, built on a core of runaways with a *kid* at tactical," Coleborn replied, gesturing toward Roslyn. "Does she even know how to fire the weapons? All she's done so far is run away!"

"Lieutenant, may I remind you that the officer you are slandering is the *only* person on this ship with the Mage-King's Medal of Valor—and she got it for a damn good reason," Kulkarni snapped. "I suggest you apologize to Mage-Lieutenant Chambers before I have you up on charges for undermining the chain of command in the face of the enemy!"

Seconds ticked by in frozen silence.

"My apologies, Mage-Lieutenant," he ground out. "I am...merely concerned at your lack of combat experience."

"And how many battles have you even been *near*, Lieutenant Coleborn?" Kulkarni asked. "Zero, according to your record. That's two less than Mage-Lieutenant Chambers."

"My concern is clearly unfounded," Coleborn said, though his tone made it clear he didn't truly believe that.

"Good. Because there's over ten million tons of gunships heading our way, and I'd rather we didn't do their work for them!"

"They're holding five squadrons back to guard the carrier group," Roslyn reported. "I don't know against *what;* it's not like we're going to abandon the planet to try and surprise a force that outguns us on every possible metric."

"They know we have to have reinforcements incoming," Kulkarni replied. "They might not know the details, but they know there's a chance a fleet is going to show up behind them."

The young tactical officer looked over her data and shook her head.

"Twelve hours until we're due to see Admiral Medici," she said, in answer to the Captain's unspoken question. "Gunship strike is four hours from range. They're faster than the carrier group. Their second wave will be later."

"Any chance we'll be facing their capital ships before Medici arrives?" Kulkarni asked.

"Fifty-fifty," Roslyn told her as she ran the numbers. "They'll probably be in missile range before he gets here, so it'll depend on how hard they're going to push it."

Her new Captain grunted, looking at the numbers herself.

"If they wait to see how the gunship strike performs, they might just hand us this," she noted. "It depends on what their limitations on jumping are."

Roslyn was lost for a moment, so she looked at the same data the Mage-Captain was studying.

"If they can jump out that close to the planet, they can push in, wipe out our defending fleet, and withdraw before Medici can trap them against the planet," Kulkarni explained. "If they know Medici is coming, then that has to be their plan."

"They seem to know more about what we're doing than we do," Roslyn said. It took her a moment to realize she'd been actively whining, and she swallowed down that tone with a flash of embarrassment.

"They do," the Captain agreed, in a far more adult tone of voice. "If we could take one of their ships..."

"We did just drop every Marine in the fleet to the surface," the younger woman pointed out. Her focus was on the incoming fleet, but she hadn't missed the nuke going off next to the RTA. "I don't think boarding ops are an option today."

"No. Today, regardless of what happens afterwards, our first priority is to survive that gunship strike."

The defensive force was maintaining a ballistic course toward the incoming Republic carrier group. Their velocity was low, allowing them to sort out their formation easily.

The four cruisers were forming the second line of the formation, making up a perfect square wall in space. The destroyers were more scattered, establishing a defensive line from ten thousand to fifty thousand kilometers in front of the cruisers.

"You're the only tac officer who's seen one of these things in action. What should we be looking for?"

Roslyn swallowed as she considered her memories of the disaster at Nia Kriti.

"They're primarily missile platforms," she said first. "Six launchers apiece, the same missiles as their capital ships. That formation is going to send twelve hundred missiles at us in a salvo." She shivered. "I don't know how many missiles they carry, but they launched multiple times in Nia Kriti, so it's not just one per launcher.

"I'd guess they'll adjust their course as they close to skim the edge of our missile range. They'll empty their magazines at us and break back for their carrier. They're far from defenseless, but why tangle with more of our fire than they need to?"

"That makes sense," Kulkarni agreed. "Barring orders to the contrary from the flag, Mage-Lieutenant, I want to keep our missiles for counterfire. We're not going to kill very many gunships today, and we're a lot better off if we still have a fleet tomorrow."

"Yes, sir."

For the first time, Roslyn Chambers watched an enemy charge toward her and her ship...and was doing nothing.

That wasn't entirely true, of course. She was laying in firing patterns, double-checking her data on the Republic's new missiles, making sure that her counter-missile and RFLAM programming accounted for their current acceleration...but the entire defensive fleet was simply waiting. There were small maneuvers inside their formation, just enough to prevent long-range unpowered missile fire, but otherwise, the Martian and Ardennian force just waited.

Four hours was a long time. Martian doctrine called for crew to be cycled over that kind of wait...but *Stand in Righteousness* didn't have enough crew to do that. Roslyn made sure the petty officers supporting her on the bridge took a break, at least enough for a coffee and sandwich.

Rank had its privileges, however, and today that privilege was staying on the bridge for the entire wait and having the one overworked bridge steward bring her coffee and a hot sub.

"Orders from the flag," Armbruster reported after just over two hours. "All destroyers are to use half of their missiles for defensive fire. The remainder, plus the cruisers' fire, are to focus on attempting to destroy gunships."

Roslyn herself would have preferred Kulkarni's plan, just focusing on surviving the incoming fire. She, however, was literally the single most junior officer in the entire fleet, Medal of Valor be damned. Her only response to orders she wasn't sure about was to smile and obey.

And perhaps ask for an explanation from her Captain, but in this case, she figured it was simply a matter of prioritization. The Mage-Commodore didn't want to see the Republic have this fight go entirely their way.

Montgomery might have given different orders, but Montgomery was on the surface and the fleet wasn't getting information from that mess.

He was probably alive—Roslyn was reasonably sure Hands were basically unkillable—but he had his own problems to deal with.

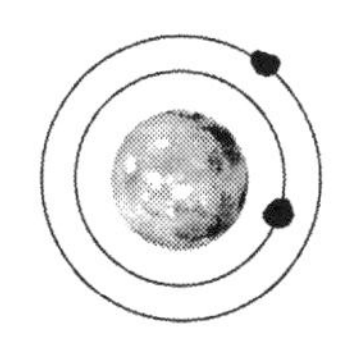

CHAPTER THIRTY-ONE

"YEAH...THOSE definitely aren't locals."

Romanov's thoughtful, almost bored observation was the only comment among the haphazardly assembled "command squad" watching the street.

Said street was now empty of locals, everyone either evacuated or sheltering in place now. It was not, however, empty of vehicles. Somebody clever on the other side had been hot-wiring the emergency remote system on every vehicle they passed, and now a solid wall of civilian trucks and sedans was rolling along the street toward the half-wrecked bank.

"Oh, I'm sure the cars are local," Damien replied. "Are we secure below?"

"Yeah, my squads are on the way back up." The Marine shook his head. "No prisoners. Where does the Republic *find* these guys?"

"Pretty sure at least some of it is suicide implants that they didn't tell them about in advance," the Hand admitted. "If we're secure below, can we reseal the command center?"

"No," Romanov told him. "They blew a damn big hole. We could probably seal it if we dropped what's left of this building on it, but reports are that we still have people upstairs. They're being moved *up* now and there's a helicopter inbound for rescue, but..."

"But that won't work for anyone if our friends out there decide to shoot it down."

"Exactly."

"Do we have a number?" Damien asked, turning back to the street. The slow-moving wall of vehicles was doing its job. It wasn't much of a barrier to the weapons available to the twenty exosuited Marines he had with him—but it was a pretty decent one against their sensors and vision.

"Somewhere between seventy and a hundred," Romanov said. "How the *hell* did they get that much armor on planet?"

"At a guess?" Damien shook his head. "They brought it in when they brought in the gear that was being sold to the resistance here. Once the rebels were working with us, we followed that chain all the way back, but we didn't think to check if anything else was brought in at the same time."

The previous Governor of Ardennes had been...problematic. The Protectorate probably would have taken longer to step in, except that he'd decided to suppress a revolt with an orbital strike—one delivered by a mutinying Royal Martian Navy squadron.

Things had gone sideways from there, and now an ex-rebel—Riordan—was the Governor, the ASDF had needed to be rebuilt, and the RMN was short a cruiser squadron. A Hand had died along the way, Damien's mentor, and Damien himself had become a Hand in the chaos of the revolution.

And now, for the second time in five years, he was looking at a street fight in the planet's capital.

"So, we're outnumbered either two or three to one, and they've had a clever idea for mobile armor," Romanov concluded. "What happened to our air support, again?"

"We're in the middle of a civilian commercial district and we wanted to avoid collateral damage," Damien replied. "Plus, *I* sent them all to help evacuate the blast zone of the *nuke* these people set off."

"Right."

There was a long silence, and the remote-controlled vehicles continued their approach up the street. They were well into the range of the heavy penetrator rifles usually carried by exosuits, which meant the Republic infiltrators were hoping for surprise by controlling the start of the engagement.

"So, what's our plan now?" Romanov asked.

Damien smiled thinly.

"Me."

Before his bodyguard could even protest, Damien calmly walked out from behind the shuttle and faced the oncoming wall of vehicles. He was wearing a T-shirt and a light armor vest, which left the platinum hand of his office highly visible on his chest.

Elbow-length black leather gloves covered his crippled hands, hopefully concealing that he could barely move anything past his forearm.

"My lord?" Romanov's voice echoed in his earpiece. "So, what's the plan?"

"You'll know when it's time to open fire," Damien told him. "It'll be hard to miss."

The Marine snorted over the radio, but he clearly understood.

Damien studied the oncoming vehicles and then used a touch of magic to project his voice.

"My name is Damien Montgomery," he told them, probably unnecessarily. "I speak for the Mage-King of Mars."

Nothing happened for several seconds, and then the entire cavalcade of remote-controlled vehicles came to a jumbled halt forty meters from him.

"I am prepared, for the moment, to assume that you were not directly involved in the war crimes the Republic has committed today," he told them. With the magic carrying his words, he spoke normally, calmly.

"If you lay down your arms and surrender now, you will be treated as honorable prisoners of war. As spies and saboteurs in our territory, you know that is *not* our obligation." He smiled coldly.

"This offers expires the moment you move forward," he continued. "I am the First Hand of the Mage-King of Mars. Do *not* underestimate my will or my power. If you do not surrender, I will destroy you."

Once, he would not have hesitated to believe his own words. He had worked outright miracles with five Runes of Power carved into his skin. With only three, however, it was easy to doubt himself.

They might underestimate his power, after all. On the other hand, so did he.

There was a moment where he thought it might have worked. The wall of vehicles was immobile for several seconds...and then started forward again.

Damien Montgomery had not picked up the moniker of "the Sword of Mars" for allowing second chances. They were already too close.

He focused his gaze on the ground beneath the advancing wall of vehicles and told about a thousandth of a gram of regular matter to "change polarity." The description was easy. The spell, less so.

It was still easier than producing antimatter without magic. The tiny amount of antimatter he created wasn't much in the grand scheme of things...but when it annihilated against regular matter, it triggered the equivalent explosion of several tons of high explosives.

The advancing wall of civilian vehicles disintegrated, debris scything out in every direction. Damien had a shield in place already, though, channeling and deflecting the explosion and debris back toward the advancing Republic infiltrators.

One moment, they had a defensive screen of stolen vehicles.

The next, Damien had turned those vehicles into a massive claymore aimed right at them.

The wave of debris smashed over the approaching troops, but even as he unleashed the spell, Damien knew it wasn't actually going to be enough against exosuits. Even before the debris cloud had begun to settle, the approaching Republic soldiers were opening fire.

Heavy tungsten penetrator slugs, designed to punch through exosuit armor with only a little bit of luck, cut through the smoke and chaos. Damien was almost impressed—despite the heat and the debris and the clouds, several of the shots would have actually hit him.

Instead, they crashed into a barrier of solidified air that crossed the entire street, an intentional leftover of the shield he'd used to shape the claymore. The clouds dispersed and more gunfire emerged as Damien walked forward to the edge of the shield.

There was no undamaged portion of the street. The area behind him had been savaged first by the explosion that had broken into the command center and then by the crashing shuttle.

"You had a chance," he told them, his voice gentle as he gathered power again. "You should have listened."

More gunfire smashed into his shield, and he shook his head sadly. The shield swept forward at a thought, clearing the street of debris and hammering the soldiers to the ground.

Romanov knew him. The Marines knew they couldn't punch through his shield from this side either and had been waiting until he'd dropped it—and Damien had done so in a way that bought them time.

As the Republic forces struggled to regain their feet and formations, the Marines charged out of the wrecked building. They were still outnumbered at least two to one, possibly more. Romanov was the only Combat Mage, but at this point, all of them were support.

A gunshot rang out as one of the Republic troopers regained his footing. It slammed into the personal shield he'd kept up—and then Damien snapped his arm out in an old gesture he apparently hadn't unlearned. A thin line of white fire flashed across the street-turned-battlefield and cut the soldier in half.

Fire began to flicker across the battlefield as Damien stepped forward. The First Hand of Mars was all but immune to their weapons, and each time someone fired, the shooter dropped.

Fewer than a dozen of the remaining Republic troopers died, to either Damien's power or the Marines falling in behind him, before it finally sank in how screwed they were.

Exosuited soldiers began to throw down weapons, rising with their gauntlets up to show they were unarmed. Some continued to fight, but Damien was watching. At this point, he started disabling weapons and locking soldiers inside their own personal shields.

It was over in a few minutes, the last of the Republic soldiers stepping out of their suits and surrendering.

"What do we do now, my lord?" Romanov asked.

"They're POWs," Damien replied calmly. "We are the *Protectorate of Mars*, Mage-Captain Romanov. We won't be the ones to mistreat prisoners."

"No, my lord," the Marine agreed. There might have been relief in his tone, but Damien wasn't sure.

"We're being jammed," Romanov continued after a moment. "We've got limited local coms, but we can't reach anyone in orbit."

"Then let's get these people rounded up and coordinate with Julia's people," Damien ordered. "There's nothing I can do for the space battle from here, but if they think they can take this planet from me..."

Romanov turned away from him and surveyed the destroyed road.

"They're going to need a bigger army," the Marine observed.

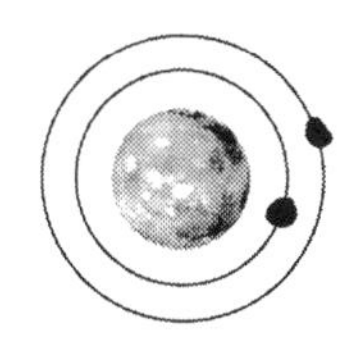

CHAPTER THIRTY-TWO

"IT'S CONFIRMED, PEOPLE," Mage-Commodore Jakab's image said grimly on the hologram on *Stand of Righteousness*'s bridge. "We believe that the situation in Nouveaux Versailles is fundamentally under control, but the infiltrators have activated several high-power jammers.

"Until those are shut down, we have no communication with Hand Montgomery or the local government." He shook his head. "Hand Montgomery was on the surface to attempt to secure the local command center, which is now cut off from us. Fortunately, *Duke of Magnificence* is more than capable of acting as a command nexus for the combined fleet without assistance from the surface."

Roslyn was only paying half-attention to the Commodore's communication with the ships' captains. Her focus was primarily on her console as she dug through the recordings of the ill-fated clash between the gunship strike and Mage-Admiral Palmeiro's squadron.

She also had the information on the fight between Hand Montgomery's recon force and the Republic battle group that had come after them.

The one thing she'd managed to confirm was that the missiles used in each case were identical. That wasn't particularly *good* news: the missiles the RIN had sent against Hand Montgomery were less maneuverable than the RMN's, but they were a *lot* smarter.

There were a lot of clever electronic warfare tricks available to her as *Stand*'s tactical officer. She could jam missiles, attempt automated hacking sequences, try and decoy them off...but she had recordings of a *cruiser* trying those stunts on the Republic's new missiles.

And failing.

An alert flashed up on her screen and she double-checked it.

"Gunships are adjusting vector as expected," she reported. "If we don't change our course, they'll reach zero velocity relative to us at about twelve point three million kilometers."

She shook her head. "They'll have enough time to dump all of their missiles at us, and we'll get a few good salvos in ourselves, but it's a hit-and-run."

"Given their range advantage, why would they let us shoot at them at all?" Kulkarni asked. From her tone, she wasn't expecting an answer, but...

"They'd still be well outside range of the Phoenix VII, which is all that the ASDF is supposed to have," Roslyn pointed out. "I'd guess their intelligence isn't up to informing them that we set up production lines for the VIIIs and opened up our stockpiles to the locals.

"Given that three of our cruisers and half of our destroyers are ASDF ships, they're probably counting on most of our weapons not having the range."

The Mage-Captain nodded slowly.

"That would make sense. And they don't lose out much if they're wrong, either. Worst-case scenario is they lose all of the gunships, which would take a *miracle* on our side."

"And if they're sending them out like this, they've got gunships to spare," Roslyn guessed.

"It won't matter too much," Kulkarni concluded. "But that's a good thought, Lieutenant Chambers. Keep that brain of yours turning, and if you see anything else..."

"Only thing I can think of, sir, is to make sure the rest of the fleet doesn't try and use any complex electronic warfare," Roslyn told her boss. "I'm relatively sure everyone should draw the same conclusions as me, though."

"How so?" the Captain asked.

"Looking at our data from Nia Kriti and Mage-Commodore Jakab's data from their ambush near Santiago, the Republic's missiles are *much* smarter than ours—and basically have our full electronic warfare suite programmed into their databases. None of our clever tricks are going to work.

"We can jam their scanners, but anything more subtle than that is going to fail."

Kulkarni sighed.

"I'll drop that note into the tactical network," she said calmly. "You're right that we all have the data, but habits are habits. We're not used to fighting an equal enemy."

Roslyn nodded, her eyes on the oncoming gunship strike.

The Royal Martian Navy had no experience in fighting an equal foe... and she was starting to suspect they might be fighting a *superior* one.

"For what we are about to receive, may the Maker make us truly thankful."

Kulkarni's words seemed oddly formal to Roslyn. She didn't recognize the words—probably a prayer, she guessed, but her own family were Mages by Blood. There wasn't much religion left in the scions of Project Olympus.

The prayer was, in any case, a strange response to the fact that the Republic gunships had finally opened fire. Twelve hundred missiles leaped into space, suicidally eager electronic brains seeking out the Protectorate fleet facing them.

"Eight minutes, thirty seconds to impact," Roslyn reported. "Now we get to see the cycle time on the gunships' launchers."

"At least their vector change bought us more time," Armbruster noted. "I make it eight hours to Mage-Admiral Medici's arrival now."

"For the first time in my career, I'm wishing it was remotely likely we'd miscalculated a Navy task force's arrival time," Kulkarni said whimsically. "Until we're in our own missile range, please use our missiles in defense mode, Lieutenant Chambers. I'd like to live through this if we can."

Roslyn activated one of the programs she'd been working on. The destroyer was linked in to the sensors of every other ship in the defending fleet, and those sensors were giving her detailed information on the incoming fire.

Give it a few minutes to build a vector and a performance for the salvo, and she'd have a decent chance of interception with each of her missiles. Of course, she only had twenty-four launchers. Even a hundred percent kill rate wasn't going to make that much of a dent in what was coming.

"Second salvo launching," she reported aloud. "I make the cycle time forty-five seconds."

That was basically identical to their own cycle time. Another area where the Republic ships weren't superior, at least.

"Time until our range?"

"They'll hit us first, we'll launch, then they'll hit zero vee and go the other way," Roslyn reeled off. "About nine minutes."

There was a good chance they'd have to weather the entire missile capacity of the gunship strike before even one of their missiles reached the enemy. A third salvo lit up on Roslyn's screens as she spoke, with the *first* salvo still seven minutes out.

"Counter-missile targeting distributions coming down from the flag," Armbruster reported. "Transferring to tactical."

"Got it," Roslyn confirmed. "And...firing."

The destroyer shivered as she opened fire. These missiles didn't have the endurance to reach the gunships yet. They were just heading out to intercept the missiles coming toward them.

"Flag has ordered five counter-missile salvos," she reported aloud, continuing to sequence up her fire. That was a third of *Stand in Righteousness*'s magazines. Mage-Commodore Jakab clearly agreed with Kulkarni on their priority: survive.

"We are past the forty-five-second mark from salvo three," Roslyn continued after a moment's check. "There is no fourth salvo. Enemy gunships appear to only have three rounds per launcher."

The counter-missile salvos were doing their work. The first intercept was always the most effective, as hundreds of gigaton-range antimatter warheads had their own natural jamming effect.

None of the first Republic salvo even made it to the Protectorate force. That took almost the entirety of the five salvos they'd launched in defensive mode, though, and the second salvo still had almost a thousand missiles as it plunged into the intercept range.

"Targets from the flag for offensive fire," Roslyn reported. It was almost an afterthought. She flagged the ship in question and told *Stand*'s systems to fire.

Her own focus was on the incoming missiles. She had more RFLAM turrets than she had missile launchers, and automated as they were, targeting priorities and programs were her responsibility.

The destroyer's electronic warfare suite came to life as well. Transmitters intended for complex siren songs in normal battles were reduced to jammers, blasting the incoming missiles' sensors with massive amounts of garbage returns.

Despite everything, missiles made it through. *Stand in Righteousness* flipped in space as the first missiles crashed toward her and Lieutenant Coleborn earned *some* measure of forgiveness for his attitude as he danced the warship around the two missiles Roslyn had missed.

As the last salvo charged in, he synchronized his maneuvers to her active defenses. It felt like there were *far* too many missiles coming at them for one single destroyer, but that was the battlespace they were in.

She shot down missiles and he dodged missiles, and for a few seconds they were working like a finely-honed team...and then one missile made it through.

Stand in Righteousness jerked in space like she'd been kicked by an angry mule...and then it was over.

For now.

They were one of the lucky ones. There were ships in the defending fleet that hadn't been hit, but over three-quarters of the ships present had taken at least one missile.

Their armor was good—*Stand in Righteousness* hadn't even lost anyone to the warhead that had hit her hull—but nothing could stand against that kind of firepower for long.

Four RMN and two ASDF destroyers were gone. One of the ASDF cruisers was badly damaged. The rest of the fleet was rattled and damaged—but combat-capable.

Roslyn held her breath as their own fire swept down on the gunships. The Republic ships hadn't had the advantage of counter-missile salvos like the Protectorate fleet had. What they *did* have, it turned out, was three lasers apiece that served perfectly well in the antimissile role.

Hundreds of lasers lit up space, slicing through the incoming fire with terrifying ease. Like their missiles' electronic brains, it seemed the gunships' computers were better than the Protectorate's equivalent.

Roslyn was unsurprised. Every trick in the Protectorate's electronic warfare arsenal was known to the Republic, and they'd built their systems to counter them. None of the clever tricks programmed into their missiles did anything except cost power.

Sheer numbers, at least, did something. The gunship strike had handled the defenders roughly, but it by no means went entirely their way. Over two hundred gunships had come after Roslyn Chambers and her comrades.

A hundred and fifty escaped. A poor trade, perhaps, for over twice their mass in destroyers, but it was what the Protectorate would have to take.

"It won't go as much their way next time, I suspect," she told Kulkarni as Armbruster listed off the damage to the fleet. "We know their computers now. Until we come up with some new clever tricks, we're stuck with brute-force jamming—but that's hardly useless."

"Better than wasting power, I suppose," the Mage-Captain said, her tone cold. Thousands of people had just died. It wasn't going to be a good day.

"The capital ships and remaining gunships are maneuvering now," Roslyn reported. "Heading our way, three gravities. If they're heading for the planet, turnover in six hours. Twelve hours until they're in orbit."

"We'll see what Jakab orders," Kulkarni said. "In his place, I'd pull us back to Ardennes orbit. Let the bastards come.

"We know our reinforcements are on their way. They don't."

"We hope," Roslyn muttered. They hadn't seemed to have very many surprises for the Republic so far, after all.

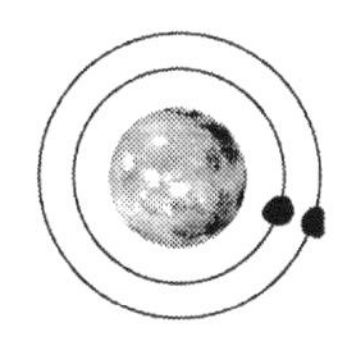

CHAPTER THIRTY-THREE

"THAT'S THE LAST JAMMER, MY LORD," the exhausted-looking Marine Major reported. She'd taken off her exosuit helmet and had locked the suit's muscles in place. The armor was the only thing holding her in place as she leaned against it.

"We should have contact with everybody now."

"Thank you, Major," Damien told her. He looked over at Romanov, who looked only slightly less exhausted than the other Marine. "Romanov, can you get us a link, please?"

They'd done a lot with his wrist-comp...but not enough for him to be able to establish a communication link with it. Not without using voice commands he wasn't going to trust sitting in the back of an APA armored personnel carrier, anyway.

"Your Marines saved a lot of lives today," the owner of said APC told him. Brigadier General Seoirse Frank was the unlucky individual in charge of the rapid-response brigade positioned next to the Ardennian capital. It was an odd honor for a man whose main claim to fame had been *surrendering* his then-battalion without a fight when the rebellion had happened.

He'd earned it, however, by being one of the few senior officers whom the ensuing criminal investigations *hadn't* flagged as guilty of something and then stepping up when a lot of those left were retiring.

"Our job," Major Porcher replied. "Not often we have to drop into nuclear blast zones, thankfully, but we train for it."

Damien was grimly certain they couldn't have saved everyone. They'd saved a lot of people, but a fifty-kiloton nuclear bomb going off on the edge of a residential neighborhood didn't spare many people close by.

He'd almost have preferred that this set of infiltrators *had* managed to get the bomb into the RTA. The same solid stone exterior that had saved the RTA from the external explosion would have saved the innocents around it if they'd managed to smuggle it in.

"We've got a link to the Mage-Commodore," Romanov told him. "Transferring to your wrist-comp."

"My lord, you're all right?" Jakab asked.

"Nouveaux Versailles stands," Damien replied. "I'm fine. A lot of innocent people aren't. There are going to have to be consequences for that. What's your status?"

"We're not doing much better up here," the naval officer replied. "We lost six destroyers to their gunship strike. The rest of the fleet is battered, too. *Appalachian* is basically crippled, so we're down a cruiser. Keeping her in formation mostly as a bluff."

"Understood." Damien gestured to Romanov, who was already bringing up the downloaded telemetry on the APC's screens. "I'm heading for the rapid-response brigade facility near the city. Seemed wisest to get my over-promoted butt out of the line of fire."

"I don't know about the locals, but I'd be *extremely* relieved to see you and your abilities back aboard my flagship *before* I go into combat with a few times my tonnage of Republic warships," Jakab replied. "This is just a delaying action at this point, my lord, and your help could make all of the difference."

"I'm meeting one of Major Porcher's shuttles at the brigade's armor depot," Damien told him with a chuckle. "If you want one semi-functional Hand on your bridge, I can be there in an hour or so."

"'Semi-functional?'" Jakab asked with a tired chuckle. "You, my lord, underestimate yourself. If we can accelerate getting that shuttle up here, let me know."

"And the fleet?"

"We're falling back to Ardennes orbit. With Ground Command Alpha still in the locals' hands, that gives another sixty or so launchers from the orbital platforms, and I need to restock ammunition. We shot off two-thirds of the destroyers' missiles against the gunships."

"I'll meet you in orbit, then, Mage-Commodore. We'll see how brave our friends are feeling—and how punctual Mage-Admiral Medici is today."

"Good luck, my lord," Brigadier General Frank told Damien with a crisp salute. "The shuttle is refueled and should be able to get you to *Duke of Magnificence* as quickly as possible."

"Thank you. Will you be all right?" Damien asked.

Frank shook his head.

"It's bad," he admitted, "but we have the situation under control. We're rounding up the remaining infiltrators, and we have the rad medications and hospital space to take care of everyone. We're airlifting some of the lower priority-radiation cases to other cities for treatment.

"We can't bring back the dead, but the living are going to stay that way. I promise you that."

"So long as we hold in orbit," Damien murmured.

"That's on you, Mage-Commodore Jakab, and Admiral Vasilev," Frank told him. "If you fall, we'll fight. They won't take Ardennes easily, not after this."

"I hope it won't come to that. Good luck to you, too, Brigadier General Frank."

Frank saluted and Romanov led the way onto the shuttle. The landing field was covered in the spacecraft, RMMC assault shuttles haphazardly parked wherever they would fit. Mobile refueling trucks were moving across the space, carefully loading the ships with more fuel so they'd be ready to go if needed.

The Marines themselves were scattered across the city and surrounding area now. Some of the worst radiation cases were being handled in military hospital units set up next to the blast zone. Marines couldn't expect to find friendly doctors, so they dropped with their own. Today, those doctors were mostly dealing with the locals.

"We're getting a vector cleared," the pilot reported as Damien boarded. "It's an honor to fly you, Hand Montgomery."

"Let me know if you still feel that way after we've been shot at," Romanov told the other Marine with a chuckle. "When do we get upstairs?"

"Five minutes to takeoff, forty-three-minute flight," the pilot replied after a moment's hesitation. "Roughly fifty minutes and we'll have you back aboard *Duke of Magnificence*."

"Good." Damien checked his wrist-comp. There were only two things on the screen: the estimated time until the Republic carrier group ranged on the ships in orbit...and the time until Mage-Admiral Medici was supposed to arrive.

Once back aboard his ship, Damien went straight to the bridge. Carefully keeping out of Jakab's way, he dropped into an observer's seat. He hadn't really meant to go unnoticed, just without bothering anyone—but he was still surprised when the seat screens and controls mirrored his flag-deck setup a moment later.

The entire crew, of course, knew about his injuries. No one seemed willing to stop him getting into the middle of a firefight, but they were still going to baby him when they could.

It was more heartwarming than anything else, most of the time, and he carefully tapped in commands on the touchscreen buttons sized for the heel of his hand.

"All ships have completed rearming," Petty Officer Rustici reported. "Everyone except *Appalachian* is reporting eighty percent or better combat-readiness."

"And *Appalachian*?" Jakab asked.

"Mage-Captain Bonaparte has ordered the evacuation of all but a minimum crew," Rustici told him. "She reports she has fourteen launchers online in central control. If there's any further issues, well..."

"She no longer has the crew to fix them," Jakab concluded. "That's a brave woman. Not sure how *smart* she is, but she's damn brave."

The Commodore turned his chair to look at Damien.

"It's good to have you back aboard, my lord," he greeted the Hand. "The moment of truth is fast approaching. The enemy will make turnover in an hour. Mage-Admiral Medici should arrive between one and two hours after that. It is entirely possible, my lord, that the Republic may decide that their only safe way out is through us."

"Or to jump out close to the planet," Damien replied. "Either way, this is going to be educational."

"'Educational,'" Jakab echoed, repeating Damien's words back to him for the second time in as many hours. "I'm not sure that means what you think it means, my lord."

"Have they attempted to communicate at all?" Damien asked, brushing aside Jakab's feeble joke.

"Nothing. We've heard more from the prisoners on the surface than we have from the fleet moving against us...and no one is so much as sending me interrogation transcripts yet."

"Well, I guess the missiles were a communication of a sort," the Hand said with a sigh as he leaned back in his chair.

"Fight your fleet, Mage-Commodore. Let's see if we can get out of this alive!"

"Turnover."

The murmured word echoed like a dropped pin in the silence of *Duke of Magnificence*'s bridge. Damien should *probably* have returned to the flag deck and taken his usual place, but this battle was already decided. If the Republic Interstellar Navy decided to press their attack, everyone in orbit above Ardennes would die.

"I make it just over seven hours to zero velocity in Ardennian orbit," another officer reported.

"How long until they couldn't jump if they were our ships?" Jakab asked.

"Depends. There are officers who'd risk a jump straight from orbit if they had a reason," the navigator pointed out. "They'll hit our usual safety margin for even emergency jumps in about three hours."

"So, they'll be able to jump when Medici—"

"Jump flare! Multiple jump flares."

The sky lit up with the bright blue of Cherenkov radiation as Task Group *Peacemaker* arrived, almost two full hours early. It took a minute for it to resolve into a fleet of twenty warships, led by the immense hulls of two Royal Martian Navy battleships.

Damien closed his eyes in relief.

"Check the masses, decrypt the IFFs," Jakab ordered. "Get me IDs."

"We're making it two battleships, six cruisers and twelve destroyers." There was a long pause. "It's *Pax Marcianus* and *Peacemaker* with the Third Destroyer Squadron."

There was another pause.

"That still leaves a cruiser squadron and a destroyer squadron," Jakab pointed out. "Who am I looking at, people?"

"Sorry, sir," Rustici cut in. "Had to double-check the codes; our system didn't have them in the active IFF listings.

"That's the Second Heavy and Fifth Light Defense Squadrons of the Tau Ceti Security Fleet. Six *Dragon*-class heavy cruisers and six *Cataphract*-class destroyers."

System Militia ships. It hit Damien like a supernova. He'd been focused on the Royal Martian Navy and the Ardennes System Defense Force without even *thinking* about it. Tau Ceti had sent half their cruisers and a sixth of their destroyers to relieve Ardennes, and while Tau Ceti had the largest System Militia, they were hardly the only one.

"When this is over," he murmured aloud, "I need to get to the RTA."

"I think I see why," Jakab replied. "Do we have coms from Admiral Medici?"

"Yes, sir, just finished decrypting now."

The main hologram dissolved into the form of the Mage-Admiral. Medici was a small man, barely taller than Damien himself, but the grim set to his face warned of terrible things for the Republic fleet in his way.

"Hand Montgomery, Commodore Jakab, Commodore Cruyssen, Admiral Vasilev. Task Force *Peacemaker* has arrived in Ardennes. We are moving in pursuit of the RIN battle group. We'll see if they have the nerve to stick around and fight."

He shook his head.

"If they come for you—and they may still—I don't need you to beat them. I don't even need you to hold them in place. That battle group is outnumbered and outgunned, and they have to know it. This battle is already decided, officers.

"I need you to stay alive until I get there."

The transmission ended and Jakab chuckled aloud.

"I think we can follow those orders, don't you?"

"If you were going to have a problem, I'd have to reiterate them," Damien told him. "Set your missiles for self-defense and watch that fleet. They can still range on you before Medici ranges on—"

"Republic force is changing course! They're vectoring to retrieve their gunships and evade us."

"Time to intercept?" Jakab asked.

"Depends on how rough they're prepared to handle the gunships," the tactical officer responded. "Thirty minutes if they can handle a couple thousand KPS velocity differential."

"We don't know enough about their engines," Damien admitted slowly. "It's possible they can jump with the gunships simply nearby.

"In any case, people, it looks like our part in this battle is over. Let's keep to battle stations for a bit yet, but we can start to breathe. Admiral Medici just saved our butts."

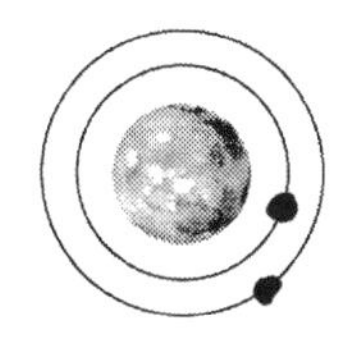

CHAPTER THIRTY-FOUR

"FIRST HAND, ARRIVING!"

It had taken Damien at least half a year to stop *Duke of Magnificence*'s crew from insisting on ceremony every time he left or came aboard the battlecruiser. He wasn't really surprised to find himself greeted by a full formal greeting party of dress-uniformed Marines when he exited his shuttle onto *Peacemaker.*

That, at least, was the extent of the formality. Mage-Admiral Medici and his flag captain, Mage-Captain Eilish Estevez, were the only people waiting for him.

Medici was barely taller and no more heavily built than Damien himself, which made Mage-Captain Estevez a study in contrasts. She shared her Admiral's dark coloring in skin and hair, but where he was at most only a hundred and fifty-five centimeters tall, Mage-Captain Estevez easily topped two meters.

She towered over Damien and the Admiral alike as she saluted the First Hand.

"I see at least some of my opinion of ceremony is starting to make it around the Navy," Damien observed as he returned the salute. "It's damn good to see you, Mage-Admiral. Things were getting dicey."

To no one's surprise, the Republic carrier group had declined to engage multiple battleships. They'd jumped clear of Ardennes well before they would have been engaged by either Protectorate force. From the speed of their maneuvers and escape, Damien had half-expected them to leave their gunships behind.

They hadn't, but they'd jumped clear of the system as soon as they'd picked the parasite craft up. Ardennes remained in Protectorate hands, though he wasn't sure how much longer that would last.

"I'll admit I had hoped that we'd catch them a bit more out of position," Medici told him. "This battle is, for all intents and purposes, a draw. I think the Protectorate could use an unquestionable victory now."

"I agree, but I'm as happy to still be here," Damien said. "We'll want to set up a meeting with all of the flag officers to establish what our plans going forward are, but I think we can assume the Republic will be back."

"We'll be waiting for them," Medici replied. "Both my Protectorate and Tau Cetan forces have been seconded to your command until you no longer need us, Hand Montgomery. I don't think anyone is expecting this to be over soon."

"Agreed." Damien glanced around the landing bay. They could probably trust the Marines in the area, but taking security for granted was dangerous. The Republic had already demonstrated their ability to infiltrate assassins into spaces he believed to be secure.

"Can we speak in private?" he continued. "I want to make sure you and I are on the same page before we begin to plan our next steps."

Medici inclined his head.

"Of course, my lord Montgomery. My office?"

"Assuming it has coffee and a holo-display, that will work perfectly."

"I assure you, my lord, that it has both," Medici said with a chuckle.

By the time Damien had sorted out where his Secret Service detail was going to wait for him and Captain Estevez had returned to running her ship, Medici's steward had produced two heavenly-smelling cups of coffee and a plate of pastries.

Medici looked at Damien in concern.

"Do we need to get you anything specific for you to be able to..."

Damien floated the coffee cup across the room to him and took a sip in answer to the unfinished question. He carefully set it down on the Admiral's desk and then took a seat across from Medici.

"You should know better," he suggested. "I may lack the use of my hands, Admiral, but I still command the Gift in full measure."

"It's easy to forget," Medici replied. "Such things grow in the retelling, after all. The story of your saving the Council has spread far. Such acts are things of legends, after all."

Damien snorted, shaking his head uncomfortably.

"Protecting the Council was part of my job," he pointed out. "Hardly legend. Simply the task before me."

"Right." Medici let the one sardonic word hang in the air as he took a drink of his own coffee.

"I have to ask, Admiral. Was bringing Tau Cetan ships your idea or theirs?" Damien said.

"Theirs," he admitted. "I was busy running around, trying to scrape up any ships we could spare beyond the battleships when Admiral Sakshi Felix approached me. She commands the Second Heavy Defense Squadron of the Tau Ceti Security Fleet; I imagine you'll be meeting her shortly."

Medici chuckled.

"She was actually *offended* that we hadn't asked the TCSF for help," he noted. "It took me five minutes to talk her down from being angry at me and convince her that we hadn't even thought of it."

"A blind spot hardly unique to you," Damien admitted. "I've been building my plans for defending Ardennes around their Militia without even considering the wider potential."

Medici paused, then sank his face into his hands.

"I'm a moron," he said, only partially joking. "God, Admiral Felix promptly offered me her entire command as soon as I convinced her we weren't insulting the TCSF, and the thought of reaching out to the other Militias..."

"A Hand comes with certain authority," Damien told him. "I'm going from here to the RTA; I'll reach out to as many systems as I can, but I need to talk to you first. Will the Navy cause problems if we bring in... well, Militia and mercenaries and whoever else I can find?"

Medici spread his hands wide.

"Some people may *have* a problem, but I swear to you: they will *not* be permitted to *cause* a problem," he said fiercely. "God, right now I'd shake hands with Mikhail Azure if you could resurrect the Blue Star Syndicate and bring their fleet here."

Damien chuckled.

"I wouldn't go that far," he admitted. "But then, Azure did come quite close to killing me personally."

It had been Mage-Admiral Medici and Hand Alaura Stealey who had prevented that. Of course, Damien had killed Mikhail Azure himself, but the mob lord had hunted his old ship across half the Protectorate.

The Blue Star Syndicate hadn't survived that clash, though its death throes had been...impressive.

"If you can get the System Militias here, I will gladly share command with whoever you order me to," Medici told him. "I, at least, think it would make the most *sense* for me to be in ultimate command, but I understand political reality: if you pull together this force, *you* will be in command. I will serve as you direct."

That thought hadn't even occurred to Damien. He'd assumed he'd put Medici in command.

"We will do what we must," he finally allowed. "No matter what, Admiral...Ardennes must not fall."

"We serve His Majesty," the Mage-Admiral confirmed. "What use is his Protectorate if we don't protect people?"

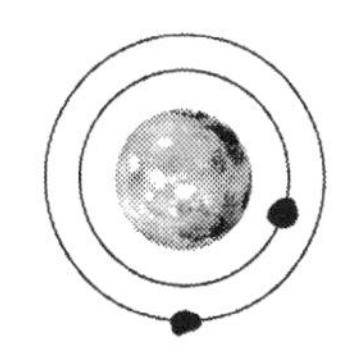

CHAPTER THIRTY-FIVE

AT THIS POINT, Mage Alanna O'Malley seemed completely unbothered by having the First Hand of the Mage-King arrive on her doorstep. Given everything else that had occurred around the Ardennes RTA, Damien was no longer that big a deal.

The old landing pad was gone. A new one had been set up by the Marines to help run search-and-rescue and supplies into the blast zone, and exosuited troopers with Geiger counters were everywhere.

The Marines didn't need to worry about exposure. Their job was to make sure that no one *else* got too much exposure. Especially not, say, a Transceiver Mage or the First Hand.

Damien allowed himself and O'Malley to be hustled inside the massive sphere of the RTA, his own bodyguards trailing in their exosuit armor.

"It's getting better," the other Mage told him as the new airlock sealed behind them. "They're moving in with cleaning gear now; the civilians have all been evacuated." She shook her head. "I almost wish they had managed to deliver the bomb into the array, though. A lot fewer people would have died."

Damien nodded silently as he followed her. Unmentioned in O'Malley's wish was that *she* would have been among that "a lot fewer" people who died. The RTA's shell had survived the blast unscathed and would likely have contained the blast if the bomb had managed to get inside.

Everyone *inside* the stone sphere would have been vaporized, however. He understood where O'Malley was coming from. The current count was over fifty thousand people who had died in the explosions, and tens of thousands more were being treated across the continent.

"And we'd be out of touch with the rest of the Protectorate," he pointed out. "That connection may save a lot more lives." He sighed. "I agree, though. No one ever wants to see this kind of wreck in their home."

"At least no other arrays have gone off the air," O'Malley told him. "We've started a system of regular check-ins. If the Republic hits any other RTAs, we'll know in short order."

That knowledge might not be enough to save anywhere, but that was why the Navy was deploying everywhere instead of just to Ardennes. Damien could see the logic, but he also couldn't help feeling that this would be the turning point.

"That only helps us with the systems that have RTAs," he pointed out. "We need to stop them, hard."

"That's outside my expertise, my lord," O'Malley admitted. "Can we?"

Damien grimaced.

"That's what I'm here to talk to people about."

Damien had done all of the calculations he needed aboard the shuttle, using a large wall screen to make up for his lack of fine manipulation. All of the results were loaded into his wrist-comp with a series of voice commands.

O'Malley left him alone in the central chamber and he took a few minutes to study the runes around him. The Transceiver Mages assured him the Array was intact, but he had advantages they didn't. They knew what it was supposed to do and whether it was doing it.

He could look at the runes and see what they *were* doing. There was damage, he noted. Nothing that was affecting the ability of the Array to project his voice across the light-years, but cracks in the rune matrices would cause problems in the future.

The RTA was fully functional, but the bomb had cut its life expectancy from centuries to years. He'd have to take some time to fix that once this was over.

For now, however, it would do what he needed it to.

"System, display calculations for Sherwood RTA," he ordered aloud. The holographic projector built into his wrist-comp calmly chirped to life, hanging the numbers in front of his face. He studied them for a few moments, then channeled power into the runes around him.

"Sherwood RTA, this is the Ardennes RTA," he announced softly. "First Hand Damien Montgomery speaking. Please verify receipt of this transmission."

Several seconds passed, then a voice echoed out of the silence around him.

"This is the Sherwood RTA, my lord. Transceiver Mage Gordon Elliot speaking. How may we assist?"

"I need a message recorded and relayed to Governor Miles McLaughlin," Damien told the Mage. "Please confirm when you are ready to record."

A few more seconds of silence passed.

"Understood, my lord. We are now recording for forwarding to the Governor. You may begin your message when ready."

"Governor McLaughlin, this is First Hand Damien Montgomery," Damien said firmly. "I'm sure you are aware by now that the Republic has launched an unexpected offensive against Protectorate space. The Navy is deploying across the border to protect our systems, but I have reason to believe that Ardennes will be the focus of the next attack.

"We have already stood off one attack here, but with the broad defensive deployment, the RMN doesn't have enough ships to reinforce me here." He paused, considering how to phrase his request.

He could, he supposed, formally draft the Sherwood Interstellar Patrol and *require* McLaughlin to send him ships. That struck him as a terrible idea, though.

"Sherwood is clear of the likely areas of the Republic's next offensives but is close enough that the Patrol's frigates could reach us before

I expect the next attack to arrive. While it is our responsibility to protect you, I find myself with no choice but to ask for your assistance.

"Any ships of the Patrol that you could spare and deploy to Ardennes may help turn the tide of the battle to come. I fear we will see a major Republic deployment within days, a week at most.

"I understand that all must look to their own defenses in these times, but I must ask for your help regardless. Anything you can spare will be appreciated. Please, Miles...this may be our darkest hour. Send help."

He swallowed, then spoke more formally.

"That is the complete message, Mage Elliot. Please forward to the Governor as soon as possible. I am ending the connection on my side now."

It cut out before the Sherwood Mage could respond, and Damien sighed. He had no idea how McLaughlin would respond, but Sherwood was his homeworld. He had faith in Governor McLaughlin—and even more than that, he had faith in Commodore *Grace* McLaughlin, the commander of the Sherwood Interstellar Patrol.

And his ex-girlfriend.

Shaking his head, he looked at his wrist-comp. There were three more systems on his list, the only ones near enough to Ardennes to get there in time who had both RTAs and significant System Militias.

Well, Míngliàng and Condor had System Militias. Amber... Amber was a different case entirely. The Amber Defense Cooperative had some jump-capable ships, but the main thing Damien was counting on was that Amber was the home base for many of the Protectorate's semi-legal mercenaries.

Amber's laws, after all, were best described as "lax."

He sighed.

"System, display calculations for Amber RTA," he ordered.

He had two messages for Amber. One was for the government, such as it was. One was for an old friend.

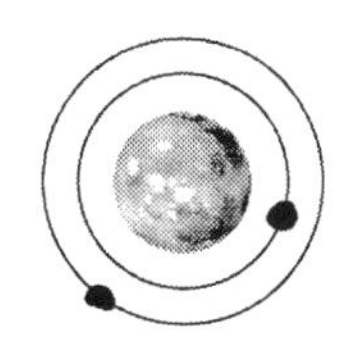

CHAPTER THIRTY-SIX

ADMIRAL GRACE MCLAUGHLIN was swamped. Saddled with an overambitious title and an even more overwhelming job, it was the job of the petite redheaded woman in the dark blue uniform to protect the Sherwood System and provide security for the surrounding jump zones.

Not to mention being jointly responsible for the security of the Antonius System, a star system–sized mineral motherlode that her government shared with the Míngliàng System's government. She and Admiral Yen Phan of the Míngliàng Security Flotilla were as close to friends as two women who'd almost started a war with each other could be.

With the latest construction, the Sherwood Interstellar Patrol was now up to twenty frigates, big ships not quite up to the weight of a cruiser but out-massing anything *else* in space. Even Grace had thought that level of construction was overkill, but now she was grateful for it.

It also meant that she had three subordinate Commodores and barely even saw the decks of *Robin Hood*, her theoretical flagship. She lived in an office buried in the new military orbital, crushed under approximately twenty metric tons of paperwork.

When her aide stepped into her office, she barely managed to avoid biting his head off. The Navy was, quite reasonably, asking for a dramatic increase in the antimatter stockpiles the MidWorlds kept on hand for them. It was falling to Grace to be sure that their production could handle that *and* the demands of the Patrol itself.

"What is it, Joseph?" she asked after swallowing her initial unnecessary reaction.

"The Governor is on a direct encrypted channel," Joseph Manderley told her. The stuffy man was at least twice her age, and she'd never met anyone less military than him. On the other hand, he was an *extraordinarily* efficient bureaucrat and was probably the only reason her office resembled anything other than an ongoing tornado.

"Your grandfather wants to speak to you immediately," Manderley continued. "Shall I tell him you're available?"

Grace chuckled, hoping it sounded only partially forced.

"My grandfather is also my boss and runs this damn star system," she replied. "Put him through. He's seen the state of my office before."

Manderley bowed and withdrew. A moment later, the wallscreen came to life with the face of Miles James McLaughlin, patriarch of the McLaughlin clan, elected Governor of the Sherwood System...and Grace's grandfather.

"I thought I hired you a damn staff," the old man said gruffly. His hair had gone from pure white to wispy and translucent over the last few years, and age was starting to drag his face down. His eyes were bright and sharp, but Grace couldn't help wondering just how long he could keep up the current pace.

This had been planned as his last term—but no one had expected it to involve a war.

"You did," Grace agreed. "A staff, three competent subordinate staff officers, and an entire administrative structure." She gestured at the mess around her. "This is what's *left* for me."

"You need more staff," the McLaughlin told his granddaughter. "Paperwork shouldn't be trapping you in an office; you have a job to do."

"This is part of the job. I figure you know that as well as anyone," she replied.

"That's fair. But it's not the most important part of the job, and *you* know that," he countered. "We've received a message from Ardennes. You need to listen to it."

"Ardennes?" Grace asked. "What's at Ardennes?"

"Possibly our only hope of not losing this war?" the Governor shrugged. "And, just as important, Montgomery."

"Oh."

Grace listened to the entire message, but by the time the recording was over, she was already pulling up the readiness reports on her ships.

"We *will* deploy," her grandfather said fiercely. "Montgomery has the authority to order us to. He has chosen not to...and it doesn't matter. He is a son of Sherwood and we owe him."

"We owe him," Grace agreed. Jurisdiction conflicts over Antonius—plus some carefully calculated intervention by Legatan spies—had nearly brought Sherwood into war with Míngliàng. Damien's intervention and refusal to let *either* system jump to war had probably saved tens of thousands of lives, if not more.

They owed him. And Grace wasn't going to pretend she was over him, either. They'd had less than a week together after the Battle of Antonius and she knew he'd dated others, as had she, but...she wasn't over him.

Even if that felt irrelevant and minor compared to the scope of the disaster the galaxy was facing.

"We have twenty frigates in commission, but four are at Antonius right now," she told the McLaughlin. "We don't have a *lot* of corvettes left, given the way I've been raiding them for frigate crews, but we've still got a solid dozen defensive ships that can't go anywhere."

She knew that her grandfather understood the value of those defensive ships too. The dozen of them left massed roughly half as much as one of her frigates.

"So, you have sixteen frigates in the system, plus the corvettes, correct?" he said.

"Exactly." Grace continued running numbers. "If we concentrate Mages from all sixteen onto say...twelve, leaving only the Captains on the remaining ships, we'll have five Mages per ship. Our people aren't Navy

Mages, but with five Mages per ship, we can make it to Ardennes in just over two days."

"Do you have twelve ships fueled and ready to go?"

"No," Grace admitted. "It'll take twelve hours for us to have two full squadrons ready to deploy."

"It'll take you almost that long just to move your Mages around," the McLaughlin pointed out. "Who will you leave in command here?"

Grace noted that he hadn't even *suggested* she not command the deployment herself.

"McTaggart," she said instantly. Commodore Ishbel McTaggart had been promoted past other officers who had been senior, primarily for keeping her head in the middle of the *disaster* when one of their Captains had turned out to be a traitor.

"I'll take Commodore Arrington with me," she continued. "That'll give me two flagships and twelve frigates total. The intel we've seen on these bastards is terrifying, I'll admit that...but I'll match eighty-odd million tons of our frigates against the same mass in the Republic's ships. *We*, after all, have magical gravity."

"That is your area of expertise now," her grandfather confirmed. "Do whatever it takes. Any resources you need, any assistance we can provide, let me know immediately. I want the Patrol underway in twelve hours, Admiral McLaughlin. Mars has called, and Sherwood *will* answer."

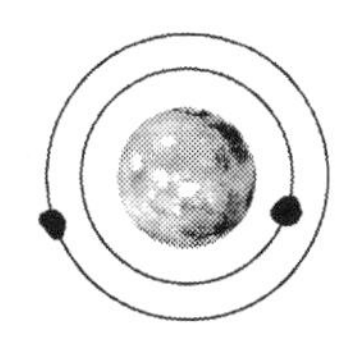

CHAPTER THIRTY-SEVEN

"I'M NOT EVEN CERTAIN you're in Amber, Captain Rice, but if you are...I need your assistance."

Damien Montgomery's recorded voice echoed in the hotel room as Captain David Rice listened to the message. The burly merchant captain turned spy had been asleep when the message arrived, but he wasn't going to let a message from the First Hand go ignored.

He wouldn't have ignored a message from Montgomery, regardless of the young man's rank. Damien Montgomery had been his Ship's Mage for only a handful of months, but they'd saved each other's lives a lot in that short time.

"Ardennes looks to be the pivot point where the next six months to a year of this war will turn," Montgomery continued. "If we hold here, we have a chance. If we don't... I can't say what happens next, but I doubt it will be pretty.

"So long as we have this beachhead, this position from which to counterattack, they will focus here. If we lose Ardennes, we may just lose the war. I want to think that couldn't be that bad, that the Republic is reasonable. They were us until a few short months ago. And yet...I cannot help but fear what the victorious Republic would do.

"I need you to recruit every mercenary you can, Captain Rice. You have the word of the First Hand. Their fees will be met. Their service rewarded. If you have allies who can put pressure on the Defense Cooperative to send ships as well, I beg of you...do what you can.

"I face an enemy stronger than our worst fears. I need every ship, every weapon I can gather. You are far from my only hope, old friend, but I need your help regardless."

David exhaled a long breath as the message ended, and pulled up a map with the ease of long practice. Twelve light-years from Amber to Ardennes. A ship with one Mage would take four days to cross the distance. That time dropped if the Mage was Navy-trained, and dropped further if there were more Mages.

A lot of the mercenaries and ships in Amber, though, only had one Mage. Jump Mages were expensive, and mercenary companies ran on surprisingly thin margins.

"David?"

He looked up as his lover reentered the hotel room. Keiko Alabaster *owned* the hotel they were staying in. He was a starship captain, which meant his assets and resources easily qualified him as wealthy even before counting the fact that he now owned *four* ships.

Keiko Alabaster was an Amber shipping magnate. She owned ten ships and leased or hired at least four times that many. She also owned at least one of the planet's orbitals—even now, he wasn't sure which one—and swathes of planetside businesses and real estate.

He hadn't known most of that when he'd fallen into her bed, and hadn't really cared once he *had* learned. That, he was sure, was a good chunk of why the statuesque woman kept him.

"You had your message; I had mine," he told her. "I'm guessing yours was also from Montgomery?"

The pale redheaded woman dropped onto the bed next to him, wrapped in a dark blue terrycloth robe as she leaned against his bare shoulder.

"That's supposed to be confidential," she said lightly. "But...yes."

"And what is the ADC going to do?" David asked.

"That's *definitely* confidential," she said. "On the other hand, how long does it take MISS to find out our decisions?"

Keiko was still far from reconciled to David's second life as a covert agent of the Martian Interstellar Security Service, but she was accepting enough about it to joke.

"Honestly?" David chuckled. "I have no idea; they keep me out of that loop unless absolutely necessary. Conflicts of interest and all that."

"That's probably wise." She kissed his shoulder, then sighed. "Montgomery knows us," she told him. "Well enough that he put a dollar figure on things. A big one. They're sending the jump fleet, such as it is."

David nodded thoughtfully. The Amber Defense Cooperative was exactly what it sounded like—a semi-private military force that provided system security for Amber. Along with the Judicial and Medical Cooperatives, it was part of the triad of "insurance" organizations that made up the closest thing Amber had to a government.

And since their purpose was entirely to provide security for Amber, funded by service fees and the purchase of membership shares, they had kept the vast majority of their forces limited to sublight ships. On the other hand...

"*Rameses* alone will be a significant contribution," he pointed out. He had no idea how the ADC had convinced Tau Ceti's Nova Industries to sell them one of the *Dragon*-class heavy cruisers—they weren't supposed to be available for export at all—but he suspected that Keiko had had something to do with it.

"*Rameses, Osiris, Isis* and *Horus*," she confirmed, reeling off the names. One cruiser, three destroyers. One of the destroyers was *ancient*, an ex-Navy ship, but the rest of the ships were brand-new. The new destroyers had actually been built in Amber herself, a test of their shipyards.

"What did Montgomery want from you?" Keiko asked. "Since I've spilled all of *my* secrets."

Again went unspoken.

"Well, in respect of that, I have a question that I suspect you know the answer to better than I," David told her. "How much to hire every mercenary in Amber?"

"More than you have," she replied after a few seconds' thought. "You might be able to come up with the deposit, but the bosses would know the limits of your resources." She snorted. "They probably wouldn't trust that *I'd* be able to come up with the liquid assets to pay them, not on that scale."

"This isn't your problem," David said slowly.

"Like hell it isn't," she snapped. "I may not work for Mars like you do, love, but I live in the damn Protectorate. I can find the people we need to talk to, but like I said...a lot of them are going to want money up front, and they're not going to trust that even I could liquidate assets in time to pay them."

"I don't think that'll be necessary," he told her. "You know these people better than I do. Think the First Hand's word is good for them?"

Keiko was silent for several seconds.

"He pledged his word. The word of the First Hand of the Mage-King."

"He did," David confirmed. "I have the recording, specifically what he said. 'Their fees met, their service rewarded.'"

"That's a blank check, David. He realizes that, right?"

"Damien Montgomery is many things," he told her. "I doubt he is as naïve as he once was, but even if he was, he was *never* stupid. He knows what he just wrote...and I know he meant it. He needs a fleet, Keiko, not a cruiser and three destroyers."

"If he's prepared to write Amber's mercenaries that kind of blank check..." His lover smiled and kissed his shoulder again. "I think we need to get dressed, David. We have work to do...but I think we can deliver the First Hand his fleet."

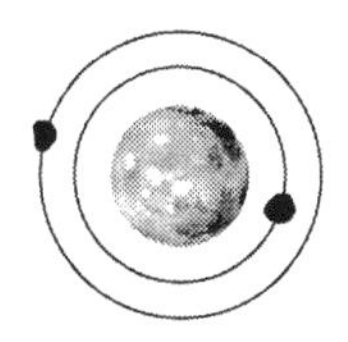

CHAPTER THIRTY-EIGHT

KELLY LAMONTE let herself sigh openly in relief as *Rhapsody in Purple* emerged into the Ardennes System. Despite running from an entire Republican battle fleet, she hadn't let herself or her crew feel safe until they made it here.

That relief didn't last long.

"We're receiving an automated transmission," Milhouse told her. "It's on a loop, making sure everyone gets it."

"Play it," Kelly ordered, and the familiar voice of Damien Montgomery echoed across her bridge.

She'd known him well enough once to be able to tell how tired he was.

"All civilian shipping, the Ardennes System has become a war zone," the recording announced. "Warships of the Republican Interstellar Navy have been present in the system and may have left behind automated munitions or mines. We also cannot guarantee that RIN parasite vessels are not present in the system.

"We are organizing convoys for in-system shipping, and your safest approach is to rendezvous with one of those convoys. An attachment to this recording will provide you with the locations of the current protected convoys."

The recording paused, then resumed after a moment's thought.

"Unfortunately, the Royal Martian Navy cannot guarantee your safety in the Ardennes System outside of those convoys. If you cannot safely reach a secured zone, I recommend that you withdraw from this system and promise that any penalties for late delivery will be covered by the Protectorate.

"If you remain, please attempt to rendezvous with a convoy as quickly as possible and we will do all within our power to keep you safe. Regardless, good luck."

The recording stopped for several seconds, then resumed. Milhouse cut it off.

"They've already been attacked," he told her. "It can't have been the fleet we saw at Santiago, or the system wouldn't still be in our hands."

"No, they probably tried to rush them with a single carrier group," Kelly guessed. "And it looks like the RMN got here first."

She haloed the two massive signatures hanging in orbit above the planet.

"Those are battleships. Ours. I'm picking up ten cruisers backing them up, too—and there's destroyers bloody everywhere. I don't know where he found them, but Damien dug up reinforcements."

"That's good, isn't it?" Xi Wu asked. Kelly looked up as her wife crossed the bridge, replacing Liara Foster at the Mage station. Foster promptly abandoned the bridge with the zombie walk of a post-jump Mage.

"In theory," Kelly allowed. "I make it over two hundred million tons of heavy warships. That's a hell of a fleet."

"I'm hearing a *but* here, my love," Xi admitted.

"Yeah." The covert ops commander studied the chart. "Except there are four carrier groups in Santiago. We *confirmed* four hundred million tons of heavy warships, and we only got a clear look at two of the task groups.

"Assuming the RIN extracted any significant portion of the strike force they hit Ardennes with, we're probably looking at the best part of a *billion* tons of warships heading this way. That's a good chunk of the tonnage of the entire Royal Martian Navy.

"We need to abandon Ardennes...but if Damien has battleships, that argument is going to be a lot harder to win."

Rhapsody in Purple wasn't pretending to be a civilian ship this time. They were diving toward Ardennes at fifteen gravities, and Kelly was sending her MISS codes on ahead.

"Any response?" she asked Milhouse after they'd been in-system for half an hour.

"Nothing yet... Wait, I've got a pair of destroyers detaching from the orbitals," he told her. "Incoming message."

"Put it on."

"Captain LaMonte, this is Commodore Cruyssen," a uniformed officer told her from her screen. "We have received your codes and are sending two of my ships out to bring you in safely. Please transmit your sensor records from Santiago to *Peacemaker*.

"We are arranging a briefing once you arrive. You'll be speaking to Admiral Medici and Hand Montgomery at least; we'll see if we can pull anyone else in."

"We're glad you made it back safely, Captain. The more data we have on the enemy, the better able we are to defend Ardennes."

The message ended and she shook her head.

"I don't get the impression anyone is going to like our data," she said aloud. "I don't think we *can* defend Ardennes."

"Don't we have to try, sir?" Milhouse asked.

"I don't know." Kelly sighed. "If the Republic is coming with overwhelming force, can we justify losing the ships needed to even try? I don't think we can."

"We need a victory," her tactical officer said quietly. "But if all that trying to hold will get us is another defeat..."

"This war isn't going to turn on one battle," she agreed. "It'll turn on whether or not the Protectorate still *has* a navy over the next few months. We can afford to lose another system better than we can afford to lose the fleet I'm seeing on my screens."

Or than they could afford to lose Montgomery. The death of a Hand was bad enough. Kelly had no idea how the Protectorate would take the loss of Damien Montgomery now.

She snorted, and Milhouse looked at her questioningly.

"I just realized that the thing in this system we can afford to lose least is probably Damien Montgomery, but I know him well enough to know that is *not* an argument I can make to him!"

Duke of Magnificence wasn't the first cruiser Kelly LaMonte had ever set foot on, but it was still an unusual experience for her. There was no formal boarding party as she came aboard. She was met by a small squad of Marines who escorted her to a conference room where several officers waited for her.

There were two men and a woman linked in by video screen. She recognized Commodore Cruyssen from her earlier conversation and Mage-Admiral Medici from when the RMN officer had rescued the crew of *Blue Jay* back when the people hunting Damien had almost finished them off.

She didn't know the tall woman in a business suit, but Kelly guessed she was a civilian member of the Ardennian government linking in from the surface.

There was another Commodore in the room with her, along with a Marine officer—she didn't recognize either, but she was focusing on the other occupants of the room to distract herself from the one person in the room she most definitely *did* recognize.

Damien Montgomery looked like he'd aged a decade in half that time. He was more formally dressed than she'd usually seen him when he was *Blue Jay*'s Ship's Mage, a black blazer over a tight-fitted white turtleneck.

He still had the gold medallion that designated him a Mage, but that symbol was almost secondary compared to the platinum-cast fist that hung on his chest. Kelly's ex-boyfriend looked...happy to see her but utterly exhausted.

She'd heard about everything, and her eyes were inevitably drawn to his hands. He wore thin black leather gloves, long enough to disappear under the sleeves of his jacket. The gloves hid any visible scars, but his hands were immobile.

He spotted her look, however, and lifted his hand and slowly, carefully flexed it.

"I am healing, Captain LaMonte," he told her. "I am perhaps in better shape than I look." He took a moment to study her in turn. "You look good. Command agrees with you. As does marriage, I hear."

"It does. Both of those," she said, stumbling over her words. She then half-forced a chuckle as she glanced around the room.

"My apologies, gentlemen, Julia," Damien said levelly. "Captain LaMonte and I are old friends; it's been a while but I don't believe we have time to reacquaint ourselves." He gestured her to an empty seat.

"The console is loaded with the data you sent us," he told her. "Why don't you walk us through what you found?"

Kelly nodded and swallowed as she took a seat. A glass of water floated its way over to her elbow from the sideboard, and she gave Damien a reproving look. He shrugged innocently.

When she'd first met him, he'd rarely openly used magic for minor effects. Sherwood had a tradition of Mages being low-key, and he'd been trained in that practice. She guessed that his broken hands didn't leave him much choice anymore.

"We arrived in the Santiago System roughly five days after Lord Montgomery did," she told them as she pulled up the data. "They'd clearly heavily reinforced their position there, in terms of both ships and ground troops. Our best guess is that these ships"—she haloed the two transports in orbit of Novo Lar—"are troop transports."

"Built on the same hull as their warships, as we suspected," Admiral Medici noted as they studied the ships. "We were correct that the Republic seems to be mass-producing as many components as they can."

"Our intelligence suggests that there are now roughly a hundred thousand Republican troops on Novo Lar alone," Kelly continued a moment later. "It sounded like most of the fighting was done. Certainly, the local government didn't have the forces to withstand an invasion of that magnitude."

"No one would," the woman on the screen replied. "We're pretty typical here, and the entire Ardennes Planetary Army is only about thirty thousand men and women. Even with control of the orbitals, we couldn't stand off a hundred thousand soldiers."

"The naval situation is worse," Kelly told them all. She haloed each identified group as she spoke. "When we arrived in Santiago, there was a carrier group positioned above Novo Lar. We didn't get as detailed a look at them as we'd like, but several vessels did appear to be damaged. I'd guess that was the carrier group that clashed with Lord Montgomery.

"A second carrier group arrived in-system while we were making our initial scouting pass, and when we scouted the cloudscoop, we found two more."

"Twenty-three starships, all told," Medici concluded.

"Plus the ships that just evacuated Ardennes," Montgomery added. "Twenty-eight warships." He met Kelly's eyes.

"You think they're coming here." It wasn't really a question.

"I don't see anywhere else they could be gathering that kind of force to strike at," she told him. "My guess would be five carriers, eight battleships, fifteen cruisers. Eight hundred million tons or more."

"Where did they get the Mages for this kind of fleet?" Medici asked. "The maneuvers they've made suggest multiple Mages per warship. Even if this is their entire jump-capable fleet..."

"It almost certainly is not," Montgomery said sharply. "I think, ladies, gentlemen, that we must accept the fact that the Republic has cracked the holy grail of technology research from the last few centuries: they now not only have a technological interstellar communicator but some form of technological jump drive."

"Given the Republic's maneuvers, I'd guess we're looking at one or two more groups on the offensive at minimum, and two to four held back for defense," Cruyssen concluded.

"If they're bringing half of their damn fleet to Ardennes, what do we do?" the woman on the screen asked. "Neither I nor Governor Riordan will ask the Martian Navy to die pointlessly for us."

Kelly wished someone had bothered to introduce her. The woman seemed to be playing the same game she was—no matter what else happened here, *Damien Montgomery* couldn't be allowed to die pointlessly here.

"Julia..." Montgomery sighed. "My apologies. Kelly LaMonte, this is Julia Amiri, Ardennes's Minister for Defense. Also a former Secret Service Agent who headed my detail for two years."

He turned his attention back to the other woman, Amiri.

"We have taken steps and organized deployments," he told her. "Yes, the enemy is bringing a larger force than our worst projections, but remember that the larger the force they're bringing, the longer it will take to organize."

"That doesn't buy us much," Medici noted.

"We have reinforcements coming, people. If the Republic will give us the time we need, they'll learn the Protectorate is far from defenseless."

"Are you really going to get enough to stand off *this*?" Kelly asked, gesturing at the estimates she now had on the hologram. "That's not a single task group, Damien. That's half the Republic's fleet. They're coming for Ardennes...but they're also coming for *you*. For the First Hand."

"I know," he admitted. "And it doesn't matter. You're all correct," he continued with a familiar wry grin. "In the cold logic of war, we should withdraw. Concentrate more ships, assemble a full squadron of battleships before we clash with the Republic on this level.

"But the cold logic of war does not speak to the duties inherent in the name of our nation. *We are the Protectorate of the Mage-King of Mars.*"

His words were fierce and Kelly looked around the room. Her ex-boyfriend had everyone's attention.

"We could retreat. Perhaps we should retreat. But I cannot. We need Ardennes as a beachhead to strike back at the Republic, but even more than that, we need it as a symbol. We need to show the people of the Protectorate that there are lines that we will not retreat from. That we will not yield them into the hands of their enemies without resistance.

"So far, this war has gone the Republic's way. That ends here. We gather the reinforcements I have called for, we assemble our fleet, and we meet the Republic's best with our best. We may still have to yield Ardennes; I won't pretend otherwise.

"But we will *not* yield one more system without a fight. Not Ardennes, not anywhere else."

Kelly sighed, but she was nodding along with everyone else. She knew when she'd lost an argument.

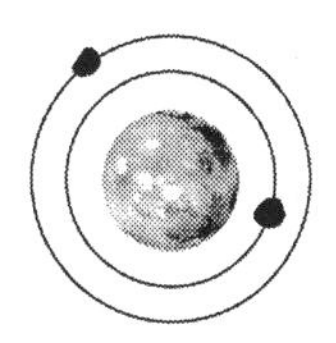

CHAPTER THIRTY-NINE

ROSLYN WATCHED the orbiting fleet with something close to awe. She'd seen battleships before—well, *a* battleship, making a close pass of the Tau Ceti Academy to show off to the cadets—but there was something more to seeing those behemoths of steel and firepower and knowing they were there to fight.

There were a *lot* of ships in Ardennes now. *Peacemaker* and *Pax Marcianus* were the most noticeable, but cruisers were nothing to sneer at. Neither were the multiple squadrons of destroyers, including *Stand in Righteousness.*

She'd half-expected to be replaced when Mage-Admiral Medici had arrived, but she remained aboard *Stand* as the tactical officer. Someone had faith in her abilities. It was probably Commander Katz and Captain Kulkarni.

It certainly wasn't Roslyn!

For the fourth time in the last hour, she checked in on the sensor network scattered around the star system. Destroyers escorted sublight convoys between Ardennes and the other planets in the system, most importantly the gas giant hosting the Transmuter facility and the Navy logistics base.

She'd have been surprised to see anything different or unexpected, but she was all too aware of how junior and unprepared for her current job she was.

"Still obsessively checking for threats?" Katz asked, the Commander having apparently drifted in while she wasn't looking.

"It's part of the job, isn't it?" Roslyn asked carefully as she turned in her seat to look at the black woman. "Making sure no one sneaks up on us?"

The Commander chuckled.

"And even paranoiacs have real enemies," she agreed. "You've spotted the problem before everyone at least once too often for me to dismiss your instincts, Lieutenant. What's itching at the back of your neck?"

Roslyn considered that thoughtfully, yanking on a loose bang as she studied her console and the tactical display.

"The logistics depot, I think," she admitted. "Every warship we have requires antimatter. We're keeping everyone fueled, but our main stockpile is out there with the Transmuter station—and a grand total of three destroyers."

"I agree," Katz said. "It's our biggest vulnerability, but I haven't seen a solution to it yet. Do you?"

"Because the brand-new Lieutenant is going to see what everyone else missed, huh?" Roslyn asked with a chuckle of her own.

"You never know," the older woman replied. "Sometimes, it takes a new set of eyes to see what everyone else missed. So, any thoughts?"

"We either need to commit to protecting the station or accept that we're writing it off," the young Mage said slowly. "Three destroyers won't make any difference to the fate of the logistics base or the Transmuter station. But they *could* provide enough missile defense to change the fate of the fleet when the Republic comes for us."

"From a strict tactical perspective, you're right," Katz agreed. "And believe me, Lieutenant, everyone up to Admiral Medici realizes it. Hell, I don't know how much tactics and strategy training the Hand has, but I'd be surprised if even Montgomery doesn't realize those destroyers aren't going to achieve anything there.

"Tactics, however, aren't the only thing in play. There are twenty-two Mages aboard that Transmuter station. Seventeen of them are convicted criminals serving sentences of various lengths, but the others are volunteers and even the prisoners are far from expendable. There are another two-hundred-odd people on that station, and about three thousand across the rest of the logistics base.

"We owe them protection." Katz shook her head. "We can't provide them with anything *effective*, but we need to make the effort. So, we send what we can spare and keep the fleet ready to jump to their relief if necessary."

"They're a...political gesture?" Roslyn asked.

"Basically. They're also a tripwire, there to protect the logistics base from long-range fire while the fleet moves in." The Commander sighed. "It's a terrible job, but make no mistake: those men and women know what their job is."

"Die protecting civilians until the rest of us get there?" Roslyn replied, a bit more bitterness slipping into her tone than she meant.

"Exactly," her boss told her gently. "To a certain extent, Lieutenant, that's the job of this entire fleet now. I've been told there are reinforcements coming, but I'm guessing the RIN is reinforcing as well. It's a race, Chambers.

"And if the Republic wins, then it falls to us to die standing to honor His Majesty's word."

Roslyn found herself staring at a different screen, the one showing Ardennes itself orbiting beneath them.

"I guess if we couldn't take the joke, we shouldn't have signed up," she breathed. It was an old quote from a book she'd read as part of her studies at the Academy.

"Nobody ever said the joke was going to be funny."

What was frustrating for Roslyn, at least, was that they had no idea if the Republic was watching them. Seven operatives had been found across the fleet. If any of them had had an FTL communicator, it had been destroyed before they were taken.

At least only four of them had suicided. There were three prisoners being held on the surface. The tendency of Republic spies to suicide—or *be* suicided—on capture made Roslyn sick.

Every tactical officer in orbit of Ardennes was digging through their sensor data, trying to find any hint, any sign of an FTL communication. It was entirely possible that there wasn't even a recognizable signal when the thing was in use, which only added to Roslyn's frustration.

Technology wasn't supposed to feel more arcane and mysterious than her magic, after all.

Something flickered on her screen and she checked it. For a moment, she thought she had something—and then the computer cheerfully informed her that the meteor she'd detected was recorded in Ardennes's databases.

Roslyn was about to move on when a thought struck her and she double-checked the data. Yes...the meteor was exactly where it was supposed to be, but the reflection was wrong. She wasn't getting reflected light from the star.

She was getting reflected light from somewhere else...somewhere *behind* the distant second gas giant that went mostly ignored due to its size and distance.

And not just light.

"Commander Katz," she said aloud. "I think we've got a jump flare."

"Jump flares aren't usually an *I think*, Lieutenant," Katz pointed out—but she stepped over to look over Roslyn's shoulder anyway.

"This meteor is supposed to be here," Roslyn told her superior. "But look at the light pattern. It's reflecting light from *here*." She haloed a region of space behind the smaller gas giant. "And there's just enough Cherenkov radiation left for me to flag it as a possible jump."

"And if someone wanted to be sneaky and get a look at what we're up to, that's exactly where they'd jump in, isn't it?" the Commander murmured. "I agree. Well done, Lieutenant."

Even as Katz was congratulating her, an alert flashed up on the screen. At least one other tactical officer had drawn the same conclusion—and, unlike a freshly promoted teenager, had had the confidence to send up the warning without checking it with a superior.

"Looks like we're sending a couple of destroyers out to investigate," Katz noted as new instructions ran over her screen. "Not us; looks like *Bonnie Darling* got the short straw again." She patted Roslyn firmly on the shoulder.

"Keep those eyes peeled, Lieutenant. Your paranoia hasn't led us wrong yet!"

CHAPTER FORTY

"WELL, THE BAD NEWS IS that they got a fantastic view of everything that's in the system," Medici told Damien over the video channel.

"And the good news is that our reinforcements aren't here yet," the Hand replied. "And the fact that they sent a scouting ship means it's less likely they have an operating agent here with an FTL communicator."

"Agreed," the Admiral said. "And our destroyers chased them out, so they'll probably realize they can't pull that again." Medici sighed. "I've positioned a net of sensor drones behind Cherbourg now, with *Bonnie Darling of Sherwood* out there to keep an eye on them.

"Cherbourg's far enough out that they can't threaten us by jumping behind it, but I'll admit we assumed they already knew everything."

Damien nodded.

"As did I, Admiral. I think that's likely still a wise policy to operate under. I wouldn't put it past a clever Republic Admiral to try and use a scout ship to make us feel safe. What kind of scout are we looking at?" he asked.

"What I would have expected before all of their new toys got revealed, to be honest," Medici replied. "A refitted jump-courier. Nothing unusual beyond the sensor arrays that our ships picked up, so it's quite possible she's even still flying with Mages aboard."

"We know they have at least some," Damien said. "I don't get it myself, but some people will always work for money—and the Republic certainly has that."

"I can't think of any particular way to take advantage of that scout sweep," the Admiral told him. "You?"

"No. We know they were here; they know we're here. We have to assume they'll know when our reinforcements arrive—but if they don't, that means they may move with less force than they'll need when all is said and done."

"I wish I didn't have to rely on that," Medici murmured. "What are we getting in terms of reinforcements?"

Damien shook his head.

"Míngliàng, Sherwood, Condor, Amber and His Majesty have all confirmed that they're sending more ships," he told the other man. "Since we don't currently trust our communication security, no one is giving me more details than that."

His concerned voice earned him a disgruntled *mewp* from the floor. Persephone appeared from nowhere to headbutt his leg and he chuckled.

"My apologies, Admiral; my therapist says I'm being too grumpy."

The Admiral laughed, breathing a sigh of relief.

"That cat is surprisingly good for all of us," he told Damien. "We're staring down the barrel of one hell of a Republican fleet, my lord. What happens if our reinforcements aren't enough to make up the balance?"

"We fight," Damien said firmly. "We fight on the assumption that we'll have to retreat from the system, but we fight. I will not yield Ardennes without a battle, Mage-Admiral...but everyone who has told me to yield is correct that we cannot lose the forces we're gathering here, either.

"But the easy victories for the Republic are over. We may not stop them here, though we will do all within our power to do so...but they will pay for Ardennes, Admiral. They will learn that they are not invulnerable."

"And we will prove that to our people as well," Medici agreed. "Too many of my officers are on the verge of running scared. We have yet to see a Republic capital ship fall. We've seen them *run*, but we haven't seen them die."

"I know. It will fall to us, Admiral, to change that."

"I'm looking forward to it," Medici said grimly. "Give that cat some pets for me, my lord. If she keeps you sane, you'll be ahead of most of us."

Helpful in many ways as Persephone was, Damien was still glad to have the ability to go to the flag deck to work away from the kitten. Different types of work for different spaces, of course. In his office, he did paperwork and spoke with people—two tasks that summed up the vast majority of his job as First Hand. On *Duke of Magnificence*'s flag deck, he helped run a fleet.

He knew perfectly well he was more of a figurehead than an actual fleet commander. He'd done enough training over the years that he knew he *could* command a battle, but that wasn't his job, and since he *had* professionals, he let them do it.

"Jump flares, my lord," one of the scanner techs reported. "On the right vector to be on approach from Sol."

"What have we got?" Damien asked. Those, hopefully, were the rest of the reinforcements that Alexander had promised him.

"I make it seven flares. Sensor network is still breaking down the contacts and we're identifying IFF codes," the tech responded.

Damien nodded, checking his channel to the bridge.

"Mage-Commodore?"

"We're ready in case it's someone playing games, yes," Jakab replied, in answer to his unspoken question. "In the good news, most of the contacts look too small to be Republic warships. In the bad news, well." The Commodore shook his head. "Most of the contacts look too small to be Republic warships," he repeated.

Which meant few or no cruisers and mostly destroyers.

"We've got IFF on the lead ship," someone reported. "*Foremost Shield of Honor*, one of the *Guardian*-class battleships. Mage-Captain...Cassian Nanni in command. I'm not reading any tags to note that there is a flag officer aboard."

"So, Nanni is in command of the group, whatever it is," Damien concluded. "What else have we got?"

"Looks like one old *Minotaur*-class armored cruiser and five destroyers," Jakab told him. "That's got to be *Labyrinthine Heart of Gold.*"

"Commodore?"

"She's the only *Minotaur* left in service," the Mage-Commodore replied. "She's been fully modernized and kept up to date, but..."

"Kole?" Damien demanded.

"She's primarily a training ship for the Sol Academy," Jakab said quietly. "I doubt His Majesty has sent her out with cadets aboard, but she'll have a scratch crew at best. His Majesty found us another battleship, but the rest of the task group out there..."

"Is the bottom of the barrel," Damien concluded. "Well, I know the Royal Martian Navy, Kole. I have faith in even their worst."

"So do I," the Commodore agreed. "And I'm certainly not turning down a third battleship. Mage-Admiral Medici will make contact with Captain Nanni. Do you want to be involved in the meet-and-greet?"

"Yes," Damien confirmed after a moment. "Regardless of who shows up to help us, those three battleships are going to carry the brunt of the fighting. Their Captains need to know I realize that."

And if all the First Hand could do was tell people their efforts were valued, well, at least that made *Damien* feel useful!

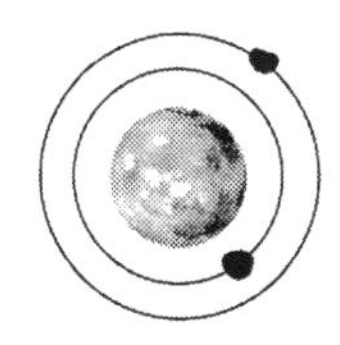

CHAPTER FORTY-ONE

DESPITE THE FACT that her grandfather had contacted her about Damien's message, Grace McLaughlin was still surprised he'd let her take a full dozen of Sherwood's frigates. The trip from Sherwood to Ardennes had passed relatively quietly as well, with startlingly few questions from her notoriously obstreperous captains.

"Jump to Ardennes in T minus five minutes," her operations officer, Captain Gunther Meadows, reported. "All ships have confirmed readiness to jump in sequence."

"Good." Grace considered the situation. "Let's get the task force to battle station, Commodore Meadows," she told him, giving him the courtesy promotion due everyone with the rank of Captain aboard a ship who wasn't the ship's actual Captain.

"Feeling paranoid, sir?" he asked.

"We know the Republic wants Ardennes," she reminded him. "While our last news is only forty-odd hours out of date, it's entirely possible the RIN has moved in since."

"What do we do if they have?" he asked carefully.

"We run. But since I'm not prepared to wait until we have *two* Mages ready to jump aboard each ship, we'll need to stay alive for at least six hours first," Grace pointed out. "So, let's bring the task force to battle stations."

Meadows grinned at her.

"Already sent the command, sir," he noted. "I was *questioning*. I wasn't *arguing*."

"Good boy," she told him. *Boy* was a misnomer. Meadows was the same age as she was. When she'd been going through university for her Jump Mage certification, he'd been studying to join Sherwood System Security.

She'd then poached the triple-S's top precinct chief as a staff officer for her new fleet shortly after the Antonius Incident. If nothing else, she'd needed a top-tier investigator to dig out the rot the Legatans had managed to insert into the Patrol.

"Nervous, huh?" he asked a few moments later, and Grace realized she'd been unconsciously drumming her fingers on her seat's arm.

"We're about to jump into a war zone," she replied, stilling her fingers. "The Patrol has only ever been in one real battle—and I was in Medical for it. But I know our people and I know the Navy and I know Montgomery."

She shook her head.

"We'll be fine."

"I know that," Meadows replied, his tone careful. "I was asking if you were nervous about seeing the First Hand again."

Grace concealed a sigh. If there was one problem with the relative ages of most of her officers, it was that many of her Captains and up were either older than her...or the same age as her. And a lot of the latter didn't *quite* understand that being in charge of the entire Sherwood Interstellar Patrol meant she wasn't dating anyone *in* the Patrol. Meadows was one of the tiny subset who had actually gone far enough to try *asking*, though he'd taken being shut down gracefully.

Mostly.

"The last time I saw the First Hand, he prevented a war that would have shattered two star systems," she told Meadows. "I'm hardly nervous to be seeing him again. He's a hero and we've worked well together in the past."

"I meant more on a personal level."

"Damien and I understand the limits of the lives we've chosen," she said calmly, but she let a frigid anger leak into her tone. "Anything else is none of your business, *Commodore*."

"Of course, sir," he admitted. "I just... Is your personal history with the Hand going to be a problem?"

Grace laughed.

"For the operation? No. Damien and I work well together. Regardless of the current status of our *personal* affairs."

"Jumping."

Mage Adrianna Luna was *Robin Hood*'s senior Ship's Mage after the Captain himself. They'd been "reinforced" by Grace herself, who had made one of the first jumps.

Now Luna finished the trip, delivering them into Ardennes with the aplomb of an experienced Jump Mage. A pulse of Cherenkov radiation temporarily overloaded the frigates' sensors as eleven other ships jumped out around her.

At the Antonius Incident, the failure to jump in formation had contributed to the loss of several of Sherwood's frigates and thousands of lives. Grace had made *very* sure that failure wouldn't recur, and this time, all twelve of her ships emerged within ten thousand kilometers of each other.

"Jump flare is fading; we are sweeping the system," Meadows reported cheerfully. "Whoa."

"Commodore?"

Grace was already pulling up his data on her own repeaters when he flicked it to the main holodisplay on *Robin Hood*'s flag deck.

"Three battleships," she noted, picking out exactly what he'd seen. "Damn, what did Damien need us for?"

"Something that three battleships isn't enough for?" her subordinate suggested. "Looks like he called Míngliàng, too. I've got two of their cruisers with a dozen destroyers for escorts making an approach. They didn't beat us by much."

Grace nodded as she found the codes. At Antonius, she'd very nearly ordered the Patrol to fire on the Míngliàng Security Flotilla. The icons and data codes attached to the other system's fleet were burned into her mind.

Two cruisers was half of the MSF's heavy warships. A dozen destroyers was *more* than half of their lighter ships. It seemed Admiral Yen Phan had taken Damien's request as seriously as she had. In fact...

"If I'm reading these codes correctly, Admiral Phan is in command?" she asked.

"I have the same," Meadows confirmed. "Phan's codes are flying from the lead cruiser, *Light of Peace*." He paused. "Is that going to be a problem, sir?"

"Do you have an obsession with anticipating problems that don't exist, Commodore?" Grace asked. "Yen and I have been in touch for years now. It's amazing how strong a foundation for a friendship almost killing each other makes.

"Send our codes to the station and request an orbit from Mage-Admiral Medici. It seems we're putting together a little surprise for the 'Republic of Faith and Reason.'"

As Grace's frigates slipped into the assigned orbit, a new set of jump flares lit up the sky.

A chill ran down her spine as she looked over at Meadows.

"Commodore? What have we got?" she demanded.

"Looks like...twelve destroyers, couple of bigger ships around the four-megaton range. Principality of Condor IFFs," her subordinate confirmed. "I'm guessing the Prince decided he needed to build some goodwill with the Protectorate."

Grace snorted. The Prince of Condor had been caught with his fingers in the cookie jar when the Protectorate had raided the Mafia's new shipping center in his system. At the very least, he'd been turning a blind eye, and from some of the confidential reports that had crossed her desk through unofficial channels, well—that eye had been pretty knowingly blind.

Condor was a wealthy system, and its no-questions-asked transshipment was part of that wealth, but there were lines the Charter wasn't willing to let be crossed. Last she'd heard, there was an entire *division* of the Royal Martian Marine Corps sitting on the Prince.

And the RMMC didn't *have* very many divisions.

"The goodwill won't hurt him, that's for sure," she agreed. Two mid-range warships and a dozen destroyers wasn't going to change the tune of the next few weeks, but she had the sinking feeling that every little bit was going to help.

"Or us," Meadows murmured.

"Agreed. We're here to pay a debt forward, but believe me, the goodwill this will earn us with Mars was considered," Grace replied. "Get in touch with Mage-Admiral Medici's staff. I'm sure there's some kind of planning session they're going to want us to show up for."

"There's what, three Admirals here? Four?" Meadows shook his head. "Who's in charge of this mess?"

"Medici," Grace said instantly. "We don't argue with the Navy. And if anyone else decides to argue with the Navy, they'll get to talk to Damien."

She remembered a meeting during the Antonius Incident with a shiver. Her grandfather had enough presence and charisma to constitute an unstoppable force in negotiations...and all of that had collided with Damien Montgomery's will and just slid off.

"I don't envy them that conversation," she concluded after a second. "Damien is a kind man, a good man.

"I have no pity for anyone who assumes that means he's a *weak* man."

Meadows was silent, focusing on his communications, then looked up at her.

"I never met him," he admitted. "But he has a reputation at this point. Anyone who thinks the Sword of Mars is *weak*...deserves what they get. *Kind* and *good* aren't most people's first description of Montgomery, sir.

"More like *terrifying*."

She chuckled as that thought collided with her image of her ex-boyfriend.

"I also don't envy the person who is expecting a great and almighty warrior and gets Damien Montgomery," Grace told Meadows.

"Well, I guess that'll probably include me," he replied. "We're invited aboard *Duke of Magnificence* for a meet-and-greet with all of the Militia and Navy flag officers, along with the flag captains and battleship captains. Sounds like a party."

"It does. I assume aides and ops officers are expected as well?" she asked. Otherwise, he wasn't coming and he knew it.

"Yes, sir. They want us flunkies along to serve coffee, I'm sure."

Grace grinned.

"I'm mostly planning on making you take notes so I don't have to," she told him.

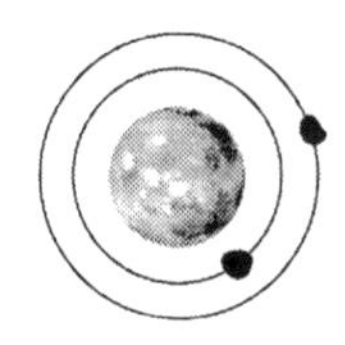

CHAPTER FORTY-TWO

"I'M NOT SURE I've ever dealt with this many Admirals in one place," Mage-Admiral James Medici noted to Damien as they stood together with Mage-Commodore Jakab in the waiting section of *Duke of Magnificence*'s shuttle bay.

"It's a logical title for the head of a system fleet to hang on themselves," Damien replied. "I was always surprised that the Patrol went for *Commodore* to begin with, though I see they've updated that."

"Three squadrons and change now?" Medici asked. "They *needed* levels of flag officers."

"It's not like we listen to that logic," the Hand said. The Royal Martian Navy had two flag ranks: Commodore and Admiral. The Royal Martian Marine Corps only had one more: Colonel, Brigadier and General.

Now that they were finally facing a real war, Damien was considering the flaws in the Protectorate's military structure. There were a lot of them, he realized. Most were rationalizations or cost-saving decisions or specialization choices inherent to being primarily a police and peacekeeping force.

For a warfighting navy, however, things as simple as the Royal Martian Navy's *ship names* were going to be a problem. Not a big problem...but a problem.

The first shuttle tucked itself into the bay before their conversation could continue. Admiral Yen Phan was out of the spacecraft as soon as it was safe for her to exit, crossing the still-steaming floor to the safety barrier and saluting Damien and Medici.

"Welcome aboard *Duke of Magnificence*," Jakab said brightly, offering Admiral Phan his hand.

The tall black woman in the black-and-blue uniform took his hand for a firm shake, then bowed slightly to Damien and saluted Medici.

"It's good to see you again, Lord Montgomery, Commodore Jakab," she told them. "And a pleasure to meet you in person, Admiral Medici."

"And this time, Lord Montgomery isn't even being threatening," Jakab replied. "Except to the Republic, at least, and we have no sympathy for them."

A flash of emotion crossed Phan's face.

"I had friends in Nia Kriti and Santiago," she admitted. "I have no idea when I'll find out their fate. This 'Republic of Faith and Reason' can be damned."

"We will beat them back," Damien promised, shaking his head gently. "We were expecting a conflict with the Republic, yes, but this is so far beyond what we were prepared for. We will teach them the meaning of *His Majesty's Protectorate* in the end. I promise you that."

A second shuttle, with the sigil of the Principality of Condor, slid into the shuttle bay. Its engines cut off the conversation for several seconds, and then the hissing steam of the water spraying over the shuttle maintained a forced silence.

The first person out of the shuttle was an absolute giant of a man with disturbingly pale skin and blood-red eyes. The albino had shaved his head to add to the starkly disturbing effect and wore a dark burgundy uniform.

He had the same two stars on his collar as Admiral Phan and Admiral Medici, and bowed as he approached.

"Admiral Darzi," Damien greeted him. He hadn't realized just how large Shahrokh Darzi was, but there was only one albino Admiral in the Principality of Condor, let alone in the detachment they'd sent.

"My Lord First Hand," Darzi greeted Damien, nodding to the other flag officers. "My Prince sends his regards and his hopes for healing of both your personal injuries and the grave wounds inflicted upon our Protectorate."

Damien half-unconsciously checked that his gloved hands were tucked behind his back. Even now, he *usually* knew where his hands were, but there were moments.

"We can only hope for both of those," he agreed. "It's getting crowded in here, Admirals."

Not least because every Admiral had shown up with at least one aide. Those junior officers hadn't even been introduced, to Damien's minor displeasure, but they were still filling up the waiting area.

Of course, the space was designed for major formal welcoming parties. It would take at least two more Admirals' parties to fill it up, but there was only one left.

"Admiral Vasilev is already waiting for us in the main conference room, and Commodore Jakab's people should have dinner ready to serve shortly. If I may suggest that we begin moving in that direction? I'll wait for Admiral McLaughlin."

And if that allowed him to avoid an audience the first time he saw Grace in two years, well, the First Hand was allowed some misdirections.

Damien was far from alone when Grace's shuttle finally landed. He'd managed to bring the audience down to his bodyguards, led by Romanov, and Admiral Medici. He was, at least, not going to make a fool of himself in front of too many people.

He was more than a little amused at himself for it, too. He'd faced down fleets and armies alone and unarmed, but this one woman made him feel like he was going to embarrass himself just by the knowledge that she was *arriving*.

The steam from the cooling sprays dissipated, and Admiral Grace McLaughlin, her aide and a Patrol MP bodyguard crossed the shuttle bay and entered the waiting area. From the moment he could see Grace, everything else faded into insignificance.

Fortunately for his nerves, her gaze was locked on him at the same time. Her salute to Admiral Medici as she entered the room with them was almost an afterthought.

"Lord Montgomery," she greeted him in a gentle voice as she bowed slightly.

"Admiral McLaughlin. Grace," he allowed himself—a concession that earned him a familiar bright smile.

Wait... Was *Grace* nervous? She was the one who'd initiated their on-again, off-again relationship through college and their later fling after the Antonius Incident. Though, now he thought about it, she'd been nervous when they first met during the Incident, too.

"Damien," she replied, and for a moment, the two of them just stood there staring at each other.

Then Romanov coughed delicately.

"Adorable and awkward as this is for the rest of us, my lord, we do have quite the collection of other Admirals waiting for you," the bodyguard noted.

Damien flushed and looked away—but not before realizing that Grace was *also* blushing.

"Of course," he agreed quickly. "Mage-Admiral Medici, if you could lead the way?"

James Medici was probably the oldest person in the room right now, and if the pair of thirty-somethings stumbling over their own tongues was a surprise or bother to him, he didn't show it.

"Of course, Lord Montgomery, Admiral McLaughlin. Follow me."

Six Admirals, a Commodore and a First Hand of the Mage-King gathered in the conference room. Four Captains and a dozen aides, assistants and bodyguards filled out the space, which was thankfully designed for at least twice as many people.

Having regained his equilibrium after seeing Grace again, Damien stood on the stage behind a lectern with Mage-Admiral Medici at his right as he surveyed the collection of stars filling the room.

"Officers, thank you," he began quietly. "Only Admiral Medici and our Navy captains are truly subject to my authority. Admiral Vasilev doesn't really have much of a choice, with his system in the line of fire, but the rest of you don't need to be here.

"So, thank you. Your presence here may well turn the tide of the battle to come. We now represent the single largest concentration of warships the Protectorate has ever gathered outside the Sol System."

He smiled thinly.

"I want one thing to be very clear from the beginning: Mage-Admiral Medici is in command of this naval force. You are assembled here under my authority, but I am a civilian with military oversight, not a naval officer."

Damien waited long enough to be certain that the other Admirals were going to fall into line, then let his smile warm.

"Our mission objective is very simple: we hold Ardennes against the Republican Interstellar Navy. Our current intelligence suggests that we will be facing five full carrier groups of the RIN, the largest force concentration of theirs we are aware of.

"We have no choice but to assume that the RIN is fully aware of our strength and deployments. All evidence suggests that we have been quite thoroughly infiltrated by agents equipped with FTL communicators of some kind. While there are some hints that we may have neutralized at least the communication capabilities of the local spies, we cannot rely on that."

"Is it truly that bad, my lord?" Admiral Darzi asked. "I've...more direct experience with the competence of the MISS than most of you here, I suspect."

"The Republic managed to infiltrate an Augment assassin onto this ship," Jakab told Darzi. "During our last action against the RIN, that Augment attempted to kill Lord Montgomery."

"And had used an FTL communicator to bring the RIN to us," Damien added. "Yes, Admiral Darzi, it is quite possible that, despite the number of agents the MISS has successfully neutralized, the Republic remains fully aware of our actions.

"We do have more reinforcements en route from the Amber System, but due to our new systems of communications security, I don't know the magnitude of that force yet," he continued. "Until they arrive, what we have is what we have. And on that point, I'll hand this briefing over to Mage-Admiral Medici."

He nodded to the Admiral and took a seat at the side of the stage, hopefully concealing the sigh of relief as he was able to lay his hands on his lap. They were starting to bother him again.

"As of the arrival of your contingents, people, we now have the following ship strength," Medici told them, bringing up an organized hologram of the new fleet.

"We have three battleships of the Royal Martian Navy, *Peacemaker*, *Pax Marcianus*, and *Foremost Shield of Honor*. We have two RMN cruisers, two ASDF cruisers, two MSF cruisers and eight TCSF cruisers. The Sherwood Interstellar Patrol has brought us twelve seven-megaton frigates, and the Condor Royal Fleet has provided us with two four-megaton guardships. Combined, our force musters sixty destroyers."

He shook his head.

"For those who don't have the math to hand, we muster eighty-nine warships massing just over four hundred and fifty million tons. We also have a damaged ASDF cruiser we may or may not be able to get back into action before the Republic arrives.

"Unfortunately, our current best guess—as Lord Montgomery noted—is that the Republic will be bringing five carrier groups. A total of twenty-eight ships massing over *eight* hundred million tons."

Medici grinned.

"What we need to sort out tonight, people, is how we're going to win that battle."

Medici waited for the responding uproar to die down, gesturing for calm.

"The situation is not nearly as bad as the numbers may make it appear," he noted once the Admirals had quieted. "Our best estimate is that the enemy sacrifices a significant amount of their tonnage to maintain rotational gravity and for whatever system they are using for FTL.

"The Republic has also consistently proven to be extremely loss-averse. Commodore Jakab has now clashed with them twice, and both times, they refused to commit to an action that would have destroyed his ships—at the certain cost of several of the Republic capital ships.

"They have so far proven willing to lose gunships, but their capital ships clearly represent an investment they are unwilling to take risks with. We can almost count on them opening with a gunship strike to try to wear us down and use up our munitions."

"That strike will likely consist of at least a thousand gunships," Vasilev pointed out. "That's a *lot* of missiles."

"And that's the situation we need to plan for," Medici agreed. "If we can't survive those salvos from the gunships, we can't win this fight. We need to find a way to deal with that initial strike. I'll match our people against the battleships and cruisers. It's that six-thousand-missile salvo from the gunships that's going to be a headache."

"How do we deal with that?" Darzi asked. "If we haven't already written this off, you have to have a plan."

"Part of a plan, at least," Medici agreed. "The Republic so far has relied on superior electronics to counter the fact that we have magic for missile defense and they don't. Their missiles are smarter, their sensors are better, their software is cleaner and their hardware is faster.

"Demonstrably, however, their missiles are no more immune to the antimatter hash of the modern battlespace than ours. The more degraded the space between us becomes, the more degraded both of our missiles are—but the Republic's missiles have more to lose."

"So, we fill space with antimatter explosions and hope?" Darzi said. "That seems...basic."

"It's a starting point," the Mage-Admiral agreed. "We've also got some of the best programmers we can find coding new electronic-warfare routines for our systems and missiles from scratch. The Republic, it turns out, has our complete ECM databases. Anything more complex than outright jamming isn't going to work."

"So, we build new routines. What about decoys?" Grace asked. "Rig up some engines and emitters on a bunch of empty cargo containers; we can pretend we've got extra destroyers at least. They won't make a lot of difference, but every missile that blasts a decoy misses a ship with people aboard."

"Admiral Vasilev?" Medici asked as he and Damien both turned to the local commander. "Do we have anything we can repurpose like that?"

"Almost certainly," Vasilev agreed slowly. "I'll have to ask, but I think we can get something into place quite quickly."

"Everything needs to be done quickly," Damien pointed out. "We don't know how much time we have, but it's on the order of days at most. Admiral, what about prepositioned missiles?"

"We'd need a better idea of where the Republic will come out of jump," Medici told him. "Otherwise, they'll be out of position for us to be able to engage them."

"I wasn't thinking in terms of firing on the Republic," Damien said. "Prepositioning them as counter-missiles. We know where we're going to be."

"That...makes sense," the Mage-Admiral allowed. "Every little bit helps today, people. We have a lot of work to do, but I don't think we can dismiss any idea out of hand. We're going to be outmassed almost two to one.

"That means we need to be that much smarter than them."

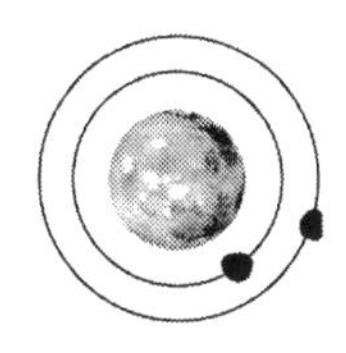

CHAPTER FORTY-THREE

AS THE MEETING wrapped up, Damien found himself facing a somewhat amusing dilemma. Amusing to him, at least. He was relatively sure that Grace wanted to spend more time with him, but given the professionalism of the current situation, he wasn't sure how to approach her.

The other Admirals drifted out in assorted order. Grace lingered, making a show of reviewing her aide's notes, until it was only her staff, Damien and his people.

Jakab's kick in the shins was gentle but pointed. Damien shook his head reprovingly at his former flag captain, now effectively his naval chief of staff. For all the grand power and authority vested in the First Hand, his *staff* seemed to be utterly lacking in appropriate respect.

"Admiral McLaughlin," he said clearly as he stepped over to where the Sherwood contingent was waiting. "Could I impose on you for a few minutes of your time in private?"

Her aide—Meadows, Damien thought his name was?—made a valiant attempt to *not* roll his eyes out of his head.

"Everybody in the room knows your two's history," Meadows pointed out. "I'm assuming Commodore Jakab's people have an office I can borrow with a link back to the Patrol?"

"We can manage that, I think," Jakab said, with admirable professionalism. "If the First Hand and the Admiral's consultations run late, we also have some spare visitors' quarters you can use."

Grace laughed, a familiar warm sound that sent gentle shivers down Damien's spine.

"And just which of us is being thrown to the wolves here for politics?" she asked sweetly.

"Both of you," Jakab told her brightly. "If nothing else, your force represents the single largest contingent here except the Navy itself. Making sure that you are on the same page as Lord Montgomery is important. If that allows for old friends to catch up as well, that's a bonus."

Damien needed to work on his emotional control, he reflected. He was pretty sure he was blushing—and Grace had a flush to her cheeks as well.

"Of course," she said. "My time is at your disposal, Lord Montgomery. Your office?"

"That seems wise," he agreed. "The peanut gallery in here seems surprisingly active."

Grace was all of two steps into the observation deck Damien used as an office before Persephone announced her presence. The kitten came streaking out of the cat door linking the office to his quarters, bounced off the desk she wasn't supposed to climb on and landed on Damien's chest with a surprisingly gentle impact.

He carefully moved his arms to keep the cat from falling, and she purred her way into an appropriately safe position on his shoulder.

"You have a cat," Grace noted with a chuckle. "I didn't take you for the type to have a long-term pet."

"Technically, she's a therapy animal," Damien told her. "One of my doctors happened to make the suggestion where Princess Kiera could hear her. The next thing I knew, I was being presented with an extraordinarily purr-y box."

"Therapy for your hands?" Grace asked, perching on his desk herself.

"Yeah. Petting her is the right kind of low-intensity activity to help stretch my fingers." He shook his head and waved a free hand. "They don't move much still, but they're getting better."

"Do you need a hand with the kitten?" she asked.

"If you'd be so kind," Damien admitted.

Grace plucked Persephone from his shoulder, snuggling the kitten as she leaned into Damien's personal space.

"What's her name?"

"Persephone," he replied. "I did name her myself, I'll admit."

"I figured from the mythology."

Grace hadn't left his personal space. She was still holding the kitten, but she was only a few centimeters away from him.

"Thank you for coming," Damien finally said. "This whole situation is terrifying. I know it's not my fault, but...damned if I wasn't the one who triggered the Secession."

"Even you can't blame yourself for that," she pointed out. She gently put the kitten down on the floor, where Persephone happily jumped up into Damien's chair and purred loudly at them. "They'd been preparing for this for years. I don't care how much pure Sherwood Scot stubbornness you've got, Damien; that's not your fault."

He chuckled.

"I know." He sighed and gave in to temptation, settling on his desk next to Grace and leaning his head on her shoulder. "Been a long few years, Grace."

"It has." She leaned her head against his. "I won't pretend I was waiting for you, but damn, does being in charge of a military not leave you much time for the personal."

"The last person I got personally involved with tried to kill me," Damien said with a chuckle. "Different problems, same result, I suspect."

Grace chuckled.

"Now, *that* I haven't had to deal with since we last saw each other," she confirmed. "I missed you, though."

"I missed you," he admitted. "Our lives don't allow for much else, though. You've got the Patrol and I..."

"You have the Protectorate," Grace told him. "All of it, from what I can tell."

"I did *try* to resign," Damien said with a chuckle of his own. "*Twice.*"

She tapped the platinum icon on his chest.

"I see how well that went. You're, what, the second-most powerful man alive now?"

"I figure third," he admitted quietly. "Mostly because Gregory and I have very different portfolios, and I'm more likely to need to follow his instructions than the other way around."

Her hand was still on the platinum fist. Her fingers were warm against his chest as she wrapped them around the chains.

"Everyone has been very cooperative in making sure we have this time together," she pointed out. "Now, I'm not going to make you do anything you don't *want* to, but..."

Grace pulled gently on the chain of his symbol of office, and he let her pull him around into a long kiss.

"My arms may work, but my hands still don't," he said quietly.

She smiled.

"I can deal with that," she promised.

It took Damien a moment to work out what was going on when he woke up. It had been a long time since he'd slept with anyone else in the bed, and Grace had wrapped herself around him like a limpet when they'd actually fallen asleep.

The unusual, though pleasant, situation left him unsure of what was going on for several seconds, but then he remembered. Carefully, so as not to injure himself, he wrapped an arm around her in turn and smiled.

Then the sound that had woken him repeated. An incoming message alert from his wrist-comp. With a sigh, he kissed Grace's head and extricated himself.

Thankfully, she woke up quickly and helped. The inability to use his hands was less of an obstacle to cuddling—or other activities—than he would have expected, but it definitely caused trouble getting *out* of bed from cuddling.

Once sitting up, Damien gestured and floated his wrist-comp back over to him so he could tap the Accept Call button.

"Sorry to wake you, my lord," Jakab's voice said grimly. Damien had forgot to engage the call in audio-only mode, but the Commodore had called in that mode. He knew what was going on.

"We need you on the flag bridge and, well, Admiral McLaughlin needs to get back on her shuttle ASAP."

He and Grace were both fully awake now and Damien swallowed.

"What's our status?" he asked calmly.

"Twenty-five jump flares," Jakab replied. "Big ones. The Republic is here. Guessing we'll have a gunship strike on our porch in about four or five hours."

"Understood," Damien told the Navy officer. "We have time, but I'll be on deck in ten minutes."

"I'll be waiting for you."

The channel cut off and he looked up at Grace. She was already half-dressed and gave him a gentle smile as she pulled her shirt on.

"Duty calls for us both."

"That it does," he agreed. "I guess we're used to that."

"Yes," she confirmed. "But this time, Damien..." Grace paused in thought. "This time, it better be more than just tonight, okay? I know that may mean only one *more* night before life drags us apart, but I'm going to insist on at least that!"

He laughed and stepped over to kiss her.

"I can live with that," he agreed. "We'll make it work...somehow."

They both knew even that was a promise they might not be able to keep...but Damien also knew that they would at least *try*.

CHAPTER FORTY-FOUR

"ALL RIGHT, PEOPLE, it looks like the Republic has finally shown up to play," Captain Kulkarni declared on *Stand in Righteousness*'s bridge. "Chambers, get me some details. Everybody else, check your departments, check your stations. We're not going to battle stations yet, but we'll be there pretty darn quickly."

Roslyn was already going through the data and comparing it against their recordings from the previous encounters. They had a growing database of information on the Republic's new warships, one that at least let her classify them.

"Five carriers," she reported. "Three are fifty megatons, two are forty. Five forty-megaton battleships, two thirty-megatonners. Eleven cruisers; all but three are twenty megatons. Three are fifteen."

She shook her head.

"Seven hundred and thirty-five megatons," she totalled it up aloud. "Not sure on the gunship numbers; we'll see shortly, I guess. The big ones definitely have over two hundred apiece."

"We've blown enough of the little buggers to hell over the last couple of weeks that they should be short a few," Kulkarni suggested. She paused. "Orders from the flag. All destroyers are to move forward into screening positions. Cruisers, guardships and frigates to form the second line. Battlewagons are the hammer."

Sixty destroyers made one hell of a screen, but Roslyn was grimly aware of what their true purpose in this battle was going to be. Her screen showed the formation Admiral Medici had ordered them into, a wall of light warships ten wide and six high. Any incoming fire was going to have to make it past those escorts.

It let them bring their own RFLAM turrets to bear well before the incoming weapons were a threat to the heavies—but it also meant that the destroyers were going to take the brunt of the gunship strike. It was going to fall to *Stand* and her sisters to take the fire of those massed salvos to spare the bigger ships that would be needed to fight the Republic's capital ships.

"We're ready, sir," Roslyn reported to Kulkarni. "All launchers are online. All missiles are primed. All capacitors are charged. I've linked in to our share of the preplaced missiles as well."

"We'll be in formation in two and a half minutes," Lieutenant Coleborn reported as well. "Heavyweights are falling in behind." He paused. "That is a *lot* of cruisers."

"If only the Republic's cruisers weren't twice as big," Kulkarni replied. "Plus twice as many battleships. Watch your maneuvers and your safety lines, Helm. The last thing we want is to accidentally run into a friendly—but any missile we can dodge is a missile we don't have to shoot down."

An alert flashed on Roslyn's screen and she swallowed hard as she updated her scanners.

"RIN fleet has launched gunships," she reported. "I'm reading one thousand units, even. Repeat, one-zero-zero-zero enemy gunships."

She kept running through the details.

"Looks like their bigger carriers have two-fifty aboard and the smaller ones have one-fifty," Roslyn noted aloud. "They're fifty short on one of the carriers. That could be us, that could be Montgomery...that could be any of the systems they took along the way."

"I'd hope they lost more than fifty gunships getting this far," Kulkarni said, "but I'll take what I can get. Stand by for target allocation from the flag. What are we expecting them to pull, Chambers?"

"They've learned their limits versus ours pretty well, I suspect," the Lieutenant admitted. "I'm guessing they'll hit zero velocity relative to us inside their missile range and outside of ours. We can close the range, we have the acceleration advantage, but...that's the Flag's call."

"That it is," Kulkarni agreed. "And it would give up the preplaced missiles. No, Lieutenant Chambers, I think you're right. We get to take this one and smile—but we'll pay it back with interest when it comes time for the real fight."

"Gunship strike acceleration dialed in at ten gravities," Roslyn confirmed a few minutes later. "Assuming they're going for a zero velocity within their range, they'll begin deceleration in about two hours and range on us in four."

Their fleet had formed up into their assigned positions but weren't accelerating. They'd leave the entire approach to the Republic. It was always possible, after all, that more reinforcements would arrive. Roslyn had to presume that someone on the surface had used the RTA to inform the rest of the Protectorate of what was happening.

Even she hadn't truly believed that the Republic would muster a more powerful force than the one Hand Montgomery had gathered to protect Ardennes. She'd have to look it up to be sure, but she suspected there had never been a larger space battle, at least as far as tonnage went, in human history.

The Eugenicist Wars between Mars and Earth, back before the Protectorate, had seen more *ships*, but the largest ships in those fleets had barely massed a million tons. The Great Armada that Earth had thrown at Mars in the final days of the war may have been a thousand ships, but it had been closer to the incoming gunship strike in terms of mass than to either of the actual fleets.

For all of the firepower the gunships mustered, the combined strike only massed as much as one of the bigger carriers. The sixty destroyers positioned to guard the Martian fleet outmassed them and certainly had more *sustained* firepower.

Six thousand missiles in one shot, however, was a tad more dangerous than twenty-two thousand missiles fired over almost twenty minutes. The gunships wouldn't be a match for the destroyers in a beam engagement, but then, a quarter of the destroyers had amplifiers.

The gunships would be massacred if they entered the range of the Royal Martian Navy's amplified Mages. Unless Roslyn was mistaken, though, they had no intention of doing so. They hadn't even been designed to do so.

The Protectorate might still be learning the tricks and tactics of their enemy, but the Republic knew the Protectorate's manual inside and out. The Republic's fleet had never trained with the Protectorate, but the Legatus Self-Defense Force had.

"If it's going to be four hours until we get to play, then let's stand down the alpha crew," Kulkarni announced. "All of you, call in your replacements and go grab a sandwich. Make sure you're back in two hours when these bastards hit turnover—or don't. Either way, things are going to get *much* more interesting at that point."

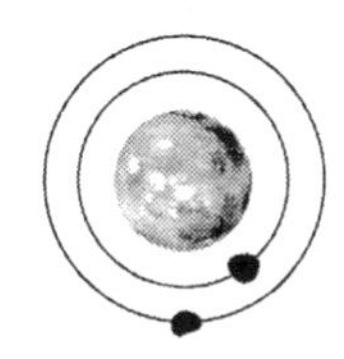

CHAPTER FORTY-FIVE

"YOU KNOW, I almost wish they'd summon us to surrender," Damien said conversationally.

Duke of Magnificence's flag bridge was as still as the grave, every eye focused on the tactical display showing the oncoming gunship strike—and the slower, but in many ways more ominous, approach of the Republican capital ships.

The gunships were sprinting toward the defenders at ten gravities, a crushing experience for the crews aboard the small ships no matter what tech they were using. The main battle line of the Republic fleet was advancing at one gravity.

Presumably, whatever internal structure they rotated for pseudogravity while immobile could adapt to allow them to function under acceleration as well. The Republic ships' need for that structure was one of the few advantages Damien's fleet had.

"Why bother?" Jakab asked. "We know they're here to take the system. They know we're not going to let them. We've each gathered one of the largest fleets seen, well, ever."

"No subtlety to their approach, either," Damien pointed out. "They've got a hammer of three-quarters of a billion tons, and clearly, they don't see a need for anything fancier."

"Would you?" his subordinate asked.

"Yup," the Hand replied. "Save as many of my people as possible, avoid any tricks we had waiting for them. They have to know we've got surprises waiting for them, and given their loss aversion so far..."

"There's only so much clever maneuvering you can do when you need to take a planet and your enemy is in orbit of it," Jakab noted. "Not to mention that this fleet is as much a strategic target as Ardennes at this point. Every deployable warship several of the most powerful System Militias have, plus three of the RMN's battleships? I don't care how risk-averse they are; that's a target they'll take on."

"I still feel like they've got something planned we haven't anticipated," Damien said. "I'm all too aware of our vulnerabilities."

"And they may not be. They could easily not have expected our reinforcements," Jakab said. "You got a lot more people to show up and help than even *I* expected."

"Part of why I want to play for time is that we were promised more," Damien countered. "I don't know how much Amber's going to put in play, but I pulled some strings there we didn't have anywhere else."

"I don't expect much from the Cooperatives myself," the Commodore told him. "I wouldn't rely on them to turn the tide."

Damien smirked.

"You haven't been to Amber, have you?" he asked.

"No. Why?"

"I expect the ADC to send everything they can, but you're right. They won't have much. I also put out an open call for mercenaries, Commodore, and while there may not be very many ships *in* Amber... well, I suspect that there are people there who can get their hands on a few."

"It still won't be enough," Jakab said after a moment's thought.

"No," Damien agreed. "We're going to get hammered, Commodore. But we have to show everyone—Republic and Protectorate alike—that the running is over. We have to stand, my friend."

He grimaced.

"Even if all that means is that we die on our feet."

"Turnover is on schedule. Gunships are decelerating for zero velocity relative to us at twelve point seven million kilometers. Capital ships are continuing to accelerate towards us at one gravity."

"A good light-second or so outside of our range," Jakab noted. "We could try and close, see if we can pick some of them off."

"It's Medici's call, Mage-Commodore," Damien told him. "But the gunships aren't our target. We could obliterate every last gunship they've brought with them and still lose Ardennes."

"I know." Jakab sighed. "And I agree with the Mage-Admiral. It just pisses me off to have to take their fire and let them walk away."

"I don't think anyone is walking away today, Commodore."

Two hours to the gunships being in range. There were at least half a dozen clever tricks Damien could think of, but none of them had a potential reward worth the risks. The best thing that the defenders could do was hold position and let the Republic make the mistakes.

"I'll have coffee and sandwiches brought up," Jakab said after a few minutes of watching the displays in silence. "Rank hath its privileges... and today, I think that means that none of us are leaving the flag deck until this is over."

The gunships launched roughly a minute before they hit zero velocity, again as they hit zero velocity—and once again a minute later as they fled back toward their motherships.

Eighteen thousand missiles hurtled through space, and Damien made a conscious show of leaning back in his chair and relaxing. He had enough scanners and displays built up around him there on the flag deck that he could intervene once the range dropped, but for now, he needed to *visibly* have faith in the people and ships he'd gathered around him.

"Gunships are fully out of range," Jakab said quietly. "First stage initiating."

Two thousand missiles had been quietly drifting outward from the planet since the formation change after the Republic had arrived, their initial engine flares concealed behind the maneuvers of the warships. Now millions of kilometers ahead of their motherships, their drives came alive.

Sparks of antimatter fire lit up across the void, and the weapons flung themselves through space towards the incoming fire...and detonated. They weren't even trying to hit the Republican missiles. Their purpose was to create a shield of radiation through which the RIN warships couldn't control their missiles.

The missiles were smarter than the Protectorate's missiles. But they weren't *enough* smarter to make up for not having shipboard support when the defenders' missiles did.

"All ships are firing in defensive mode," someone announced. "Flag has ordered five salvos, then hold."

Duke of Magnificence trembled under Damien's feet, an almost-imperceptible vibration as her dozens of launchers flung weapons into space.

Hundreds of preplaced missiles came alive alongside the missiles launched by the warships, and thousands of missiles blasted into space toward the salvos from the gunships. Five salvos from the defenders put over twice as many missiles in space as the gunships had deployed.

The first two salvos simply evaporated in the firestorm. The third made it through, vastly diminished, and collided with the destroyer screen. Sixty destroyers mustered thousands of RFLAM turrets, however, and the last of the missiles died well short of the screen.

They came closest, however, against the Navy ships, and Damien took note.

"I don't think the amplifier really makes up for the lack of RFLAM turrets on our destroyers," he pointed out to Jakab. "The Tau Ceti ships have a lot fewer battle lasers but more defensive lasers. We may want to consider adapting our own designs."

"As opposed to mass-producing an upgrade of the same design we've used for a hundred years, I suppose," his subordinate noted. "We probably should have thought of that."

"Why?" Damien snorted. "The *Honor*-class ships have served in their designed role perfectly. We've upgraded our cruisers and our battleships all along. I don't think we ever really considered our destroyers as screening ships, after all. More anti-pirate ships."

"War teaches a lot of lessons," Jakab said quietly.

"It does. And if we want to survive, we need to learn them. What's our timeline looking like?"

"They'll pick up their gunships in just over three hours. At that point, we'll see just what they're planning—they won't have time for another gunship strike before they get into range unless they change their course, but they'll still be well short of turnover for reaching Ardennes."

"Based off their approach so far, I'm expecting them to assemble everything into one giant hammer and come right at us," Damien admitted. "But underestimating them is a bad idea. Let's use that time, Commodore."

He shook his head.

"Let's work out how they can hurt us the worst, and then see if we can counter it."

CHAPTER FORTY-SIX

THEY WERE STILL ALIVE.

That was something of a surprise to Roslyn. The entire purpose of putting the destroyers out in front, after all, was to protect the heavy warships. The Republic's new gunship strike had come in and done their worst...and the defenders hadn't lost a single ship.

They hadn't even taken a single hit.

"Well, let's hope they think we can do that again," Captain Kulkarni murmured. "We shot off every spare missile we had to do it."

The young Lieutenant checked the status reports for both *Stand in Righteousness* and the fleet and saw the Captain's point.

Everything smaller than a battleship carried fifteen missiles per launcher, a standard the RMN had decided on long before and the System Militias had copied. They'd fired off a third of their magazines to stop the gunship salvo...and the weapons they could have reloaded those magazines with had been preplaced in orbit and fired as well.

Roslyn checked the vector data on the enemy ships.

"The gunships are vectoring to rendezvous with the carriers," she reported. "We don't know how long rearming will take, but they almost certainly have missile reloads aboard their motherships."

"And the rest of the fleet?" Kulkarni asked.

"Advancing at one gravity. Just over three hours to gunship pickup; ninety minutes after that before they enter their missile range. Assuming we don't go out to meet them, anyway."

"That's Medici and Montgomery's call," the Captain replied. "I don't expect us to, though. If they're prepared to come straight at us, we'll sit here nice and pretty and wait for them."

"Shouldn't we be doing *something*?" Roslyn asked. Just...sitting didn't feel right.

"I imagine the Admiral and his people are going over scenarios as we speak," Kulkarni agreed. "And they're at least as smart as I am and there's more of them than me...but I don't see any option where the rewards would outweigh the risk.

"No. We wait, Lieutenant. Four and a half hours, then kick the sons of bitches with everything we've got."

Roslyn nodded silently, checking on the formations around them again. Eighty-eight other warships drifted in space, maneuvering at random intervals. Just enough to throw off any long-range missiles trying to come in on ballistic courses.

Engaging this close to Ardennes meant that they were "under the guns," so to speak, of the planetary fortifications. Another eighty-odd launchers should have been a game-changer, and yet...they were so badly outgunned today that Roslyn wasn't sure anything could make that much difference.

Her career in the Royal Martian Navy was looking like it was going to be short and eventful. She couldn't see herself having done anything different at any step of the way, though. This was where she was meant to be.

"And until then, sir?"

"We indulge in the mixture of terror and boredom that is unique to space combat in my experience," Kulkarni told her with a chuckle.

The process of the carriers collecting their gunships was fascinating for Roslyn. She didn't have a perfectly detailed view of it, but with the number of sensor platforms watching the Republican fleet, she had a decent one.

The two classes of carrier the Republic had fielded were based around fundamentally the same structure: two of the cylindrical hulls all of the RIN warship designs shared, linked by a one-hundred-meter-wide central deck.

The smaller of the two carriers had a pair of thirty-meter diameter airlocks at the front and back of that deck. The larger carrier had two offset rows of two on each side, giving it twice the landing or launch capacity of the smaller ship.

When the RIN fleet had launched gunships for the attack, they'd deployed the entire contingent of a thousand ships in barely five minutes. It rapidly became clear, as Roslyn watched the recovery, that the carriers were far better set up for launch than for recovery.

It took almost thirty minutes for the last of the gunships to disappear into their designated airlocks, and Roslyn had to wonder if they were being rearmed any faster than they were being recovered.

"I don't think we need to worry about a second gunship strike, sir," she reported to Kulkarni. "Even assuming that they can rearm them fast enough to get them out, they wouldn't have time to carry out a strike, return and be recovered. They'll deploy them before the fleet action, but they aren't going to send them out again."

"Not that an extra three thousand RFLAM turrets and six thousand launchers are going to be meaningless in the fleet action," the Captain said. "I'd almost rather they tried to send them in alone again."

Roslyn was selfish enough to silently disagree. Another gunship strike *would* hammer the destroyer screen—a screen that included the ship carrying one Roslyn Chambers.

"I'll watch for the first launches," she promised the Captain. "That will give us a good idea of how long it takes them to rearm the parasites."

"Every scrap of data is worth something," Kulkarni agreed. "No one has said anything specific to me, but my understanding is that we've got that MISS stealth ship swanning around out there somewhere, picking up our telemetry and recording everything in case things go wrong."

Roslyn swallowed.

"So, at least if we die, Mars will know what happened," she said levelly.

"Exactly. Can't say that's how I would prefer this to end, but at least it won't be for nothing." The Mage-Captain shook her head. "I'm still hoping to find out we overestimated the bastards somehow."

Roslyn kept her peace. About the only trick left in the Protectorate's quiver were the decoys positioned throughout the cruiser line. When the fleet brought those online, it would look like an extra two hundred cruisers had appeared from nowhere.

They wouldn't fool anyone in the RIN formation—but if the rest of the defenders were throwing enough jamming into space, those extra two hundred targets should screw up their missiles pretty badly.

"Fifty-five minutes to Republic missile range," Roslyn stated. "Unless we start moving shortly, almost twenty minutes after that before we're in range."

"It's the Admiral's call," Kulkarni replied. "If we push too soon, though, we'll lose the decoys. I'd guess we'll start accelerating after the Republican launches."

Roslyn wasn't sure the decoys were worth the risk inherent in the near-immobility of the defending fleet, but she wasn't the one making the decisions. She was just the one watching the sensors...and what was *that*?

"Jump flare!" she reported loudly. "Multiple jump flares...more jump flares. Dear gods...I'm reading over a *hundred* jump flares."

"The *hell*?" Kulkarni demanded, the Mage-Captain rising from her seat to study the scanners. "Get me better resolution, Chambers!"

"I make it...one hundred fifty signatures," Roslyn said slowly as she ran the numbers. "They're at the same one light-minute mark that the Republic arrived at. They're *in range* of the Republic fleet!"

Five million–plus kilometers meant that amplifiers or battle lasers were useless, but even police-grade fusion-drive missiles could cross that range. Roslyn didn't have enough data to say just who had arrived—but neither did the Republic.

The newcomers hadn't even opened fire before the Republic battle group vanished in the bright blue flares of outgoing jumps.

Roslyn waited, letting her scanners drink up the data, then looked up at Mage-Captain Kulkarni.

"Lead unit is a *Dragon*-class cruiser flying Amber Defense Cooperative IFFs, sir," she reported. "Only three ships are under ADC codes, though."

"Who are the *rest* of them?"

"I'm seeing at least forty different mercenary company codes, sir," Roslyn told her boss. "Everything from corvettes to guardship-mass medium warships.

"It seems our Amber friends made it in time after all."

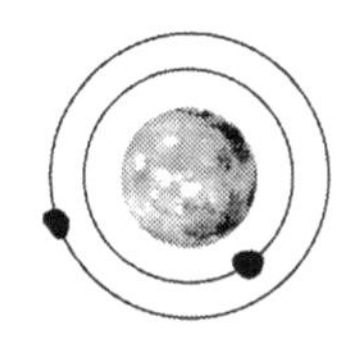

CHAPTER FORTY-SEVEN

"INCOMING TRANSMISSION, MY LORD," Rustici announced as Damien breathed a sigh of relief.

"Put it on screen," he ordered. The Amberite contingent was still a full light-minute out, regular safe-emergence distance, but they'd spooked the Republic. It was possible that it was over.

Damien wasn't counting on it, but it was possible.

He was relieved to see the stocky figure of Captain David Rice appear on the screen, flanked by an unfamiliar older man in a dull white uniform and a woman Damien knew by image and name. He'd never *met* Keiko Alabaster, but he knew who she was.

"Lord Montgomery," Rice greeted him. "Damien. I'm sorry we're late. Apparently, if you offer *enough* money, Amber mercenary companies are willing to take cancellation penalties. We had to stop off at a few places to pick up friends.

"I hope the wait was worth it," he finished with a grin. "I also hope you're going to honor that promise with regards to fees met and service rewarded, because I have promised these folks a *lot* more money than I am ever going to be able to conjure up on my own!"

The grin faded.

"I doubt we've seen the last of our friends from the Republic. I make it eleven hours until we're in orbit, so I'm hoping they'll give us at least that much. Full specifications on the ADC and mercenary units accompanying me are included in an attachment to this message."

Rice shook his head.

"I'm glad we spooked them, because we couldn't have won the fight we accidentally courted. On the other hand, I put together a fleet of a hundred and fifty warships. Do I get to call myself an Admiral now?"

Alabaster gently elbowed him, and the white-uniformed officer coughed.

"Lord Montgomery, I am Admiral Alistair Casanova from the Amber Defense Cooperative. As *Captain* Rice has so eloquently put it, most of our companions are here based on the promise of money. And, well, frankly, some of them could probably use pardons, though I'd strongly recommend that they be *highly* conditional."

He shook his head.

"You should also be aware that the majority of the mercenaries are only carrying Rapier missiles and my own magazines are only loaded with Phoenix VIIs. From the amount of radiation I'm seeing, I guess that you don't have any munitions to spare to rearm us, so those limitations must be considered in your planning.

"I look forward to meeting you in person, Lord Montgomery. Your reputation precedes you."

The message ended, and Damien chuckled.

"Damn good to see them," he said aloud. "Rustici, record for transmission."

He faced the camera with a smile of his own.

"Captain Rice, Admiral Casanova, Ms. Alabaster," he greeted each of the trio in turn. "The Protectorate is in your debt. I pledged my personal word and the word of our nation that the service called for would be rewarded, and your mercenaries need have no concern. If the ADC could provide me with a listing of each mercenary company's standard rate for full-hire operations, I will see them compensated..."

He paused, letting the implication that he would only be paying the standard rate sink in, before his smile widened and he continued.

"...at, I think, four times that standard rate," he concluded. That would be expensive, he was sure...but it was cheaper than losing another star system.

"In any case, I look forward to meeting with the three of you as soon as you make orbit. While I hope that your arrival has sent the Republic running with their tail between their legs, that seems unlikely and we will need to prepare for continued combat operations."

He ended the recording, nodding for Rustici to send it, and leaned back in his chair.

"Mage-Commodore."

"My lord?"

"Are we even going to be able to reload our own magazines?" he asked flatly.

"No."

"Then I don't think we're giving the mercenaries missiles." Damien chuckled again softly. "It's good to have an excuse. I *need* them. I don't necessarily know if I can *trust* them."

From Jakab's expression, he would have very much doubted the First Hand's sanity if he had decided to trust Amber's mercenaries.

The sheer quantity of ships that David had brought from Amber was deceptive for more reasons than one, Damien realized. The most obvious was the inferiority of the missiles they were carrying. Most of the heavier warships had at least one salvo's worth of old Phoenix VIs or Phoenix VIIs, but the rest of the missiles aboard the Amber fleet were Rapiers.

Rapiers were fusion-drive missiles, with a third of the acceleration of the Phoenix VIIIs Damien's main fleet carried—and roughly the same flight time. Their range was under four million kilometers from rest.

Then there were simple mass and number of launchers. Sure, the mercenaries and ADC had a hundred and fifty starships, but their total weight was barely a hundred and twenty megatons. David and the ADC command had arrived aboard *Rameses*, a *Dragon*-class ship from Tau Ceti.

At twelve million tons, *Rameses* was a tenth of the mass of the fleet and almost as large a portion of their firepower. Larger, really, given that the ADC ships were the only ones carrying a full load of antimatter missiles.

Including the two ADC destroyers, Amber-built copies of the Tau Ceti *Lancer* design, the Amber force mustered twenty-nine destroyers. There were ten larger ships, too. At four megatons, the Amber-built "heavy destroyers" were on par with the guardships Condor had sent.

The remaining hundred-plus ships ranged from two hundred thousand-ton ships, specially designed to use pack tactics against Navy destroyers, to seven hundred thousand-ton monitors designed to fight anything *smaller* than a Navy destroyer.

A hundred and ten ships that massed less than forty million tons, all told. Their presence wasn't meaningless—if nothing else, they would fill in a lot of the missile-defense gap that Medici was worrying about—but they weren't going to contribute to the kind of long-range missile duel this battle had been so far.

"Those hunter-killers make my teeth itch," Jakab murmured in Damien's ear. "Most of the rest are probably at least somewhat legitimate, but *those* are pirate ships."

"I know," the Hand agreed. "And I've all but promised them pardons." Damien smiled coldly. "We're also going to use this opportunity to get hyper-detailed scans of them. If they decide to fall back into habits we disapprove of, we'll be able to find them."

Jakab nodded, but he still didn't look happy.

"Look on the bright side, Commodore," the Hand said. "They are the most vulnerable target on the board. If we get into a knife fight, I'll be glad to have their battle lasers, but right now, they're going to be screen. And they're the least likely to survive that role."

The Commodore sighed.

"That might be too cold-blooded, even for me," he admitted.

"I have no intention of intentionally sacrificing anyone," Damien said levelly. "But I'm not going to shed tears for people manning ships *designed* to murder our Navy."

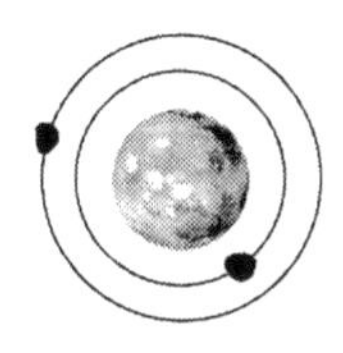

CHAPTER FORTY-EIGHT

RHAPSODY IN PURPLE drifted in an unpowered orbit, closer to Cherbourg than Ardennes and well out of the way of the battle that had taken place. Kelly LaMonte *wanted* to be pacing her bridge, but informal as *Rhapsody*'s command structure was, that remained a bad idea for the Captain.

Instead, she occupied her seat, studying every scanner around her with a watchful eye as she twisted a now-onyx-black strand of hair around her fingers.

"Should we be bringing up the engines and coming in from the cold?" Jennifer Hilton asked, the stealth ship's navigator equally locked to her screens. "Milhouse isn't showing me any trailers from the RIN fleet. It looks like it's over."

Kelly shook her head with a sigh.

"It's not over," she told them. "The Republic jumped out, yes. But they'll review their sensor data before they keep running, and they'll realize just how lightweight the force Amber sent is. They couldn't risk staying in-system with an unknown force in weapons range, and they already had their gunships aboard."

"But once they go over their data, they'll realize it was a bunch of corvettes," Milhouse agreed. "Hey-diddle-diddle, straight up the middle again, you think?"

"No. I was surprised enough when they pulled that stunt once," Kelly admitted. "They had the force for it, but it was setting them up for losses—losses they clearly aren't willing to take."

"So, what then?" her tactical officer asked.

"Their commander is going to have to decide if she is willing to court a full fleet engagement," the covert ops Captain replied. "She's been over-hesitant once already. If her orders are to avoid losses above all else, she's going to try something clever."

"And what exactly are we expecting that to be?" her subordinate said.

Kelly chuckled softly.

"If I knew that, the odds of it working would go *way* down," she told him. "We've got the best view of half the star system from here, and we're pretty sure the Republic didn't see us. Keep your eyes open, Milhouse. What we see could make the difference between victory or defeat today."

The tactical officer snorted.

"You do realize that we're still outmassed by over two hundred million tons, right? I don't know what I can see that will change *that* calculation."

"Opportunities, Guns," Kelly said. "I want you to find me opportunities."

"To do *what*?"

"Ram a battle fleet up the Republic's ass while they aren't looking."

Despite her fears, Kelly sent most of her crew to their bunks an hour after the Republic fleet retreated. She didn't know how much time they'd have, but she'd be better off with rested officers than with exhausted ones.

Not that she was sleeping herself. The Amber fleet was still eleven hours out from Ardennes orbit, and the hairs on the back of her neck were tingling.

"So, does the Commander ever sleep?" her wife asked, Xi Wu dropping herself into the seat next to her. "The bridge is looking rather empty."

"Nothing is going to happen fast enough that I need my crew on deck immediately," Kelly pointed out. "But someone has to be here, so it's me."

"Right." Xi's hand snaked across to squeeze Kelly's. The Mage didn't let go, either. "And how far into the center of this are you planning on throwing us?"

"A long bloody way away, if I can manage it," Kelly said with a chuckle, squeezing Xi's hand in turn. "Our job is to be Damien's eyes and ears, not to take on battleships on our own."

"Always good to be sure we know our limits," Xi replied. "How are you doing on that?"

"Doing what? Knowing my limits?"

"Exactly."

Kelly sighed.

"I can keep going for a while yet," she told her wife. "And someone has to keep their eyes open out here."

Xi leaned her head on Kelly's shoulder.

"There are over two hundred warships in this system, my love. What makes you think we're indispensable?"

"Because we're the ones the Republic hasn't seen. The set of eyes they're not anticipating when they try and be sneaky. They've tried to sneak in behind the gas giants before. They may try it again."

"That's not going to do them much good with a *fleet*."

"Maybe not. But just because I'm not seeing it doesn't mean there isn't an opportunity there."

"Promise me you'll sleep once Milhouse is up again?" Xi asked. "Someone has to be on watch, but it doesn't need to be you."

"I will," Kelly promised. "Happy?"

The Mage snorted.

"My wife commands a covert operations stealth ship, and my husband commands the flight ops for the shuttles aboard it," she said. "I'll be happy when I can wrap you two in cotton wool and keep you *safe*."

"Yes...but I seem to recall someone *else* in this marriage being the Ship's Mage aboard said covert ops ship," Kelly replied. "*Safe* isn't part of our job. We made that decision a long time ago."

"I know." Xi kissed her hand. "Since I can't get *you* to rest, I'm going to go fall over. Make sure that our Mage is ready to go when everything comes apart."

Kelly nodded and pulled Xi's hand to her own lips.

"It's not over," she warned quietly.

"I know. We'll be ready."

Ten hours later, all of Kelly's bridge crew were back on the bridge, rested and ready. Even she'd managed to get six hours of sleep before returning to the bridge to check on everything.

The two fleets in-system were an hour away from rendezvous and the system was quiet. No Republican warships, no accidents, no strange reflections off passing meteors, nothing.

"We're about ten minutes from Cherbourg eclipsing Ardennes," Milhouse reported. "We'll be out of direct communication for an hour after that."

Kelly nodded and studied the map. The logistics base was currently on the "inside" of the gas giant, but *Rhapsody of Purple* was on a long, eccentric orbit. They'd wrap around the outside of the gas giant about ten light-seconds clear.

"Let's drop some relays and get them accelerating in the opposite direction," she ordered. "Make sure we've got them dialed in for tightbeams and can reach Ardennes."

"Still think this isn't over, boss?" Milhouse asked. "Surely, if they were coming back..."

"They'd be waiting to be sure they could jump in and out if they got ambushed," Kelly replied. "We don't know what they're using for FTL, but it seems to follow much the same rules as a Mage jumping. So, we can guess that there's a cooldown period of some kind involved.

"Drop the relay, Milhouse."

"Yes, sir."

A new green icon appeared on their screens. The relay dropped with all of *Rhapsody*'s velocity but rapidly brought up its own engines. Smaller than the ship and not needing to worry about fragile humans, it blasted back along their course at several hundred gravities.

"Tightbeam link established," her subordinate confirmed after several minutes. "Relay link set up with the fleet. We're getting their telemetry; they're getting ours."

"Good. Time to eclipse?"

"Five minutes and counting." Milhouse shook his head. "If I were being paranoid, I'd be worrying that they were going to jump us while no one else could see."

"That's part of what I'm worried about, yes," Kelly agreed. "Bring the ship to battle stations and go to full stealth. We can run the heat sinks for an hour. Let's make ourselves invisible."

The lights dimmed slightly as her staff executed her commands. The lighting aboard a starship didn't consume *much* power, but in full stealth mode, every joule of energy—and the associated waste heat—mattered.

"And...eclipse," Hilton announced from navigation. "We no longer have a clear line of sight to anybody. Welcome to the dark side of the moon, people."

Kelly snorted. "The dark side of the moon" wasn't a place very many humans visited in this day and age, a poetic metaphor for being out where planets blocked almost all communication.

"Scanners are clear?" she asked.

"Scanners are clear," Milhouse confirmed. "Calibrations are aligned for full stealth; we are drinking starlight and asking questions. Link to the fleet is intact."

"Thank you, Guns. Now tell me...what do our invisible eyes see?"

He shrugged.

"Starlight and shadows, mostly. The Ardennes System's colonization and industry ends on the inside of Cherbourg's orbit. There's nothing out here but u—JUMP FLARE!"

Milhouse's snapped report echoed through the bridge like a falling anvil, and Kelly swallowed a curse as she saw the scanners. Her hand unconsciously went to the silver pentacle around her neck, and she murmured a silent prayer to the gods.

The entire Republican fleet had just jumped back in—on the dark side of Cherbourg, where no one would see them...and barely eight million kilometers from *Rhapsody in Purple*.

"Xi," she said calmly, opening a channel to her wife. "I need a Mage on the bridge *now*. Every stealth spell you've ever learned."

A moment of silence.

"How on top of us are they?" Xi asked.

"We're in missile range. *Well* in missile range. Please come make us invisible."

"I'm on my way. What do we do?"

"We disappear...and then we tell Lord Montgomery *exactly* where to find his enemy."

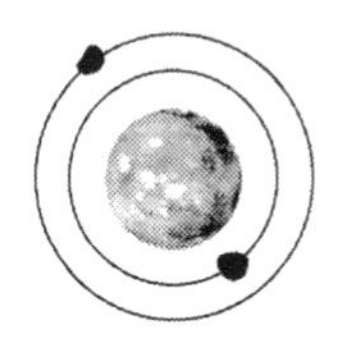

CHAPTER FORTY-NINE

"WELL, THAT IS SNEAKY," Medici said grimly over the conference link. "They'll hit the refueling station in just under eleven hours, and if *Rhapsody* hadn't been out there, we wouldn't have seen them for at least ten."

"How bad will that be?" Damien asked. He had a pretty good idea, but with half a dozen Admirals on the call, someone needed to make sure they were all on the same page.

"There's both civilian and military cloudscoops, plus a large Transmuter station," Vasilev told them. The Ardennian looked even more tired than the rest of them. "There are some defenses, but it's traditionally a Navy facility with Navy defenders."

"And right now we've got three destroyers out there," Mage-Admiral Medici observed. "The Republic will run right over them and obliterate everything. There're no missiles out there anymore, but that's the only thing we've used up.

"There's enough fuel and other consumables to maintain this entire combined fleet for six months. With the cloudscoops and the Transmuter station, combined with Ardennes's industry and agriculture, we could support a fleet of almost any size indefinitely."

"That logistics base is part of the key to Ardennes," Damien said. "Without it, our intention of using Ardennes as a launch pad against Legatus becomes much harder."

Not impossible. Far from impossible—but they'd have to bring in a lot of infrastructure and supplies from the rest of the Protectorate. It would cost them time...time he wasn't sure the Republic of Faith and Reason would give them.

"*Rhapsody in Purple* reports they're pushing three gees, relying on Cherbourg to hide them from everyone," he continued. "If they sustain that for ten hours, their crews are going to be hammered. They also jumped in closer than normal to try to keep themselves hidden. Unless their jump tech is superior to two hundred years of Mage experience, I doubt that was easy on their crews, either.

"They're not trapped in Cherbourg's gravity yet, but give them a couple of hours and they're not getting out of there easily."

The Admirals were silent.

"You have a plan, my lord?" Vasilev asked slowly.

"Several," Damien said with a chuckle. "But they all boil down to one basic concept: let's pin the Republic fleet against Cherbourg and smash them to pieces."

"They'll run," Casanova noted. "We don't have enough force to cut them off—not to mention they'll see us coming hours away. Even if the entire fleet could pull the same acceleration as the Navy ships, we couldn't get to Cherbourg before they could run."

"The same gas giant they're hiding from us behind will hide us from them," Admiral Phan replied. "We could sneak up on them with relative ease. A high-velocity pass, without decelerating, would negate many of their advantages over our forces—and then we could jump back to Ardennes once we were clear."

"And any of them that survive are completely unopposed while we decelerate to do so," Vasilev said. "We'd hurt them, yes, but they'd be able to complete the destruction of the logistics base and seize control of Ardennes's orbitals. We'd take a handful of pawns and hand them a checkmate."

Damien met Grace McLaughlin's gaze and realized she'd picked up at least part of his plan. He smiled.

"Ladies, gentlemen, you're all missing one key part of my plan," he told them. "*Two hundred years,* people. That's how long Jump Mages have been teleporting starships around. We know this game, better than they do.

"Most of our ships only have civilian jump matrices, not amplifiers, but every Mage in your forces is a fully-qualified Jump Mage, at the very *least.* Many of you employ Mages that are on par with those of the Navy for power and training.

"We can do things no other force in the galaxy can. I don't care what technological solution the Republic has developed. It seems to run on the same rules as our jump spells—which means I *know* we can jump circles around them."

Damien's smile got colder.

"And most importantly, people, we can jump directly from Ardennes's orbit to *behind* the Republic fleet."

Five Admirals started arguing across each other, while Grace and Jakab both just waited quietly.

Damien held up his hand.

"We all know it can be done," he told them. "The Navy trains for it and that's the difference, not the amplifiers. To pull off a short jump like this, especially into a gravity well, we'll need detailed scans of our emergence points' gravimetric status.

"But we have *Rhapsody in Purple* in position to do that already. We're already getting detailed information from Captain LaMonte's ship. They can get us the gravity data we need to finalize the calculations—and we have time, people. We'll want to give the Republic at least two to three hours to get deeper into Cherbourg's gravity well."

"We can't come in that close," Darzi finally objected. "I'm not sure we can even risk coming in as close as they did."

"We don't need to," Damien told him. "They came out at eleven million kilometers and we want them inside about nine and a half million klicks to keep them trapped. If we jump in at twelve million, they'll be within amplifier range of our capital ships and laser range of everybody."

Everyone on the conference except Damien winced. That meant he was probably overestimating the ability of the Militia crews, since he knew most of the Navy crews could do it.

"Fifteen," Medici countered. "I don't think we could do it closer than that."

"We can do closer," Casanova said with a sigh. "My mercenaries practice for the closest insertion they can get, and our missile ranges suck. If we can come in at thirteen million kilometers, we're in missile range, but..."

"My people can't do it," Darzi said flatly. "Even if they could, my orders from my Prince are not to risk my fleet more than necessary—and jumping in closer than is safe to allow for these mercenaries to range on the bastards definitely counts as unnecessary to me."

"We can do the calculations for everyone," Medici said. "My people are practiced and trained at that, but we can't make a Mage jump closer than they're prepared for. We'll end up with a mess of a formation."

"We'll lose the decoys as well," Vasilev noted. "They're just cargo containers. They can't jump."

"We can bring them with us," Grace pointed out. "They'll lose some effectiveness, as we'll have to launch them after jump and the Republic will have the data as to where the jump flares were, but we can play some games to screw with that."

"We can probably do fourteen million kilometers from Cherbourg," Vasilev said slowly. "That would get us into position to cut them off, hit them with long-range laser fire and close into their teeth with the fusion missiles."

"We could do that, but they'll still be able to run," Casanova noted. "I don't know how deep the First Hand's pockets are, but keeping the mercenaries here is going to cost a *lot* of money. I don't think any of us want to be sitting here playing watchdog for Ardennes forever."

"No," Damien confirmed. "My pockets are deep, Admiral Casanova, but you're right. We need a victory. Not just the RIN running with their tails between their legs, but those carrier groups *smashed*."

"We're not going to get that," Medici said bluntly. "They'll recognize any attempt to pin them against the planet. We can force an engagement, but we can't force them to fight to the death. They'll do everything in their power to avoid amplifier range."

“If we can’t force them, then we’ll need to fool them,” the First Hand replied. “They’re not expecting us at all, people, not until much later in their approach. At the very least, we have surprise.

“Surprise begets panic. Panic leads to mistakes. I think I know what we need to do.”

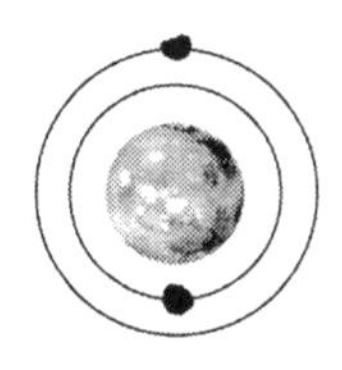

CHAPTER FIFTY

THE MONTHS OF PRACTICE since the Antonius Incident paid off for the Sherwood Interstellar Patrol. Despite towing a dozen decoys apiece, all twelve of Grace's frigates appeared exactly where she'd needed them to—fourteen million kilometers from Cherbourg and just over four point seven million kilometers from the Republic battle group.

A hundred and forty–plus decoys spread out from the hulls of her ships, and a full salvo of over seven hundred missiles blasted out moments later. Most of those missiles wouldn't make it through the RIN's defenses—and over a hundred of them didn't even try. They blasted well clear of Grace's ships and then detonated.

Sixty seconds after the Patrol arrived, the *rest* of the fleet arrived, led by the six twelve-megaton battlecruisers of the Tau Ceti Security Fleet. There was no screen or vanguard this time. There wasn't even truly any *organization* to the defending fleet.

Almost two hundred starships flashed into existence around Grace's command, the bigger ones towing more decoys. By the time the explosions from the Patrol's salvo faded, the decoys had more than doubled the number of targets on the Republic's screens.

Thirty seconds after the emergence of the rest of the fleet, a second salvo of missiles blasted into space. This wasn't the paltry six hundred they'd sent hurtling ahead to get the carrier groups' attention.

Almost three thousand missiles blasted into space, scattering the launches across the disorganized fleet with nearly random abandon. The salvo was concentrated together enough to overwhelm the Republic's defenses but the flight pattern was random enough to prevent the Republic from picking the *actual* ships launching out from the decoys.

Long-range laser fire followed, and they finally saw the first response from the Republic. A dozen decoys disappeared as the Republic demonstrated that they'd mass-produced a battle laser, too.

A twenty-gigawatt battle laser, as powerful as anything the Martian battleships mounted. The mercenary heavy destroyer *Red Fox* took three hits from the massive beams and simply...vanished.

They weren't alone. Four destroyers and half a dozen corvettes joined *Red Fox*—but the Protectorate fleet had lasers too.

Grace's frigates didn't match cruisers for guns, but their custom-designed beams outweighed anything a destroyer could carry. The twenty mercenary "monitors" had light missile armaments for their mass—because they were built around cruiser-weight lasers.

The *Phoenix*- and *Dragon*-class cruisers built by Tau Ceti carried their own weight, and dozens—*hundreds* of heavy battle lasers flared across the Republic fleet.

The big ships had withstood antimatter fire from Montgomery's fleet before, but they had barely been evading. They hadn't expected missiles, let alone lasers. They hadn't been ready to be attacked yet.

One of the big fifty-megaton carriers came apart, and two of her escorting cruisers went with her. It was barely a tithe of the Republic's strength, but the loss of one of their biggest ships clearly broke their nerve.

"They just tripled their acceleration," Meadows reported. "That's going to hurt...but they've got enough of a velocity advantage that they can break free of our beam range, at least. Fifteen minutes or so."

He paused.

"A lot longer before they're clear of the gravity well. Assuming they slingshot and keep going...a bit over four hours after they're clear of beam range."

One of the Condor guardships leapt sideways as a beam hammered into her flank. Her engines flickered and then cut out.

"*Sky Burial* is out," a coms officer reported. "Her engines are down; she can't keep up with the acceleration."

As the Protectorate fleet sorted themselves out, they were stabilizing at ten gravities. That was all the Amber mercenaries' ships could manage—*and* it was all the tow-cables they were hauling the decoys with could handle, too.

And if they lost the decoys, the Republic might start asking questions that Grace *really* didn't want them to.

"Can *we* hold this up for fifteen minutes?" she asked. "Let's get those decoys out as wide as we can and make sure everyone is maneuvering. Are they launching gunships yet?"

"Maybe; yes, sir; and no," Meadows reeled off in answer to her rapid-fire questions and orders. "So far, only the bigger and, frankly, less advanced ships are taking real hits. We're losing lighter ships, but that's basically pure bad luck."

"Pure bad luck" had half the Protectorate's corvettes and heavy corvettes damaged or destroyed already, Grace reflected. Those were mercenary ships, not hers, but that didn't mean she wasn't going to miss those losses.

"Get them to tuck in behind the decoys," she ordered. "Our bigger ships can at least *take* a hit. The sub-megatonners can't."

As she spoke, *Rameses* lurched in space as two lasers struck home. The Amberite cruiser seemed to hang in space for a moment, then brought her engines back online as she spiraled away from the hit. She was losing atmosphere, but she was still in the fight.

"There goes a battleship!"

Meadows was right. The focused fire of the mercenary hunter-killers wasn't doing much on its own, but those dozens of five-gigawatt beams had just herded one of the forty-megaton ships into the crossfire of the entire Tau Cetan cruiser squadron.

It didn't matter *how* tough the Republic built their ships. No one was surviving that.

"We have incoming missiles," her aide reported a moment later. "And we're half-through our magazines ourselves." Meadows shook his head. "If we win this, it's going to hurt."

"They're running, Commodore Meadows," Grace said levelly, watching as thousands of RFLAM turrets added their weaker beams to the chaos on her screens. "I think that means we've already won."

"Well, we're still here."

Meadows's voice was sardonic, and his comment was followed by a cough as acrid smoke wafted its way through the flag bridge of *Robin Hood*. A power surge had blown a series of the protective fuses throughout the ship, leaving a scent of burnt plastic throughout the frigate's hull.

Their frigate was one of the lucky ones. Three of Grace's frigates were just...gone, taking over four thousand of her people with them. Four more had been left behind along the way, along with an equal number of cruisers and over two dozen lighter ships. They'd only *lost* one cruiser, *Himalaya*, but over three dozen destroyers and corvettes weren't going home.

"And the Republic?" Grace asked, watching the enemy fleet draw away from beam-weapon range.

"They're down to three cruisers and they've lost over half the carriers," Meadows replied. "But they've still got most of their battleships and two carriers. Probably four hundred gunships left, easy."

The RIN hadn't deployed their gunships in the vicious running battle over the last fifteen minutes. Grace had expected them to use the parasite craft for missile defense, but the Republic commander had clearly judged them too vulnerable for the risk.

Given that missiles had only taken out a couple of the cruisers, she could see the point.

"Do we have any missiles left?" she asked.

"We've got the Rapiers on the mercenary ships," Meadows replied. "They're even shorter-ranged than our lasers, but if we keep chasing the

RIN, we'll eventually get into range to use them. Of course, the Republic will almost certainly jump out of the system before then, given that we're potentially talking *days*."

She snorted.

"Do *they* have any missiles left?"

There'd been enough of the weapons thrown around. The decoys had proven worth their weight in gold or anything else you named. The rigged-up containers were all gone now, but they'd served their purpose—and the Republic hopefully overestimated how much damage they'd actually done.

"Well, they've stopped *shooting* them at us, and they've fired off at least twenty salvos apiece between the first go-around and this one, so...I hope not?" Meadows replied. "I mean, they've probably got missiles aboard the carriers for the gunships, but they seem content to run for now."

"We'll keep chasing them," Grace ordered. "Let any of the damaged ships still with us drop back to the rear of the formation, but we need to keep the pressure up. Don't want them stopping to think. Or, well, count heads."

Meadows shook his head.

"We've already hammered them harder than we hoped," he pointed out. "Do we need to keep this up?"

"A dozen occupied systems say yes, Gunther Meadows," Grace told him. "We can't just beat them. As Montgomery said, we have to smash them. And that, Commodore, is why we'll stick to the plan."

"And if they do decide to launch those gunships at us?" he asked.

"At this point, I think we can take four hundred gunships," she said. "But there are still five battleships and two carriers over there, and that fleet can take on anything else in the Protectorate.

"So, we keep chasing them."

"Yes, sir," Meadows replied, turning back to his console. "Hounds are on duty. Woof-woof."

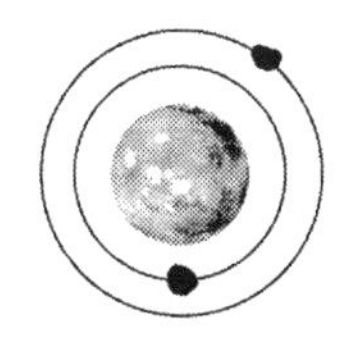

CHAPTER FIFTY-ONE

"AND...NOW."

The presence of Cherbourg between the original fleet position and the Republic force had ended up being more of an advantage for Damien than for his enemies. He'd held the entire RMN task group back, trusting in the decoys and the System Militias to spook the RIN into running.

They'd succeeded. The price was going to haunt his dreams for a long time, but they'd succeeded. Now, however, the Republic fleet was about to make their slingshot, coming around Cherbourg at a higher velocity and staying well ahead of the pursuing Militias.

And they'd be able to see the battleships and cruisers he hoped they believed they'd destroyed. It wouldn't matter if they did, to be fair, but if they saw Medici's fleet coming, they might realize what he was about to do.

He didn't need to have worried.

The Militia ships had pulled off exactly the jump they needed to, and the Navy wasn't going to be shown up. Hours of acceleration at fifteen gravities had got them far enough clear of Ardennes that they weren't jumping from one gravity well to another. They were jumping from relatively flat space into a gravity well—with perfect data on the target.

Three battleships, two cruisers and seventeen destroyers disappeared from the void of the Ardennes System and appeared two million kilometers from Cherbourg—and barely one point five million kilometers from the Republic battle group.

Lasers and missile launchers spoke as soon as the Martian fleet emerged. Phoenix VIIIs screamed across space, and the battleship's twenty- and twenty-five-gigawatt beams spoke in anger. The destroyers and cruisers couldn't match the overwhelming power of the heavy battle lasers, but they didn't need to.

Not at this range.

Precious seconds passed as the Mages who'd jumped the ships stumbled away from their simulacrums. This wasn't an evolution they practiced nearly enough, Damien reflected in the back of his head, and those seconds were paid for in the only currency accepted by war.

All three battleships lurched under heavy beam fire and several destroyers disintegrated—but then the Mage-Captains slammed their rune-marked hands down on their ship's simulacrums and fire lit up the sky.

This was the environment for which the amplifier matrix had been designed. At this distance, missiles and even battle lasers paled into insignificance as the Mage-Captains of the Royal Martian Navy unleashed their magic.

The only missiles in space were their own, and they'd have ignored missiles even if they were there. Their targets were the enemy. Arcs of plasma and lightning flashed across space, and fireballs erupted inside enemy ships.

The carriers died first, the battleships' lasers focusing on them even as the Mages tore into their consorts. The Republic had built big, powerful ships, ships that could withstand even the amplified power of a Mage...for a few seconds.

But Damien had *twenty* Mages and amplifiers. Both carriers vanished, obliterated by magic. The last cruisers disappeared, almost an afterthought. A battleship died. Then another. A third turned in space, *flinging* its forty-million-ton mass in front of the remaining two ships at a dozen gravities.

It bought a few seconds—a few seconds where every weapon and Mage in the RMN task force focused on one ship.

But when the shattered debris of that warship cleared, the surviving two battleships were also gone. The fading radiation of two jump flares lit up the wreckage around them.

Then new explosions and rads lit up their screens. A trail of fire traced itself back around Cherbourg, back to where the Republic ships had first emerged.

"What the hell?" Damien demanded.

"Suicide charges," Jakab said after a moment. "Probably nuclear, hidden in the drive systems and remote-detonated by one of the battleship commanders before they fled."

"Or by remote control from Legatus itself," Damien said in a sick voice. They'd seen that at the Antonius Incident; Legatan Agents had used suicide devices on the ships of their patsies—or implanted in their patsies' *heads*—to make sure there was no evidence. "They have an interstellar com, after all."

"And the Navy commanders wouldn't even need to know they were aboard," Jakab agreed. "As soon as some officer in a bunker fifty light-years away sees the battle is lost and their ships are clear...he pushes a button."

"We need to search for survivors regardless," Damien ordered. "They may have wrecked the jump drive, but they *probably* didn't kill all of their crews. Regardless of this damn war, we're all human. We owe them that much mercy."

"Yes, sir. I'll make sure the order is passed on."

"Let's make sure we get our own people as well," the Hand added, almost certainly unnecessarily. "Our friends paid an ugly price to set this up. Let's make sure as many people get to go home as possible."

CHAPTER FIFTY-TWO

***RAMESES* WAS NOW** definitively lacking in "new ship" smell to David's nose. Even twelve hours after the battle, the smell of burning smoke was distributed throughout the ship—or at least the parts of the cruiser that still had atmosphere.

His and Keiko's quarters were *not* in those parts of the ship, and she was looking at a damage control map with a somewhat lost expression on her face.

"Keiko?" he asked.

"David." She turned and leaned against him. She was taller than he was, but he was more than solidly built enough to hold her up. "What do we do now?"

"*Rameses* is heading back to Ardennes orbit," David told her. "You and I get a shuttle down to the surface and grab a hotel for a few days, at least, while Admiral Casanova and his people establish whether or not they'll be able to fly her home or will have to repair her here."

"Can we repair her here?"

"Yeah. Ardennes can't build cruisers, but they can definitely fix them. I checked," he confirmed. "And the Protectorate will pay for the fixes, too."

"And death benefits for the mercenaries."

David looked up to see Admiral Casanova joining them.

"Admiral?"

"I'll admit, Captain Rice, that I wasn't sure how reliable the ships we collected along the way would be," Casanova said. "But now..." He shook his head. "I'll take anyone who thinks they didn't earn their pay and their pardons out into a dark alley and change their minds."

David winced. The Amber Defense Cooperative ships had been damaged, quite badly in *Rameses'* case, but they'd all survived.

Of the hundred and forty-seven mercenary ships he'd brought to Ardennes with him, sixty-two had been completely destroyed. Another thirty-five were cripples, probably not economical for their for-profit owners to repair.

"How many of them *were* pirates?" he asked.

"Not as many as you're afraid of," Keiko told him. "I wasn't going to hire anyone with *that* bad of a record. A few crews with issues in their pasts and definitely more than a few in need of pardons, but no active pirates."

He arched an eyebrow at her.

"Okay, very *few* active pirates, and only ones I knew wanted out," she admitted. She shook her head with a sigh. "They're all dead, if that makes you feel better."

"Not really," David admitted. "We just gutted Amber's mercenary economy. Was it worth it?"

"Yes," Casanova said flatly. "Montgomery and the Protectorate will see the ships replaced. The dead...no one can bring back the dead, but they died doing the right thing. Even Amberites value that, Captain Rice."

David snorted.

"I never doubted that, Admiral, even if I'm only an occasional resident still. Was this...all worth it, in your opinion?"

"We held Ardennes. We stopped the Republic and shattered an entire battle fleet." Casanova shook his head. "Their losses will hurt them worse than ours hurt the Protectorate. The logistics base will let the RMN launch offensives to retake the lost systems.

"I don't plan on staying," he admitted. "We were an emergency band-aid, a stopgap to hold the line until the Navy could act. Once we're sure *Rameses* can safely jump, we're going home."

The white-uniformed Admiral smiled.

"But we're going home with the knowledge of a job well done."

Despite everything, *Stand in Righteousness* had come through the Battle of Ardennes with only minor damage. They'd been hit with the aura of a battle laser in the final clash, and an entire face of the pyramid was missing sensors and no longer white, but that was repairable.

Roslyn still concealed a sigh of relief as they slotted the destroyer back into orbit of the planet. A lot of ships hadn't survived the last few days, and as theirs was one of the undamaged ships, search-and-rescue had fallen heavily on them.

"We have a final count, sir," Chief Chanda Chey told her as she stepped into the tactical officer's office.

"Chief?" Roslyn asked carefully.

"Of rescues," the noncom clarified. "We—or our shuttles—pulled three hundred and forty-six escape pods and about a thousand loose vac-suits out of the wreckage. All up, four thousand eight hundred and fifty-two people."

"Damn." That brought the first smile to the young officer's face in a while. Five thousand people were going to live because *Stand in Righteousness* had been there to save them. Someone else might have saved them if they hadn't been, but still...five thousand lives.

"I can feel better about that than a lot of our job," she admitted. "I saw the estimate on Republican losses, too."

The RIN fleet's twenty-eight ships and thousand gunships were estimated to have had the better part of a *million* people aboard. Two ships had got away and the Protectorate had pulled almost a hundred thousand RIN crew from the wreckage, but that still put the death toll at around half a million.

"Largest fleet battle in human history," Chey agreed. "Hell of a baptism by fire for a brand-new Lieutenant, if I may say so, sir."

Roslyn shook her head.

"We're still here," she pointed out. "I'd like to think that means I did okay."

"'Okay,'" Chey echoed. "Brought *Stand* home, almost on your own. Stayed in command of a department that thought you were too young. Saw the scout ship before anyone else."

She snorted.

"Yeah, I'd say that was passable, sir. Potentially adequate."

Roslyn gave the Chief a gently reproving look, then caught the older woman's broad grin.

"Of course, remember that I'm judging on the standards of *holders of the Medal of Valor*." Chey stepped back slightly from the desk and gave Roslyn a crisp, Academy-perfect salute.

"I'm honored to be under your command, Lieutenant Chambers," she concluded. "I look forward to seeing what trouble we get into in the future."

Roslyn laughed.

"Be careful what you wish for, Chief," she warned Chey. "I didn't get rammed into the Academy by a Hand for *avoiding* trouble, after all."

Grace McLaughlin's flagship was the last one to leave the battlespace. *Robin Hood* had taken a few solid hits, but her sensors and boat bays were intact. They'd kept up the search and rescue sweep for three entire days.

"Sir, that's the fourth sweep that hasn't found anything," Meadows said quietly as she continued to look over the scans. "Pretty much everyone out here was using the same standard emergency vac-suit. Forty-eight hours. Life pods had more, but they also have beacons and, well, power sources."

"So, we've found everyone we're going to find," she murmured.

"Almost certainly," her aide agreed. "It's possible there's still someone in a chunk of debris with atmosphere that we've missed, but we're down into fractional percentages." He sighed. "Sooner or later, we have to stop looking."

Thirty shuttles and a pair of destroyers from the ASDF continued to sweep around them as well, but everything was being coordinated from *Robin Hood.*

"We still have ships that need repair before we're going anywhere," Grace pointed out.

"Yes. And, frankly, those ships might be better served by having their Admiral on hand to negotiate repairs and parts," he replied. "I don't know what more we can do out here."

"We can save the damn people I led to their deaths," she said bitterly.

"I think we did that," Meadows said. "You led, they followed. Everyone knew the plan, Grace. There was a reason Montgomery put you in command, and it was because he trusted you to judge how hard to press. We did it right. We won, smashed the bastards to hell. You helped save the Protectorate, which does—last time I checked—include our homeworld."

She snorted.

"You're not my therapist, Commodore Meadows," she told him.

"No, but you should probably talk to her, too," he replied. "Right now, I'm one of your senior subordinates telling you that even if the search-and-rescue effort continues, *you* don't need to be here. In fact, you *shouldn't* be here."

Grace was silent as she glanced around her flag deck.

"I'll admit to being a bit worried about...other motivations for returning to Ardennes," she admitted.

"Gods, McLaughlin—and you accused *Montgomery* of Sherwood Scot stubbornness?" Meadows demanded with a laugh. "You did your job. You've kept doing your job. No one is going to begrudge you and the Hand grabbing a hotel room together in an orbital around Ardennes. If either of you would let sleeping together get in the way of your duty, I haven't seen any sign of it!"

Grace flushed but nodded.

"We can leave our shuttles with the ASDF ships for a bit longer, I think," she decided. "A little bit more help can't hurt, even for these final no-chance sweeps. But once we've sorted that out, I suppose we can set our course back to Ardennes."

"Oh, thank Gods," Meadows said. "I'm *trying* to help coordinate the repairs, but a thirty-plus-minute turnaround time on coms is giving me a headache."

That managed to get a chuckle out of Grace.

"I see you have ulterior motives of your own, Commodore."

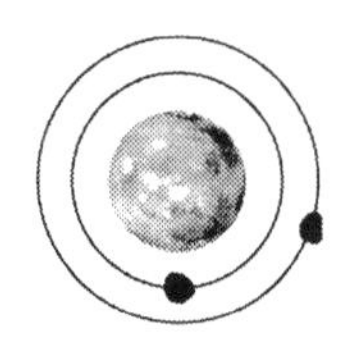

CHAPTER FIFTY-THREE

AFTER THREE DAYS of sharing a bed at night, if barely seeing each other during the day, Damien was *almost* used to the degree to which Grace held on to him at night. She hadn't clung as hard when they were younger, but he understood that it was different now.

And it wasn't just the fact that they were only going to have days until they were separated again, he reflected, while he gently stroked her hair as she gasped her way awake from another nightmare. Duty tended to drag people into many places where life was not so kind.

"Shh, shh, I'm here," he murmured. His hands couldn't *bend,* but he could at least touch her and help calm her down.

"That was at least...not a new one," she said slowly, exhaling into his shoulder. "Remember getting blasted out of my office and having to keep air around us in vacuum with our magic?"

Damien winced.

"Yeah. That one features in my own nightmares," he admitted. "We made it through it, though. And we made it through this battle."

"Still get to watch my ships blow up when I close my eyes," Grace told him. "Gods. We won. Should it feel this bad?"

"In my experience?" He sighed, then kissed the top of her head. "Yup. Never won a victory that didn't cost more than I was prepared to pay."

"Like your hands," she said quietly.

"I'll get them back," Damien said. "It sucks for now, but they're healing."

Realizing that they were awake, Persephone arrived on the bed with a sudden thump and a loud purr.

"And that is what your cat thinks of our moping," Grace told him.

"It's not moping," he replied as he petted the cat. "PTSD is a known career hazard. I'm guessing you have a counselor aboard your ship?"

"Yeah. Only managed one appointment so far. Time, after all."

"Make it, my love," Damien told her softly. "It's worth it. You don't have anything as precious as your sanity."

"I can think of a few things you probably value as much," she said with a lascivious wink. He chuckled and gently poked her.

"Value, yes, but not *that* much," he told her, earning himself a throaty chuckle as she slipped herself along him.

Things were progressing quite positively, to Persephone's disgruntlement, when his wrist-comp chimed.

Sighing, they extricated themselves and Grace passed him the computer.

"This is Montgomery," he answered it, careful to activate it in voice-only mode.

"My Lord, we have a new sequence of jump flares. Current IFFs are reading at least two battleships and twelve cruisers with destroyer escort...under command of Mage-Admiral Alexander."

Damien inhaled and met Grace's eyes.

"That's Jane Alexander, correct?" he asked.

"Yes, my lord."

"Let me know when she reaches orbit," Damien ordered. "I'll meet with Her Highness immediately once she has."

Her Royal Highness Mage-Admiral Jane Michelle Alexander was the Mage-King's younger sister and one of the handful of other Rune Wrights alive. Apparently, *she'd* managed to convince the Navy to come up with a real force to help hold Ardennes.

"Yes, my lord. The Admiral's ETA is about eight hours."

"Thank you."

The channel closed and Damien turned to find Grace sitting on his bed, stretching. Still naked.

She grinned at him.

"So, where were we?"

Damien was reasonably sure that the Mage-Admiral knew his reputation well enough to realize that he wasn't a fan of ceremony. That didn't seem to have changed anyone's mind on whether to meet him with a full welcoming party.

Dress-uniformed Marines saluted and a greeting party of *Righteous Shield of Valor*'s senior officers waited for him at the end of the carpet they'd rolled out.

There was no question who Mage-Admiral Alexander was, though. Even if he'd never seen pictures of her, he'd have recognized her instantly. She looked like her brother's twin, sharing his height, his eyes and his gunmetal-gray hair.

That wasn't really a surprise. Damien knew, better than most, the degree of genetic engineering that was going into making certain the Mage-King's family remained Rune Wrights. Jane Alexander and her brother weren't quite clones...but they were far closer to that than to naturally-conceived humans.

"My Lord Montgomery," Alexander greeted him.

"Your Royal Highness, Mage-Admiral," he replied. "It's good to see you—and your ships."

"I imagine it would have been better to have seen us, what, a week ago?" she admitted. "I am somewhat immune to the displeasure of my fellow Admirals, so my brother asked me to come here." She shrugged. "Unfortunately, I was on the other side of the Protectorate on other business."

"After the losses we took, we're glad to see you regardless," Damien said. "You'll take over command?"

"Once Admiral Medici has had a chance to fully brief me," she told him. "Until I'm entirely up to date, I'd rather not get in the way. May we speak in private, Lord Montgomery?"

"I am at your disposal," he said.

It was an open question which of them had authority over the other, but the easiest solution was to treat each other as equals. The only person who could resolve an actual conflict between them, after all, was on Mars.

"I take it your presence here doesn't represent a change in the Admiralty's strategy," Damien said as he took a seat in her office.

"In and of itself, no. The Battle of Ardennes, however, has forced some rethinking," Alexander confirmed. "My current task is to continue what you and Medici have done so dramatically: hold this system. I've been promised reinforcements, because eventually I intend to take the fight directly to Legatus."

"What about the systems in Republic hands?" he asked.

"We'll be scouting those over the next few weeks, seeing if we can establish what kind of force the RIN is protecting them with," she said. "The hope is that we can liberate them with lighter forces while I take most of our battleships and cruisers on a direct strike at the heart of the Republic.

"If we can capture or otherwise neutralize the Centurion Accelerator Ring, the lack of antimatter should bring their war effort to its knees in short order. I doubt it will be *easy*, but since you just smashed at least half of their offensive forces, it should be more straightforward than before."

"A siege, most likely," Damien suggested. The Centurion Accelerator Ring was a massive particle accelerator built around Legatus's main gas giant, Centurion. It was the primary source the Republic had for antimatter, and cutting it off from the RIN would drastically reduce their ability to fuel gunships and missiles.

She winced but nodded.

"Both Legatus and Centurion are heavily fortified. Dividing the two from each other will eventually deprive one of manpower and the other of antimatter, but it won't be a quick or clean process. That's my job now, though."

"Thank you," he told her. "I'm no fleet commander. That's what I have Mage-Commodore Jakab for—and Medici did an exemplary job."

"As I understand it, you're the one who found the fleet," she said. "Speaking of which, how long are we planning on keeping the Militia here?"

"They do have jobs of their own, and the mercenaries are getting expensive," Damien conceded. "Though compared to what we've paid in death benefits and ship replacements, the daily cost of keeping the ones left isn't much. If we're up to five battleships, we can probably send most of them home."

He'd miss Grace, but they'd known what they were getting into this time.

"We'll want to talk to the commanders, see if we can hang on to some of the heavier ships for a while," Alexander said. "At least until the next wave of Navy reinforcements arrives. We've been promised every battleship that isn't effectively nailed down but...well, that's still only ten of them."

That was still half of the Protectorate's battleships—and half a *billion* tons of warships.

"It seems like Ardennes is in good hands," Damien said.

"From what I have seen, Damien, Ardennes was in good hands all along," she said with a chuckle. "I'll take over the war, but I definitely still see value in having you along if you're available. I'm a soldier, not a politician. There's a reason I avoid Mars."

"I'm a glorified cop, not a politician," he objected.

"Sure you are," she told him. "Whatever label you'd like, you're still the First Hand, which makes you a better choice for arguing with system governments than I am. Plus, if we start punching into Republic space, *you* have full plenipotentiary authority to negotiate for Mars. I don't, officially at least."

"I wasn't planning on going anywhere else," he admitted. "This war is the most important thing currently going..."

Damien's wrist-comp buzzed and he stared at it in surprise. He'd muted it. There wasn't even a priority code that could get through the lockdown he'd activated, since he was aboard a Navy warship and they could get in touch with him regardless if the system came under attack.

"Excuse me, Admiral, the fact that my wrist-comp shouldn't be notifying me of *anything* makes me curious," he confessed.

"Go ahead," she said. She looked curious enough herself.

Damien brought up the holographic screen with a gesture. His wrist-comp wasn't requiring precise hand motions right now, which made it slower than most people's...but usable for Damien.

"That's strange," he observed aloud. "Apparently, one of your ships' post databoxes picked up a message for me somewhere along the way that got bounced to the surface when you arrived. Just got sorted by the post computers and sent back my way."

Every ship, even the Navy ones, carried an encrypted post databox that picked up massive dumps of data and mail from each system they traveled through. With the RTAs only capable of voice communication, the automatic-post databoxes were what truly held interstellar communication together.

"The origin is garbage data," he continued. "But the wrapper included some kind of code that forced my wrist-comp to notify me. That's... strange."

"Wrist-comps are pretty standard," Alexander pointed out. "My understanding is that the notification function is disturbingly unsecured by their standards, too."

Damien nodded and flicked a screen aside, opening the message. It was very short. And very impossible.

Damien Montgomery.

We met once before and worked well together. Now it seems my nation has gone mad and I have received orders I never expected to see. Meet me on Amber. The bar of the Six Red Seasons Hotel on Heinlein Station.

You may be my only hope. What I have learned may be the Protectorate's.

James Niska, Legatus Military Intelligence Directorate

They both stared at the message hovering in the air.

"You know an LMID operative?" Alexander asked.

"Back before I was a Hand, I was a Jump Mage," Damien reminded her. "We hauled gunships for LMID. Major James Niska commanded a contingent of Augments put aboard our ship to protect them. I knew he was more than he pretended to be, but I never expected to hear from him again.

"Especially not now."

"It seems, Lord Montgomery, that I'll need to find someone else to argue with governments for me," the Admiral said. "This is suspicious as hell, but..."

"But we need to act on it," Damien agreed. "Conveniently, we have an MISS stealth ship to hand."

He shook his head, then smiled.

"I wonder if Captain LaMonte has space for my cat."

CHAPTER FIFTY-FOUR

"DAMIEN, HOW CAN WE HELP YOU?" Kelly LaMonte greeted the face on her screen.

"I need you to clear space for an extra shuttle, two Mages, thirty Secret Service Agents and Marines, one cat and supercargo of one First Hand," Damien Montgomery told her with a chuckle. "I'm commandeering your ship and crew for the good of the Protectorate."

Kelly was taken aback and stared at him in silence for a second.

"You're serious," she responded.

"We're on our way over aboard an RMMC assault shuttle. We need to be on our way in short order, and this needs to be covert. My people can stay on the shuttle if we need to, but..."

"No, we have space," Kelly replied as she thought it through. "It'll be a tight squeeze, though. I can put you and the Mages up in visitor quarters, but the Agents and Marines will have to share space with my cyber-commandos."

"I am quite certain I can make sure there are no problems," Damien said calmly. "We'll compress ourselves into whatever space you can give us. As soon as we're aboard, you need to set your course for Amber...but if you can get us out of Ardennes without anyone knowing where we're heading, that would be preferable."

"What's going on, Damien?" she asked.

"I'm not entirely sure," he admitted cheerfully. "But what I can promise is that it's important—and the entire fate of the Protectorate may hang on it. I need your ship and I need your brains. Can I count on you?"

"Always," Kelly told him. "What about *Duke*? And...McLaughlin, for that matter?"

"*Duke of Magnificence* will rendezvous with us one light-year away from Amber after we're done," he replied. "I'm not giving up our backup, Kelly, but I think we need to keep what we're doing under wraps—and *Rhapsody in Purple* is designed for that."

He sighed.

"As for Grace, well. I've spoken to her already. We both understood what we were getting into. That's more than I can say for some of my other relationships."

Kelly snorted. Damien had left her behind to head to Mars and the Mage-King's service. She'd understood even then. It had still hurt.

"So, Amber, huh?" she asked. "What's in Amber?"

"If I'm reading between the lines correctly, a spy who wants to come in from the cold."

ABOUT THE AUTHOR

GLYNN STEWART is the author of Starship's Mage, a bestselling science fiction and fantasy series where faster-than-light travel is possible–but only because of magic. His other works include science fiction series Duchy of Terra, Castle Federation and Vigilante, as well as the urban fantasy series ONSET and Changeling Blood.

Writing managed to liberate Glynn from a bleak future as an accountant. With his personality and hope for a high-tech future intact, he lives in Kitchener, Ontario with his partner, their cats, and an unstoppable writing habit.

OTHER BOOKS BY GLYNN STEWART

For release announcements join the mailing list or visit **GlynnStewart.com**

STARSHIP'S MAGE

Starship's Mage
Hand of Mars
Voice of Mars
Alien Arcana
Judgment of Mars
UnArcana Stars
Sword of Mars
Mountain of Mars
The Service of Mars
A Darker Magic
Mage-Commander (upcoming)

Starship's Mage: Red Falcon

Interstellar Mage
Mage-Provocateur
Agents of Mars

Pulsar Race: A Starship's Mage Universe Novella

DUCHY OF TERRA

The Terran Privateer
Duchess of Terra
Terra and Imperium
Darkness Beyond
Shield of Terra
Imperium Defiant
Relics of Eternity
Shadows of the Fall
Eyes of Tomorrow

SCATTERED STARS

Scattered Stars: Conviction

Conviction

Deception

Equilibrium

Fortitude (upcoming)

PEACEKEEPERS OF SOL

Raven's Peace

The Peacekeeper Initiative

Raven's Course

Drifter's Folly (upcoming)

EXILE

Exile

Refuge

Crusade

Ashen Stars: An Exile Novella

CASTLE FEDERATION

Space Carrier Avalon

Stellar Fox

Battle Group Avalon

Q-Ship Chameleon

Rimward Stars

Operation Medusa

A Question of Faith: A Castle Federation Novella

SCIENCE FICTION STAND ALONE NOVELLA

Excalibur Lost

VIGILANTE

(WITH TERRY MIXON)

Heart of Vengeance
Oath of Vengeance

Bound By Stars: A Vigilante Series
(With Terry Mixon)

Bound By Law
Bound by Honor
Bound by Blood

TEER AND KARD

Wardtown
Blood Ward

CHANGELING BLOOD

Changeling's Fealty
Hunter's Oath
Noble's Honor
Fae, Flames & Fedoras: A Changeling Blood Novella

ONSET

ONSET: To Serve and Protect
ONSET: My Enemy's Enemy
ONSET: Blood of the Innocent
ONSET: Stay of Execution
Murder by Magic: An ONSET Novella

FANTASY STAND ALONE NOVELS

Children of Prophecy
City in the Sky

Made in the USA
Las Vegas, NV
28 April 2021

22136561R00208